G000275441

THE
RED
GENE

BARBARA LAMPLUGH

THE
RED
GENE

Urbane
PUBLICATIONS

urbanepublications.com

First published in Great Britain in 2019
by Urbane Publications Ltd
Suite 3, Brown Europe House, 33/34 Gleaming Wood Drive,
Chatham, Kent ME5 8RZ
Copyright © Barbara Lamplugh, 2019

The moral right of Barbara Lamplugh to be identified as the author of this work has
been asserted in accordance with the Copyright, Designs and Patents Act of 1988.

All rights reserved. No part of this publication may be reproduced,
stored in a retrieval system, or transmitted in any form or by any means,
electronic, mechanical, photocopying, recording or otherwise, without the prior
permission of both the copyright owner and the above publisher of this book.
All characters in this book are fictitious, and any resemblance to
actual persons living or dead is purely coincidental,
other than those in the public domain.

A CIP catalogue record for this book is available
from the British Library.

ISBN 978-1-912666-42-3
MOBI 978-1-912666-43-0

Design and Typeset by Michelle Morgan
Cover by Dominic Forbes

Printed and bound by 4edge Limited, UK

URBANE
urbanepublications.com

CONTENTS

MAPS

ACKNOWLEDGEMENTS

To the 300,000 women, living and dead, whose babies were stolen from them in Spanish hospitals and prisons during Franco's dictatorship and beyond.

PART 1 ROSE 1936 -1939

Murcia, February 1939

Miguel was standing by the open door, beckoning to me. 'Rose, we must talk.' I knew from his clenched muscles, the urgency in his voice, what this meant. The moment had come.

He led me outside where we would not be overheard. I could barely make out his face in the gloom of advancing nightfall. With my fingers, I traced his features, trying to imprint them on my memory, saying nothing, waiting for him to break the news I'd been dreading.

'Listen, *cariño*,' he said, his voice a hoarse whisper. 'I can't stay here any longer. And neither can you.' Was he suggesting we flee together over the border to France? My fingers paused on the bristled surface of his cheek as I clutched at the tiny flicker of hope his words offered.

'I'm leaving at dawn tomorrow. And you must go back to England without delay. At Gandia there are British boats.'

I turned away, disappointment like a stone in my chest. It was just as I had expected. Dr Jolly's skilled surgery and the long period of convalescence meant his stomach wound was all but healed. Having nursed him, I was as familiar with the lines and textures of his scar as if it marked my own body. All week I'd been waiting for him to announce his return to the fighting. I guessed he would head for Madrid, now Catalonia was taken.

Miguel lowered his voice even further. 'The war is lost, Rose. Madrid will fall; it's useless to hope otherwise. And there'll be no negotiated peace. You think those fascist bastards will show mercy? To survive, we have two choices: to flee or to continue the struggle. It's not in my nature to give in. I'm staying.'

'Staying?'

'I'm joining the guerilla. We're making for the Sierra de Segura, Eduardo and I. He's from a *pueblo* in those parts; he knows the area well. He knows the *enlaces*, the safe houses. He says the people there are loyal, there's already a strong network we can trust. And those hills are mostly forest, we'll have good cover.'

'Miguel...' He would die, gunned down like a rabbit by the *Guardia Civil*, and I'd never see him again, I was certain of it. My legs had begun to shake; they had no more strength than those of a newborn foal. I sank my head against his chest, struggling to think clearly, to form a plan, a way to stop him or... I could scarcely breathe, let alone speak, yet my mind was racing.

'Believe me, I've thought about this.' Miguel grasped my hands and took a step backwards. In the little light that remained, I could see how his eyes blazed, their intensity reflecting the conviction in his voice. 'They've sealed the border with France. Thousands of refugees are heading towards a closed frontier. My uncle was in Málaga. He saw what happened in the days before it fell: the sad trails of people trudging with all their possessions, their children, their animals... He told me how they were strafed by German and Italian planes, killed indiscriminately – women, children, the mules pulling their overloaded carts. Others dying of hunger or sickness or exhaustion. They say five thousand died, trying to make it to Almería.'

I knew. I had worked with some of the traumatised survivors.

'It will be the same again with those fleeing Barcelona. We have to go while there's still a chance, while a red zone still exists in this part of Spain. It's only a matter of time: days, weeks, who knows? There's a lorry setting out for Albacete early tomorrow. The driver has agreed to take Eduardo and me part of the way. He can drop us off further north and we'll make our way westwards across country.'

'But how can you hope to...?'

'You won't stop me, Rose. My mind is made up.'

'Then I'm going with you.'

'My love, are you crazy? It's no life for a woman. On the run, sleeping in the open or in caves, living on God knows what, there'll be danger in every moment.'

'I'm used to danger. Haven't I risked death every day of this barbarous war? I won't go back to England, not when my skills can still be of use here. What if you or Eduardo get injured?' I covered his mouth with my hand to stifle his protests.

Gently he removed it and kissed each of my fingers. 'Rosa, *mi amor...*'

We stood facing each other. Miguel looked directly at me, reading my eyes as if to measure my courage, my steadfastness, my sanity perhaps. I did not flinch. For several minutes neither of us moved. Then he took me in his arms and I knew my choice was the right one, the only one possible.

'Be ready at six,' he said.

I nodded and turned to go inside. 'Till the morning then.'

CHAPTER 1

Rose, Evesham 1936

'For food in a world where many walk in hunger;
For faith in a world where many walk in fear;
For friends in a world where many walk alone;
We give you thanks, O Lord. Amen.'

Mother frowned at Bertie and Ralph, who had already picked up their knives and forks before the last word of the grace was out of Father's mouth.

'I thought your sermon went down well today,' Mother said. 'People understood your message.'

'The words of Jesus, his parables, are not difficult to understand. The difficulty is living by his example.' Father paused in his eating. 'Humility, forgiveness, tolerance... For most of us, these are not attained without struggle.'

Rose inspected her plate, where several islands rose out of a sea of thick gravy: to one side the pale grey slices of lamb decorated with blobs of mint sauce, to the other three roast potatoes, glossy and golden, and a heap of wet cabbage. She lifted a small piece of lamb to her mouth and chewed it, swallowing with difficulty. Eating wasn't usually an effort but today nerves were playing havoc with her digestion.

After dinner she would tell them. All she had to do was remember the words of the speaker, the depth of emotion in her voice as she described the suffering of the Spanish people and their desperate need for food, for medicines and above all for trained nurses; how her breath caught as she implored the audience at the packed hall in Oxford for help. Newly arrived from Spain, the young interpreter was anxious only to gather supplies and return there as soon as possible. All were moved by her speech. Several volunteered to help with the campaign immediately; others pledged money, food, clothes, blankets...

'What's the matter with you, Rose? Don't you feel well?' Mother was regarding her with concern, Father with mild curiosity.

'I'm not hungry, that's all.'

Her two younger brothers stared at her in disbelief. 'Not hungry? You can give *me* your meat then.'

She speared a slice of lamb with her fork and deposited it on Bertie's plate. A splash of gravy fell on the tablecloth.

'Rose!'

'Sorry, Mother.' She forced herself to eat and even to join in the conversation – about the christening of her cousin's twins, about cricket, about the new organist – but her mind was elsewhere.

Father laid down his knife and fork, taking care as always to place them exactly vertical in the centre of the plate. He was a good man; everyone said so. His name, the Reverend Arthur Tilly, was always spoken with respect. They compared him to other vicars who didn't live by their beliefs as Father did. So he, more than anyone, should understand her reasons for going. She was obeying her conscience.

Maisie popped her head round the door to see if they were ready for dessert and started to clear away the plates.

The vicarage lawn had been recently mown and the scent of cut grass mingled with that of the late summer wallflowers, phloxes and sweet peas. A few of the Michaelmas daisies were beginning to unfurl their petals. Rose and her father strolled arm in arm along the path edging the lawn.

'So what's troubling you, Rose?' Father stopped and turned to face her. It was impossible to hide her moods from him: he knew her too well.

She had meant to soften her announcement by first describing the terrible plight of the Spanish people so that her parents would understand what impelled her; would approve her decision. But in the end she just blurted it out. 'I'm going to Spain.'

She could tell immediately, before Father even opened his mouth, that he understood. Of course, he read his *News Chronicle* every day; he would be aware of the situation. Relief flooded through her. She flung her arms around him. 'I have to go,' she said. 'You do see, don't you? They're crying out for nurses. I'd never forgive myself if I just turned my back on them.'

'You're a good girl, Rose.' He paused and she read on his face a succession of different emotions. 'Your response, what you intend to do, is a Christian act from which I won't try to dissuade you if you've truly made up your mind – even though I fear for your safety. But think hard; be sure before you commit yourself. Consider the dangers.' He smiled. 'I know how impulsive you are. And how soft-hearted.' A shadow passed across his face. 'War is a terrible thing. What you'll see and experience… it will change you forever.'

Rose knew where his thoughts lay. Two of his brothers had been killed in the Great War and another had lost a leg. His family, like so many others, had been deeply affected; grief, it was said, had sent his mother to an early grave. Rose had no memory of her grandmother but she remembered Uncle Tom, whose stump had fascinated and repelled her as a small child. He too had died young, some years ago.

'Mother won't take it well, you realise.' Father pulled off a few dead flower heads and tossed them onto the rubbish heap. 'It's natural for a mother to worry.'

'I know,' Rose said, taking his arm again. 'But if you approve, she'll accept it.'

'Maybe. And what about Harry? Have you told him yet?'

'Not yet.' There was no doubt in Rose's mind about how her fiancé would react. He'd make a big fuss and then, after a heated argument, go into a sulk so that she'd end up feeling guilty for leaving him. 'If Harry loves me, he'll wait,' she said, but with more hope than conviction. Father squeezed her hand. He had understood that too.

'I suppose this is Mabel's doing.' Rose had waited till late in the evening to break the news to her mother, slipping into the kitchen where she was making their usual nightcap. Although her back was turned, the emphatic rattling of the spoon as she stirred cocoa and sugar into the splash of milk in each cup revealed Mother's feelings clearly enough.

'I haven't joined the Communists, if that's what you mean,' Rose said. Her friend Mabel, who had accompanied her to the Aid for Spain meeting, was a keen member of the Communist party, as were many of the others present, but that had nothing to do with her decision. 'Mother, I'm a nurse. Men are dying for lack of nurses. Women and children too. Isn't this what I trained for, to save lives, to care for the sick and wounded?' She touched her mother's arm, willing her to turn.

'The milk, it's boiling...' Mother caught the pan just in time and filled the two cups. Rose waited while her mother ran water into the pan, leaving it to soak in the sink before finally sitting down with a heavy sigh at the scrubbed wood table.

'I understand your desire to help' she said, 'but there are other ways, less dangerous ways. A country at war – it's not the place for a young girl. I've seen pictures in the newspapers, women in overalls marching with rifles...'

'But Mother, I'm not going there to fight, I'm going to nurse.' She reached for her mother's hand and stroked the smooth skin, noticing a small cut on her index finger. 'I won't be on the front; I'll be quite safe. And I'll write.'

'You've made up your mind, it seems.' Mother's voice was resigned, her weak smile no reflection of her feelings.

'But you do understand, don't you?' Her parents' approval mattered to Rose. She realised she was squeezing Mother's hand rather too hard and loosened her grip. 'The conflict probably won't last long, there's such solidarity among the people, they say, that the rebels can't succeed.'

'Well, I hope you're right,' Mother said, rising to her feet. She placed the two cups of cocoa on a tray and picked it up. 'I must take this through to Father and then we'll be off to bed. Sleep on it, Rose. Big decisions shouldn't be made in a hurry.'

Upstairs in her bedroom, Rose took a pad of writing paper, an envelope, her fountain pen and a bottle of blue ink from the drawer and sat down at her dressing table. Having cleared a space where she could write, she addressed the envelope to Harry at the Royal Military

College, Sandhurst. He would be home next weekend but giving him a few days to get used to the idea might make the inevitable scene to come less explosive.

The envelope was the easy part and she took her time over it, shaping the letters with care. Then, sucking the top of her pen, she sat, pondering how to phrase the letter. In the end, she dashed off a couple of brief sentences, simply informing him of her decision and making it plain she would not be dissuaded. Posted first thing in the morning on her way to work, it should reach him on Tuesday.

'Prove you love me then.' Harry pressed himself against her so that she could feel the heat and hardness of him against her stomach. He pushed his tongue further into her mouth, insistent, clamorous, until what had started as a seductive kiss became tainted with aggression.

Rose broke away and looked at him standing there amongst the tombstones, breathing hard, his face set. The cemetery was deserted, the bereaved visitors with their offerings of garden flowers having long returned home for tea. In the fading light, Harry appeared more handsome than ever. He had the look of an officer: his erect posture, along with his height, gave him a commanding presence. Long-legged, with an athletic, well-proportioned body, hair the colour of wheat and eyes that recalled exactly the 'sea-blue' in her childhood paint-box, he would also, Rose thought, conform to Hitler's notion of the ideal Aryan.

She had wavered just a little when she saw him striding towards her down the station platform, a warm, confident smile lighting up his face. Hers were not the only eyes turned towards him. He could have any girl he liked. What if he wouldn't wait? What if his parents prevailed, persuading him that a girl of his own class would make a better wife for him? That niggle of uncertainty had grown stronger still when he took her in his arms and looked into her eyes with a softness that was now quite absent. It was not what she had expected as she waited for his train to arrive. She had feared a much chillier encounter. Had he received her letter? 'Oh that...' Harry had dismissed the letter as if the message it contained were mere fantasy.

'We can do it, we're engaged,' he said now, recovering his composure enough to shape his lips into a smile, a smile contradicted by his eyes. 'Come on, Rose, don't be so heartless. If you're serious about going away, it will give us something to remember, something to keep us close.'

'And what if I fall pregnant, Harry? What use will I be then to the sick and wounded in Spain? Not to speak of the shame and sorrow it will cause my parents.'

'You won't fall pregnant,' he said, taking a step towards her. 'I'll be careful. Come...' He pulled her towards him. 'But if by some fluke you did, we'd just bring our marriage forward. Don't make me suffer, Rose. God, you're so lovely...' He began to kiss her again, more gently this time, stroking her hair, whispering words of love in her ear. She was melting, her body yielding to his caresses, her resolve faltering.

She let him lead her to a patch of grass away from the graves, partly shielded by a hedge of holly. He pulled her down beside him and started to unbutton her blouse, at the same time nuzzling her neck, his mouth moving lower as more of her flesh was exposed.

'No Harry, we mustn't.' He took no notice, if anything intensifying his efforts to reach inside her clothing. 'Stop it, Harry. At once!' Her attempts to wriggle free were useless against his superior strength. 'I said stop!' She slapped his face – not hard, but hard enough to shock him.

He pulled away and leaning on one elbow, passed his other hand across his reddening cheek. She could see the effort it took for him to control his anger. But she was angry too – with him for ignoring her pleas but also with herself for letting things go this far. She had allowed her feelings, the attraction she felt for him, to take precedence over caution and common sense.

He took a deep breath. 'Did you really think I'd force myself on you? I would never do that, Rose. I respect you far too much. But you were enjoying it too, admit it.'

She bent her head to fasten the buttons of her blouse. 'Maybe I was, but I asked you to stop. I meant it, Harry. I can wait and you must wait too. When we're married...'

'Then let's bring our marriage forward. Forget Spain. I want you as my wife, and the sooner the better. If you really care for me, you'll forget your silly ideas of helping those Spanish Commies. Stay, and look after me instead.'

For a moment, Harry's selfishness robbed her of words. Then she let fly at him. 'So your impatience to possess me, your... your *lust* is more important than the lives of those who're prepared to sacrifice everything in the fight against fascism.' In her head, Rose heard again the earnest, impassioned words of the speaker in Oxford on Friday, saw in vivid detail the images of suffering and privation evoked by her stories. 'You talk of Commies? They're ordinary people like us: men, women and children in desperate straits. How can you be so selfish?' At that moment she despised Harry.

'Rose, don't look at me like that. I'm sorry. It's only because I'm so crazy about you. I can't bear the idea of you putting yourself in danger. You know I'll worry like billy-o.' He gestured for her to take his arm. 'Come on, we'd better go back. It's almost dark.'

Mollified to some extent by his hangdog demeanour and soft words, she put her arm through his and they moved slowly towards the vicarage. 'You're right,' he said as they reached the garden gate. 'I'm a selfish brute. But I love you, Rose. You'll forgive me, won't you? Say you will.'

Rose nodded. 'I'll write to you, Harry. And once this wretched war is over, there'll be nothing to stop us getting married.' She tilted her face up towards his and smiled. 'I love you too.'

But that night, as she lay awake and restless in her bed, reflecting on their conversation, she could not dismiss her deep disappointment in Harry. She had wanted his support, wanted him to understand, as Father understood.

CHAPTER 2

Evesham/Aragón, 1936

On her last Sunday in England, the church was filled to capacity. Rose knelt with the rest of the congregation as prayers were said for her safety. Father had been keen to give her a good send-off. She sensed he was proud of her, while her mother could only focus on the perils she faced. Earlier, Rose had found her in tears, a copy of *Woman Today* open in her lap. She had already read the article that upset Mother. It described the *milicianas*, the 'ordinary housewives with husbands and children and homes not unlike our own' who leave their domestic duties to fight at the front, 'shouldering their muskets' in defence of their elected government.

'Mother, can you honestly imagine me carrying a gun?' Rose put an arm round her mother's shoulders. 'Don't worry, please. I won't be anywhere near the fighting.' But Mother remained unconvinced.

The last two months had crawled by as Rose waited with increasing impatience for the time when she could leave. While Mabel was busy organising collections and helping set up a workshop to make medical splints, Rose was forced to wait. Matron had refused to release her from her job without giving the full four weeks' notice, making it clear she disapproved of Rose's decision to help the 'reds' in Spain. There had been further delays getting hold of the anti-typhoid serum and her uniform. Then the Medical Aid Committee suggested she hang on a few days longer in order to travel with three London men volunteering for the newly formed International Brigades.

Now at last the time had come. Early tomorrow morning she would take the train to London, where she would meet her travelling companions at Victoria station. From there they would make their way to Paris and onward by train to an as yet unknown destination in Spain.

'Are you scared?' Ralph asked her.

She would never have admitted it to her brother but the question made Rose aware that fear, although largely eclipsed by excitement and her eagerness to play a part, lurked not far below the surface. The queasiness of her stomach confirmed it.

It was excitement that fuelled Rose through the long hours on packed trains as they trundled southwards through France. She was still sore from her typhoid shots but the warm welcome their small group received at the Spanish border and at every station they passed through kept her spirits high. Cheering and raising their closed fists, the country people showered them with gifts of peaches, grapes and pomegranates. A girl of about six with enormous dark eyes tapped Rose on the arm, holding out her offering of bunched sprigs of lavender. Bright sunlight painted the landscape in vivid colours.

After a few hours' rest in Barcelona, she was woken at dawn and put on a lorry taking her to Grañen on the Aragón front, while the London men continued south to Albacete. They bumped along rough roads, dust irritating her eyes and nose and choking her lungs. The boiled sweets she had brought from England proved a godsend, helping soothe the scratchiness in her throat. She shared them with the driver, a volunteer from Poland. In Lérida they stopped to pick up some Spanish recruits on their way to the front at Huesca: young boys eager to join the fight. For the last few hours, they had been driving in darkness, the lorry's weak headlights occasionally picking out a village with its church and a cluster of shabby dwellings or some animal running across the road and disappearing into the undergrowth.

Rose longed to arrive at the hospital, to wash the dust from her skin and hair and get a decent night's sleep. After that, she would be ready for whatever duties were required of her. Thora Silverthorne, who had also trained at Oxford's Radcliffe Infirmary and had gone out with the first medical contingent, was based there, she'd been told. Rose knew her by sight. She had a reputation for her political activity on the left.

They drew up outside a rambling old farmhouse on the edge of yet another down-at-heel village. 'Thank goodness you've arrived.' Thora had the hollow, shadowed look of someone who hasn't slept for days. 'Scrub up – water's short but you can have half a bucketful – then come and help out as quickly as you can. We're expecting another ambulance from the front any time now.'

Every bed was occupied, while more injured men lay on stretchers on the floor. Some were moaning, calling out for water or shouting for their mothers. Rose joined two other nurses and buckled down, doing what she could for them. She held the hand of a Scottish volunteer, who had come round from anaesthetic to find his leg amputated. The ambulance arrived with another twelve wounded, some of them seriously. One was rushed off to the theatre, where Dr Saxton had just finished operating on a chest wound, assisted by Thora. Another, with half his face blown away, died within minutes. It was mid-morning by the time Rose was relieved, given a cup of tea and shown to the loft where she could at last collapse onto one of the wire mattresses laid out on the floor. Sleep overtook her in an instant.

For the first time in days, Rose was free. Longing for an hour or two of solitude, she walked down to the river, which turned out to be little more than a muddy stream. The poplars lining it were still golden though the leaves had begun to fall, carpeting the ground. In the fields, she could see the remains of barley and maize crops. A man was ploughing with two mules. It had rained yesterday but now the sky was a cloudless blue. Rose took off her cardigan and rolled up the sleeves of her blouse, relishing the feel of the sun on her skin. She looked across to the mountains, the foothills of the Pyrenees, and back to the road where an endless procession of small covered carts was passing. A group of women with big baskets of soiled bed linen from the hospital were heading towards the river further down where there must be more water. How peaceful it all appeared.

She had written to her parents, telling them she had arrived, that she was safe, that they shouldn't worry. She wrote about the flocks of goats and sheep with tinkling bells that passed by every morning at the exact same time, driven by an old goatherd; about the generosity of the Spanish peasants, the dedication of the medical team and of how useful she felt.

She didn't feel safe. Air raids had been deliberately targeting the hospital, which had only narrowly escaped damage. Not surprisingly, the bombs caused utter panic among the patients, while the staff, equally frightened, tried to remain calm and reassure them. However, the last few nights had been quiet with no planes coming over. Fighting at the front had also stopped for the moment, but no one expected the lull to last long. In the meantime, there was little to do except wait for the next onslaught. With the pressure off and not enough work to occupy all the staff, solidarity was beginning to unravel, tensions and petty jealousies to emerge. Thora brewed tea and tried to smooth over the quarrels.

A donkey brayed from somewhere on the other side of the river as Rose found a spot to sit on the riverbank. The voices of the women busy with their laundry drifted faintly towards her on the still air. Taking a pen and exercise book from her bag, she tore out the centre pages and began the letter she had promised her friend.

Dear Mabel, she wrote, *I think of you often, remembering that meeting we went to in Oxford and how stirred I was by the speaker – stirred enough to follow her example and come to Spain! I don't think I knew the meaning of hard work before. We work 15-hour days, with few if any breaks. Men with dreadful injuries are continually arriving from the front. Some die before we can do anything for them; others need arms or legs amputating. But Mabel, they are so astonishingly brave. They brush off their injuries, however terrible, and talk only of returning to the front as soon as possible. They're convinced that if fascism can't be stopped here, the whole of Europe will be forced into another war.*

We're short of everything – medicines, blankets, stretchers, ambulances, decent food – so please spread the word and send what you can. We're training half a dozen Spanish girls as 'practicantes', what we would call orderlies. It's touching how keen they are to learn. They look up to us as if we were gods. Trained nurses scarcely exist in Spain. Hospitals have always been staffed by nuns.

I'm determined to work on my Spanish while I have a little time; I've picked up oodles already. One of the nurses is leaving for England today so I'm going to sign off now and give this letter to her. Keep up the good work.

Much love, Rose.

CHAPTER 3

Spain, 1937

Rose screamed, and immediately felt ashamed. It was only a rat scampering away from under her bed as she approached. She brushed the rat droppings from the blanket with her hand and kicked off her shoes before throwing herself down, too tired even to undress.

Jarama had proved a disaster for the British Battalion with at least a hundred and fifty killed and almost twice that number wounded. Working day and night with hardly a pause, Rose kept going on Spanish cigarettes and black coffee, a sandwich if she was lucky. Beds and stretchers filled every inch of the floor; some injured men lay on stretchers outside in the bitter cold, waiting till space could be found inside. It was hard not to trip over them. Several times Rose had stumbled over what turned out to be a dead body. An old man with a donkey cart ferried the dead in batches to the cemetery.

The doctors worked miracles but they could barely cope. Chloroform and ether ran out so they had to perform major operations using only local anaesthetics; surgical instruments became blunt with overuse; there were not enough bandages, dressings, needles or sutures. Working through the night, the electric lights failed regularly and they would be forced to work by torchlight. Once Rose had used a cigarette lighter to illuminate the opened belly of a soldier while the doctor operated. She no longer baulked at sleeping on the bloodied stretcher occupied only minutes before by a dying man. Like most of the staff, she, had an upset tummy from the lack of clean drinking water.

Time had become elastic, stretching or shrinking at random, so that the hour of the day, the day of the week, no longer had meaning. Five minutes at the side of a dying man, listening to his screams of agony, could feel like an eternity. Meanwhile, the days blended together in a seamless flow. The present moment was all that counted. The future could not be relied on. The past – before Spain – had no reality. There were times when Rose thought she had been in the country forever and others when it seemed she had arrived just days before. Only the changing seasons told her of the year's progress.

When a letter arrived one day from Harry, she could scarcely conjure up his face. He felt more of a stranger than the patients who passed fleetingly through her care. She regretted having let slip to one of the other nurses that she had a fiancé. Inevitably, word had spread and they would regularly quiz her about him. Rose responded snappily. She could not endure their teasing, however well meant. Romance was the last thing on her mind.

Then, to dispel her irritation, she would walk out and find a place to sit alone amongst the almond trees now bursting into delicate pink and white blossom. Surrounded by the unsullied beauty of nature, she could momentarily forget the horrors of war, the pervasive smell of blood and iodine. A snatch of bird song, the smell of damp earth, the feel of the breeze blowing through her hair would restore her sense of proportion, enabling her to shrug off the insistent questions of her colleagues as harmless banter. A few minutes usually sufficed to calm her.

They were no longer working with the British Medical Aid Unit. Now their team was attached to the 35th Division of the Republican Popular Army, following them about from front to front, wherever the need was greatest. It was becoming almost a routine, the moving from one base to another. They'd be given the order and would immediately start packing up. Each time, they would have to search for a suitable building, fetch water – rarely was there a direct supply – and then frantically scrub, scour and mop before setting up their operating tables, boiling their instruments and preparing to receive the steady flow of casualties.

Day after day, Rose watched as Spanish boys scarcely older than her brothers were stretchered in with the most ghastly injuries: eyes ripped out by grenades, bones shattered to splinters, flesh torn apart. She held their hands as they died still defiant, still convinced the rebels would be defeated and that death was a price worth paying. Their courage was inspiring but it moved her to tears. What a waste of young lives. Like many others, she felt angry and ashamed that the British government, along with the French and others who had signed the non-intervention treaty, were just standing by while Nazi Germany and Italy, who had also signed, supported Franco with bombs and weaponry and soldiers.

A steady trickle of deserters from Franco's side had been joining them in recent weeks. Most were simple farm lads, conscripted when their villages were taken, and felt no great loyalty to the rebels. Like many others, they were just young boys drawn in to this war either against their will for arbitrary reasons of geography or swayed by propaganda to join up. The same must be true in all wars.

'Leave him to die.' Rose thought at first that she must have misunderstood the muttered comment of the injured Catalan. A patient with a perforated kidney was being brought to the operating table. She exchanged glances with the Spanish doctor about to operate, who frowned and shook his head in a gesture of exasperation. She had heard griping from some of the men as he was stretchered in but only now did the reason dawn on her. The patient was from the fascist ranks, one of a group of their wounded brought in as prisoners earlier on. The order to treat them with the same care and courtesy as the Republican casualties had come from above but for Rose and the other medical staff, a patient's allegiance never made any difference: they were all just human beings in need.

After an eighteen-hour stint without rest and nothing to sustain her but dry bread topped by a sliver of corned beef, Rose had finally managed to escape and snatch a few hours' rest. She was woken by the most blood-curdling shriek, immediately followed by several more. Alarmed, she struggled to her feet, still bleary with sleep, to find Trinidad, one of the Spanish *practicantes*, trying to clean the wounds of a young soldier from Extremadura. Trinidad gave her a despairing look.

'Be quiet and stop wriggling about,' Rose said sharply to the patient. 'Do you want to lose your leg from an infection?' Her bullying nurse manner, though entirely feigned (had she missed her vocation as an actress?), worked like magic to subdue him. The British men rarely made such a song and dance. She was secretly amused that these Spanish fighters, so fearless in battle, tended to kick up an almighty fuss when faced with injections or the sting of having their wounds cleaned. A recent outbreak of typhoid had led to the decision to inoculate everyone; Rose and her colleagues had had to lock a couple of the officers in the Mess to stop them running away.

The suffering of the local population angered her more than almost anything. The bombing was indiscriminate. Shells were dropped on the streets and houses of poor villages as people went about their everyday business. A small girl was brought in with her arm hanging off, bleeding profusely. Her mother held it, still attached but only by a sinew. A weeping man rushed in, carrying his wife, her brains oozing out. One night Rose saw from the hospital windows a village some distance away consumed in flames.

She recalled her father's warning about the brutality of war. He had considered her too soft, but he was wrong. Many times she would catch herself thinking *I can't bear any more* as she tended the injured or watched helplessly as the life drained out of them. But then some small gesture of generosity or courage or kindness would renew her faith in humanity and give her the strength she needed to carry on. The people she was living amongst must be every bit as impoverished as the African poor for whom Father appealed when he passed round the collection plate in church. They had nothing, but still they insisted on bringing gifts. It might be only a handful of almonds or dried figs, a small round of moist goats' cheese or a pumpkin but they gave it proudly, eager to show the appreciation they felt. How could she turn her back on them?

There were happier interludes too, enjoyed all the more for their rarity. On May Day, while the Division was enjoying a brief rest, Rose heard the strains of music coming from the village. She ran out with one of the Irish nurses to join the celebration. Seeing the parade of girls dressed all in white, carrying bouquets, they plucked bunches of white mayflowers from the hedgerow and joined in with the Spanish girls. For a day, the war could be forgotten, sorrows put aside. A military band led the way, followed by hundreds of people, young and old, healthy and lame. Singing filled the air as the procession wound its way through every street and square.

The local women had baked cakes for the hospital patients and as she helped the village girls distribute them, it seemed to Rose that even the badly wounded imbibed something of the happy atmosphere. A couple of the girls had woven flowers into her hair, which inspired some jocular comments from the patients, used to seeing her austere in her uniform, with hair pinned back. Later, games were organised for the children and one of the nurses brought out a package of chocolate bars sent from England by her mother. By breaking up the Aeros and Kitkats into tiny pieces, they were able to give each child a sliver. Rose observed the delight on their faces as they savoured the unfamiliar taste and sweetness.

With everyone relaxed and in buoyant mood, the fun continued into the evening. The villagers had gone home but in the hospital, doctors, nurses, ambulance drivers plus a few of the recovering patients rustled up whatever outrageous garb they could find to dress up in. Then Kathleen, the Irish nurse, called for music. One of the doctors produced a guitar; a boy from the village, who'd had his appendix removed, took out a mouth organ; the theatre nurse joined in with a tin can and comb. Rose wished there was a piano for her to play – how she missed her piano – but at least she could sing. Their voices rang out, exuberant and fearless.

Singing worked wonders for morale. Singing, laughter, silly games all served to defuse the tension. Without that release, Rose thought, she would have gone mad; they would all have gone mad. The soldiers sang too, as they marched. Bolstering their courage. Sometimes she heard them singing softly in the darkness before dawn, as they passed on their way to the front.

Rose had never coped well with heat. During the occasional summer heatwaves in England, discomfort made her irritable. Her pale skin turned red, she sweated and itched and found the slightest activity an effort. As much as possible, she skulked indoors, avoiding the sun.

July in the baking plains of central Spain was beyond anything she had previously experienced. The temperature soared to well over a hundred degrees. She marvelled at the men's endurance, fighting in those temperatures. Their hospital was based in a Catholic boys' school within the huge and austere complex of El Escorial, monastery, palace and final resting place of Spanish royalty. An odd base for a Republican hospital, Rose thought, but its thick granite walls and small windows were a godsend, keeping the place relatively cool.

In any case, it was not long before her own small discomforts paled into insignificance, supplanted by more serious concerns. Ambulances were being targeted, bombed as they brought the injured from the battlefield, so that every trip was fraught with danger for the drivers. Two were killed and several wounded. When she was sent to a mobile hospital nearer the front, Rose worked in constant fear.

The number of casualties was tremendous and once again she found herself working day and night, never sleeping more than four hours at a stretch. They were lucky to have a Catalan surgeon, Dr Broggi, a genius with abdominal injuries. A high proportion of his patients, even those with quite severe injuries, survived. Rose felt privileged to work with him. He had none of the airs put on by some doctors but was kind and considerate with everyone and managed to stay calm in the most difficult circumstances. But after three weeks of intense fighting, the Republicans had to withdraw. The enemy's superior weaponry and planes had reduced the British Battalion from three hundred and thirty-one to forty-two.

Rose had expected to be caught by a bomb at Brunete but it was the following month when she was once again on the Aragón front that the hit she'd been dreading materialised. And it wasn't a bomb but the bullet from a machine gun that found her. They were in tents by the roadside a few kilometres from the front, using an old abattoir for operations. The conditions were appalling; they were only able to operate on the most urgent cases. Flies buzzed about their heads in the stifling heat. Rose was shocked to discover that some of the soldiers being brought in hadn't eaten for two or three days because food had to be taken up on mules and it was often difficult to reach them as they advanced. Worse, when they arrived half-starved, there was virtually nothing to give them – sometimes only black coffee. Yet they scarcely complained. One boy had in his pocket a raw potato dug out of the ground. Spotting tooth-marks where a bite had been taken from it, Rose wanted to weep.

She was tending to a patient in one of the tents when she heard the plane. It was flying low, the drone of the engine growing louder. Emilia, the Spanish *practicante* working with her, screamed. Rose instinctively threw herself down on the nearest bed, shielding one of the patients who had recently been operated on. They lay there in terror as they heard the unmistakeable rat-tat-tat of machine gun fire.

She must have blacked out briefly because the next thing she knew, one of the Spanish doctors was standing over her, examining the bullet wound in her upper left arm. The laceration was not too deep, he said as he cleaned and sutured it – she was lucky the bullet had passed through without lodging there. He instructed Emilia, who was unhurt, to bandage it up and told Rose she must rest. 'You've lost some blood and you're going to feel weak.'

She was taken back to the hospital at El Escorial in an ambulance, shared with several far more badly wounded fighters. 'It's nothing,' she told everyone. 'Just a graze.' Surrounded by so many serious injuries, she felt a fraud.

The following day, Dr Crome came to see her. 'Why don't you take a break, go back to England for a week or two?' he said. 'You're exhausted and it will give your wound time to heal.'

'But I'm fine,' she protested. 'Fit as a flea apart from this silly old gash in my arm. I'm right-handed; I can still work.' There was too much to be done and not enough nurses. 'I'll take a few days' rest here instead.'

'Hmm.' Chin in hand, the doctor regarded her thoughtfully. 'I've an idea. If you want to make yourself useful, you could address a few meetings over there, try and get hold of more equipment and medicines. I'll give you a list. See what you can do.'

'Is that an order, doctor?' Rose was smiling. His proposal made sense. She would be performing a worthwhile task and in less than a fortnight she could be back.

With her arm still throbbing, Rose shuffled about in her bed, trying to find a comfortable position. One thing troubled her now. Although eager to see her family, she knew that if she returned wounded, Mother would be greatly distressed and do everything possible to dissuade her from coming back.

By morning, a solution had presented itself. She would go first to her friend Dorothy's in Birmingham. There she would speak at public meetings, write to every organisation she could think of, spread the word by whatever means possible about Spain's dire situation, their pressing need for supplies. She was convinced that if only people knew, they would give generously. After a week or so, when her wound was sufficiently healed and she had collected what she could, there would be time for her family – and for further appeals and talks within range of home. It was a plan that satisfied her.

A lorry was due to leave for Valencia that same day. There seemed no point in delaying. Armed with the promised list, Rose hitched a ride south. From the port, she was escorted by launch to a British naval ship – one of several patrolling along the Spanish coast – that was now heading back to England. The journey did not pass without incident. Submarines had begun launching attacks on neutral ships in the Mediterranean and a torpedo narrowly missed them as they sailed away eastwards. At the same time, they had to dodge aerial attacks from Italian planes.

The British officers took pains to reassure her she was in no danger. After what she'd been through in recent months, their gallantry and concern made her smile. She felt like a queen when at five in the afternoon they brought her tea in a bone china cup and slices of bread and butter with jam.

CHAPTER 4

England, 1937

Rose was relieved to find the front door of Dorothy's terraced house in Northfield slightly ajar when she arrived at twelve o'clock on a rainy August Sunday. She'd been unable to give warning of her visit. Dorothy had no phone and a letter would not have reached her in time. 'Anyone in?' she called.

'You!' Dorothy stared at her in amazement. 'I thought you were in Spain.'

'I was and I'll be going back there soon. It's a long story but...'

'Come in for goodness sake, Rose. You will be staying for lunch, won't you?'

Rose followed Dorothy into the front room. 'Actually,' she said, 'I was hoping to stay for a few days. I mean if that isn't going to put you out too much.'

'It will be a pleasure.' Dorothy flung her arms round her friend. 'It's been such a long time... What's the matter?'

Rose had leapt backwards with a screech. She unfastened her cape to reveal her bound up arm. 'You must swear secrecy, Dot. I don't want my family to find out. No need to look so alarmed,' she said, laughing. 'Honestly, it's nothing but you know how mothers fuss. In a week it'll be completely healed. As soon as I can dispense with the bandages, I'll head off to Evesham. In the meantime I've got loads to do. I won't be getting under your feet, I promise.'

'That's the last thing I'm worried about. In any case, I'll be out at work.' She picked up Rose's suitcase. 'Let me take this upstairs to the spare bedroom. Then you can come and talk to me while I cook lunch. I want to hear everything. And I've got some news too.'

Rose could guess what it was. Dorothy had been sweet on her boss, a bachelor, for some time. Romance was already in the air when she last heard from Dorothy; news of an engagement would come as no surprise. 'You're not!' Her friend's shy smile told Rose she was right. 'But that's wonderful. Congratulations!'

'Thanks. We're hoping to wed next spring.' Noticing how her eyes sparkled, Rose had to admit to a prick of envy at her happiness.

'But what about you and Harry?' Dorothy asked now. 'Have you set a date for your wedding yet?'

'Well, no.' Harry was a problem Rose didn't want to talk or even think about. She would have to see him – impossible to avoid – but the prospect did not gladden her heart as it should have done. Dorothy took the hint and they spoke of other things.

'I so admire what you're doing,' Dorothy told her after she'd attempted to paint some kind of picture of the tragedy unfolding in Spain and of the role being played by the internationals – both fighters and medical teams. 'I couldn't bear it, seeing so much suffering, so many young lives lost or blighted by injury. After the Great War, I thought we were finished with all that. I thought we'd learnt enough to create a Europe free from war. How do you stand it? You're such a soft-hearted creature.'

'I suppose I've become tough. I've had to, there's no time for weeping.'

Rose was soon busy arranging meetings and following up contacts. She had little experience of public speaking, nor of importuning company directors. A year ago she could not have imagined ever having the courage to do either. Now the prospect didn't give her a moment's pause. She spoke to social clubs and trade unions and the local branches of political parties. Not being affiliated to any of them helped. She knew her subject. She knew what was needed. And the passion that infused her words appeared to convince those who turned out to pack their meeting rooms and town halls.

The firm Dorothy worked for, chivvied by her fiancé Archie, donated enough money to purchase three dozen stretchers. A collection organised among the staff of one large company helped to fund much-needed medical instruments. Bird's Custard Factory contributed a large quantity of tinned milk; Cadbury's offered half a hundredweight of chocolate bars. Rose imagined the whoops of joy that would greet this unexpected gift and its effect on the morale of fighters and medics alike.

On the following Friday she unwound the bandages and examined her wound. The flesh had knitted together perfectly, all credit to the Spanish doctor. It was still a little sore and she would have to protect it from knocks and dirt, but a small pad and light bandaging, easy to conceal under a long-sleeved blouse, would be sufficient.

She took leave of Dorothy on the Saturday morning and caught the train to Oxford. From there she rang the vicarage. 'I'll be catching the next bus to Evesham,' she said when Father answered. 'Ask Maisie to make up my bed.'

'What?' There was a longish pause. 'Rose? Is that you?' She found herself smiling. 'The bus from where? Where are you?'

'It's me, Father. I'm on my way. I'm in Oxford.' She heard a sharp intake of breath and added, 'Can't wait to see you all.'

Her parents and brothers were at the bus stop to welcome her when she arrived. Rose had tears in her eyes as she hugged each of them in turn. The joy she felt at seeing them took her by surprise. She had thought only of their reaction, not of her own. Mother was crying too, Father beamed and even the boys looked pleased to see her.

'It's wonderful to be home,' she said, 'but I must tell you straightaway that I'm only staying for a week. I have to go back.'

Rose saw her mother's face drop. 'Let's not talk about that yet,' she said. 'You've only just arrived. It's such a relief to see you alive and well, Rose. And just like you to spring it on us without letting on beforehand.' She took Rose's arm – the good one. 'I told Maisie to have the kettle boiling for tea. There'll be buttered scones too if you're hungry.'

Father picked up her case. 'I think this calls for a glass of sherry,' he said.

Over lunch, Rose explained her plans to speak at meetings and appeal for donations. She forbore from mentioning the week she'd already spent in Birmingham.

'But my dear,' Mother interrupted, 'you won't be able to organise things so quickly. I'm on the committee of the W.I. so I know. We arrange speakers weeks or months in advance.'

Rose knew better. Her experience in Birmingham had shown her what was possible. 'The Women's Institute is an excellent idea,' she said. 'I'm sure they'll be keen to help. Just give me the name of the Secretary and I'll get in touch.'

Rose's friend Mabel was of great assistance with contacts and also took on some of the footslogging. Being active in the Communist party, she was better informed about Spain than many people but what Rose reported left her aghast and angry. The two of them worked with relentless zeal and Rose soon had a list of groups and companies willing to give her a hearing. Not all showed interest. Two or three were openly unsympathetic, disparaging even, but as in Birmingham, the majority responded positively.

'So when will you be seeing Harry?' Mother asked on the third day when Rose had still failed to mention him. 'I suppose he does know you're here?'

Rose walked over to the window and looked out at the garden, bright with summer blooms. It must be a year since that afternoon she'd walked down the path with Father and told him she was going to Spain. How green she had been then, how carefree. 'I'm sure we'll find time to meet soon,' she replied, turning to face her mother. 'By the way, did I tell you Mrs Dixon from your W.I. has invited me to the meeting on Thursday? She thinks they'll want to knit blankets for the men. We're terribly short of blankets.'

Mother gave her a sharp look. 'I thought about inviting Harry for supper one evening. With your permission, obviously.'

'Please, Ma, leave it to me. I haven't forgotten about him.'

'Very well, if that's what you want.' She joined Rose at the window and embraced her. 'My dear, I know what you're doing is important, but don't you think you should rest a little? I'm sure you deserve it.'

Rose sighed. 'I expect you're right; I could do with a rest. It's just...' Seeing the sorrow on her mother's face, she said, 'I'll try. How about a family picnic on Saturday? If the weather holds. And we'll invite Harry along.'

The smile that lit up Mother's face made her capitulation feel worthwhile.

'So you're home. Splendid.' Did she detect a slight unease in Harry's voice on the phone? If so, his enthusiastic response to her invitation led her to dismiss the thought. 'A picnic? Capital! I'd rather it was just the two of us but there we are.

'Tell you what, ' he added, 'I'll take you to the pictures one evening. There's a cracking film on at the Regal.'

'I'm going to be rather busy actually...' Harry's pronounced silence persuaded her to delay any difficult conversations till they could meet face to face. 'Super,' she said. 'It's ages since I went to the pictures.'

Rose was occupied every day, intent on what she regarded as her 'mission'. The results were gratifying. Dr Crome had arranged for her to return to Spain in an ambulance being driven out the following week. She spoke by telephone to an official at the HQ of the London Medical Aid Committee and orchestrated collection of the supplies she had been promised.

Once all that was in hand, Rose felt she could relax and spend the weekend enjoying the company of her family. She had long talks with Father, recounting some of her experiences in Spain and listening to his fears about the political situation in Europe, in particular the rise of Hitler. While Jewish refugees were arriving in Britain from Germany, Mosley continued to preach his ugly dogmas. Oxford University had an active fascist association. Rose told her father about some of the Jewish emigrés she had met in the International Brigades. With Mother, Rose spoke less of politics and war than of the hardships suffered by the Spanish population and their gratitude to the foreign volunteers.

By lunchtime on Saturday it had turned warm and humid with a ceiling of low cloud that Rose found oppressive after the high vault of the Spanish skies. They carried their picnic baskets to the grounds of Evesham Abbey and spread a tablecloth on the grassy riverbank.

Rose helped her mother lay out the plates, cutlery and napkins. Father poured glasses of homemade lemonade. 'We'll keep the beer till Harry arrives,' he said.

'He's coming now,' Ralph said. 'I can see him.'

Harry was heading towards them, his long swinging strides covering the distance in no time at all. He shook hands with her parents and brothers and sat down beside her on the grass, taking her face in his hands and kissing her on the mouth. Bertie stifled a snigger.

Harry's close physical presence – the smell of his hair oil, the texture of his skin and timbre of his voice – sent the blood rushing to her head. Her feelings were not as clear as she had supposed. In Spain she had rarely given him a thought. The idea of sharing her life with him, living as man and wife had seemed absurd. Now she could not rule it out with such assurance.

'So what are you going to do now?' Harry asked a little later when they had eaten and drunk and exchanged pleasantries, avoiding controversial topics like war and weddings.

'Rose, haven't you told him?' Mother chided. Turning to Harry, she said, 'Perhaps *you* can talk her out of going back. Though I'm afraid she's very determined.'

Harry's response was not the one she had expected. 'I can understand your feelings, Mrs Tilly,' he said, 'but in the end it's Rose's decision. After all, she's been out there for several months. She knows what she'll be facing.'

Rose felt even more confused. 'Didn't he care any more? Had he met someone else? Or was he being admirably (and somewhat untypically) selfless in standing up for her right to autonomy? Maybe she had misjudged him. His expression was inscrutable.

She let him take her to the cinema that evening. They saw *Captains Courageous* with Spencer Tracy, a new Hollywood film she gathered everyone was talking about. Resting her head on Harry's shoulder, feeling his protective arm around her, she felt like any other girl out for the evening with her sweetheart. A world away from the savagery of Spain.

As he walked her home after the film, he seemed distracted. 'What's on your mind, Harry?' she asked, and immediately wished she hadn't.

'A lot of people think we'll be at war before long,' he said. 'What's happening in Europe... Things are getting more serious. And as a trained army officer, I'll be involved, naturally.' He stopped and faced her. 'I still want to marry you, of course I do. But the future is looking very uncertain; it's not a time for making firm plans.'

She examined his face in the lamplight. It revealed very little, and yet some nagging intuition told her he was not being entirely frank. His eyes held hers for only a moment before flicking away. She decided to let it rest. 'That's very sensible, Harry,' she said. 'In any case, I'm leaving on Monday.' Having more time to consider her own feelings rather suited her.

CHAPTER 5

Murcia, 1937

'Franco, *Señorita*, Franco!' The little boy clutched at Rose's uniform as the air raid siren sounded its ominous screech. The children leapt out of their beds, running to her in terror. The nightmare of their retreat from Málaga was still with them. Rose could not erase from her mind the horrific scenes described by the mothers of these children – those who had survived. The nightmare of being attacked from air and sea, machine-gunned and bombed as they fled with what possessions they could carry on their backs or in overloaded carts. The nightmare of seeing men, women and children dead or dying in ditches, mules lying feet up in the air by the roadside.

On her return from England, Rose had been sent south to Murcia to work with the refugees there. A hundred thousand, two thirds of the population, had taken flight from Málaga as Franco's Italian forces prepared to invade, seeking safety in the Republican zone to the east. Many did not make it. For four days and nights as they trudged along the road to Almería, old people, babies, children and animals were slaughtered indiscriminately. Rose felt ashamed of her country. They had carried out a meticulous search of the ambulance she travelled in from England, ready to confiscate any hidden weapons, while German and Italian arms were being used to kill and maim civilians with impunity. The non-intervention treaty applied to one side only.

Almería and Murcia were now swamped with refugees. Attempts to distribute them around neighbouring villages and set up children's colonies had been partially successful. However, the local population had scarcely enough to eat and with such an influx, malnutrition was rife. Rose was horrified to see a four-year old boy with limbs no bigger than those of a six month old baby. Where there should have been muscles, repeated hypodermic injections had caused the most awful abscesses. Rose had no qualms about ignoring the Spanish doctor's order for daily injections of glucose. Instead she gave him small but frequent amounts of the fluid by mouth, a slower but far less risky treatment. The standards of hygiene also shocked the English nurses. There was little they could do about it: the doctors responded angrily to any challenges to their authority. Rose was not the only one to have been slapped down for an implied criticism.

She found the state of the children more distressing than anything she had faced up to now. Half the babies were dying – needlessly, she felt – as a result of the conditions. Many mothers, under-nourished themselves, were unable to feed and tinned milk was in short supply. The lack of clean water and proper sterilisation for the bottles exacerbated the problem. Rose was reminded of her stint in a paediatric ward during nurse training, of having to stand by helpless as children died from TB, diphtheria or meningitis. Now, once again she experienced that sense of frustration and despair. She had neither the authority nor the resources to alleviate the children's suffering in any significant way. The stressful atmosphere in the hospital was also taking its toll. At the end of a shift, she would often break down in tears.

Rose felt wretched as she tried to comfort yet another distraught mother. 'I'm sorry, we did all we could.' Breaking the news no mother wants to hear. As if these women had not suffered enough. Some had already lost children on the long trek from Málaga. No wonder they screamed or refused to believe their babies were dead. After waking in anguish from a dream in which the limp, lifeless body she cradled in her arms was her own infant, Rose asked if she could be transferred.

The convalescent hospital in Castillejo was housed in a summer palace formerly used by royalty. It was run by the American medical services and had a Dutch doctor in charge, while the patients were from a dozen different nations and political shades. After working mostly on or near the front, Rose was relieved to be in the more relaxed atmosphere of a convalescent hospital and a fairly luxurious one at that. No one had to share a bed or sleep on a blood-soaked stretcher. There was enough to eat and although she was kept busy, there were no twenty-hour shifts. She realised how worn down she had become before her break in England. Now her energy was returning and with it her sense of humour.

As in the other hospitals, they relied on volunteers from the local population to carry out many of the routine tasks like laundry, cleaning, fetching water from the river, preparing food and washing up. Patients were also expected to help, once they were back on their feet. Lini, the Dutch woman charged with organising the hospital, told Rose how she had persuaded the men to scrub floors, peel potatoes and wash the dishes alongside the girls. 'Once they were reminded of the Republic's ideals – that women were their comrades and should be treated as equals – it was hard for them to refuse,' said Lini, laughing. 'Though some of them still tried, especially the Spanish men.'

The Italian patients from the Garibaldi brigade volunteered to supply food. Bored with a diet of endless chickpeas, they hobbled down to the nearby stream on their crutches and came back with trout or other fish. Occasionally one of them would arrive with a live chicken in his arms. 'I hope you haven't stolen that from some poor peasant,' Rose said to Salvatore. His outraged denial didn't ring true but the chicken was received with such cheers that she had to smile and let the matter rest.

Women from the village would sometimes sneak in with rabbits or chickens hidden under their shawls and beg the man in charge of the stores to exchange them for soap, tinned milk or sugar. Once there were roasted mule ribs for dinner. But mostly it was chickpeas – in soup or with a little onion and tomato paste – and rather tasteless bread. One day a group of the local men, who lived in caves nearby, came to offer seeds and the loan of a plough so that the fertile land surrounding the hospital could be put to use to grow food. Some of the more mobile patients volunteered to work the land. The spirit of cooperation heartened Rose. These people were living out their ideals.

In the trenches when it was quiet, the Spanish men, many of whom had never had the chance to go to school, were learning to read and write. The girls too, especially those working alongside the nurses as *practicantes*, were eager to learn. Two of the more educated Spanish men – one with both legs amputated, the other recovering from a lung injury – volunteered to set up literacy classes for them.

Now there was less pressure, Rose found time to write home – to her parents and to friends. She took care to focus on the positive. *Dear Dorothy,* she wrote, *Our hospital is in a palace, would you believe! It's surrounded by gardens, there's a ruined Arab castle nearby and a trout stream running past. Last night we organised a musical evening. It was so jolly. I played a horribly out of tune piano that had been left there. A Hungarian patient with a head wound played the violin, a carpenter from the village had a guitar and Miguel, a rather good-looking Andalusian with a badly wounded thigh, played a kind of accordion called a bandoneón. He was injured at Brunete while I was on the front there but we never met as he was taken to another hospital. (I would have remembered him!). Well, our little band was swelled by all kinds of improvised instruments; you can imagine the racket we made. Everyone wanted tunes and songs from their own country and naturally we sang the Internationale – several times in several languages. We'd bought some of the local 'vino' and we all got quite merry, the villagers included. But could we find partners for our patients to dance with? Absolutely not! For the village girls, physical contact with men is considered scandalous. They insisted on partnering each other. We've been training some of them as orderlies but getting them to touch the patients – washing them and so on – has been quite a challenge.*

Rose finished her letter and lit a cigarette. She was thinking about Miguel, wondering what it was about this sturdy, dark-eyed accordionist with his intense gaze that had made such an impression. As she stood outside in the afternoon sunshine, she noticed a couple of the village women watching her.

'Do all women do it in your country?' one of them asked.

'Do what?'

She pointed to Rose's cigarette. 'Women don't smoke here.'

Her friend giggled. 'Only whores. The priests tell us it's wicked. Yet they see nothing wrong in men smoking. Why should the rules be different for men and women?'

'Yes, and they tell us a lot of things are sins but it doesn't seem to apply to them,' the first one added. 'Padre Teófilo regularly visits the widow of Arsenio the carpenter late at night, or so I've heard. Are the priests the same in your country?'

'My father is a priest,' Rose said, 'and he's a good man. He practises what he...' They were staring at her, open-mouthed. It didn't take long to figure out why. Amused, she explained, 'He's a Protestant, not a Catholic. They're allowed to marry.'

'*Ay*, Virtudes, did you hear that? Priests allowed to marry!'

Virtudes considered. 'Maybe it's not such a bad idea. It might stop them ogling the young girls.'

Rose could converse in Spanish quite easily now. Working alongside the Spanish girls and with patients of all nationalities, she had absorbed the language without even trying. If she didn't understand a word, she would ask. The patients, with plenty of time on their hands, liked to engage her in conversation. Their stories, especially those of the Spaniards, inspired her and made her understand why they were prepared to sacrifice themselves for the Republic.

Miguel often sought her out. He told her how, like many of the children in his village in rural Granada, he could only attend school – two rooms in the Town Hall – after several hours of work on the land, starting before dawn. When the school day finished, his work would resume. On many days, half the children were absent because they were needed for agricultural work; otherwise the family would not eat. His father had never been to school and was determined his children should have the education he lacked.

'He was a sharecropper but we were lucky in that we owned a tiny patch of land where we could grow vegetables. My mother worked as a *recovera*, buying eggs in the village and taking them to Granada to sell. She would set out in the early hours to reach the city by midday, just to make a few pesetas. Then she would have to walk all the way back.'

During the Republic, he had helped build a school for one of the neighbouring villages. 'There were seven thousand new schools built in less than a year – secular schools free of the Church and religion.' He told her of his ambition to be a teacher once the Republic was re-established. Rose was struck by the passion in his eyes when he spoke of these things. She pictured Harry's eyes, cool, detached, expressionless.

'Consider this, Rose,' he said to her another day as they surveyed the newly planted vegetable garden. 'My mother's sister Remedios gave birth to a little boy, my cousin. A few days later, one of the *señoritas* in the town also gave birth. For reasons of vanity, she preferred not to feed the baby and asked my aunt to be wet-nurse to her child. You must understand, the people were poor, often eating only once a day – sweet potatoes, bread, never meat. Remedios couldn't refuse the *señorita* but she didn't have enough milk for both babies. Her own son became weak; he was losing weight. She tried giving him goats' milk but he wouldn't take it. He died at two months.'

Rose lay in bed that night haunted by Miguel's tale. She was haunted too by his eyes, by the way they could turn from burning ferocity to tenderness in an instant. She could feel them blazing into her soul, branding her. She knew her own eyes lit up when she saw him.

'I'm being discharged,' Miguel told her one morning. He stood square and straight-backed in front of her, full of confidence. 'The doctor says I'm fit.'

Rose had been expecting it. His wound had healed well and like most of the men, he was impatient to return to the front. His natural gait was fast and now he was like a hound straining at the leash, 'I'll miss you,' she said and averted her eyes so that he wouldn't see her sadness. He took her by the hands, kissed her forehead and walked quickly away without turning to look back.

CHAPTER 6

Teruel / Ebro, 1937 - 1938

Teruel in winter was cold, bitterly cold. When Rose arrived there in December, the winding mountain road was already deep in snow. Halfway up, they were caught in a blizzard that forced their lorry to a halt. Rose thought she would freeze to death. They brewed tea by melting snow on their primus and warmed their hands on the tin mugs, praying for the snow to ease off before nightfall.

The hospital had been set up in an old water mill. Ambulances struggled to reach it; sometimes they had to be dug out of the snow. In the trenches, the men turned blue with cold and when there was action, they battled in a slippery mash of snow, slush and mud. Some died of exposure; others had limbs amputated due to frostbite.

On top of the cold, they had to contend with lice. Everyone was infested, staff and patients alike. Day and night they were scratching, scratching... There was little chance to wash because of the cold. All you could do was scratch. It drove Rose mad, especially at night. She would lie awake scratching till she bled.

She thought often of Miguel. She had no idea of his whereabouts. Any day he might be brought in dead or dying to her own hospital or another. He might already be dead. It was better not to think of him. Nothing had been said, no kisses exchanged or promises made. But in war, promises were as flimsy as a moth's wings; only a child would believe them. All she knew was that she wanted to see him again. In the meantime she worked – dressing wounds, assisting with operations, holding the hands of the dying. And scratching, forever scratching.

News took time to reach them. They could only judge the level of activity at the front by the number of casualties being brought in. A Republican victory at Teruel in early January saw little respite in the fighting. Franco launched a counter-offensive and the following month retook the town, along with fifteen thousand prisoners and a great deal of military equipment. The war was not going well and morale, so strong up till now, began to falter.

Rose cursed as she banged her leg on one of the hundred or so metal camp beds lying higgledy-piggledy on the uneven floor of the cave hospital above the river Ebro. It was summer now and outside there would be at least another two hours of daylight, but in the cave, protected by a hefty overhanging rock, darkness came early. The only light they had to work by came from tiny oil lamps made from tin cans with a wick, which flickered and kept going out. She still felt slightly dizzy after giving blood yet again. Everyone – lorry-drivers, doctors, nurses, villagers – was called on to give blood. The transfusions were saving many lives. Often they were carried out directly, arm to arm.

Night was when the casualties came in. With the constant heavy bombardment, it was too dangerous to move them by day. The ambulances brought batch after batch of wounded to the valley below, where the nurses would examine and sort them. A grievous number were beyond saving. Those with a chance of survival were carried on stretchers up the steep, rocky slope to the cave and the operating theatre, which was lit by a couple of electric bulbs run off an ambulance. They included women and children from the nearby village, caught in the bombing raids.

Rose felt sick at heart seeing the procession of lorries high on the opposite bank, making their way to the Ebro crammed with men, ammunition and materials while ambulances transported the dead, dying and wounded down to the valley. These men now singing with gusto would be tomorrow's casualties. The injuries were worse than anything Rose had seen before. Although the doctors succeeded in saving some lives against all the odds, many died. Rose watched one man after another fade away.

Even outside, the smell of death hung in the air. The dead were buried in an unmarked common grave in the village cemetery. They competed with the living for blankets, as usual in short supply. More than once, Rose had argued with the Spanish stretcher-bearers who wanted them to wrap the dead; she had insisted they were needed for those who might recover.

Here it was not lice but scabies that affected the wounded. Rose scrubbed her body with Lysol and then meths to protect herself. But there was worse: an outbreak of typhoid that had started in the local population and was now spreading among the patients. Two of their nurses had to be sent home to England. Rose slept on a mattress in the open just outside the cave's long cleft of a mouth.

Heavy bombing from the air and the repeated destruction of the pontoon bridges and boats meant that often the wounded would be waiting for hours on the opposite bank before they could be brought across. As soon as the bridges had been repaired, more bombs would demolish them. They urgently needed a safe place for a hospital on the other side.

A team of them set off early one morning in several ambulances to find a suitable building. Dodging the constant bombardments from enemy planes, they drove into the hills. Their first attempt to set up a hospital, in the white hermitage of Santa Magdalena, lasted only a week before the order came to evacuate. Bombs and shells were raining down on them without respite; it was simply too dangerous.

The search resumed. After driving around most of the night, often without lights to avoid being spotted, they were about to give up when they came upon an old, disused railway tunnel on the edge of the river. Half in ruins, its walls were coated in soot and grime, but it would be safe. By now it was almost dawn. Rose felt in desperate need of food and sleep; her body protested at the task confronting them. Still, the work had to be done. Together they scraped and scrubbed in the dark, trying not to trip over the railway lines, working against time until their new hospital, equipped with sixty-five beds, was ready. A quick cup of black coffee and a hunk of bread were all they had time for before the casualties started arriving.

Rose watched bleary-eyed as the stretchers were brought in – one man after another, some groaning or calling for water, some with blood dripping through their bandages, some unconscious. The doctor, with a patient already on the operating table, called her to assist him. The patient was barely conscious. A severe abdominal wound – one of the worst she'd seen. Rose glanced at their one lamp. Its poor light would have to serve for all three operating tables. 'Chloroform,' Dr Jolly ordered as she assembled the instruments. 'And we may need blood. What group are you?' Only then did she turn her gaze from the patient's wound to his face. It was Miguel.

'*Curandera! Curandera, ven aquí.*' Rose began to hear the cry even in her sleep. For many of these men lying stacked in rows one above the other on the hospital train parked in another tunnel behind the front lines, this was their first taste of a professional medical service. They were calling for the 'healer'. In their villages, there would be a woman, an expert in plants and herbs, to cure whatever ailments they suffered.

The operation on Miguel had gone better than expected. His chances of survival were slim, Dr Jolly had warned as he prepared to operate. And it was still touch and go, he told her, when the ambulance took Miguel off to one of the base hospitals away from the front that was better equipped and safer. He had recognised her when he came round from the anaesthetic. She was holding his hand and as he opened his eyes, took in the surroundings and began to piece together what had happened to him, he smiled at her and spoke her name.

The fighting raged on. The Republicans' successful crossing of the Ebro had blocked Franco's attack on Valencia but with such vast air power at his service, a Republican retreat was clearly only a matter of time. Soldiers were being blasted off the rocky hillside in appalling numbers and the reserves weren't infinite. Already, they were conscripting sixteen and seventeen-year-olds.

At the beginning of October, foreign volunteers were withdrawn from the lines. There was to be a farewell parade in Barcelona at the end of the month, Rose heard. She was at the base hospital now – the same one to which Miguel had been sent. She'd been relieved to find him alive, though weakened by an infection that had taken hold after the operation and threatened his life. Now he was over the worst, slowly regaining strength and refusing to be disheartened by the situation, which was looking ever more hopeless. The talks at Munich, the policy of appeasement, meant they could not look for help from outside Spain.

'I'll be fighting fit in no time,' Miguel told Rose as he and some of the other recovering wounded left by ambulance for a convalescent hospital in Murcia. It was late November and the Ebro battle had been lost. The foreign soldiers – and many of the medics too – were returning to their countries.

'It feels like a betrayal to leave when there's still so much work to do,' one of the other nurses said to her, 'but I don't think I can take much more.'

Rose nodded. 'I know how you feel. It's grim.'

'What are you going to do when you get home to England?'

'Actually,' Rose said, 'I'm planning to stay on a little longer.'

Three days after Miguel left, she had written to Francesca, the Quaker woman with whom she had worked at the refugee hospital in Murcia last year. Reports had reached her from another nurse about the excellent work Francesca was doing with the children there. Rose admired her greatly. Already in her mid-fifties, she had more energy than many of the younger nurses and was a born organiser. Nothing could ruffle her: even in the face of complete pandemonium among the refugees she remained poised and elegant.

Dear Rose... Francesca wrote back with typical enthusiasm, describing the sewing workshops she had set up for refugee girls and her idea for a farm colony for the boys. *It would be a pleasure to have you with us. The children's health has improved greatly since you were here but refugees are still arriving and among them many cases of typhoid, pneumonia, whooping cough, TB, measles and the usual childhood illnesses. Most of the nurses have already gone home so please do come, whenever you're ready.*

CHAPTER 7

Murcia, 1938

Murcia – and the children's colonies nearby where Rose now spent some of her time – was like paradise after the Ebro, after Teruel, after Brunete. She no longer had to survive on four hours' sleep a night or deal with dreadful injuries in dire conditions. Most of the children were recovering. Once their health had improved sufficiently, they were taught new skills in the workshops. There, in an atmosphere of purposeful activity, they thrived.

Rose loved visiting the different colonies, seeing the young girls busy at their sewing machines, often singing as they worked. She was touched by their proud smiles as they turned out garment after garment for other refugees who had arrived with only the clothes they stood up in. In the evenings, the girls were learning to read and write. Sometimes they would ask her to listen as they read aloud. Another group – mainly older men – were being taught to make *alpargatas*, the rope-soled shoes with canvas tops that everyone wore in the countryside.

Francesca's idea for a farm colony for boys was becoming a reality. They had acquired an old flourmill with a spring behind it at Crevillente in the mountains between Murcia and Alicante and had started to convert it to accommodate the boys and staff. On the terraced hills around the mill, once well cultivated, only a few almond, fruit and carob trees remained, because the land was no longer watered as it had been when the mill was in use. Here the boys would work, learning to irrigate and farm the land, and growing vegetables. Rose wrote to Miguel, knowing how much he would applaud these projects.

His reply was exactly what Rose had hoped for without daring to suggest. He wrote that his wound was healing well but he was impatient and longed for some useful activity until he could return to the fighting. *Please ask if I can help at one of the colonies or workshops.*

I could teach the children to read and write or train them in agricultural skills at the farm colony. Or I could show them how to make alpargatas – my uncle was the alpargatero in our village and I often helped him as a boy. Besides, I miss you…

'When the Republic is restored…' Rose and Miguel were walking hand in hand along the beach. *The Republic… When Spain is a republic again…* He started so many pronouncements like this, so many plans. She let him talk. She wanted to believe in a future, as he did. And walking was good; it was part of his cure now the wound was almost healed. The sun and the salt air were good. Good for her too: her skin had recovered a healthy glow. A diet of vegetables from the farm, occasionally rabbit, along with corned beef sent from England, and plenty of oranges suited her well. Miguel had progressed from liquids to soft foods to a normal diet and was getting stronger with each day.

Miguel was recovering and Rose was afraid. He still talked of defending the Republic, of a return to the front. Now Catalonia was under attack. If what she heard was true, the Republic had no chance. The Republic was all but defeated. Still he would go, she knew he would go, and next time he might not return. She wanted to bask in their new love, but it was too precarious.

Rose and Miguel walked slowly, bare toes sinking into sand warmed by the mild winter sun. They had taken off their *alpargatas* to let the sea lap at their feet. Mountains to one side, the sea and the distant horizon to the other. Fishing boats were pulled up on the beach and a fisherman sat mending his nets. They stopped to watch him. Miguel lifted her hand to his mouth and kissed it. She closed her eyes and breathed in the salt tang of the sea, trying not to think of anything beyond this moment. In her ears the shrill cries of seagulls and the rhythmic slapping of waves on the shore.

Very soon they would have to turn back. The doctor they had travelled with would be waiting at the girls' colony established in a villa here on the coast, where one of the girls was recovering from suspected pneumonia. Rose was to stay until the girl's health had improved sufficiently, while Miguel would return to Murcia with the doctor.

'I wish we had more time.'

Rose knew what Miguel had in mind. On her last day off, in a lemon grove in the quiet countryside, they had spread a blanket on the earth and lain there among the fallen lemons, feeling the sun on their faces as they talked; as they learnt the contours and textures of each other's bodies, exchanged caresses. Soft, gentle, unhurried caresses. Unhurried until Rose looked at her watch and realised she had to be back on duty. As she folded the blanket, Miguel started singing. '*Y el verde, verde limón...*' He pointed to an unripe lemon on the tree above them. 'Like your eyes, the same colour exactly.' She began to laugh but he shook his head. 'No, I'm quite serious. I thought of your eyes when I was half-delirious with fever after my wound became infected. I was afraid I'd never see them again.'

Now once more, Miguel was looking at her in that intense manner of his. 'I want to marry you, Rose. When the Republic is restored and we don't have to ask permission of a priest.' He turned her to face him and took both her hands. The fisherman continued to mend his nets, no longer within hearing. 'Tell me yes. Tell me we'll be together. We will, won't we, *cariño*?'

Rose nodded her assent and squeezed his hands tight. Somehow, by force of will they would make it happen. They would be married and make a future together: a future built on rock, not sand. 'In my country you can choose a civil marriage. Or you can live together as man and wife without any formal process.'

'In our Republic too. But you must decide, Rosita. Whatever you prefer. I just don't want you to feel shame on my account.'

'What I'd like...' She spoke without the slightest hesitation. 'What I'd like is to be married in Evesham by my father.' He took her in his arms and they clung to each other. 'And when the Republic is restored,' she added, pulling away and looking into his eyes with a playful smile, 'we'll come back to Spain.'

'Yes. And our children can decide for themselves if they want to be Catholics or Protestants or have no religion.'

It was Christmas but no one had much stomach for a celebration; nor was there much food. Jaime, one of the convalescents helping in the workshops, talked with longing of his family. He wanted nothing more than to return to his *pueblo* once the war was over, as it surely must be soon. 'We'll be safer with our families and friends in the villages where we grew up,' he said. Listening to him, Erich, the German volunteer, shook his head. He knew better. 'I think not,' he said. 'Not while Franco rules. I think you go where they know you and you are dead.' Eduardo and Miguel said nothing, but Rose sensed that Miguel also yearned to be with his family in the mountains of the Alpujarra.

Still, it was Christmas and for the sake of the children, the staff did their best to enter into the festive spirit. They put up a Christmas tree in the hospital and decorated it with scraps of bright material from the sewing workshops. Some of the girls made little animals or dolls with the remnants. A few days ago, a parcel had arrived with toys sent by the children of America, so each child in the hospital could be given a present.

Francesca, Rose and the Spanish helpers organised games for those well enough to be up. Watching the children laughing and having fun, Rose found her own spirits rising. Christmas dinner was modest but everyone's helping included a tiny portion of rabbit or chicken. For most of the children, the taste of fresh meat was a distant memory. After lunch came the music and entertainment. Well fed and content, the children joined in with raucous voices as Francesca led a series of carols and popular songs, accompanied by Miguel on *bandoneón*, Eduardo and Jaime playing guitar and Erich his mouth organ.

On a mild January afternoon when Rose had finished her shift, she put fresh bread, tinned sardines in olive oil and a few oranges into a basket and set off with Miguel towards the hills. They walked up a streambed lined with oleander bushes and wandered among pine trees where the ground was littered with fir cones.

Sitting in the sun behind the wall of a ruined *cortijo*, they fed each other segments of orange. Then they broke off crusts of bread and ate them with the oil and sardines. Miguel had filled his tin flask with the rough local wine, which they took turns to sip. Afterwards they stretched out on the ground, heads resting on Miguel's jacket. She closed her eyes, breathing in the smell of the pines.

Miguel was leaning over her, kissing her face, her neck, her ears. His hands were brushing her breasts, finding a way into her blouse, fondling her nipples. She relaxed, allowing herself to enjoy the shivery pleasure of it. He was undressing her, pushing her skirt up…

'Wait.' She raised herself on one elbow. 'I'm… I've never done this before.'

'Do you want me to stop? I will if you want me to.'

'No.' She wanted him to make love to her. It felt right and natural. It felt… *Sacred* was the word that came into her mind. 'No, don't stop.' She pulled him back down and kissed his mouth, twining her tongue with his.

'You're quite sure?' When Rose nodded, he said, 'I'll be gentle, I promise. I don't want to hurt you.'

He *was* gentle and afterwards she felt no regret, no shame, no fear. Only a deep gratitude for their love, for the wholesome, life-giving beauty of their love.

When news reached them that Barcelona had fallen, Miguel stopped talking of victory. He talked scarcely at all. And then for two days no one saw him.

PART 2 CONSUELO 1945 - 1952

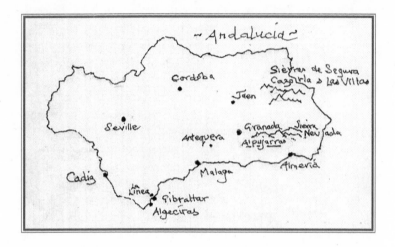

CHAPTER 8

Antequera, 1945

Mamá hung the cross round Rafa's neck and stood back with the rest of the family to admire him in his white communion suit. The admiral's jacket with its gold braiding, shiny buttons and epaulettes made him look so smart and grown-up, Consuelo could hardly recognise him as her brother.

She pointed to the big gold cross. 'Can I hold it?' she asked Rafa.

'If you want,' he said. 'Feel how heavy it is.'

Mamá shook her head. 'No, Rafael, you know how clumsy your sister is. She'll only drop it.' Turning to Consuelo, her face hardened. 'Out of the way, now. And get Encarna to brush your hair again. Can't you keep it tidy for five minutes?'

Last year it had been the turn of José María to celebrate his First Communion. Consuelo remembered sitting in church for what seemed like hours as the rituals were performed and the priest talked about purity and sin, about fighting the enemy Satan who was sent to tempt them. Then one by one, the boys in their sailor suits, the girls in their white dresses, proceeded to the altar to receive the sacraments, followed by the grown-ups and older children.

Mamá had hissed at her for not sitting still but she was afraid of wetting herself, which she very nearly did. Freed at last when the service ended, she had moved with too much haste, fallen and dirtied her clothes. As a punishment, instead of sitting down at the table for hot chocolate and pastries with the other children, she was made to stand against the wall. It was only because Concha's *papá*, the doctor, felt sorry for her and spoke to her own *papá*, saying they were too harsh, that she was fetched to join the others at the table. Or so Concha told her later.

In church, Juanito whispered, 'It'll be my turn next year. And then yours.' Consuelo stared at the girls in their white dresses and veils, looking as clean and pure as the Virgin herself. Last year one of them had fallen down in a faint, having had nothing to eat since the evening before. Listening to the priest as he intoned the familiar words, Consuelo hoped that when it came to her turn, Jesus would accept her, despite her many sins.

She looked forward to her first confession. By reciting all her bad deeds and thoughts to the priest and repenting of them, she might be saved. 'The sooner the better for that one,' her grandmother had whispered to Mamá when she visited them last. Consuelo often had nightmares about Hell. She would wake up screaming as the flames licked up all around her and the Devil brandished his pitchfork and cackled in derision at her terror. She couldn't help envying the Virgin for being born without sin. Even her parents, even priests were born with original sin, but the muttered comments of the grown-ups around her suggested she had more than her fair share of it. That was without taking into account her own transgressions. She tried to be good but it was so hard... There seemed to be different rules for her. Was it because she was a girl?

Now, as they filed slowly out of the church, Consuelo looked forward to her cup of chocolate, hoping she wouldn't spill any on her frock. In the patio, several tables had been pushed together to make one long one. Some of the children were already seated on benches either side. She took her place between Juanito and cousin Bea. Behind her, several of the adults were clustered together, talking in hushed tones. She heard the name Serafín and knew they were referring to the pharmacist.

'He's been taken away,' one of the women said. 'Two *civiles* came for him late last night.'

Consuelo liked the pharmacist. He had a kind face with big, sad eyes and his head was bald except for two tufts of black hair behind his ears. He would often wink at her in a friendly way or pat her on the head, which made her feel special. She strained to hear what Aunt Inma was saying but could only catch the odd phrase.

'Listening to *Radio Pirenaica*,' someone else whispered. 'They say it was... reported him...'

'Reds, the whole family...'

'Never liked them...'

Rojos. Consuelo had no idea what they were. She only knew that 'reds' were to be feared. Like monsters or wild animals, they lived in the hills and shot or kidnapped you if you were unlucky enough to be caught. How could Serafín and his family be *rojos*? And why was it wrong to listen to the radio? She wondered where the *Guardia Civil* had taken him and who would give people their medicines until he came back. Also, what would happen to his wife Aurora and their four girls, especially if they were reds too? Or could only men be *rojos*? But she had a vague memory from when she was younger of groups of 'red' women, their heads shaved, being paraded through the streets for everyone to jeer at. Their legs were smeared with *caca* and they stank; she'd had to hold her nose. Nothing was ever explained to her. Asking questions usually provoked either laughter or a scolding. The safest course was to keep her mouth shut and make herself as inconspicuous as possible.

A cup of chocolate was placed in front of her and perked up by the sweet taste, she devoted herself to the serious task of drinking it without spilling a drop.

CHAPTER 9

Antequera, 1949

'Hey blondie.'

Consuelo tried to slip past her older brother but Francisco's muscular arms and legs were spread, blocking the doorway to her bedroom. She turned, intending to retreat, but Francisco grabbed her arm, pinching the flesh so it hurt. He was taller than Papá now and at fifteen, considered himself a man. She hated him.

'Let me go!'

He laughed. 'Why should I?' Without slackening his grip, he flicked at her hair with his other hand. 'Blondie,' he repeated. 'Look at you, your green eyes…'

'So what?' Consuelo tried to stamp on his foot but he was too quick and her foot hit the clay floor tiles with a force that stung.

'You're not my sister,' he said, lingering on each word, his mouth twisted into an ugly sneer.

Consuelo stared at him – at his slicked-back hair, greedy eyes and the bulge of his Adam's apple. 'What are you talking about? Of course I'm your sister. Let go of me, you're hurting my arm.'

'Haven't you ever wondered why you look different? You're nothing like any of us.'

Consuelo frowned. It had never occurred to her but he was right: everyone else in her family had brown eyes, and their hair and skin were much darker.

'I'll tell you why.' He brought his face closer to hers. She cringed and tried to turn her head away. The down lining his upper lip disgusted her. 'You're adopted.' He was grinning stupidly. It wasn't fair that he was vastly bigger and stronger so she couldn't hurt him back.

'No I'm not!'

'You don't belong in our family at all. Mamá and Papá took you in out of pity, so you wouldn't burn in hell as a sinner. Because they're good people – unlike *your* mother.'

'I don't believe you. You're making it up.' But a part of her did believe him; a part of her was scared he might be telling the truth. 'Who is my mother then?'

'Want to know who your mother was? OK, I'll tell you. Your mother was a red. A *puta*. You understand? Immoral, wicked, unfit.' Francisco paused, watching her reaction, gloating over the effect his words were having on her. 'And you know what happens to reds: they get shot.'

Consuelo dodged past him and slammed the door of her bedroom shut. She threw herself down on the bed and buried her face in the pillow, trying to erase the vision of his sneering face. She asked Lola, her secret friend, to help her find a way of taking revenge on Francisco and Lola came up with some tempting ideas that made Consuelo smile even though she would never have the nerve to carry them out.

Lola thought her green eyes were beautiful and wished her own were a more interesting colour instead of boring old brown. Some of the girls at school made comments about her eyes. They'd sing that song of Concha Piquer's, *Aquellos ojos verdes*, about a girl with green eyes, eyes like basil, like green wheat, lemon green… pointing at her and laughing, but not in a nasty way; not like her brother. Except for Puri, who had teased her once, saying only cats had green eyes so she must be a witch's cat, put under a spell that gave her the form of a girl. It wasn't even as if she were the only one in town. The draper's son had green eyes too. And there were several with blue eyes, like Eufemia and Paquita and Paquita's sister, and no one made fun of them. It wasn't fair.

'Francisco said I was adopted.' Consuelo faced Mamá. She folded her arms and stood as tall and straight as she could to give herself courage. 'Is it true?'

'You're nothing but a nuisance, always bothering me with *tonterías*.' Mamá spoke in her cross voice and wouldn't look at her but Consuelo just stood there, waiting.

'I'm not being silly. Just tell me. Is it true what he said?'

Mamá stopped twisting her fingers and brushed a hand over her face. 'Very well, let's sit down for a moment.'

Consuelo could feel her heart beating faster than it should. She knew Francisco had been telling the truth and now Mamá was going to admit it.

'It's true.' Mamá still wouldn't look at her. She was fingering the pearls on her necklace. Any minute the string would snap and the jewels go spinning off all over the floor. 'We saved you from a harsh and wretched life.' Mamá took a deep breath. 'Your natural mother abandoned you. Uncle Rodrigo, who worked in the hospital where you were born and helped bring you into the world, asked us to raise you rather than send you to an orphanage or leave you to die. Lucky for you that he had such a kind heart. Otherwise...'

'Why didn't you tell me before?' There was much more she wanted to know but all her efforts were directed at fighting back the tears of confusion threatening to spill out in a humiliating flood.

Mamá ignored her question. 'It was our duty,' she said. Then, finally turning to face Consuelo, she added more kindly, 'And we wanted a little girl.'

Mamá wasn't her real mother. That meant Consuelo didn't have to like her. It meant she was a stepmother like the one in her favourite storybook, *Cenicienta*, about the girl whose stepmother and ugly stepsisters mistreat her, making her do all the work, dress in rags and stay at home while they go to the ball. Until Cenicienta's fairy godmother turns up and gives her a beautiful gown and slippers and a carriage to take her to the Prince's ball. And there she dances with the Prince and he falls in love with her.

Consuelo thought about that time last summer on the feast day of 18th July, the anniversary of the Glorious Uprising, when the family went to El Chorro and she was left behind with the servants as a punishment because she'd accidentally torn her dress, playing outside. She had cried bitterly that day – the gorge at El Chorro was one of her favourite outings. Ramona, the cook, had comforted her and made *natillas* specially, knowing it was her favourite dessert. She'd played with Ramona's son, Jorge, and some of the other servants' children, even though she wasn't really allowed to.

When the family came back from El Chorro, Rafa gave her some flowers he'd picked. Of her four brothers, he was the only kind one. Francisco, José María and Juanito made her life miserable, each in a different way – by teasing or hurting her or putting her down. They were sneaky about it so their parents didn't see. Or maybe they did see but they didn't care. Consuelo wished she had a sister to play with and take her side. Sometimes she pretended Lola was a sister, but mostly she thought of Lola as a friend, her best friend. Lola would never let her down.

CHAPTER 10

Antequera, 1950

'*Ave María purísima.*' Consuelo was still out of breath, having run most of the way to school, but managed to join in with the other girls as they recited the familiar words.

'*Sin pecado concebida,*' Sor Francisca responded and signalled for them to be seated. Consuelo tugged at her skirt as she sat down. Mamá complained she was growing too fast. Already the hem of her blue tunic had been fully let out and soon it would be indecent, she said. The cuffs of her white blouse were also creeping further and further up her arms. But even Mamá couldn't claim it was her fault she was growing. Juanito, who was more than a year older, hated the fact she was as tall as him. He'd lift her up or hold her arms behind her back or even push her to the ground to prove he was stronger.

At school yesterday, one of the nuns had slapped her cheek for talking in class so now she kept her head down and didn't look around at all, which was hard. She concentrated on the page in front of her, trying to make her writing neat, with the loops all the same size and no mistakes or smudges. Sor Francisca paced up and down between the rows of desks, stopping now and then to peer at one of the girls' work. Two rows in front of Consuelo, she stopped at Resu's desk, seized her exercise book and waved it in the air. 'What are all these crossings out? This is deplorable! You must start again and continue during *recreo* until you're finished.'

Consuelo commiserated with Resu for missing the break. Outside in the patio, girls were skipping and playing tag or four corners. The poor girls in their striped uniforms played the same games but separately. She noticed their cook Ramona's two daughters amongst them but went to join some of the girls in her own class, asking if she could join their game of four corners. Even though they were one girl short, Ernestina said no at first. She had to wait while they discussed whether to let her play. As usual, she seemed to be in the middle more often than the others, however fast she moved. But that didn't bother her too much; she was grateful to be included.

Afternoon school was always the same. When they returned after having lunch at home, it was embroidery, which she quite liked. What she didn't like was the *Visita Santísima*, when they all had to line up and troop in silence to the church. It was colder, darker and more oppressive than the one her family went to on Sundays. The musty smell reminded her of all the old bones buried under the floor. She imagined even the Virgin in her niche must feel chilly and uncomfortable here.

After the prayers, it was a relief to emerge into the fresh air. Padre Lázaro stood at the door as they filed out. She always tried to sneak past quickly because, as all the girls knew, he sprayed spittle when he spoke and it was best to keep out of range. She wondered if Padre Venancio Marcos, the priest who came on the radio every day and spoke with such fervour about chastity and the dangers of sin, did the same. She thought he probably did.

The next day was Saturday and she saw the usual queue of poor people lined up at their door, hoping for a coin so they and their families could eat. The queue was longer than usual because it had rained most of the week, which meant no work for the day labourers. Papá was always generous – unlike some of the other *señoritos* with big houses in the town, so her father said.

Consuelo went out to the back of the house, where one of the horses was being saddled up for Papá to ride to their *cortijo*. She patted his glossy brown flank and stroked the mane. She wished Papá would take her with him. She loved sitting in front of him high up on Galán's back, riding through the countryside with the wind rippling her hair and the animal smell of the horse in her nostrils. More often though, he took one of her brothers and she rode in the cart with her other brothers and the produce. Today none of them were going. They were expecting visitors, Mamá said. Her brother Rodrigo and his wife were arriving later this morning by motorcar, all the way from Jaén.

'Can you remember Uncle Rodrigo?' Consuelo asked Rafa. 'Has he been here before?'

Her brother wasn't sure; he couldn't picture him either. 'Maybe a long time ago,' he said. 'You'll have to ask Mamá. She said he was a doctor so he's probably very busy.'

'A doctor, did you say he was a doctor?' Bells were ringing in Consuelo's head. Mamá's brother Rodrigo. The one who sent her here after her real *mamá* abandoned her. It must be him.

'What's the matter?' Rafa asked. 'You've gone white as a sheet.'

'Nothing. I'm fine.' But Consuelo's heart was battering her chest and she felt dizzy. She rested her hands on the back of a chair to steady herself and smiled at Rafa so he'd believe nothing was wrong. Her mind was whirling. Uncle Rodrigo had known her mother. He'd be able to tell her things about the woman who'd given birth in his hospital: what her name was, what she looked like, where she came from...

'Tell me about my mother.' Consuelo had waited till the next morning to approach her uncle with the questions she longed to ask. She'd had to wait to catch him alone and even now they had no more than a few minutes.

'Your mother?' Rodrigo smiled condescendingly and patted her on the head. 'What can I tell you that you don't know already? Do you mean when we were children?'

'No, not María Angustias. My *real* mother.'

Uncle Rodrigo's smile abruptly vanished. 'I don't know what on earth you're talking about.' He laced his fingers over his fat stomach as if it needed holding in.

'My birth mother,' Consuelo insisted. Why was he denying it? Mamá had admitted she was adopted and that her brother Rodrigo had arranged it. He must remember. 'You helped her give birth to me in your hospital.'

'I think you're confused, child. I'll admit my memory isn't so good any more, but it seems an unlikely story. I'm sorry to disappoint you but now if you'll excuse me, I have to get ready for Mass.' He took his hat from the stand in the hall and called to his wife. 'Elena, it's time to go.' Turning back to Consuelo, he said, 'I suggest you forget your peculiar ideas. Angustias and José are your parents and very lucky you are to have such a fine *mamá* and *papá*.'

CHAPTER 11

Antequera, 1952

'I've been waiting an hour for that wretched dressmaker. Where can she be?' Mamá was pacing up and down, pausing every now and again to peer out of the window. 'The fitting was promised for five o'clock!'

Hearing the rage in her mother's voice, Consuelo tried to creep away. Making herself scarce was a skill she had learnt young, but this time Mamá had seen her and wasn't going to let her escape.

'Consuelo, where are you off to? Get your coat and run down to Manuela's house. Tell her to come immediately and don't listen to any excuses she might use to pull the wool over your eyes. I will not be treated with such lack of respect.'

There was no disobeying Mamá. Consuelo made her way through the streets to the small, ramshackle house in the poor district where Manuela lived with her six children, and called out her name. She felt sorry for Manuela who, according to Mamá, had come down in the world since her husband, a clerk in the Town Hall, disappeared after the War and her two brothers were killed. The dressmaking wasn't sufficient to support her family, so only one of the children could attend school. The others all worked on the land – sometimes for Consuelo's father, sometimes for other landowners.

Occasionally, when she came to their house for fittings, Manuela would bring the youngest girl, Charo, and Consuelo would play with her. Charo liked to see her toys, especially the toy kitchen, which she thought was marvellous. She'd never seen one before. Her only toy was a tatty old papier-mâché doll called Pepona, which she nearly always brought with her. Pepona's hair was just painted on and her dress was nailed to her back so you couldn't change it. Her own doll, Mariquita Pérez – a present from Grandma on her Saint's Day the year she was four – had real hair and eyelashes and several different dresses.

After shouting a few times to no effect, Consuelo pushed open the door and took a step inside Manuela's house. It appeared deserted, completely silent except for the pecking of a small caged bird. Then from down the street, she heard running footsteps and loud sobs. Manuela flew into the house, her hair wild, her face ravaged with tears and grief.

'They've taken him away!' Her voice was choked. She hardly seemed aware of Consuelo standing there. 'They've taken my Fernando, I'll never see him again. *Ay Dios*, what will we do now?' She beat her fists against the wall until blood started to drip from them, streaking the wall red.

'What are *you* doing here?' Manuela had suddenly woken up to her presence.

Consuelo stepped out of the shadows. What could she say? In the face of Manuela's distress, it was impossible to deliver the message she'd been charged with.

'I'm sorry about Fernando,' she said. But that only started Manuela off again, weeping and wailing and calling on all the saints to help save her eldest son, who'd done no wrong in his whole life, the eighteen years since his birth. God knew he was a good boy...

Consuelo edged towards the door, hoping to slip out unnoticed. She would tell Mamá Manuela was away from home and couldn't be found.

But just as she reached the doorway, Manuela grabbed her arm and pulled her back in. 'What am I to do, child?' she beseeched, clinging to Consuelo. 'Haven't I already lost my Reynaldo and two brothers? What have we done to deserve this? *Ay*, six of us still to feed and no man to help me...'

Consuelo knew Mamá wouldn't pay Manuela, even though the dress was nearly finished – not unless she came quickly for the fitting. 'My mother was expecting you.' Her voice faltered. 'The dress...'

Manuela clapped her hands to her head. 'Today was it, child?' she cried. 'But how can I think of these things when my Fernando...?' She seemed about to resume her lament, but realising the likely consequences if she ignored the call, she abruptly pulled herself together. 'Then I must go,' she said. 'Run home and tell your *mamá* I'll be there in fifteen minutes.' A final sob escaped her as Consuelo nodded and backed out of the house.

As she hurried past the other workers' hovels in the direction of her own home, which now struck her as a palace, Consuelo spotted Charo in the distance. She was walking barefoot with a slight limp, heading back from the fields, and Consuelo thought how sore her feet must be from the rough ground. Didn't she even have any rubber *albarcas*? They would have been better than nothing. She supposed the family were too poor to buy *alpargatas*. If she could find a pair of her old, outgrown ones, she would give them to Charo.

We saved you from a harsh and wretched life. Consuelo still remembered Mamá's words on that day three years ago when Francisco told her she was adopted. Although no more had been said on the subject, the words had stuck in her mind. Now, thinking about the harsh life endured by Manuela and her family, it occurred to her that perhaps she *had* been lucky to have Mamá and Papá take her in and save her from a life of poverty and deprivation.

Besides, her real mother didn't want her. For weeks after being told, she had cried herself to sleep every night – until finally she had managed to push the hurt and anger away and harden herself, leaving only a lingering bitterness that mostly stayed buried. Perhaps Uncle Rodrigo had wanted to spare her the pain of knowing her mother was wicked and that was why he pretended not to remember. Because according to Francisco, her mother was a red. Consuelo wondered if, like the pharmacist and others she knew in the town, her mother had been taken away to prison and never seen again.

PART 3 ROSE 1939 - 1940

CHAPTER 12

Jaén, February 1939

Rose covered her mouth and nose with a handkerchief, trying not to breathe in the choking dust that blew into the back of the lorry as it bumped along the unmade roads in the direction of Albacete. The canvas roof and sides offered little protection from either the dust or the cold February air. Although the sun had risen soon after they set off, it did little to warm her frozen hands and feet. She was only half listening to the men's animated talk of routes and contacts, weapons and supplies. Her impulsive decision to join Miguel and Eduardo now seemed foolish, now it was too late. She tried to hide her terror as they discussed the munitions they would need and their means of obtaining food and other requisites, by force if necessary.

Hearing her name, she began to pay more attention and blanched as she grasped their meaning. They were speaking fast in the sloppy accent of Andalucía, dropping consonants and slurring words together, but she understood well enough.

'Rose will need to be armed too,' Miguel was saying.

'Of course, the girl should have a pistol at least.'

Of course. She should have anticipated this, thought everything through properly.

The driver dropped them on the edge of a small town. 'We're in Cieza,' he said. 'The river Segura runs through here. If you follow it westwards towards its source, you can't go wrong.' He shook their hands and wished them luck.

Rose hitched up her corduroy trousers and tightened the belt another notch as they started walking. Designed for a man, they hung on her, ridiculously baggy. Miguel had bought them at the store in Murcia, along with a kind of hunting jacket, also far too big for her slight frame, and a beret. Although there was little difference in their height, Miguel was much broader and stockier, with strong muscular legs.

'You look like a boy,' Miguel said, casting his eyes over her approvingly as she tucked her hair up inside the beret. She felt like a child – fearful and uncertain – but this was no game. She would be armed, as the men already were; to defend herself she might have to kill. She remembered the conversation with her mother. *Can you honestly imagine me carrying a gun?* Her hands shook as she adjusted the knapsack on her back. It held a few provisions, a block of soap, spare shirt and underwear and a rolled up blanket. An aluminium flask with water was slung on a strap round her neck. They had a little money, each of them having saved some of their monthly wage of three hundred pesetas. When that was gone… She would rather not think of what they might resort to then.

'You two wait here while I go and shop,' Eduardo said. 'One person will attract less attention than three, especially with a *chica*. I won't be long.'

He returned within a couple of hours. Rose did not ask what he had bought but she knew the bulky package he carried was not food. She was glad to be on the move again after hanging about in the cold, waiting. Her nerves began to abate with the rhythm of their feet on the ground, the calming effect of momentum. Crossing fields, some of them ploughed, others fallow, they made their way down to the riverbank, lined with poplars and willows.

They had been walking for five days when Eduardo pointed to some thickly wooded hills in the distance. 'The Sierra de Segura,' he said. 'We'll be there in a few hours.' He turned to Rose. 'You might be lucky and sleep indoors tonight. I have friends with a *cortijo* this side of the mountains. With luck we'll be able to rest there a day or two, get some hot food inside us.' He licked his lips. 'Felisa makes a good stew.'

After several nights sleeping in barns or grain stores, on beds of straw if they were lucky, often sharing the accommodation with mules or other animals, Rose perked up at the prospect of a more substantial roof over her head. Although in truth, despite the discomfort and the cold, she had treasured the nights. It was only at night, with Eduardo asleep at a discreet distance, that she and Miguel could enjoy some moments of intimacy, lying curled up together, warming each other's bodies, whispering their love.

So far she had managed to keep pace with Miguel and Eduardo, but her legs ached. Unlike those of the two men, her muscles were not adapted to the unremitting exercise of a route march. As for food, stale bread formed a major part of their diet. Rose had been constipated since leaving Murcia. They were eking out their provisions with a few vegetables and on one occasion some eggs, bought from the small farms they passed, but there was scant food to be had anywhere. The peasants ate poorly; they had precious little to spare. Once, as they passed an isolated farm, the wife had invited them in to share the family's communal bowl of chickpeas. Seeing they had six hungry children to feed, Rose and her companions dipped their spoons in only once or twice before thanking her and leaving.

It was late when they arrived at the *cortijo*. Eduardo had forgotten the precise location and two or three times they had to retrace their steps before he finally spotted it on a hillside over to their left. As they approached, their presence was announced by the clamorous barking of dogs. The noise brought Felisa running out.

'*¡Anda! Eduardo*, what a surprise!' She embraced him and welcomed them into the kitchen, where a few logs were burning in the fireplace. 'Juan and the boys haven't yet returned from the fields but they'll be back soon, when the light goes. Eulalia is sick with a fever.' Felisa indicated an open doorway into the next room, where in the shadowy gloom Rose could just make out a bed with someone lying in it. 'I'm worried about her. Conchi has gone to the doctor for medicine but already we owe him money.'

'Let me see her, I'm a nurse.'

'*Ay*, thank the Lord. Maybe you can do something for her.'

They stayed three nights, sleeping by the fire, sharing the family's meals and making themselves useful on the land. Miguel and Eduardo helped rebuild a collapsed wall and worked with the men in the fields. Rose assisted Felisa in the house and tended to her daughter, a pale sixteen-year-old with eloquent eyes and a head of unruly black curls.

The girl was suffering from a severe chill but her fever gradually abated and by the time they left, it was clear she had turned the corner and would soon be back on her feet.

'Truly, you were a gift from God,' Felisa said to Rose on their last morning, after she'd seen to the youngest boy's badly cut foot and advised Juan's elderly father on how to deal with a digestive complaint he'd been enduring for months. 'Here, take these. Our last pig was killed in January.' She handed them sausage and black pudding, bread and some dried figs. 'At least you'll have something to fill your stomachs for the next couple of days.'

As they were leaving, they met Juan with one of his sons, returning from the nearest small town.

'Any news?' Miguel asked.

'Bad news,' Juan answered. 'Alfredo can read a little – he went to school for a couple of years during the Republic – and he saw a newspaper in the bar. They were talking too. It seems that Britain and France have recognised Franco's regime. *Ay*, things will get worse, much much worse.'

'But Madrid is still holding out?'

Juan nodded. 'For the moment, yes.'

They were in hilly country now, making their way through vegetation of holm oak, juniper and pine. Above them, rocky outcrops stood out against a deep blue sky while below, narrow river valleys threaded the landscape with silver. The walking was harder here and several times Rose stumbled on a rock or tree root or missed her footing on loose earth and stones. Although Eduardo said nothing, at times she sensed his impatience. They were heading towards his village of Beas de Segura. He knew people there, they would be safer, he said.

Often they saw no one all day. At night they slept on beds of dry leaves in hollows between the trees, wrapping themselves in blankets and huddling all three together for more warmth. They washed when they could, in rivers studded with boulders. One afternoon they stopped at a waterfall where the cascade gushed into a deep clear pool. The men stripped off and stood for a few seconds under the full force of the torrent. After dipping her feet in the pool, Rose washed the rest of her body as best she could without immersing herself. The water was icy.

On the morning of the third day, Miguel handed her a pistol. 'You need to learn how to use it,' he said. 'Look, hold it like this. Your finger on the trigger here.'

She shrank back. 'Is it loaded?'

'Not yet. Come on, practise pulling the trigger.'

Rose took the gun from him and did as he instructed, trying not to flinch.

'You must be prepared to use it without a second's hesitation and aim well. Otherwise you put all our lives at risk.' He added more kindly, 'You can't afford to be fearful, Rose. Once the fascists are in control, the whole place will be swarming with *Guardia Civil* and they'll show no mercy, you can be sure.'

Eduardo took a cartridge belt from his knapsack. 'Look, this goes round your waist, and the pistol here. Put it on.' He showed her how to load the gun. Then he took it and fired a shot into the air. The loud report made her tremble. 'Now you. That tree trunk over there.' She steeled herself and took aim. The bullet scraped the side of the tree trunk.

'OK, that'll do. We can't spare any more ammunition. Just remember, it's our lives or theirs.'

They had been walking for some hours when Miguel suddenly stopped. Ahead of them a thin wisp of smoke was rising from a clearing in the trees. He signalled to her and Eduardo to wait and moved forward cautiously. A moment later Rose heard him call out a greeting that was followed by a muted response. He whistled to them to come forward. An old man was squatting there, making charcoal.

'You're not with those from Granada, are you?' he asked. Staring at Rose, he added, 'That one's a *chica* if my eyes don't deceive me.'

Rose greeted him and acknowledged that she was indeed female.

'We've come from the front,' Eduardo said, 'but tell me, who are you referring to? Are there fugitives from Granada here in these mountains?'

'Six or seven of them hiding out here. I spoke to them yesterday; they can't be far off. They'd made their way from the Sierra Nevada, said they had dozens of *Guardia Civil* after them there. I'm damned if I know how, but they managed to get clear. It's a fair distance from Granada, two hundred and fifty kilometres, I reckon. They hit lucky and hitched a ride on a lorry part of the way but they still had eight nights walking to reach here. In any case, you'd better be careful. If the *Guardia* get wind their quarry are up here, they'll be combing these *sierras* and they won't be too fussy who they pick up.'

'Thanks for the warning.' Eduardo offered the old man the last of their *chorizo* but he shook his head. 'You'll be needing that yourselves.'

It was almost dark when they finally saw Beas ahead of them. As they followed a path leading towards the town, a fox ran across in front of them. 'They say there are wolves in the *sierra* around here,' Eduardo said, 'though I've never seen one myself.' Earlier, near a river, they had spotted footprints that Miguel said were those of *jabalí*, wild boar.

Determined not to show any signs of feminine weakness, Rose ignored him and walked on. Wolves, wild boar, the Civil Guard: she might have to face any or all of these at some point, but she had made her choice and it was too late now to give way to fear. Much better not to think of the dangers.

She had grown accustomed during their three-week stay with Eduardo's family in Beas to Eduardo and Miguel disappearing for days at a time. They were 'getting organised', Eduardo said. Which meant, she gathered, liaising with others preparing to form a guerrilla or willing to support them in some way. He had many contacts scattered in villages, small hamlets and isolated *cortijos* in the countryside round about as well as in the town. Only those he judged a hundred per cent trustworthy would be informed of their plans.

Meanwhile, Rose helped his mother, a woman who like so many others in Spain, looked worn out and prematurely aged. She was forty-seven. Rose had guessed sixty at least. Her husband had been an invalid since a young age; of their nine children one son had died in infancy, two had been killed in the war, another had lost both legs; a daughter had recently died in childbirth. One of her brothers and a nephew had disappeared, presumed dead. As Rose walked about the town, she was struck again by the number of women dressed in black. She had noticed it before: it was the same in every village. They were all in mourning. Eduardo's family had a small *taller*, a vehicle workshop where his uncles and the remaining brother worked. It barely brought in enough to feed the family. Working as day labourers when they could, the family just about survived.

Now Rose and the two men were on the move again, better armed and provisioned, more cautious. News had reached them of the rebels' entry into Madrid. Any day now, Franco would be in control of the whole country; the war would be over and their situation infinitely more dangerous.

'We'll have to move by night,' Eduardo told her. 'In silence. No talking, no coughing, no snapping of twigs underfoot. During the day we stay hidden. Do you understand?'

Catching the tension in his voice and demeanour, she nodded. 'I understand.'

'You need to learn the signals,' he said. Putting his hands to his mouth, he imitated the call of an owl, followed by that of a hoopoe. Even the birds would be deceived, Rose thought, impressed.

'Practise until you get it right every time. And make sure you can recognise them too.' She listened carefully as he explained their interpretation: how many repetitions, how long the interval between them… 'Getting it wrong could mean death,' he added.

Their plan was to join with a larger group camped on a rocky summit high in the *sierra* where the cover was good and it would be easy to see anyone approaching.

'You'd better not let us down.' Eduardo had been friendly towards her up till now but in the last two days she had noticed a change in his manner. 'Some of the others were reluctant to accept a girl,' he said by way of explanation. 'We had to persuade them you were strong and could handle arms like a man. We're counting on you, OK?'

CHAPTER 13

Jaén, March - August 1939

The war was over and many men from the villages around Cazorla, in fear for their lives, were fleeing to the mountains. Those from the Civil Guard were not far behind. Eduardo's warnings had been no exaggeration. In the encampment where Rose and her companions were based with the group from Beas, the rules were strict. Fires were not allowed – the smoke would give them away immediately – so they were limited to cold food day after day. Using soap to wash themselves or their clothing in the rivers was forbidden in case the bubbles were detected. Any breach of the rules was dealt with severely. Already two of the men had been confronted by a patrol of the *Guardia* as they were heading to a farm lower down to stock up with food. One man had got away but the other had been fatally shot. Three of the guards had been injured too.

To reach their camp on a summit of flattish rocks, they had to crawl through a tunnel of brambles. They were safer than in a cave, from which there was only a single exit. Rumours had reached them of a group in one of the caves nearby being trapped as they slept, and smoked out. Occasionally Rose would hear gunshots in the distance. She had been taught how to distinguish the sounds of different arms and identify which were likely to be *Guardia Civil* and which the fugitives. Arms and provisions were kept in a deep crevice in the rocks, but any time they left the camp, they would be armed, and that included Rose. She prayed she would never have to use her gun.

Most of the men had accepted her – it helped that she was a nurse – but she sensed hostility from one or two of the eight. She was allocated the less dangerous tasks: looking after the stores, cooking, washing and mending the men's clothes. Once she had been left to guard the camp while they carried out a raid for supplies.

'Rose, is this yours?' Miguel was holding out a small, embroidered handkerchief, a parting gift from Felisa. For a moment, the anger in his voice robbed her of speech: he had never addressed her in such harsh tones. 'It was in the brambles, close by our camp; I could see it from two hundred metres away. Two hundred metres! And the *Guardia* will have excellent binoculars, you can be certain.' He flourished the handkerchief in her direction before ripping it across several times and stuffing the useless shreds in his pocket. 'How could you be so careless? You might have had us all killed.'

Mortified, she groped in vain for words to appease him. Miguel was right to be angry. 'I'm at fault, I'm sorry. I can't think how...' The contempt in his eyes dismayed her.

'Just as well I was the one to find it.'

'Yes. Just as well.' They both knew the likely consequences of its discovery – even by one of their own band.

'*Bueno*, it had better not happen again.' She was relieved to see his eyes soften.

'It won't.' She pointed to the stream some way below. 'I need to fetch water. Will you come?'

They stayed in the hilltop camp for several weeks more, until Lorenzo, their designated leader, judged it too dangerous. There were signs their hideout had been rumbled, he said. Someone, probably under torture, must have betrayed them.

That same day, they packed everything up and prepared to move on as soon as night fell.

Rose, like all of them, had a heavy load to carry on her back. She struggled to keep pace with the men, especially in the pitch dark. The moon was a mere sliver – an advantage according to Lorenzo: with little moonlight, they were less likely to be seen. For Rose every step was an effort. She knew she must not complain or ask to stop; she knew also that there would be no chance of rest for many hours. Her energy had been flagging for the last week or two. She could think of no obvious reason; the strain must be getting to her.

They were making for a spot in the range of hills to the west of their previous camp. Miguel took her hand as they started to ascend again after crossing a river valley.

'*Ánimo*, Rosita. Try to move faster. We must reach there before daylight.'

'I'm sorry.' She wiped away a tear, hoping Miguel hadn't noticed. 'Is it much further?' She was missing her step more frequently as she forced herself forwards, dragging her feet, fighting her exhaustion. She noticed Rubén turn his head to look at them.

'I'm not sure. A couple of hours, maybe,' Miguel whispered.

'Shh.' Rubén's furious rebuke silenced them both instantly.

Head down, Rose stumbled on up the slope, following the others as they zigzagged their way between trees and through undergrowth. Her lower legs were covered in bruises where she had knocked them against invisible rocks.

It started to rain – not heavily but enough to soak their clothes within an hour. The sky was beginning to lighten when Lorenzo finally called a halt and allowed them to make camp and rest in a clearing surrounded by vegetation. They hung their oilskin cloths between the bushes and laid others on the ground before wrapping themselves in blankets to sleep for a few hours, leaving two men on guard.

When Rose woke, the sun was still low in the sky and her companions – apart from the two guards – appeared deep in sleep. She threw off her blanket and made a sprint for the trees, knowing with absolute certainty she was going to be sick. Something she'd eaten yesterday must have disagreed with her. Afterwards she felt better, though weak. Cocooning herself in the blanket again, she managed to sleep for another couple of hours.

'What's wrong with you, Rose?' She was washing some clothes at a small spring when Miguel came up behind her. He took the shirt she had just rinsed and squeezed the water out of it.

Rose pointed to a tree. 'You can hang it on one of those branches,' she said, ignoring his question.

'What's the matter?' he repeated after following her instruction. 'Are you ill? Rosita, I'm not blind. I can see something is up.'

Rose put down the trousers she'd been scrubbing and looked around to make sure no one was close enough to overhear. Then she turned to face Miguel.

'I'm pregnant,' she said. It had finally dawned on her a few days ago as the nausea and fatigue continued and her monthly bleed still did not come.

He took her in his arms and held her close without speaking. A huge wave of relief swept over her at having shared her burden. 'I was going to tell you,' she whispered. 'I'm so frightened, Miguel. What are we going to do?'

'I don't know, I need time to think. We must keep it from the others – at least for the moment, while it's not yet showing. In any case, we should probably move on soon, the three of us. The group is too big and there are tensions. But Eduardo… maybe we should tell him? *Ay*, I don't know, it's complicated.'

'I know, it's the worst time, but… are you just a tiny bit happy, Miguel, that I'm carrying your baby, that we'll have a child?'

'Listen *cariño*, I'm only concerned about how to protect you and the baby. If the circumstances were different…' He wiped the tears from her cheeks with his hand. 'We'll find somewhere you can stay when the time comes,' he said. 'One of our safe houses where the women can look after you, bring a midwife if necessary. Don't worry, we'll think of something, make a plan.'

She realised Miguel's eyes were wet too. It was not the first time she had seen him cry. His emotions – whether of sadness, joy or anger – were close to the surface. She remembered how he had shed tears when talking of his family and of his village, Cañar. It was more difficult now to find opportunities for such conversations but in their earlier days at the convalescent hospital, he had described them often. She knew the names of all his brothers and sisters; could visualise the streets and squares of Cañar where he had grown up: the herds of goats stopping to drink every evening as they were led past the old stone fountain in the *plaza*; the postman they called el Tío Pocoveo, who came by donkey from Órgiva; or the women bringing their dough to bake in one of the public ovens in the street.

'When is the baby due?' Alba and Rose had been left to guard the camp while the men were out negotiating for supplies with some *señoritos* in one of the villages.

'Early October.' It was easy to lose track of time here in the *sierra*. Rose was doing her best to keep a tally of the days and weeks as they passed. She patted her stomach. 'I've felt something once or twice, a little flutter that could have been the baby moving.'

Alba smiled at her. 'How exciting.'

The sickness had passed and Rose felt surprisingly well considering the limited diet and tough living conditions. She was determined not to let pregnancy hinder her from the usual tasks, so as not to be seen as a liability. Later it would be more difficult. She knew Eduardo was concerned about what would happen in the months to come. His muttered comments to Miguel had not escaped her.

After several months living exclusively with men, both Rose and Alba had been delighted to find female company. Their two groups had teamed up a few days ago but they were still only eight: a better number than four, Miguel and Eduardo felt. Tomás had joined their trio after falling out with Lorenzo. Alba was César's sister and the wife of Mariano. The other member of their band was Pedro.

'I'd better have a scout around.' Rose put down her mending. 'I won't be long. When I get back – if it's all quiet – I'll cut your hair, and you can do mine too.' Short hair was more practical; Rose had long ceased to lament the wavy locks she had cultivated with such care in England.

'Good idea. Mariano's hopeless at cutting.'

Rose skirted the camp, scanning the trees and bushes that surrounded it for anything that moved, listening carefully for voices, rustlings or footsteps. A rabbit scuttled away and she spotted several squirrels amongst the trees. Overhead an eagle rode the air currents. Occasionally they came across villagers gathering *esparto*, the tough grass used to make baskets and *alpargatas,* but today there was no sign of human presence.

She was far more worried about the men. The *señoritos* were scared of the *maquis* living in the mountains, Miguel said. They preferred to concede to their demands for food or money than risk being kidnapped or killed. Still, no matter how much he tried to reassure her, she knew these expeditions were fraught with danger. The rich *señoritos* were naturally on the side of the victors and under pressure from the Civil Guard to talk: an ambush was always a serious risk. She would watch, heart in mouth, as Miguel and the others set off with sub-machine guns slung from their shoulders, each time wondering how many would return.

Up until now they had relied mainly on their *enlaces*, the sympathisers in the local population, for supplies and information, but it was becoming more dangerous. Those suspected of collaborating were beaten and tortured; some had even been executed. Pedro told them of homes and *cortijos* burnt to the ground because their owners were thought to be helping the guerilla.

By August, Rose was unable to fasten her trousers at the waist. The belt, at its full stretch, just about held them up, for the time being. She knew the others were talking about her, discussing a split in the group. It was clear that Mariano and César were no longer prepared to accept the risk posed by a heavily pregnant woman. She lacked the necessary agility and speed should they have to move fast. The *Guardia* were not far away. If the rumours they heard were correct, Lorenzo and some of his men had been caught. César had stayed out twelve hours yesterday – until well past nightfall – to avoid giving away their hiding place. It was high time to move on again.

Over supper one night, Mariano put forward the strategy they had worked out. 'We'll split into two groups,' he said. Pedro, César, Alba and myself in one group, Eduardo, Miguel and Rose in another.'

Eduardo fidgeted with his rifle. 'I'll go with you,' he said to Mariano.

'Very well. And you, Tomás? Have you decided yet?'

'I'll go with Miguel and Rose. Five and three, it's a better division. Safer.'

Rose turned to him in surprise and gratitude. His local knowledge would be a huge asset to them. Tomás was only nineteen but as mature as any of them, solid and dependable. They would indeed be safer with him. But for Tomás… She was uneasily aware that for him, accompanying them would bring greater risks.

'What are we going to do?' she whispered to Miguel as they rested, waiting for darkness to fall. 'I mean when the baby comes.' They couldn't avoid talking about it indefinitely. For the first few months it had been easy to put her fears in abeyance but now she woke each day in dread and went to sleep in dread. Miguel's comforting presence by her side was no longer enough. Her optimism had run out and been replaced by a deep sense of foreboding. Now she needed a plan.

'Don't worry, *mi amor*.' He cupped her face with his hands and looked into her eyes. 'I've been thinking about it. There's a woman I know, absolutely *de confianza*. I'd trust her with my life. If we can reach her village or get a message to her… It's not so far away, maybe fifty or sixty kilometres. You'll be safe there.'

'And what about you?' There was no safe place in this country – not for those on the wrong side. They both knew it. She wanted desperately to believe in his plan, to make that blind leap of faith.

'I'll join you later when it's over, when we have a republic again. I tell you, the fascists won't last long. Europe will never stand for it.'

Rose sighed but said nothing. She closed her eyes and tried to get comfortable in Miguel's arms. They had a long night's march ahead to a new camp that might or might not be safer.

On and on, hour after hour, they had trudged through the night, stopping only to strain their eyes for movement amongst the trees or for the glint of metal in the moonlight, to listen for the sound of snapping twigs or muted voices. The two men walked ahead, burdened by heavy loads while Rose carried only her gun, a flask and a small knapsack. The grey light of dawn had crept up on them too soon and their failure to find a safe place to set up camp was causing tension. Tomás thought they should wait, lie low for another day. Miguel disagreed. The cover was poor, he argued, and there was no source of water. 'We have to carry on.' Both men looked grim: moving in daylight was always risky.

Had they made the right decision? Rose knew she was slowing them down, increasing the danger. The weight of the baby, her fear of falling, the need to watch her footing... With every step, she battled against exhaustion, against the longing to subside onto the bed of pine needles and tangled undergrowth beneath her feet and give way to sleep. Hunger gnawed at her but there was no time to stop and munch at the bread she carried in her pack. How much longer could she carry on without a rest?

Voices from somewhere to their rear. She saw Miguel's head turn abruptly, a look of alarm on his face. He pulled at her hand, urging her forward.

'Run!' she hissed. Why didn't he go? She stumbled on behind him, knowing it was hopeless, screaming at him to make a break for it. A tree root caught her and she fell, landing on a clump of some coarse grass. Its spikes dug into her as she lay sprawled there, too stunned to move.

It took a second for the sound of the shot to register. Then she was aware of a flurry of movement, shouts, a muttered curse from very close by, footsteps running, another shot. And when she dared raise her head to make sense of all this confusion, it was to the sickening realisation that the figure now lying a few paces away, one hand to his chest, was Miguel.

CHAPTER 14

Jaén, September 1939

'Shut up or you'll get the same treatment as him.' The two burly men of the *Guardia Civil* gripped Rose's arms yet more tightly as she struggled to break free.

'Miguel! Miguel!' She twisted her neck round again and again as they dragged her further from his body, now completely inert. She had not moved fast enough; they had seized her from behind before she could take a step towards him, to where he lay helpless on the hard ground with the blood from his wound staining the earth red. She must go to him, he might still be alive, he might still be saved... 'Let me go!' she screamed. 'Let me go, you bastards.' With as much force as she could muster, she gave the younger one, the one with the thin face and protruding ears, a kick in the shins.

He swore and removed a hand for just long enough to slap her hard on the face. It could have been her moment to escape but he was too quick. 'You're lucky I didn't give you one in the belly,' he said with a sneer. '*Puta.*'

Her cheek smarted but the pain was nothing, nothing at all. Tears of grief, anger, despair ran down her face. *Miguel, oh my love*. With every step, they were moving further from where he lay, dead or dying amongst the scrubby bushes, the jutting rocks. Alone on the hillside without even a goodbye, a word of comfort, a last kiss. He should have run; he might have got away. Tomás had run, two of the guards on his tail. She had heard more shots...

The sun moved behind the mountain. Soon it would be dark. What if a wild boar found him? Vultures or other birds of prey could already be hovering. Just another dead animal left to rot on the hillside. *Miguel.* Several times she tripped on a tree root and was jerked upright. She was so weary, so sad. Her baby. Her baby, who would grow up fatherless...

'Faster, it's getting dark.'

They had been heading south but Rose had long ceased to notice or even care where they were taking her. One foot then the other, on and on in a relentless, numbing rhythm. How many hours had they been walking? She had no idea; she only knew that if any life remained in Miguel, the night would put an end to it: he would not survive in the open. She prayed his death had been instant.

Lights appeared ahead of them, a scattering of houses. They were approaching a village or small town. *Miguel.* She would never see him again. Once more she craned her neck to look back, knowing the gesture was useless: they were too far away, too far down the mountain; it was too dark. Her parched throat craved water; hours had passed since she'd last wetted her lips. The *civiles* had a flask they drank from but it was not offered to her and she would not ask.

They came out onto a stony track and moments later entered the town. The streets were almost deserted. A woman wrapped in a black shawl hurried past, taking care not to look at them. A young boy chased a scraggy chicken into his house and quickly shut the door. They passed an old man with a bundle of firewood under his arm, who nodded to the guards.

Her captors had been mostly silent during their march but now they became more voluble, Alberto, the one with the moustache, anticipating with relish the stew his wife would be preparing for him in the *cuartel* and inviting his comrade to share it. Rose listened, hoping for a clue as to their whereabouts. She heard 'Quesada'. The name rang a bell: Miguel had talked about it, about a contact there.

The barracks were on the far side of the town. As she was led inside, a sudden spasm of pain seized her and she clutched her stomach. It couldn't be… No, it was too soon: three weeks before her time. It must be the chickpeas she ate last night; or else her guts rebelling against the rigours of the long march, the unspeakable trauma of today.

'Come on, move. What's the matter with you?'

The pain passed and Rose walked on, the two *civiles* still holding her by the arms. She was taken to a desk, where a sergeant barked questions at her and wrote her answers on a form. Name, nationality, date and place of birth…

'Civil status?'

'Married.'

He gave her a hard stare, pen poised over the page. Rose stared back defiantly. She didn't care if they believed her or not.

'Widow,' Felipe said with a smirk.

'Who were you with? How many of you?'

She would not say Miguel's name, not give them anything more.

'Come on, answer me, woman.'

Holding his gaze, she tightened her lips, refusing to turn away or speak. Then another contraction gripped her stomach and she gasped.

'You might as well answer, we know who he is.' The one they called Alberto jabbed her in the back with a finger.

'Then you don't need me to tell you.'

Felipe drew a hand across his throat. 'He's dead, we made quite sure of that. Another *canalla* down. But there were others, at least one more.'

The officer nodded. 'Put her in the *calabozo* for tonight. She'll talk in the morning; a night in the cells and the usual treatment should do it. Make sure she gets a good dose of castor oil. And you can draw lots for which of you has the pleasure of wielding the razor to her head. One of those cunts killed Pepe and I want to know who.'

Be strong, be strong for Miguel. As Alberto seized her by the arm, Rose felt her belly contract once again, in a way that left no room for doubt. It must be the shock bringing on her labour. She doubled over.

'What's up? Is it the baby? Is the baby coming?'

She nodded, breathing through the pain. 'Early. It's coming early.'

The three men exchanged nervous looks. Felipe grunted. 'How do we know she's not faking it?'

'I'll get my wife, she'll know what to do,' Alberto offered.

Another pain, this time stronger. 'Can I sit down?'

'She's not faking,' their superior said. 'Take her to Jaén, to the hospital there, but tell them she's to be kept under guard and returned here after she's given birth.'

'Get in.' Rose was shoved into the cab of a small truck between Alberto, who was driving and the thin-faced youth, Felipe. Hurtling along rough roads full of potholes, she was bounced up and down, thrown against one or other of the men or forward, towards the windscreen. She gripped the seat, fearful for the baby, aware her contractions were becoming more frequent. At the hospital she was bundled out and delivered into the care of a sour-faced nun, who examined her with cold fingers and a wordless frown.

When she left the room, Rose sat up on the bed. She took deep breaths, trying to gather her resources, to find strength from somewhere. In her head she heard the kindly voice of her father, saw his face before her, and even though she had long ceased to believe in God, she prayed, the words ingrained in her youth coming back to her. She felt more helpless and alone, more frightened, than ever before in her entire life. She was totally at the mercy of those she saw as 'the enemy' and who doubtless saw her as 'scum'.

'Lie down.' The nun was back. She pushed Rose's skirt up above her waist and taking a razor from her pocket, roughly shaved her. Rose knew these nurse nuns had no qualifications, no training. If something went wrong… She was vaguely aware of other beds in the ward, of blurred voices, creaks and the distant barking of dogs. Time passed – whether one hour or many she could not have said. The pains came and went, the nun came and went. Now there was barely three minutes between contractions.

Warm liquid coursed down her legs: the waters had broken. 'Move.' A towel was placed underneath her. The pain blocked out all other thought. *Breathe. Stay calm. Go with the pain.*

The nun peered between her legs. 'Push when you're ready,' she said.

Rose shook her head. She had no energy left to push. Weren't you supposed to feel an overwhelming urge? She felt none. In a sudden panic, she asked, 'Is everything alright?'

Without bothering to answer, the nun left her and then, barely a minute later, something shifted and she had to push, simply had to. She cried out. The baby was coming.

'Quiet, there are patients trying to sleep.' The nun's voice, but Rose also saw a man, a doctor standing by the bed. She pushed, again and again, and then she felt a tearing of her flesh as the baby's head emerged. She looked down and saw the strands of damp hair stuck to it. Dark hair like Miguel's. She saw the cupped hands of the nun, ready to receive it.

Another push, a sideways turn, a slithering, and with a cry her baby propelled itself into the world.

'A girl.'

'Give her to me. Let me hold her.' Rose was smiling. Impossible not to. She loved this child. Already her heart was bursting with love for her tiny daughter, who was now placed on her chest. The baby's body was streaked with blood but she was perfect, beautiful, a miracle. Her little mouth was sucking at air, searching for Rose's breast. Rose put the baby's mouth to her nipple and she fastened on to it. Blanca. She would name her daughter Blanca. 'Look what we created,' she whispered silently to Miguel. 'Look how beautiful she is.'

'That's enough. You're not finished yet.' The doctor, a short, plump man with a bulbous nose, spoke brusquely.

'Cut the cord and take the child away to be washed,' he instructed the nun. The cord was clipped, the baby lifted from her. 'Now, push again. The placenta… Come on, push. Harder.' Faintly she heard a thin cry from further down the ward. The baby wanted its mother. *Bring her back.* She pushed again and felt the placenta slide out. The doctor threw it into a basin, then parted Rose's legs and examined her. 'A small tear not worth stitching, but you need to rest.'

She wiped the sweat from her face and neck with a corner of the sheet and lay back, physically spent but still too elated to sleep. As soon as she had recovered, she would take her baby and run. She could see no guards. The nuns would not chase her, surely. She would hide somewhere safe for a few days or weeks until she and the baby were stronger. Then she would get out of Spain, go back to England as Miguel had urged her. She imagined her parents' delight at having her safely home and how they would spoil their beautiful granddaughter.

'Here, drink this.' A small glass of liquid was thrust at her. In the dim light of the ward, its colour was difficult to discern.

'What is it?'

'Just something to help you sleep. Drink. All of it.'

As she drank, the novelty of being patient rather than nurse struck her. How often had she given medicine to the sick and wounded in just such a way? With some of them protesting, having to be coaxed and cajoled. She thought of the many who struggled violently or ran away when faced with injections. The nun held out her hand for the empty glass. Rose gave it to her and lay back, yielding to her exhaustion. She was so tired, so so tired…

CHAPTER 15

Jaén, September 1939

A familiar smell… Familiar, but from long ago, surely. A hospital, she was in a hospital. She sniffed that unmistakeable combination of iodoform and sickness that had been absent from her life for what seemed like years. Rose opened her eyes. She did not recognise this place, this hospital ward. What was she doing here? And where was Miguel? Her head was stuffed with cotton wool, she could not think. Was she awake or dreaming?

Then, little by little, the fog started to thin. She became aware of a pain in her belly, a sodden pad between her legs, an aching in her breasts and an absence, a terrifying absence… The baby! She sat up and looked around. There were other women in the ward. One was groaning, another calling out a man's name over and over: *Mateo, Mateo, Mateo*. Most lay inert and silent.

'Nurse!' Her cry echoed around the ward. A nun appeared, younger and prettier than the one who had attended her yesterday. 'Where's my baby?'

'Shh, you must rest. You'll see your baby later.'

'I want to see her now.' Rose took in the fading light from the row of small windows along one wall. 'What time is it? How long have I slept?' Her bladder was bursting. 'The lavatory…'

'Wait, I'll bring the bedpan.'

Pulling back the sheet and thin blanket that covered her, the nurse removed the soaked pad and thrust a bedpan under her.

'I need to wash.' Even with a fresh pad, the fetid smell from her lower parts could not be ignored. After months in the *sierra*, Rose was used to the lack of opportunities to wash, yet even with scant water she had managed to keep herself reasonably clean. Now the combination of dust from yesterday's long trek and the sweat and blood of the birth disgusted her. 'Please, bring me some water,' she begged the nun.

A basin of water was brought and, soon after, a bowl of thin soup, which she consumed with relish, having eaten only a dry crust of bread given her by the guards since yesterday morning. It was not enough, but feeling hungry was something else she had become used to.

Left alone, Rose determined to go in search of her baby. She had asked again, been fobbed off again with excuses. Now they said the baby had an infection. What kind of infection? Had she been fed? Rose's breasts tingled. She would find Blanca and feed her without more delay. She lowered herself from the bed and lumbered down the ward, now in semi-darkness, to where light shone through an open door.

'Where are you going?' The nun from yesterday stood barring her way. 'Get back to bed.' Her callous voice made Rose shiver.

'Give me my baby.' Frantic now, she pushed the nun aside and stumbled on, opening doors, peering into the darkness, her ears pricked for the sound of crying.

Was that a whimper she heard? 'Blanca!' Her daughter wanted her. She knew it with complete certainty even before she heard the cry.

Then someone grabbed her from behind, pinning her arms back.

'Let me go!' She struggled with every ounce of energy to break free but the doctor's grip was strong. She heard a wail, the robust wail of a hungry baby. 'Blanca!' Using all her force, she wrenched one wrist free, grabbed the doctor's hand and sank her teeth into it.

'Damn you, bitch!'

Now was her chance… But then a torrent of blood ran down her legs and a fit of dizziness overcame her. She must have passed out briefly because when she came to, she found herself being escorted back to the ward by the two nuns. Tears ran down her face as she was lifted onto the bed, examined and her legs sponged. More pads were fastened in place.

'That was a very stupid thing to do,' the older nun said. 'You must stay in bed, unless you want to suffer a haemorrhage.'

'Then bring me my baby. She's hungry.'

'As we told you, your baby has an infection and can't take the breast. We'll see she's looked after, don't worry.'

'I want to speak to the doctor. He can tell me what's wrong with her.'

'Calm down, girl. In the morning we'll bring your baby. Now sleep.'

The doctor was standing over her. Sunlight streamed in through the windows; it must be late. Rose remembered lying sleepless for hours, crying for the baby, for Miguel, for herself. Crying with frustration at her helplessness. She must eventually have cried herself to sleep just before dawn.

'My baby... Can I see her now?'

The doctor cleared his throat. 'I'm sorry,' he said. 'Your baby was very small, very weak. I'm afraid she wasn't strong enough to survive the infection.'

Rose sat up. 'What are you saying? Let me see her!'

The younger nun joined them. 'As Dr Martínez said, your baby died during the night. We tried to save her but there was nothing we could do. She was buried earlier this morning. We thought it best to let you sleep.'

'I don't believe you, you're lying,' Rose shouted. 'The baby was healthy, there was nothing wrong with her.'

'I can assure you she was far from healthy,' the doctor said more coldly. 'She was several weeks premature and in these cases it's not uncommon...'

'You've killed her!' Sobbing, Rose grabbed the doctor by his sleeve. 'You've killed my baby. You're murderers!'

He shook her off and turned to the nun. 'Give her a sedative before she gets any more hysterical.'

Rose came round slowly, trying to make sense of her surroundings through the fuzz of half-remembered scenes. Please God, let it be just a nightmare. Miguel, the baby, everything that had happened over the last two days, three days... But she knew it was not. A moan escaped her as she became more alert and took in the terrible losses she had endured.

'Are you awake?' Someone was standing by her bed. Not a nurse, a woman in normal dress holding a sheaf of papers: an administrator perhaps. She spoke sharply. 'We need your signature on the death certificate.'

Confused, Rose peered at the paper being held out in front of her. She saw her name, date and place of birth; the words: *bebé sexo hembra* and two dates: 12th and 14th September 1939. There was more but she could not make it out through the blur of her tears.

'I'm not signing anything.'

'Come on now, it's just for the records.'

Rose hesitated. What did it matter? Her baby was dead, everything was over... She took the pen.

'*¡Por Dios!* How long does it take to write your name? As if I haven't anything else to do all day.'

Incensed by the woman's impatience, Rose flung down the pen. She would not oblige this vixen, devoid of any humanity. 'Go to hell!'

'Doctor Martínez!'

He strode into the ward. 'What now? Is that bitch making trouble again?'

'She won't sign.'

'Won't sign?' He laughed. 'You do it then, Dolores. What difference does it make?'

¡Anda! Take a butcher's at what's just driven through the gates.' Rose lifted her head from the pillow. One of the other patients, a young woman with a bandaged head, was standing by the window, looking out. 'I wouldn't mind a ride in that,' she commented to no one in particular.

'In what?' A voice came from the bed next to Rose's.

'Posh motorcar. There's a couple getting out now. Fur stole, high-heeled shoes, smart suit and tie... *Señoritos*. I wonder what they're doing here.'

Rose lay back on the bed. She couldn't care less about the *señoritos*. All she wanted was to leave this accursed hospital, this accursed country now ruled by the fascists, and go home. Back to England, to her family, to safety. She was still bleeding, still sore. The doctor had told her at least a week for the tear to heal. They were watching her closely. No doubt they would send her back to the Civil Guard as ordered. And then what? Castor oil and a scalping? Prison? Or worse? She should be planning her escape but she had no energy. No energy even to talk to her fellow patients.

The head wound was still standing by the window, where two or three other patients had joined her. 'They're leaving now. Just look at them.' She nudged the girl next to her, the one who had lost an eye and who screamed for her mother half the night. 'I'll bet they've never been hungry in their lives. Probably never done a day's work either.' The running commentary continued. 'He's shaking hands with Doctor Martínez now. What's that she's carrying? I can't see, she's got her back turned. That's it, off they go in their swanky car.'

'Get back in your beds at once.'

Rose pulled the sheet over her head and covered her ears. She was sick of this hospital, the stony-hearted nuns, the rigid discipline. How she longed for news from England – from her parents and brothers, from Dorothy and other friends. During her months in the *sierra*, communication had been impossible. Twice she had given letters to their safe contacts in Beas and Cazorla, but she had no idea if they had arrived or even been posted. And what address could she give for letters back?

For days she slept, she ate the tasteless food they gave her, she cried. Her dreams, that seemed to drip with crimson, were of severed limbs and heads, of babies being slaughtered, of gigantic grinning rats. Or she dreamt of Miguel. Miguel alive, caressing her hair, singing to her. *Ojos verdes, verdes como la albahaca. Verdes como el trigo verde, y el verde, verde limón.*

But most of her waking hours were tormented by guilt for Miguel's death. Without her, they would have moved faster, he might have survived. She could not escape the visions that haunted her day and night of his body lying exposed on that stony hillside. The vultures and eagles they had seen every day soaring above the crags would now be pecking at his flesh.

Then, to escape madness, she would tell herself he had merely feigned death and that Tomás had come back for him – Tomás or one of the other *maquis* – and saved his life. She clung to the idea – clutched at it like a raft of sanity – that one day he would track her down and they would be reunited. And they would make another baby, one that would live.

CHAPTER 16

Jaén, September 1939

'Here, get dressed; your clothes have been washed. You'll be leaving in half an hour.'

Rose knew better than to ask questions. She put on the loose gown given to her by a woman sympathiser when neither her own well-worn trousers nor the slightly larger ones she'd appropriated from Miguel were big enough to accommodate her expanding girth. It hung slackly now and she noticed how the hem was torn in several places. There was no sign of her shawl. Nights and mornings were becoming chilly; she would be cold without it. Her possessions amounted to this dress and nothing else. No other clothes, no money, no blanket, soap or sanitary pads, no food or drink. Her boots were falling apart after constant wear in the rough mountain terrain. They wouldn't last much longer.

She had been expecting the same two guards who'd brought her here, but it was another pair who came for her. 'You'd better not try any silly tricks with the *Comandante*,' one of them warned as they marched her through the streets of Jaén to what must be the provincial headquarters. 'He's not a patient man and today he's in a foul mood.'

Rose could hear him shouting from halfway down the corridor. A group of guards were being chastised for some neglect of duty. 'I've lost more men on your watch...' he yelled. She heard the scraping of furniture across the floor and cries. Were they being beaten? Her guards appeared edgy and she realised they were scared of their boss.

'Out of my sight!' The door opened and four or five men stumbled past her, their faces flushed. One had blood dripping from his nose, another held a handkerchief to his mouth.

'Hurry up, bring the *puta* in,' a voice thundered from inside the room. The *Comandante*, a corpulent, jowly man with close-set eyes and a ruddy complexion, faced her across a massive, heavy desk.

He looked her up and down with contempt. '*Malditos rojos*. Scum! Traitors! I've lost fifteen men in the *sierra* since the war ended. Fifteen! Good, loyal men, at the hands of you red vermin. But I'll settle the score, don't you doubt it.' He glared at her. 'Where did you say you're from? You're not Spanish, that's for sure.'

'I'm from England.'

'Then what in God's name are you doing here?' He kicked at his desk and stood up. 'Well, don't think you'll be treated any better for that!' Turning to the guards, he shouted, 'Take her away. Be generous with the castor oil and shave her head – we'll get a good price for those blonde locks.' He came up close and pulled her by the ear. 'Ever been to Madrid?' He spat the words in her face. 'We've a very popular prison there. Ventas, it's called. You won't be seeing your country again. No, *Señora*, not for a very long time.

'Come on, what are you waiting for?' he bellowed at the two guards. 'Take the bitch out of my...'

The Commander's sentence remained unfinished as he fell to the floor, clutching his chest.

The young guards eyed each other in alarm. 'What's wrong with him?'

'Quick, get help.'

While one of them bent over his boss, the other rushed out of the room. Rose stood rooted to the spot, breathing hard. She noted the open door. While all attention was focused on the Commander, she had her best – probably her only – chance of escape. If she acted quickly... Her eyes swivelled towards the burly figure sprawled on the floor. A heart attack, almost certainly. 'Is he breathing?' she asked the guard.

'No.' There was panic in his voice. 'I don't think so.'

She was a nurse. A life was in danger. Rose knelt on the floor and felt the man's pulse. It was still detectable but very weak. His face was taking on a distinctly blue tinge. She must get him breathing again and fast. Resuscitation may not be enough to save him but it was all she could do. She moved into position and began, pressing down on his chest, raising his arms; repeating the familiar actions. A number of other men had entered the room and were watching in silence, though she was only vaguely aware of their presence.

She paused. He was breathing. She helped him sit up and at once a violent fit of coughing seized him, convulsing his whole body. Rose took his wrist, felt the beat of his pulse getting stronger. She'd seen it before, how coughing could trigger a stopped heart.

'Get a blanket,' she ordered the bumbling guards. Two of them collided as they ran for the door. The bull-necked one with the crooked teeth pushed his colleague aside. 'Stay,' he hissed.

Dazed, the Commander looked around him, taking in the scene, taking in Rose. Any minute now he would remember his plans for her, repeat the order to his men to haul her off to prison. She glanced at the knot of *civiles* standing around gawking uselessly. These were the men who would draw lots to shave her scalp, who would jeer as the castor oil took effect on her bowels.

'Fetch my wife.' The Commander's voice was weak.

'Yes sir, immediately.' Another of the guards left.

'Now help me up.' He was hauled to his feet and manoeuvred into the large office chair. Rose draped the blanket over his shoulders. While she listened to his breathing, observed the colour return to his cheeks, her mind was on the doorway behind her. She thought of the razor and the castor oil, of the kind of life she could expect in one of Franco's prisons, and edged backwards a step.

'*Ay, madre mía.* What happened to you, José Luis?' Rose heard the door bang shut and turned to see a bird-like woman with thin lips, a high, nervous voice and skin like creased silk, hurrying forward to the Commander's side. She had missed her chance.

'Don't fuss, *mujer*. I'm still alive.' Rose flinched as he jabbed a fat finger in her direction. 'Yes, I'm still alive, thanks to this English *señora*. She'll come home with us today. See to her, Esperanza. Make her comfortable and give her whatever she needs.'

The inspector entered their compartment and stared at Rose with obvious suspicion despite the presence of the two *civiles*, Vicente and Eugenio, who sat either side of her in their uniforms. 'Papers.' She passed him her *salvoconducto*, signed by the *Comandante*, along with her passport. He examined it for several minutes then handed it back without a word. Addressing Vicente, he said, 'Make sure you don't lose sight of her when you get to La Linea.'

Carriages rattling, the train steamed through the countryside at an unhurried pace. As they puffed past neglected fields devoid of crops and villages steeped in poverty, Rose mused on the implausible sequence of events of the last twenty-four hours. Instead of being scalped, dosed with castor oil and sent off to prison, here she was on her way to Gibraltar (and with any luck a British ship that would take her to England).

At the Commander's quarters, she had been treated like royalty. She had not eaten so well for months, nor slept in such a comfortable bed. Recovered from his attack, he had been a different man, courteous and gentlemanly, though his wife had hinted that the earlier behaviour was closer to his true nature. Rose had been shocked by the bitterness in Esperanza's voice as she said, 'I wish you'd left him to die. Don't be fooled, he's a tyrant. What you see now, it's put on. In private he treats me worse than an animal.' Nevertheless, she had obeyed her husband's orders and provided Rose with all she needed for the journey: spare clothes including a warm shawl, soap, sanitary pads and ample provisions. Most important of all, Rose was in possession of the 'safe-conduct' that would get her out of Spain.

They changed trains at Antequera. '*Mi pueblo*,' Eugenio said with longing and a touch of pride in his voice. He couldn't be more than seventeen, his cheeks covered in a soft down. She observed him scanning the passengers who waited on the platform, hoping perhaps to catch sight of a familiar face.

Bobadilla, Campillos, Ronda, Benaojan... Rose gazed out of the window at the landscape of densely wooded hills and limestone outcrops, the dramatic river valley below. She recalled a young Spanish soldier whose last moments she had shared at the Ebro, whose hand she had held as he talked with longing of his village here in the Serranía de Ronda. She unwrapped the bread and sausage Esperanza had prepared for her, remembering how Miguel would always make sure she had the best of whatever food they managed to procure. 'For the baby,' he said. Meanwhile, she had watched his body become thinner and more wiry, any spare fat turned to muscle.

The other occupants of the compartment brought out their own rations and shared them round. She noticed how meagre were the provisions of her escorts and offered them some of her sausage. When they had finished eating, Vicente took out his packet of *tabaco* and Zig-Zag papers and rolled cigarettes for himself and Eugenio. As the compartment filled with smoke, Rose felt a sudden, intense craving for tobacco. She had given up while she was expecting, finding it repugnant – and besides, tobacco was hard to obtain – but now she longed for a cigarette. 'Can you spare a little of that?' she asked. Vicente nodded and rolled one for her. She drew on it, savouring the taste, the feel of the smoke in her lungs.

The train stopped at Jimena de la Frontera and a well-dressed man carrying a copy of ABC under his arm entered their compartment. He greeted them and sat down opposite Rose. For months she had heard no news of the outside world. When the man opened his newspaper, Rose could not resist peering at the headlines. *British destroyers sink German U-boat*, she read and further down the page, *First Air Battle between RAF and Luftwaffe*. Was Britain at war with Germany then? By sticking to their misguided non-intervention treaty in Spain, they had allowed the fascists to gain hold. This – all-out war in Europe – was what the volunteers who had come here to fight had tried to prevent. War, she thought bitterly. Hadn't she seen enough of it to last her a lifetime? In Spain, albeit disastrously, the war had ended. Now she would be returning to a country in the thick of another war, with no guarantee of a better outcome. The possibility of a fascist Europe horrified her.

She thought of her parents and of her brothers – thankfully still too young to fight. And also, briefly, of Harry, who would no doubt be leading a unit somewhere. For months she had put Harry out of her mind, having decided long ago to put an end to their engagement. Miguel's death made not a jot of difference to that decision: the thought of him repelled her. He had written a few times, saying how he missed her and couldn't wait for their wedding, and she had replied, but without reference to either her feelings or their future. Instead she had described the hard work and long hours, the bravery of the volunteers and the terrible plight of the people of Spain. It was cowardly; she should have told him.

The light was beginning to fade as Vicente informed her La Linea was the next stop. 'Let's hope you can cross the frontier this evening. Otherwise you'll have to stay at the barracks with us.' He pulled out a letter with the Commander's signature. 'Once you're in Gibraltar, you're on your own. You're on British territory.' Rose wondered how the war would affect her chances of finding a passage to Britain – and how safe it would be. But then hadn't she exposed herself to danger countless times since arriving in Spain? She had become inured to it.

CHAPTER 17

Evesham, October 1939

Rose ran upstairs to her bedroom and pulled the door shut behind her. It was all too much. The pitying looks on their faces, the whispers exchanged, the endless questions, spoken and unspoken. Nothing felt real, she hardly felt real herself. A part of her was still in Spain, in a hideout somewhere in the mountains of Andalucía with her lover close by and a baby yet to be born. A world so utterly different...

Everything here was familiar yet at the same time alien. Bewildered, she found herself touching the objects around her, testing their solidity. But she knew it wasn't the vicarage or her family that had changed. She looked in the mirror and struggled to recognise the image she saw there: a woman bearing little resemblance to the one who had stared back at her from that same mirror three years ago – or even two, when she'd returned briefly from the Aragón front after her injury.

Arriving in Evesham, she had been overwhelmed with relief and joy at seeing her family, at being in the comfortable, safe environment of her old home. She had revelled in the warm embraces of her parents, in the comforting movement of the old rocking chair by the fire (usually reserved for Father) and in her mother's home cooking. Her parents' relief and joy equalled her own. They had assumed the worst and were content to postpone some of their questions for a few days – though they could not entirely disguise their shock at her haggard appearance, the lines of grief that now marked her face.

Rose was thankful they had granted her this respite. She was well aware it could not last, that she would have to offer explanations, an account of some sort. During her time on the ship, a naval destroyer returning to Portsmouth for an overhaul, she had pondered how much to tell her family and constructed in her mind a story that did not lie but omitted a great deal, including her pregnancy.

There were too many gaps, too much ambiguity, she now realised. Her parents had listened but were not satisfied. She felt battered by the barrage of perfectly reasonable questions that erupted on her fifth day. *Why didn't you leave with the other nurses after the war ended? Where did you spend those months? Who were you with? Where did you sleep? What happened to your companions?* Without knowing the whole story, how could they understand? She craved understanding yet felt unable to reveal the traumas she had suffered. *You've changed*, they said. Everyone she met repeated those same words. *You've changed.* Of course she had changed. All the brigade volunteers, all the medical staff and administrators had been changed by their experiences in the war, she told them. How could it be otherwise?

Still, Mother especially remained unconvinced. It was the physical changes that concerned her most. 'You must see a doctor,' she insisted. 'I'll make an appointment for you.'

'Leave it to me. I'll phone first thing tomorrow, I promise.' Rose had already decided to confide in their doctor. The bleeding hadn't completely stopped and she wanted to make sure nothing was amiss.

Persuading Mother not to accompany her wasn't easy but Rose stood her ground and visited the surgery alone. Dr Baines assured her he would respect patient confidentiality despite being an old family friend. He examined her and found no cause for anxiety. 'Come back if you're still bleeding at the end of next week,' he said. 'There shouldn't be any problem with future pregnancies.'

'No no, I don't expect to get married.'

Dr Baines raised his eyebrows. He knew about her engagement to Harry. 'Losing a baby is always traumatic,' he said. 'And in your case, alone in a foreign country without a husband to support you… But time is a great healer. You may feel different in a year or two.'

Rose shook her head. 'It was a girl,' she said, fighting back the tears, 'a perfectly healthy baby girl. She was so beautiful… I fed her, but then they took her away and refused to let me see her again. They said she'd caught an infection, that because she arrived early…'

'You say she was born three weeks prematurely? Are you sure about the dates? Three weeks isn't much – not enough in itself to account for her death. But without knowing her weight, her general health, the state of her lungs – and of course the kind of infection… Do you have the death certificate? It should give more details.'

'No, there was one but they didn't give me a copy.'

Again the doctor's eyebrows went up. 'Tut-tut. They really should have done. Well, Rose. Best to try and put it behind you now and start to think about the future. We're at war here and your skills will be much in demand – when you feel ready, that is.'

'I've decided to break off my engagement to Harry.' Rose was sitting with Father in the drawing room.

His face showed no sign of surprise. 'You know best, Rose. I'm sure you've thought carefully about it and if that's your decision, better to act now than marry and regret it. Have you told him?'

'Not yet but I will when he's next home on leave.'

Father put down his newspaper. 'I don't want to pry, Rose but is there someone else? Someone you met in Spain?'

Without specifically mentioning Miguel, she had dropped enough hints for her parents to guess. 'There was someone, yes.' She swallowed and took a deep breath, trying to control the grief that surged up. 'I loved him very much, but he was killed.'

'My poor girl.' He reached for her hand and clasped it in both of his. 'I'm so sorry.'

The door opened and through her tears Rose saw her younger brother Bertie gape at her before making a rapid retreat.

Rose sat facing Harry in the Oxford café she had chosen as a meeting place on the assumption that neutral territory would be easier for them both. They had exchanged news and small talk, of the kind that might pass between friends or strangers. He told her he was stationed on the Belgian border, where they were expecting the Germans to attempt an invasion imminently. His three-day leave was provisional – he might be recalled at a moment's notice to lead his unit.

Now he leaned towards her across the table and his voice, lower but more venomous, dripped sarcasm. 'So, my dear Rose. *Red* Rose. Did you miss me?' The malice in those steely eyes shocked her. How could she ever have promised herself to him? As she sought for the least hurtful way to reply, he asked, 'Do you have something to tell me?'

She reached into her bag for her engagement ring and handed it to him. She had not worn it for over two years. 'Forgive me, Harry. I hate to hurt you but I can't go through with this.'

'Ha. Do you think I hadn't guessed?' He took the ring and put it in his pocket. 'I'm not a fool, Rose. I've seen this coming for a long time and acted accordingly. In fact… Well, to put it simply, there's another girl, a sweet young thing, who'll be only too willing to take your place. I'll be a married man soon, I can guarantee you.'

'I'm glad for you, Harry. Genuinely.' Rose felt only relief. 'We were never really suited. I'm sure this girl will make you a much better wife than I would have done.'

'Maybe so. Though I disagree that we weren't suited. The thing is, you've changed. I saw it when you came back from Spain the last time and I see it even more clearly now. To be frank, I already had doubts when you decided to go off in the first place, rather than get married. Putting it bluntly, I expect the girl I marry, my wife… I expect her to put me before anything else, before any abstract ideas about… You know what I mean, Rose.' He offered her a cigarette and lit one for himself.

She had hurt his pride, that much was plain. Whether his deeper feelings had been affected she could not tell. Of one thing she was certain: she had not truly loved him. Miguel had shown her what it was to love. She could not imagine feeling that way again about anyone, and certainly not about Harry, whose selfishness had never been more apparent.

A warm fug of cigarette smoke, tea and rancid lard filled her nostrils. The café windows were misted over, contributing to her sense of suffocation, of being enclosed in a space that was becoming ever smaller and more oppressive. She finished her tea and pushed aside the uneaten scone Harry had insisted on ordering for her.

'I have to go, but let's part as friends,' she said, managing a weak smile. 'Please try to stay safe. And… I want you to be happy, really I do.'

CHAPTER 18

England, 1940

The war had given everyone a sense of purpose, Rose noticed. They talked of 'the war effort', of 'pulling together' and of 'battening down the hatches'. She ought to share this sense of common purpose but she could not. A kind of numbness had overtaken her. Purpose and effort were exactly what she lacked. The loss of Miguel and of her baby had also left her bereft of purpose. And without purpose, she could not spur herself to make an effort.

Sporadically and without warning, shafts of pain would pierce the numbness. Memories of an imagined future, of what could have been: a vision of happiness stolen from her, irretrievably. When she woke in the mornings or during the restless nights, flashes of half-remembered dreams ensnared her. Dreams of Spain – of dying patients, broken bodies, the roar of bombs and whine of bullets. And of silent marches in the night through the rocky, forested mountains, with Miguel in front of or behind her and the weight and promise of a baby girl in her womb.

What are you going to do? Everyone advised her to find some useful work that would take her mind off whatever traumas she had suffered in Spain. Rose knew they were right, in theory. If she could only summon up the energy, she would like to put her skills to a useful purpose. There was need enough for nurses. But a more personal need was pressing on her: the need to make contact with some of the medical staff she had worked with in Spain, those who had returned in the autumn or winter of '38. Their common experience made a bond that no one else could share.

She wrote to Margaret, Annie and Patience and arranged to meet them in London. Margaret had thrown herself into nursing again; Annie was in charge of an air-raid station; Patience had a job teaching war nursing. They had all adapted to life in wartime England although, as Rose was well aware, they too had been touched by personal sorrows. At a table in the Lyons Corner House, she was able for the first time to recount her story in full – of life in the guerrilla, Miguel's death, her pregnancy and the loss of her baby. It left them speechless for a long moment while she rummaged in her bag for a handkerchief. Despite the tears, she felt some relief, a slight lessening of the pain through having shared her sorrow. There was no need for words of comfort from her former colleagues; she could read the understanding in their eyes.

Annie was the first to speak. 'You must be kind to yourself,' she said. 'Give yourself time.' The others nodded their agreement.

'Spain has changed all of us, I think,' Margaret said. 'Seeing so much suffering, so many lives lost in vain. But what you've been through… Look, why don't you come and share our flat? If you don't feel ready to nurse, there are plenty of other jobs you could do. Take your time, look around and see how you feel. The flat has four bedrooms and we're only three at the moment. It's cheap and with four sharing, the rent will be even less. I'm sure Eileen and Gladys would be only too happy.'

'I'll think about it.' After nearly a month resting at home, Rose knew she needed to move away. She was feeling physically stronger but that didn't help in dealing with the looks of pained concern on her mother's face or the silent pressure to 'pull herself together' emotionally.

Now, at least, she was not the only cause of concern in their household. Ralph, having turned nineteen in the autumn of '39, had been called up for service and declared himself a conscientious objector. He would happily drive an ambulance or volunteer for some other non-combative role but he would not fight. He was planning to join the Quakers. Their parents respected his decision. Bertie, three years younger, expressed disgust. He couldn't wait to play his part in the fighting, preferably as an airman in the RAF. Rose understood both brothers' points of view, though she hoped the war would be over before Bertie reached eighteen and could join up.

She was on the verge of accepting Margaret's offer of a room when Mother heard of a residential job at a home for handicapped children in Oxfordshire, now expanding to take evacuees. She went for an interview and was impressed by the Matron's dedication and manner of treating the youngsters in her charge.

'I take it you like children?' The Matron fixed a shrewd gaze on Rose. 'I feel that's more important than almost anything else.'

'Oh I do.' She described her experience with the refugee children in Murcia.

'You can start tomorrow if you like. We're terribly short-staffed.'

Rose knew after the first week that it was a mistake. She did like children and was popular with them too. The younger ones were affectionate, the older ones found her a sympathetic confidant. Naturally the children missed their families, but a warm, caring atmosphere and cheerful staff ensured that laughter alternated with the tears. The children's disabilities were mainly physical; Rose admired their bravery, their attempts at independence.

The problem, which she should have foreseen, was the babies. There were half a dozen little ones, some as young as six months. She could not bear to set eyes on them, to hear their cries, to inhale their milky baby smell or touch their velvety baby skin. One in particular upset her: a girl called Mary who suffered from a rare digestive condition that meant she could not take solid food. She was eleven months old, her birthday just a month before Blanca's. Outwardly, she appeared normal, with round blue eyes and the most dazzling smile. When Rose started the job, Mary was on the point of walking and beamed with delight at every tottering step she made. If Blanca had lived… The thoughts and images tormented her; there was no escape. She simply could not endure it.

After Matron found her sitting on the stairs sobbing one night, she realised she must hand in her notice. As Annie had said, she needed time. Matron's efforts to dissuade her were useless: she would take some menial job, one with no emotional demands, no reminders of what she had lost. She thought about volunteering as a Land Girl or working in a munitions factory. So when Margaret wrote to remind her of the vacant room in her flat, Rose decided to take up the offer. She needed to be among friends, and now Mabel, her very oldest friend, was also in London.

She moved in as soon as she had worked her notice at the children's home, and began looking for a job. The sign in the window of the Angel Café caught her eye one afternoon as she was passing. Without a moment's hesitation, she entered the busy café and asked to see the manager. Working as a waitress would suit her just fine, keeping her busy while paying the rent and her modest living expenses.

'So you're going to be a Nippy? What a hoot!' Rose's flatmates examined her uniform with interest – the monogrammed cap threaded with ribbon, the black bombazine dress with its white collar and cuffs, the white apron. Her employers were strict about appearance and cleanliness. She must be neat and tidy at all times, the manager stressed. Getting ready for her first day at work, she looked at herself in the mirror and wondered if any of her companions in the *sierras* would have recognised her.

Rose was used to hard work and long hours, to being on her feet all day. Unlike some of the other girls, she found nothing to complain about in the conditions: it helped to be busy and surrounded by people. What led her to quit her new job after little more than a month was the blitz of bombing that hit London that September. With so many injured, she could not ignore the call of conscience. Nurses were in demand.

Once again she found herself dealing with the casualties caused by bombs and incendiaries. She chose to work at one of the mobile medical units set up in the street, where the less serious injuries were treated, the hospitals being full to overflowing. Once again she was exposed to danger. But there were few small children or babies – most of them had been evacuated to the country. She could cope.

For a spell she was based at the tube station in Holborn where every night, as in many other stations, hundreds of people were crammed together on the platforms, in the corridors and along the tunnels. Here, the main aim of the medical unit was to avoid the spread of disease and contamination. Rose liked the atmosphere of camaraderie, the way people of all classes and backgrounds chatted to each other on an equal basis, united by their common need of a safe place to spend the night.

Mabel was working as an ARP warden, also risking her life by making sure everyone in her neighbourhood made it to a shelter. Her patch was not far away from where Rose was working. Some mornings, after Rose's station had been cleared in readiness for the morning trains and Mabel had checked that her neighbours still had homes to go to, the two women would meet for breakfast in a café.

'Couldn't you just eat a big plate of bacon and eggs?' Mabel said, spreading a thin layer of margarine on her toast.

Rose thought of the starvation in Spain and said nothing. Towards the end of the war she had heard they were trapping rats or cats and roasting them in the streets, going to work on a few lettuce leaves or a crust of maize bread. In the concentration camps where thousands of Spanish refugees were interned, they were reduced to chewing on discarded orange peel trodden underfoot and filthy.

'Oh I know we shouldn't complain but I'm so sick of dried egg and hardly any meat, and margarine instead of butter.'

'I'm just sick of war,' Rose said with feeling. 'Sick of being surrounded by death and injury, sick of having to worry about bombs all the time. I can hardly remember what normal life is like.'

'You're so much braver than I am, Rose. Weren't you scared stiff in Spain? Honestly, last night I was literally shaking when I heard them come over. Bloody Germans. And I have to stay calm and keep others calm, even though I'm usually the last to get in the shelter.'

'Of course I was scared. I was absolutely terrified a lot of the time. We all were.' Rose drained her cup. At least the tea here was good and strong. 'I'm not really brave,' she said. 'But you end up... well, as a nurse you don't have time to think of anything beyond the immediate needs of the wounded. You just have to get on with it.' She didn't want to talk about Spain. Mabel was a good friend but how could she begin to understand? 'I must get some sleep,' she said, pushing back her chair.

Mabel seized her hand. 'Rose, perhaps I'm being foolish but I have this awful premonition something's going to get me before this damned war is over.' Her eyes were pleading. 'Have you ever felt like that?'

'Often,' Rose said, smiling in what she hoped was a reassuring way. 'Come on, I'll walk with you to the bus-stop.'

The letter was sitting on the doormat when Rose opened the front door of their flat. With a Birmingham postmark, she guessed it was from Dorothy, though the handwriting on the envelope was her mother's, the vicarage address neatly crossed out. She tore it open, eager to hear her friend's news. They had not been in touch for some time.

Dearest Rose, she read. *I hope this letter reaches you as I'm not sure where you are at the moment. I hope you're feeling better and have recovered from your experiences in Spain. How rotten for you to have to face war again here. Do try and keep yourself safe. I'm so relieved Archie is exempt from service as his firm is classed as essential manufacturing. Well, I have some very exciting news to share with you. I'm expecting a baby! I know you will be thrilled too and...*

Rose leant against the wall and closed her eyes. She was not thrilled. She should be, but what she felt was anger, bitterness, envy. Her breath had quickened, her eyes were smarting.

'What's up?' Gladys stood at the open door of the kitchen. 'Are you alright, Rose? Come on, the kettle's just boiled. I'll make you a nice cup of tea, you look as if you need it.'

'Thanks. I'm...'

'I hope it's not bad news,' Gladys said, her eyes falling on the letter in Rose's hand. 'These days you always worry...'

'No, not bad news. I'm fine, honestly. A cup of tea would be lovely.' Rose folded the letter and slipped it into her pocket. She would read the rest later. It was just the shock, she told herself, already feeling guilty for her uncharitable reaction. Of course she was pleased for Dorothy. And after all, the news was hardly unexpected: they had been married for over two years. She forced herself to sit down and chat with Gladys, but her mind was far away.

In the privacy of her room, she resumed reading. *I would love you to be a godmother. Please say you will.* A consolation prize, Rose thought. Not a child of her own but a godchild. She sat on the bed for a long time, staring at the wallpaper with its pattern of roses, struggling with her warring emotions. If she could learn to see it in a positive light, form a close relationship with the child... She wondered briefly whether to tell Dorothy about little Blanca but decided against. It seemed cruel to mar her present happiness or provoke fears about the health of her own baby.

Despite her fatigue after the long night underground, she slept little. In the end she gave up on sleep and sat down to pen a letter of congratulation to Dorothy. By the time Margaret came home from work a couple of hours later, Rose was feeling more composed, able to talk to her friend openly but without burdening her.

The sirens had not yet started up when she approached Holborn station that evening but already people were making their way towards it through the streets, carrying blankets, cushions, bottles of milk. Perhaps the Germans would give them a night off but no one was counting on it. There were always some who liked to stake a place early. Rose recognised the same familiar faces.

There was one man, a tall, lanky chap who always carried a notebook and pencil – he had told her he was a poet – whom she saw every night. One of the other girls in their team teased Rose about him. Apparently he was always asking after her. 'He's certainly taken a fancy to you,' Grace said. 'What about it? He's not bad-looking.' Rose always laughed off her remarks but she noticed now that he blushed when he spoke to her. Several men had asked her out since she arrived in London. She had refused them all, kindly but firmly. She wasn't interested; she could not imagine loving another man. Besides, illogical though it might be, to take another lover would feel like a betrayal of Miguel.

'One day you'll fall in love again,' Margaret told her. 'You'll fall in love and marry and have children. I know you will, you're just not ready yet.'

Rose shook her head. 'I don't think I'll ever be ready,' she said. Although she did not share Mabel's feeling that her life was doomed, love no longer formed a part of her vision of the future. She could not begin to imagine what her life would be in five or ten or twenty years. The future was a blur, far too shadowy and uncertain to divine.

PART 4 CONSUELO 1953 - 1965

CHAPTER 19

Antequera, 1953

Don Teodoro, the owner of the sugar beet factory and a good friend of Papá's, had invited them to his house for a fiesta. Consuelo always felt intimidated by him. He was the biggest man she had ever seen and apart from his massive frame he had a booming voice that echoed around the courtyard of his house and even reached the higher floors. With only one son and seven daughters, his family was the opposite of theirs. Antonia, the third oldest, was in her class at school.

'*Mistela for the señoritas*?' The maid held out a tray with glasses of steaming punch. Consuelo took one and sniffed the rich aroma of burnt sugar and alcohol. She loved the way it warmed your throat and chest as it went down. Mamá said it wasn't strong – you wouldn't get tipsy unless you drank an awful lot.

'Have you tried the *roscas*?' María Teresa, the oldest girl, pointed to the big plate of pastry rings on the table.

Consuelo took one and bit into it. 'Delicious,' she said, although in her opinion those their own cook Ramona made were much better.

María Teresa was sixteen and had already been engaged for two years, to Joaquín, the bank manager's son. As he still had another four years of his Law studies in Granada to complete, they wouldn't be able to get married for ages. María Teresa didn't mind. He'd have a good job when he finished. In the meantime, she was happy with the company of her girlfriends. Being a housewife and having babies could wait, she said.

Consuelo wondered if her parents had anyone in mind for her. She hoped they would allow her to choose her own *novio*. She wanted one who treated her nicely, who took her out – and not just on Sundays. Eighteen would be a good age to get married, nineteen at the latest.

It wasn't that she particularly liked boys. What appealed to her was the freedom to do as she liked instead of being ruled by her parents and bossed around by her brothers. She would be in charge of the household. A little house with just two rooms and a kitchen like the one her cousin and his new wife lived in would be perfect to start with, until they had children. She wanted lots of babies, though they'd better not all be boys.

She wished Francisco would go away to university in Málaga or Granada like Joaquín and Antonia's brother, but he hated studying and preferred to stay and help Papá with the estate. Giving out orders to the day labourers and shouting at them if they were slow was right up his street. He wasn't in a hurry to get married either. According to Rafa, he and his friends went to a house of *putas* on Saturday nights. But that didn't stop him molesting her. If she had a *novio*, he wouldn't dare.

She threw a surreptitious glance at the boys on the other side of the room. She couldn't imagine being married to any of them. Antonia's brother Bartolomé was passing round a packet of Camel cigarettes. The boys all smoked American cigarettes now you could buy them at the tobacconist's instead of only on the black market. They cost eight and a half pesetas but everyone said they were much better than the cheap Spanish ones. Jose María had offered her a puff of his Chester to try once. She'd been disappointed: all it did was make her cough. Yet women smoked too in the Hollywood films and seemed to enjoy it.

The girls were talking about Ava Gardner, the American actress who had visited Spain the week before. Of course she hadn't come anywhere near Antequera – nobody important or glamorous ever did – but it was exciting all the same. Consuelo had seen her in a couple of films and thought she was very beautiful.

Mamá wasn't beautiful like the American actresses but she did look glamorous when she was all dressed up in her furs, with a hat and lipstick and perfume. Consuelo had been allowed a few spots of Mamá's eau de cologne today. She couldn't wait to be old enough for lipstick. One or two of the other girls had painted their lips – those whose fathers and *novios* were more liberal.

'Joaquín doesn't like me using make-up,' María Teresa said, 'especially when I'm not with him. He won't let me cut my hair short either.' She had lovely thick hair that she fastened with grips and wore tied back.

'None of the men like short hair,' Pilar said. 'My uncle made a big fuss when Aunt Josefa had hers cut.'

Consuelo noticed that nearly all the girls were wearing the new nylon stockings from America. She owned two pairs herself, a Saint's Day present from her Aunt Inma. One stocking had laddered the first time she wore them, which upset her a lot and made Mamá cross. She was more careful now because even a rough fingernail could ruin them.

Their group moved out of the way as tables and chairs were pushed aside to make room for the dancing. Consuelo watched Don Teodoro's sister seat herself at the piano. After imploring her parents for months, they had agreed to let her have piano lessons. She had only started a few weeks ago but already she loved it and practised every day. For once her big hands were admired. Sor Carmela said she had the perfect combination: large hands with slender fingers. None of her other girl students could span an octave.

Consuelo loved singing too. She always sang along with the *coplas* on the radio and at Christmas poured her heart into the *villancicos*, the traditional carols they all knew by heart. Juanito laughed at her for singing louder than anyone else but she took no notice. One of the nuns had told her she possessed the voice of an angel, if she would only learn some discipline.

Don Carlos, the Deputy Mayor, began tuning his guitar and was soon joined by a singer and a violinist. When the musicians were ready, Don Teodoro led his wife onto the floor and started the dancing with a *pasodoble*. They were followed by other couples, including Consuelo's parents. The girls mostly danced with each other, unless they were engaged. Joaquín was away in Granada so María Teresa danced with one of her sisters. Consuelo danced with Antonia and then Pilar. When two boys, neighbours of theirs, approached and asked to partner them for a *bolero*, they declined. Consuelo felt more comfortable dancing with her girlfriends. She knew Mamá was keeping an eye on her too.

Ever since her first period, Mamá had been warning her not to bring disgrace on the family. Did she think suffering the *regla* every month would suddenly change her behaviour? Her big breasts were a terrible cross to bear. 'Let's hope they don't keep growing at this rate,' Mamá had said grimly last spring. As if they were her fault. Ashamed, she'd tried to squash them down with strips of cloth under her dress but they continued to swell.

She had overheard Mamá talking to Aunt Inma once: 'God knows, I've done my best to bring her up right, but with her bad blood, who knows? Rodrigo warned me right from the start about her red genes. He said it was proven scientific fact, the work of an eminent psychiatrist from Palencia, that these children of *rojos* must be removed and completely re-educated if they're not to inherit the animal nature of their parents.'

Consuelo had no idea what Mamá meant by 'red genes' but the gist of the conversation was clear. She had crept away, crushed and tearful at hearing her birth parents referred to as animals. Later she had asked Rafa, but although he pretended to know what genes were, it was obvious he had no idea either. How could Aladdin and his magic lamp have anything to do with it?

Now Mamá had deprived her of even the little freedom she'd enjoyed as a child, imposing countless new rules. She wasn't allowed out without stockings, not even in the summer; she must cover her arms and wear skirts that came well below the knee; and as for her 'impossible' hair, a way must be found of taming it. Mamá watched over her like a hawk, making sure she never so much as spoke to a boy. Except for her brothers.

Francisco nauseated her; she dreaded being alone with him. 'It's OK, you're not my sister. I can do what I like to you,' he always said as he pawed her breasts and the private place between her legs or grabbed her hand and tried to put it down his trousers. It wasn't OK, it was wrong. But when she threatened to tell their parents, he just laughed. 'You think they'll believe you?' She would struggle with all her might to get away. She didn't care if she hurt him: kicking him down there gave her the best chance of escape. One day she would get her own back on him.

It was early morning and the whole family was travelling to the *cortijo* for a few days, Francisco mounted on Galán, the rest of them in the motorcar. Ramona had set out on foot even earlier with a couple of the other servants. Papá said there was another *arroba* of tomatoes to be bottled. Consuelo tried to imagine how many jars twelve and a half kilos would fill. There would be other fruits and vegetables too – plenty to see them through the winter.

'Look, thieves.' Juanito was pointing to a scene at the roadside. A couple of Civil Guards were beating a man and his son by the edge of a field. As they drove past, Consuelo noticed a pile of a dozen or so sweet potatoes, which they must have dug up from the earth. Poor people and gypsies were always thieving from the fields. She supposed they were hungry or had big families to feed and not enough money to buy vegetables in the market. All the same, it was wrong to steal.

The ruts and potholes in the road meant Papá had to drive very slowly so as not to damage the car. Although it was already hot, Mamá insisted on closing the windows to keep out the clouds of choking dust. Then a puncture forced them to stop while Papá and José María changed the wheel. Francisco on the horse had overtaken them long ago. Consuelo wished they could still ride in the cart as they had when they were younger. She felt stifled in the car and the jolting was nearly as bad. Papá said a new road would be built soon, like the ones to Málaga and Granada. Earlier in the summer as they drove back from the coast, she had seen men breaking up stones with picks in preparation for one of these new roads. She had pitied them working in the full heat of the midday sun but Francisco dismissed her concern. They were used to it, he said; it was nothing to them.

Bruno and Baltasar came running out as soon as they heard the screech of the car's brakes, signalling their excitement with raucous barking. Consuelo couldn't wait to see Princesa, who was expecting pups any time now. Guillermo, the old man who looked after the animals at the *cortijo*, was there to greet them. 'Has Princesa had her puppies yet?' she asked before she was even out of the car.

'Just yesterday, four *cachorritos*. You can go and look at them; they're in the outhouse. But don't go too close,' he warned. 'She's very protective.'

The animals were what Consuelo liked best about the *cortijo*. In town they had no animals at all, not even a dog. Here in the country there were mules, donkeys, pigs, a few goats, chickens… Her brothers mocked her for getting sentimental about them. Every winter at the *matanza* she would weep for whichever of the pigs was up for slaughter. Once they started work though, making the sausages and black pudding and other *embutidos*, no one noticed her crying because more often than not her task was chopping the onions, which always brought tears to her eyes. Everyone had to muck in that day, even Mamá; otherwise the work wouldn't get done. And she had to admit to enjoying the cakes and biscuits made from the pig fat. They were the best ever.

What she didn't like about the countryside in summer were the flies. The animals in particular attracted them and they drove her mad, buzzing about her head and continually landing on her face and arms. She hoped there'd be a chance to swim in the river, to get some relief from both the flies and the insufferable heat. There was a spot not far away where they always went – a secret place no one else had discovered – with a pool deep enough to swim in. Rafa especially loved it. The two of them used to play in the water for hours, staying in long after her other brothers had got bored and wandered off. They would use the rope hanging from a tree branch on the bank to launch themselves and jump in. Of course she couldn't do that any more. 'It's not dignified,' Mamá had ruled two years ago when she reached her twelfth birthday. 'You're a young lady now.'

Papá was thinking about buying a tractor. That afternoon, he and Francisco went to inspect one belonging to Don Manuel. They came back convinced, saying it would be more efficient than using the mules. Guillermo, who had always looked after the mules and even slept with them in the stables, didn't like the idea, but as Papá said, everyone with land used tractors now. You had to move with the times.

When they drove back to town four days later, Duquesa the mare was pulling a cart laden with provisions. As well as the dozens of jars filled with tomatoes, plums, peaches and pears, there were pumpkins, sacks of potatoes and onions, rounds of soft goats' cheese and a big slab of *membrillo*, the quince-meat they all loved.

Consuelo didn't mean to eavesdrop but with the door of Papá's office open, it was impossible not to hear him shouting and Encarna sobbing.

'How dare you accuse my son! Do you think you can fool me so easily? You're a disgrace.'

'If you don't believe me, why don't you ask him?' Encarna's voice was defiant through her weeping. 'Ask José María.'

'You're a wicked liar. Get out of my sight right now. You're sacked.'

'Oh but *Señor*, please. I have nowhere to go. *Por favor*, take pity...'

'Pity? I don't waste my pity on degenerates. Next you'll expect me to feed and clothe your bastard.'

'My bastard is your grandchild!' Encarna bolted from the room, almost colliding with Consuelo. She would have liked to comfort the maid, but Encarna sped straight past her. Consuelo was dismayed. José María had made her pregnant and now she was being dismissed for it. What would happen to her and the baby? She knew now that Francisco was right: there was no point telling Mamá and Papá about what he did – or tried to do – to her. They wouldn't believe her, just as they didn't believe Encarna.

'What are you doing here?' Papá was at the door. His lips were pursed in anger.

'Nothing. I was just passing.' Mustering all her courage, she said, 'Papá, please don't sack Encarna. She works very hard and she's kind and... Papá, she hasn't anywhere to go. It's not her fault if...'

'Not her fault? No, she'd rather blame my son than admit to her wantonness.' Consuelo took a step backwards as her father moved towards her, but he put a hand on her shoulder and spoke more calmly. 'Look, *hija*, don't squander your sympathy on the girl. I know you mean well but she doesn't deserve it. In any case, the nuns will be sure to take her in. Unfortunately there are many others like her with loose morals. The sisters, out of the goodness of their hearts, give them shelter and see they're cared for.'

Consuelo didn't think Encarna would like that at all. She had no doubt José María had forced himself on her – not that he would ever admit it, not in a million years. And then... what if one day she couldn't defend herself against Francisco? The thought made her tremble. She would have to get a *novio* sooner rather than later.

Another thought struck her. Sometimes she almost forgot Mamá and Papá weren't her real parents, but now Encarna's situation jolted her into thinking about her birth mother. Perhaps she wasn't wicked at all. Perhaps she'd been abused like Encarna – by a red or by someone in her family or by an employer. It had never occurred to her before. A deep longing surged up in her, a longing to know her real mother and hear her side of the story.

CHAPTER 20

Antequera, 1955

Consuelo examined with satisfaction her booklet from the *Sección Feminina*, stamped with the yoke and arrows emblem of the Falange and showing each day of her completed Social Service. Since leaving school six months ago, she had been learning domestic skills, like most of her friends – except for Puri, who was exempt because she had eight younger brothers and sisters she helped look after at home. Only Antonia had opted to continue her studies, at a boarding college in Málaga.

Some of the girls complained, saying their brothers had a more exciting time in the *Frente de Juventudes*, attending camps in the mountains and playing sports. Consuelo disagreed. According to Rafa, it was very strict, like being in the Army. She enjoyed sewing and embroidery and thought the skills of cooking and housework would be useful when she was married. They were taught about the importance of pleasing your husband and looking good for him. Men were superior, the girls were told, and it was women's duty to serve them, making their lives comfortable and never arguing with their decisions. That seemed rather unfair – boys didn't always know best – but it was the way of the world so she would have to accept it.

At *Acción Católica*, the activities were for both boys and girls. She went twice a week with her youngest brother. Mostly her mind wandered far away from the boring talks on religion and how to be a good Christian. Once or twice she had tried to slip off, but Juanito, the little sneak, always threatened to tell on her.

'So what are you up to these days, pretty one? I'll bet all the young men in town want you for their *novia*.' Papa Curro ruffled her hair. She hadn't seen her grandfather for some time but now he had come to stay with them for a week. 'Sixteen and no sweetheart?' he continued. 'Well, you keep them guessing and make sure you pick the right one.' He straightened his necktie. Her *abuelo* was always impeccably dressed in a dark suit made of wool with a collar and tie; outside the house he wore a hat like Papá's with a broad band around it.

She had great respect for Papa Curro. He was strict like all the old people – she couldn't imagine disobeying him – but as Mamá said, he had a heart of gold. He'd always made a fuss of her ever since she could remember, dandling her on his knee and teaching her songs. She felt sorry for him now. Since his wife died, he seemed to have shrunk. Not only had his physical bulk diminished but also the force of his presence. Once he had dominated a room without even speaking a word. Now his face often betrayed a vacant look. After the death of her grandmother, he had gone to live with his oldest daughter, Aunt Adoración, who was haughty and sour-faced, Consuelo's least favourite aunt. She and Uncle Jesús were childless, which might explain why she was so disagreeable. It must be terrible to discover you were infertile; Consuelo couldn't imagine anything worse.

It was time for the recitation of the rosary. Papá gathered the family together round the table as he did every day to meditate on the mysteries of the faith. Being a Saturday, she knew it would be the Joyful Mysteries. Her favourite part was the Visitation, when the Virgin Mary goes to visit her cousin Elizabeth, who then feels her own unborn baby leap for joy in her womb.

'*Señor, ten piedad,*' Papá began.

'*Cristo, ten piedad,*' José María responded.

It was her turn. '*Cristo óyenos,*' she recited. They went round the table, giving their responses as Papá intoned, counting off the beads.

'Lord, have mercy, Christ have mercy, Hear us Christ,' they repeated in unison. When she was very young, she used to get the lines mixed up. There were so many, it was hard remembering their order. Now she didn't even have to think about it.

After lunch and siesta, they got dressed up for their *paseo* in town. As the new maid Paloma helped Mamá into her fur coat, Consuelo stroked the glossy animal skin. She had always loved touching it. One of her first memories was of being held close by Mamá, with her cheek resting against the soft fur of her coat.

Half the population of Antequera seemed to be out, strolling down the tree-lined Paseo Real, greeting their neighbours and acquaintances and inspecting their dress and appearance. Consuelo always felt constrained, as if she were on exhibition. She had to be perfectly groomed, carry herself in the correct way and keep her eyes modestly lowered if she was spoken to, otherwise Mamá would berate her. Their progress was slower than usual because of Papa Curro. He walked stiffly, stopping often to rest, leaning on his cane. They reached the gardens at the end, with the statue of La Negrita pouring water from her pitcher, and turned round.

From the corner of her eye, Consuelo noticed one or two of the boys giving her a once-over as they walked past with their families. She didn't mind that but when she had to endure the bold stare of Timoteo, the doctor's son, who looked her up and down, letting his eyes linger on her breasts without the slightest embarrassment while their parents engaged in conversation, she wanted to sink through the floor. The baker and his family walked by while they were standing there and Enrique, the youngest son, smiled at her. She didn't dare respond although she liked him. With his long eyelashes and graceful way of moving, he reminded her of a shy gazelle. He had soft features and a hesitant manner that made him seem less threatening than some of the other boys with their thin moustaches, who strutted and swaggered as if they owned the whole world.

Back at home, while they were drinking camomile tea with squares of Ramona's freshly baked *bizcocho*, two Civil Guards called to pay their respects. Her mother invited them in and ordered Paloma to bring them tea. They took off their shiny tricorn hats and talked about the problem of peasants stealing *esparto* grass from the countryside. Even putting them in a cell for a week didn't stop them, one of the men said. And as for the contraband goods they found in the houses of ordinary workers… 'We found condensed milk in one house, coffee in another, good white bread… Unbelievable! And they tried to stop us taking away their booty – as if they had a right to it.'

'The coffee was excellent,' his companion said with a smirk. 'Not a hint of barley in it.'

Later Papá and her *abuelo* went to the casino to play cards. It wasn't a place for women. Francisco had been a few times and had told her about the secret room called the *peña* that the men could reserve if they wanted to bet on the cards. She didn't think her father or grandfather would gamble; they just enjoyed the game. All the men, whatever their class, liked to play cards or dominoes in the bars. She would see them sitting there at the tables as she walked past. For her part, she was happy to stay at home and work on her embroidery or read the encyclopaedia, which was full of fascinating facts about far-off countries, famous people in history, the science of animal and plant life… She would pore over the pages for hours until Mamá snatched the book away, saying it would strain her eyes.

Consuelo was taken by surprise when Enrique the baker's son arrived at their house with a basket of bread to deliver. Usually they sent one of their employees. She was standing outside with her father as he prepared to set off for the *cortijo*. Just as Papá was mounting Galán, she saw Enrique approaching on a bicycle and the blood rushed to her cheeks. After politely greeting Papá and herself, he walked straight past them to the kitchen entrance but she noticed how his glance had lingered on her a fraction longer than normal and that his face had reddened too.

The next week was *Semana Santa*. Consuelo was not the only one to find Holy Week tedious. Many of the girls at school complained about it amongst themselves. She was already sick of eating lentils or salted cod every day as they had to for the whole of Lent while meat was forbidden. In *Semana Santa* all entertainment was banned: the cinema stayed closed, the radio broadcast only religious music for the entire week. On the Thursday and Friday you couldn't do anything, you just had to stay indoors and keep quiet. When she was younger, each hour had felt like an eternity. Confession was compulsory for everyone – though most people she knew went every week throughout the year. Sometimes she wondered how much Francisco and José María confessed to the priest. She would have liked to eavesdrop on them.

The only good thing about Holy Week was seeing the images of Christ and the Virgin taken out through the streets after being confined in the church all year. She loved those images, especially the Virgin with her beautiful, pure face so sorrowful. Papá and all her brothers belonged to one of the brotherhoods, the *Cofradía del Mayor Dolor*.

This year Juanito was going to be a *costalero* for the first time. He was proud to be included because it was hard – you had to be strong and disciplined. They'd been rehearsing for weeks carrying the floats, free of their images, around town. The most difficult part was the timing – raising and lowering the platform as a team in perfect unison. The whole family would be taking part in the procession. Papá always carried the *bacalao*, the richly embroidered banner shaped like a fish. Francisco liked to carry the big pot of incense with its wafting fumes or one of the massive candles that dripped wax onto the street. José María and Rafa were in the band – they had been practising their trumpets every day – while she and Mamá would be accompanying the Virgin as *manolas*, dressed all in black. They had their *mantillas* and long gloves ready, along with the rest of the outfit.

But on the Tuesday of Holy Week, they heard that Mamá's brother, Uncle Rodrigo, had collapsed with a seizure. He was not expected to live. Mamá was crying, insisting they must go immediately to Jaén. Hadn't she already lost her youngest brother Elias, killed by reds in the War? And now Rodrigo, it was too much to bear…

Consuelo didn't care about her uncle. He had lied, refusing to even admit she was adopted, let alone enlighten her about her real mother. He could die as far as she was concerned. They all looked at Papá to see what he would decide. Juanito's expression made it clear he was dismayed at the idea of missing his first year as a *costalero*. Her other brothers would rather not go either, she was sure. But in the end Papá decided they should all go. He had driven to Jaén before, he said, and now the roads were better, it should be possible to reach the town in a few hours. Juanito was close to tears. Seeing his distress, Mamá spoke into her husband's ear.

'*Bueno*, five in the car is rather a squeeze now you're all so grown up,' Papá said. 'Juanito, you have an important job to do here. If you prefer to stay, you can do so.' Consuelo wished she could stay behind too.

They set off before first light the following morning. By the time they arrived at the hospital – the same one where he worked – Uncle Rodrigo was dead. 'He slipped away peacefully,' the nuns told them. Had he made a deathbed confession of his deceit, Consuelo wondered? It was something she would never know.

CHAPTER 21

Antequera, 1956

The rain came in a sudden violent burst when they were still some way from the spot on the riverbank where the picnic always took place. Having set out in warm spring sunshine under a cloudless sky, few among the dozens of their friends and acquaintances from the town were prepared. Neither the fields of wheat on one side nor the recently planted olive trees on the other provided much shelter. In moments, Consuelo's dress was soaked and clinging to her body.

'Here, put this over you.' She looked round to see Enrique holding out his jacket to her.

Overcome with confusion, she hesitated while the huge drops of rain continued to splash her face and wrists. Water was dripping from her hair, running down her bare shoulders. Surely Mamá wouldn't want her to catch a chill.

'Thank you,' she said, taking the jacket from him and draping it over her shoulders. The wet wool gave off a strong smell that mingled with the odour of tobacco smoke clinging to the garment. It felt strange and exciting to be in such intimate contact with Enrique's male scent.

Within a few moments the rain eased off and then stopped. The clouds broke up, allowing the sun to blaze down on them again unhindered. Steam started to rise from the woollen cloth of Enrique's jacket, her hair and dress dried out and the earth gave off a fresh, clean smell that brought out the scents of wild herbs, broom and lavender. Consuelo looked round for Enrique to give him back his jacket but he had disappeared. A group of her friends were walking just behind, laughing and whispering together. Everyone was in high spirits now the rain had stopped.

'We saw you talking to the baker's boy,' Mari Carmen said as they caught up with her. 'Is he your *novio* then?'

'She's a dark horse,' Resu commented. 'Trying to keep it from us. *¡Pues mirad!* Look how she's blushing!'

'He's not my *novio*.' Consuelo regretted having accepted his offer – especially now she saw Mamá and Aunt Inma approaching.

'What's that you're wearing?' Mamá was frowning at her.

'Does it belong to one of your brothers?' her aunt asked.

Consuelo would have liked to say yes but she knew her mother would not be so easily deceived.

'I don't know,' she said. 'Someone draped it over me when the rain started. I didn't see who...' She prayed her friends would keep quiet.

'Give it to me,' Mamá demanded.

She handed it over, glad to be rid of it now. Her mother had better not spoil the day. She had been looking forward to it for weeks – not only the picnic outing to the river but also the dancing at night. The May *feria* was her favourite. The *casetas* were there for a week. Every night you could eat and drink and dance in the big marquees till the early hours. She loved walking past the rows of stalls, looking at all the trinkets for sale and choosing which to buy. And best of all, she could wear her beautiful flamenco dress with its extravagant flounces and frills, and decorate her hair with flowers and combs. Unlike some of her friends, she was allowed a new dress every year. This year's was green with white spots. Their dressmaker Araceli had spent weeks working on it. When she was small, Manuela had made all her dresses. Consuelo preferred Manuela – she had never been impatient or stuck pins into her at the fittings as the new dressmaker did – but she had to agree that Araceli's dresses were more stylish. She supposed that was why Mamá had replaced Manuela.

When they reached the picnic place, the servants spread blankets on the ground and set to preparing a huge *paella*. Mamá indicated where she should sit, between various aunts and cousins. She had hoped to sit with her friends. A group of them were talking together under the poplars, not far from where the mules had been tied up. They had bottles of Coca Cola, the new American drink with a peculiar taste and colour that everyone was talking about. She spotted Enrique – in shirtsleeves – and two of his brothers amongst them and noticed how he was paying particular attention to Pilar and Mari Carmen.

'Consuelo, how did you like last Sunday's film about the Virgin of Fátima?' Aunt Inma asked.

Enrique and Pilar were laughing, their heads inclined towards each other. Some kind of game seemed to be in progress amongst the group of young people. Then the boys were called away to help carry the melons down to the river, where the water would swirl over and around them, keeping them cool. 'What did you say, Aunt Inma?' She wasn't interested in talking about the film, nor in listening to her aunt's tittle-tattle about the latest baptisms, first communions and weddings.

Much later, after they had eaten and drunk and everything was cleared away, she found an excuse to 'stretch her legs' and escape her relatives' close vigilance. Enrique was seated with his family now, in the shade of a eucalyptus tree. She sneaked a look and noticed that he had donned his jacket. One of his sisters was talking to him but his eyes swivelled to focus on her as she moved past to join a group of her girlfriends. She turned away quickly, hot with shame at being caught looking, and avoided his eye for the rest of the afternoon.

But as they were walking back towards the town in a straggling group, Pilar came running up to her. 'I've a message for you,' she whispered when she'd got her breath back. 'Enrique wants to come to your house.'

Consuelo walked on, head down. She knew what that meant.

'Do you like him?' Pilar asked, putting her arm through her friend's.

Consuelo nodded. She did like him but whether her father would allow Enrique to court her was doubtful: although his family owned two bakeries in the town, they weren't landowners. She looked over towards the *Peña de los Enamorados*, the distinctively shaped rock that rose from the flat plains around Antequera, dominating the landscape. According to legend, it had been named Lovers' Rock after a Moorish princess and her Christian lover leapt hand-in-hand from its summit when the girl's father gave chase with a band of soldiers. What would it be like, she wondered, to feel such passion that you chose to die rather than be separated?

Enrique sat stiffly in the chair next to hers. He was wearing a jacket and tie that must be suffocating on such a torrid summer afternoon. Mamá and Aunt Inma and cousin Trini were crowded into the small drawing room with them. The ceiling fan revolved, stuck in its incessant clanking motion that did little to relieve the stifling heat yet filled the otherwise silent room with its sound. Consuelo would have preferred to be almost anywhere else. She could think of nothing to say and neither, it appeared, could Enrique. If only her father had said no when he asked to come to the house. This was his second visit; the first had been equally strained and uncomfortable, although on that occasion Papá had been present and the two men had smoked, which seemed to help Enrique relax.

She had exchanged scarcely a word with him in private although it was assumed they were now officially *novios*. Papá had warned her she could not expect to live in great style with the baker's son (they were a large family so Enrique's share of the business would be modest) but he would not stand in her way if she wanted to marry him. She suspected her parents might be glad to get her off their hands.

The marriage was unlikely to take place for a few years. Consuelo hoped that by then she would know her fiancé better. In the meantime, she would have plenty to keep her occupied: sewing and embroidering the bed linen and tablecloths, accumulating kitchen utensils, crockery, towels and other essentials for their home. It was the boy's responsibility to buy the furniture. Enrique would probably need time to save up, which suited her fine. She was in no hurry and would much rather wait for a home of their own than have to live with his family.

The church clock struck seven. Sixty minutes still to wait before the start of the film at the open-air cine. It was *Marcelino, Pan y Vino*, about an orphan boy raised in a monastery, who finds in the loft a beautiful statue of Christ on the Cross and brings it to life by offering it bread and wine. Enrique had invited her to go with him to the film. Of course, her relatives would accompany them. María Teresa had confided that she and Joaquín sometimes held hands when they went out for a *paseo*, the sister acting as chaperone having agreed to turn a blind eye. Once they had even managed a furtive kiss when her mother left them alone for a brief moment to go to the bathroom. Consuelo would have liked to hold hands with Enrique but couldn't imagine such an opportunity arising. Her parents, brothers and aunts would never relax their vigilance, not for a moment.

The film made her weep, especially the part where the statue comes to life and befriends Marcelino, and again towards the end when the orphan boy says he wants to see his mother, and the statue – which is really Christ – cradles Marcelino in his arms, allowing him to die happy. She was so absorbed she almost forgot about Enrique sitting by her side.

As the credits went up, he whispered in her ear, 'Can I call you Chelo?'

She nodded, hoping her family hadn't heard. At home they never used the diminutive form of her name, though her friends sometimes addressed her as Chelo. Lola, the imaginary friend she'd had as a child always did. It sounded warmer, more affectionate. She was glad Enrique had asked.

CHAPTER 22

Antequera, 1962

Enrique's *papá* unlocked the door of the little house and the seven of them trooped in: both sets of parents, Enrique and herself and Aunt Inma. They filled the whole of the *salón*, making it seem even smaller.

'The kitchen and bathroom are at the back,' his father said, pointing to a doorway that led off the living room, 'and upstairs there are two bedrooms.'

Consuelo surveyed the newly painted walls, the *chimenea* in one corner and the small window overlooking the street. Most of the furniture was already in place: two armchairs, the sideboard where she would keep their crockery and glasses, the *mesa camilla* with a brazier underneath and four rush chairs. In a month she would be married and living in this little *casita* in the Santiago district. It was hard to believe. She stole a glance at Enrique, with whom she would be thrust into sudden intimacy in one of those two bedrooms upstairs, and wondered if he felt as nervous as she did.

Their relatives trooped up the stairs. As she made to follow, Enrique put out a hand to detain her. 'Do you like it, Chelo?' he asked, his voice betraying a hint of anxiety. 'It's not very big but I hope it will do for the moment.'

'It's big enough,' she said. 'I do like it.'

'Good, I'm glad.' Moving closer, he added softly, 'Your hair is lovely, I want to stroke it.'

Consuelo didn't know how to reply; his *piropos* embarrassed her. When he told her she was pretty or had a good figure or beautiful eyes, it was obvious he was just saying those things to please her because really she was quite plain to look at – not like María Teresa or Antonia with their thick black tresses, smooth skin and natural poise. Mamá always complained about her flyaway hair and criticised her gangling deportment, her lack of grace. She was sad to be such a disappointment to her mother, who would naturally have preferred a beautiful, elegant daughter. She had never managed to live up to her family's expectations. And yet Enrique had chosen her... She couldn't fathom it out. Her biggest fear was that he would be disappointed in her too.

'Come on, let's go upstairs,' she said.

Consuelo took another carnation from the basket and added it to the garland.

'That's long enough now,' Paloma said. She joined the two ends and handed it to one of the grooms, who placed it around the mare's ears. It was the third one they'd made this morning. Mamá didn't consider decorating the horses a suitable occupation for the bride but Consuelo had pleaded with her to be allowed to help until finally she relented.

'Shall we plait some of these into Duquesa's mane?' Consuelo suggested, looking at the pile of white carnations still remaining.

'If you like. Stand on the stool and you should be able to reach, but don't fall.' Paloma wagged her finger. 'We can't have any accidents on your wedding day.'

It was her wedding night that most preoccupied Consuelo. The task of garlanding the horses had taken her mind off it but now she was reminded again of the ordeal to come. María Teresa, who had married last year, admitted it was painful at first but you got used to it and if your husband was considerate, you might even come to enjoy it. Resu had also reassured her there was nothing to fear. She advised Consuelo to stay calm and afterwards to show her appreciation. It was all very well for Resu to say those things. She had been married three years and already had a young child, with another on the way. Consuelo could not imagine feeling relaxed on the first night with her new husband.

Before that, of course, she would put on her beautiful white wedding dress with its train that she must take care not to trip over, a veil to cover her face and the dainty white shoes that made her feel like a princess. After the ceremony and Mass in the church, she would get changed and then she and Enrique would ride together in a carriage pulled by Duquesa to the *cortijo*, where their wedding feast was to be held. Dozens of guests had been invited and she would be the centre of attention. That alone was cause enough for nerves.

About the marriage itself her feelings were mixed. A flare of excitement and pride at the prospect of being a married woman would occasionally take her by surprise, banishing for a brief time her many anxieties. She tried to remember the advice given by the *Sección Feminina*. There were so many things to remember: always to adjust your make-up and look attractive for your husband when he came home from work, as well as having his favourite meal prepared; to minimise noise in the house; not to bother him with details of your humdrum day but instead listen attentively to his affairs; to refrain from questioning him if he returned home late; not to put your rollers in or apply face-cream till he was asleep…

Cooking didn't worry her so much. She had learnt from Ramona about the different cuts of meat, how to make good casseroles, the secrets of thick nourishing soups for the winter and *salmorejo* for the summer. All the same, she hoped Enrique would be patient if her first attempts didn't come out perfect. 'At least you won't need to bake,' Ramona had pointed out. 'Not when your husband works in a *panadería*.' That was true: they would always be well supplied with bread and pastries. Some of her relatives had already made it clear they expected to share the privilege, especially as his family's bakery made the best *molletes* in town, so everyone said.

She wanted to be a good wife to Enrique, to make him happy. Occasionally she allowed herself to dream of a future where the two of them were surrounded by babies and young children – a happy family unlike the one she had grown up in. However many children they were blessed with, she would love them all equally; six or seven struck her as a suitable number. With luck, Santa Eufemia would answer her prayers and make her a mother before next year was through.

With the festivities over, the last guests had finally departed, leaving Consuelo and Enrique sitting, one each side of the fireplace, in their little *casita*. The silence in the room was broken only by the ticking of the clock, a wedding gift from Enrique's sister. It sounded unnaturally loud. Left alone with her new husband, Consuelo could think of nothing to say. The hands of the clock stood at a quarter to two but she didn't feel in the least sleepy.

'Shall we go upstairs?' Enrique said.

Consuelo lowered her eyes. 'If you like.'

The sheets of the *cama de matrimonio* had been neatly turned back on one side – by Mamá or one of the aunts, she supposed. It dominated the bedroom. Enrique switched on the light and watched her as she began slowly to undress, starting with her shoes and stockings. His keen gaze unnerved her; she would have preferred to change into her nightclothes and slip under the covers in darkness.

He came towards her, his shirt already open, and helped her undo the fastenings at the back of her dress. 'You're beautiful,' he said, turning her round to face him. 'Don't be nervous. I won't hurt you.'

The gentle kisses Consuelo had long anticipated lasted only seconds. To her dismay, he quickly laid her on the bed, lifted her nightdress and climbed on top of her, breathing hard and nuzzling at her neck. His body was pressing against the soft flesh of her breasts and belly, crushing her beneath its weight. Down below, she imagined a dog prodding at her most tender parts with its long snout, trying to find a way in. Except that a dog's snout would have been cold and damp while the creature between Enrique's legs was burning with a fierce heat.

It was over almost immediately and the pain began to subside as she felt a wetness trickle down her thigh.

Enrique rolled off her. 'I wasn't too rough, was I?' he asked anxiously.

'Oh no.' She felt an overwhelming relief that he had been the one to cry out while she had endured the pain without a murmur.

'Good.' Yawning, he said, 'Now we must sleep, *corazón.*'

She would have liked to go downstairs and wash but her husband's eyes were already closed, his limbs entwined with hers. It was too late to move without disturbing him. She lay listening to his regular breathing, feeling the rise and fall of his chest. He would always be by her side now, this man to whom God had joined her in marriage. After a while, she allowed herself to stroke the smooth expanse of his back. He slept on oblivious, and emboldened by this, she plucked up the courage to run her tongue along his neck, wondering at the salty tang of his skin. She was a married woman and everything would be different now. A new and happier life awaited her.

CHAPTER 23

Antequera, 1964 - 65

Consuelo put down her book to attend to her infant daughter, whose hungry yells could not be ignored. She held little Belén to her breast, showering her sweet face with kisses, smoothing her fine hair as she fed. As usual, Enrique was out for the evening. He never asked if she'd like to accompany him. In his view, he was fulfilling his duty by taking her with him on Sundays and feast days as custom dictated. In any case, women didn't go to the casino or the bars; she was no worse off than her married friends. He worked hard in the bakery: he deserved to go out and relax in his time off.

Meanwhile she kept herself busy sewing, embroidering and – when she managed to get hold of a book – reading. She could lose herself in books. She had read nearly all the *Lives of the Spanish Saints*. At the moment she was learning about San Juan de Dios. One of her uncles had given her a copy of Don Quijote; she'd read that twice already. For lighter reading, she looked forward each month to the next instalment of the romantic serial in her women's magazine.

Enrique didn't really understand her interest in books. He preferred watching films at the cinema or playing cards or dominoes with his friends. There was a new priest at their church, younger and less rigid in his ways, who had talked about organising dances for the young people. She hoped it would be allowed and that Enrique would take her to dance. The old priest seemed to regard dancing as a sin.

Married life had not turned out quite as she expected. She was still subject to the will of others. Enrique had lost his shyness almost immediately and did not hesitate to issue orders about what she should or should not wear and how she must behave. He was just like all the other husbands and *novios* in forbidding her to go out without him. And sometimes she felt stifled by the family, which was now twice as big as before. Now she had to put up with her in-laws as well as her own relatives interfering and trying to exert control. Besides, if there was any disagreement, her parents-in-law always took Enrique's side. She missed the company of her girlfriends too, but that was the price of becoming a wife.

She wouldn't have dreamt of complaining; she considered herself fortunate. Her husband worked hard, treated her well and was a good provider. They never had money to spare but neither did they lack anything. And although he rarely talked about his work, she knew he had ambitions to better himself. He was learning the business side of the bakery – accounts and record-keeping – along with his brothers, except for Federico, who had gone to the seminary at the age of fourteen.

They never talked about what went on in the bedroom. She relished the kisses and embraces, which kindled intensely loving feelings towards her husband, but the act that followed, though no longer painful as at first, was uncomfortable; she always felt relieved when it was over. Fortunately, Enrique's performance rarely lasted long and, as the *Sección Feminina* book had promised, her husband quickly fell into a deep sleep, leaving her free to put in her rollers and apply her face cream. She still couldn't quite shake off the notion that carnal relations were a mortal sin, even though the catechism stated that within the sacrament of holy matrimony, where procreation rather than physical pleasure was the aim, the act was sanctified. Enrique never asked if she'd enjoyed it. If he had, she would have lied rather than hurt his feelings.

With the arrival of their first child six months ago, everything had changed. For the first time, she felt fulfilled. Becoming a mother had given her a purpose in life, the purpose laid down by God and the *Caudillo*, General Franco. This was her role as a woman and she embraced it with all her heart. Early in the New Year she would give birth to another child and, God willing, several more would follow. She could wish for no greater blessing.

Consuelo gasped as the contraction gripped her belly. She would have cried out but it was important not to frighten Belén, who was playing on the rug at Aunt Inma's feet. The pains had started only an hour ago but already they were coming fast, one after another. With her first-born, she had been in labour all night long.

Mamá gave her a shrewd look. 'Go and fetch the midwife,' she instructed her son-in-law.

Enrique did not need telling twice. He cast an anxious glance at Consuelo and grabbed his coat.

'You'd better take the child now.' Aunt Inma scooped Belén up and after lavishing her with kisses, handed her to Enrique's sister Ana.

Consuelo held out her arms. 'Give her to me first, just for a moment.' She cuddled her little girl and spoke soothingly to her. 'Go with Auntie now and when you come back, you'll have a sweet, new baby brother or sister.'

Belén clung to her but Mamá quickly intervened and took her from Consuelo. 'Come now, don't make a fuss, *niña*. You'll have your auntie and your other grandma to spoil you.'

After Ana had left with Belén, Consuelo picked up the tin drum her daughter had been playing with and put it away, then walked over to the window. As she stood looking across to the familiar outline of the *Peña de los Enamorados* with its profile of a sleeping giant, she felt another contraction, the pain even stronger this time. She wondered how long the midwife would be.

'You should go upstairs and lie down,' her mother said.

'No, Mamá, I'm more comfortable moving about.' She needed an occupation to dispel her restlessness. Taking up her sewing – a romper suit for the new baby – she sat down and completed a few more stitches before the next pain took hold. Would this one be a girl or a boy? Enrique was hoping for a boy, while she had no preference so long as the child was healthy. She'd been secretly glad to have a girl first.

She hoped there would be no arguments about the name this time. Mamá had pressed her to call their first-born after her as was the tradition, but Consuelo had resisted her demands and those of their other relatives, who all pitched in with their own ideas. It was she and Enrique who had decided on Belén. Choosing a name no one else had suggested was the best way to avoid offence. Their second baby was to be Carlos (not Ernesto or José as the two sets of parents wanted); or if it turned out to be a girl, Rocío rather than Angustias or Maruja after one of the grandmothers.

Would she have felt differently had she known her real mother? Pregnancy seemed to heighten her feelings of isolation, the loneliness that sprang from her lack of roots. In quiet moments when Belén was asleep, she would fall to brooding over the woman who had given birth to her: a woman whose name and face and nature she would never know but whose existence she could not forget.

'*¡Un niño!*' Her new baby son gave a little cry as the midwife lifted him up and placed him on her chest. She smiled in gratitude and relief. His birth had been much easier than Belén's.

'Carlos,' she whispered as she cradled him in her arms. He was adorable; she couldn't wait for his father to see him. Enrique would be so proud.

'You must rest now,' the midwife said after the placenta had been expelled and the cord cut. She took the little boy from Consuelo and handed him to Mamá.

Enrique had gone to his mother's to eat. 'Please, fetch my husband,' she urged Aunt Inma.

They were not long in arriving: Enrique, his mother Maruja carrying little Belén, and Ana. Somehow they all squeezed into the tiny bedroom. The newborn slept on oblivious as everyone cooed and exclaimed over him.

Consuelo hugged her daughter. 'Belenita, my precious one, what do you think of your new brother? Do you like him?'

Belén nodded, her eyes fixed on the sleeping baby.

'This calls for a celebration,' Enrique said. 'You'll be alright, won't you, Chelo? Only I promised my friends... I'll make sure not to be back late.'

'You go, son,' his mother said. 'Your wife needs to sleep and there are more than enough of us here to take care of her.'

Consuelo would have liked Enrique to stay, but she said nothing. It wouldn't have served any purpose.

Enrique bent over the crib and kissed the baby. '*Guapísimo,*' he murmured.

'Just like you when you were born,' Maruja said. 'You were a beautiful baby too.'

Weren't all babies beautiful to their mothers? Yet her own mother had given her away. Had she ever regretted it or could a woman really be so heartless? The question had long perplexed her, but now all such thoughts were swept from her mind. Elated by the birth of her son, she soon fell into a contented sleep.

PART 5 ROSE, 1948 - 1958

CHAPTER 24

Oxford, 1948

The interview at Elmhurst Nursing Home on the outskirts of Oxford went well. Rose was impressed by the friendly atmosphere and the fact that the more capable residents were engaged in activities rather than sitting blank-faced with boredom as in so many homes. The Matron was a jolly woman called Betty Burford. 'I'm fifty-two and a happy spinster,' she told Rose with a disarming smile after offering her the job. 'I love my charges, even the cantankerous ones. I see them as my family.' Rose couldn't imagine hearing such words from her current boss, the draconian Mrs Hollis, who treated the residents of Northcote Lodge with a mix of exasperation and disdain.

After a week working at Elmhurst, her initial opinion was confirmed. The tone was set by Betty, who did indeed appear to be a happy spinster as well as a warm and caring matron. *Happy spinster*. To many people it must sound like a contradiction in terms. She would not describe herself in that way but on the other hand she wasn't looking for a husband. The pain of losing Miguel and its accompanying burden of guilt had eased. Still, it did not take much – the snatch of a song, a reference to Spain, a romantic weepy at the cinema – for the wound to pull apart at the edges. The scar tissue was thin.

'I'm concerned about Evelyn?' Rose confided to Betty one morning not long after starting the job. 'What's her story?' Evelyn was in her early forties, recovering from a hysterectomy. She was healing well and had no wish for more children, having three already. Yet on several occasions Rose had found her so distressed that she could neither speak nor eat. Tears were hardly unusual after a major operation but in her case Rose suspected some other cause.

'The only thing we've been able to discover,' Betty said, 'is that she lost her husband in the Blitz. According to her sister, she never got over it. Why don't you try talking to her? She obviously needs help.'

Rose found a quiet moment to go and sit with Evelyn, holding her hand as she sobbed. Only on the third such occasion did she hint at the source of her grief. Then, little by little, she began to open up.

'Do you know what it's like to live with guilt? To feel its leaden weight crushing you every moment of the day and night?' The anguish in her voice tore at Rose. 'It was my selfishness that killed Dick. There, I've said it now. I killed my husband.' Evelyn turned away as if unable to face the condemnation she clearly expected.

My selfishness killed Miguel.

Rose spoke gently, battling to contain her turbulent emotions. 'It's sometimes hard to know the consequences of our actions,' she said.

'If I'd known…' Evelyn let out a low moan. 'I should have done as he urged. "Go with the children," he said. "You'll be safer in the country." I didn't listen. If only I'd left London, Dick would still be alive.'

If only I'd left Spain as Miguel urged, Rose thought.

'Tell me,' she said. 'Tell me what happened.'

'The sirens started up, that ominous wail I'll never forget. We ran towards the shelter, but then I twisted my ankle. I couldn't move; my foot was floppy as a rubber toy. So Dick stopped to pick me up and he carried me in his arms. But of course that slowed him down, we were too late…' She tugged at her hair, balling both fists and examining the loose strands in her fingers as if surprised to find them there. 'He shielded me. I came out without a scratch and he was killed. So you see? I'm wholly responsible for his death.' She buried her face in her hands. 'I should have been in Wales with my parents and the children.'

I should have been in Evesham with my parents and our baby.

For days after their conversation, Rose felt unsettled. Conversely, several of the staff commented that Evelyn appeared lighter in spirit.

Since the end of the war, the birth rate had soared. Everywhere she went, Rose saw pregnant women, women with prams, toddlers clutching the hands of their mothers. The sound of crying or gurgling babies, the high-pitched voices of young children formed a constant backdrop in any public place. Not even the nursing home offered a safe refuge: the daughters and daughters-in-law of patients frequently brought their babies, much to the delight of all. Rose didn't begrudge them this pleasure: she fussed over the infants like everyone else, keeping her sadness hidden – just as she did when she saw her brother's children or her godson Frank.

Occasionally one of the patients would ask if she was married. Her reply generally elicited a sympathetic nod of the head. 'Sweetheart killed in the war?' Her situation was shared by so many. With all this century's wars, half of Europe's women must be mourning husbands, fiancés or sons. Several of the Elmhurst residents had lost sons in the First World War. Although Rose had no marriage certificate to show, privately she thought of herself as a widow. She and Miguel had lived as man and wife. In other circumstances… 'You're still young, you'll meet someone new,' everyone said; they meant well.

She was thirty-three – not so young any more – but she was fit and healthy, grateful to be alive. Her two brothers had also survived the war more or less intact, though Bertie had suffered a close brush with death and Ralph was now deaf in one ear. Mabel, her friend in the ARP, had not been so lucky. Just as she'd feared, a bomb had caught her one night during the Blitz on London as she performed her warden duties. Rose missed her.

You just had to get on with your life, the bereaved told themselves and each other. Soldier on. Look on the bright side. Make the best of things. After all, the war had been won, Hitler defeated; the country was at peace. When it came down to brass tacks, what other choice was there? So Rose got on with her life. She threw herself into her work and into her role as aunt and godmother. She visited her parents whenever time permitted. And tried to put her Spanish experiences behind her.

Rose leant her bicycle against the garden wall and rummaged in her bag for the house key. 'Hello, anyone in?' she called as she stepped into the hall. Jean was usually busy in the kitchen when Rose returned from work after a dayshift. She felt comfortable lodging with Norman and Jean in their large terraced house in Oxford. They had given her the biggest bedroom and encouraged her to make herself at home. 'Feel free to entertain your friends here too,' Norman said. 'Just let us know.' The combination of privacy and the pleasant, undemanding company of Norman and Jean were just what she needed.

'Hello love, come and have a cuppa with me.' The kitchen was warm and homely and smelt of baking.

'I meant to remind you,' Rose said as she sipped her tea. 'My friends from Birmingham are visiting tomorrow.' It was her weekend off and she'd invited Dorothy and Archie with her godson, Frank.

'I hadn't forgotten. That's lovely, dear.'

She had plans to take Frank boating, which would be much more entertaining for him than traipsing round the Oxford colleges as his parents proposed. In her opinion they were over-protective of their only son. She understood why – Dorothy had suffered a difficult pregnancy and been advised not to have any more children – but felt he needed some fun and spontaneity in his life. He was a serious, rather precocious child, probably the result of too much time in adult company.

She delved into her bag for the photo of Frank that she always carried in her purse. 'This is my godson,' she said, holding it out to Jean. 'He's six.'

'What a darling.' Jean smiled as she handed the photo back. 'I bet you dote on him.'

'A rowing boat? You want to take him out in a rowing boat?' Dorothy looked aghast. 'What do you think, Archie?'

'Well, the thing is, he can't swim.'

'I don't intend to tip us into the water.' Frank's eyes brightened, confirming to Rose that he very much wanted to go out on the river. 'But if the worst happened, I'm a strong swimmer and I'd soon have him back in the boat or on dry land.'

'Do you know how to row?'

'I'm an expert, Dot.' Not quite true but she had rowed once or twice on the Wye; there was nothing to it. 'The boats are very stable, not like those little canoes. And with no current to speak of, it's perfectly safe. You know I wouldn't suggest it if I thought there was any danger.'

At the jetty, Frank turned to raise his hand in a perfunctory wave as the boat pulled away. 'Remember not to fidget,' Archie shouted after him.

The river was dotted with boats on this spring Saturday. White clouds scudded across the sky; sunlight sparkled on the water.

'Isn't it lovely out here?' Rose said.

'Spiffing. Look, swans over there.'

'Yes and a whole family of baby ducks following their mother.'

'One two three four five six!'

Newly clothed in green, the willows lining the bank arched over the water, the curve of their branches reminding Rose of the bent backs of women scrubbing their clothes in Spain's rivers. A pleasure boat passed by, its wash rocking their small craft.

'Hey, we're going under a bridge!'

They swished through the stone arches and out again into the sunlight. Frank waved to the people walking across; a small girl and her mother waved back.

'You must learn to swim,' Rose said. 'It gives you a wonderful feeling of freedom, like being a fish. My father taught me when I was about your age.'

'I want to but my dad says not till I'm ten. My friend Billy can swim and he's only seven.' Frank's pout vanished as he added, 'I'll be seven in June. Did you know?'

'I did indeed. June 25th, I've got your birthday firmly fixed in my head.'

'How old are you, Auntie Rose?'

'You aren't supposed to ask ladies that question,' she said, laughing. 'But I'll give you a clue: I'm the same age as your mother.'

'Oh, I know how old Mummy is. She's thirty-three.'

Rose had no objection to being called Auntie. Children were often taught to address adults in that way as a sign of respect. In any case, 'godmother' struck her as a dubious title, given her views. Well before

Frank's birth, she had explained to Dorothy that her lack of religious belief might not be compatible with the role.

'Oh don't worry about that. We just want someone who'll be a good influence and take a special interest in our child. The religious part isn't important to us.'

'But I'm supposed to make a promise to educate him in the Christian faith.'

'You're a good person, Rose. You have principles. That's what matters.'

Many regular churchgoers would consider her a sinner, Rose thought, but it was true she had principles and tried to live by them – even if she'd lost her faith in God.

She observed Frank now as he sat trailing his fingers in the water, a sweet, innocent child. When he was older, she would talk to him about good and evil – but not in terms of God and the devil or heaven and hell. She thought of her conversations with Miguel; about the values and ideals he so passionately defended, the kind of society he and all the others had been fighting for. Frank was lucky to be growing up in England. For those in Spain… Her heart ached with sorrow when she thought of the continued suffering in Spain. The little news she received was grim, unbearably grim.

CHAPTER 25

Oxford, 1950

From her piano stool, Rose glanced at the clock on the wall. 'Right, time for just one more. Any requests?'

'*If you were the only girl in the world!*'

'*Tipperary!*'

'*In the mood!*'

They always wanted the same old favourites. Rose didn't mind. She loved playing for them, leading the sing-alongs that had proved so popular, especially with the older, long-term residents. It was now a regular event, highlight of the week, some said.

She hit the keys and they immediately broke into song.

'*Sometimes when I feel bad and things look blue*

I wish the girl I had was, say one like you.

Someone within my heart to build her throne

Someone who'd never part, to call my own.'

However hopeless at remembering where they'd put their glasses, what they'd done the previous day or, in some cases, even recognising a son or sister, their ageing memories never failed to produce the words to the songs of their youth.

As usual, this song left Aggie in tears, but it was plain they were tears of happy nostalgia. 'My Freddie sang it to me when we were courting,' she informed them for the umpteenth time. 'Forty-five years of wedded bliss we had and he never stopped singing it. *A garden of Eden just made for two, with nothing to mar our joy,*' she warbled.

One of the kitchen helpers passed the open door with a trolley. Rose closed the lid of the piano. 'I think supper is ready.'

'Oh give us another, Rose. Go on, dear. Just one.'

She spread her hands in a gesture of defeat. 'Now this really is the last.'

'*It's a long way to Tipperary, it's a long way to go.*

It's a long way to Tipperary, to the sweetest girl I know...'

Her shift was due to finish before supper. She had arranged to go to the cinema with Ken, a friend from the rambling group she belonged to. Ken made her laugh – he was unfailingly cheerful and a great raconteur. Rose enjoyed his company but there was no romance in the offing. He was seen as a confirmed bachelor, which suited her just fine.

The film, *Kind Hearts and Coronets* with Alec Guinness and Joan Greenwood, made her laugh too. She liked its black humour and subversive, not-so-subtle pokes at the hypocrisy of the upper classes. After the film, Ken took her to a pub by the river, where they sat in a cosy nook close to the fire, discussing their favourite scenes from the film.

His question took her unawares. 'Why haven't you got a young man, Rose? An attractive girl like you?' Seeing her startled expression, he added, 'You can tell me to mind my own business, only I wondered… Forgive me, but I wondered if perhaps you were like me.'

Bemused, she stared at him for a moment before the penny dropped. 'Oh Ken, I didn't realise. I'm sorry.' She knew there were men – and women too – who preferred their own sex. She had met several in Spain, amongst the volunteers. 'No, I'm not that way. I had a young man, we loved each other deeply but he was killed.'

Ken was fiddling with a beermat, avoiding her eyes. She felt a wave of sympathy for him. It must be so hard having to live a lie. Once or twice she had glimpsed something, a fleeting sadness in his voice that made her wonder if his outwardly jaunty manner might be a disguise, concealing some private sorrow.

'It makes no difference to me,' she said. 'Honestly.'

'Thank you, Rose. I knew you'd understand. Not everyone does.'

'Don't worry, this is between you and me.' She hesitated then reached out a hand to cover his. He let it remain there. 'I think we all have secrets,' she said. 'Things we'd rather keep to ourselves.'

Ken nodded. 'That's true but sometimes I wish… The pressure of being on guard the whole time, forced to maintain a pretence, it wears you down.' He picked up his glass and drained it.

'Well, you don't have to pretend with me anymore.'

'Good.' He smiled, his posture more relaxed now. 'Care for another beer?'

'Thanks. Why not?'

When he returned with the drinks, he was his old self, chirpy, affable and eager to revert to the subject of the film. Rose understood. The barriers had been lowered and further revelations might follow at some point in the future, but for now it was enough to feel comfortable together without the need for masks.

'Take a look at these, Rose. Bertie sent them just this week, the latest snaps of Susan.' Mother handed her a folder of photographs. 'I do so wish they lived nearer,' she added. Bertie and Prue lived up north, close to Prue's family in York. Rose hadn't seen her niece since the christening six months ago. 'Isn't she a bonny baby?' Mother was gazing at a picture of Susan on all fours, face turned up to the camera. 'You should come with us next time we go.'

Most of the photos crowding every available shelf in her parents' house were of Ralph's family, who lived only a short distance away and were frequent visitors. Ralph had met his French wife Chantal during the War, when he was billeted with her family while working as an ambulance driver in France. They had married straight after VE Day and he'd brought her back to Worcestershire. Within a year, their first child Peter was born; Helen arrived barely two years later. Chantal said Helen resembled her. True, she had the Tilly green eyes – the only one of the new generation to inherit them – but apart from that, it was too early to say.

Some of the pressure had been taken off her when her brothers married and started to produce babies, the grandchildren her parents had long been hoping for. Mother dropped fewer hints about her unmarried status, though the deliberate and all too blatant tact she adopted instead left Rose even more exasperated. *No I haven't met anyone special*, she wanted to scream in response to the unspoken questions. *Yes I know the clock is ticking.* Of course she yearned for babies – more than her mother would ever know – but like Ken, she had to hide her true feelings. They were too complicated, too saturated with pain. She couldn't begin to explain to her parents.

Now, as she flicked through the pile of photos sent by Bertie, she was ambushed again by the 'what ifs'. What if her baby had lived? Mostly she suppressed such pointless speculation but every now and again the questions rose to torment her. Would they have escaped fascist Spain or been trapped there, to languish in one of Franco's notorious women's prisons perhaps? Or if they had managed to get out, how would she have supported herself and Blanca in England? Would her parents have cared for the baby while she worked? And if not... She thought of Clark's House, the mother-and-baby home in Oxford run by Skene Moral Welfare, and shivered. The girls taken in by the religious charity were coerced into giving up their babies for adoption. A friend who lived nearby had heard them screaming as their babies were forcibly removed. The pathos of it brought tears to her eyes. What could be crueller?

Yet the stigma of having an illegitimate baby, whether in Catholic Spain or Protestant England, made you a social outcast. She imagined the scandal – worse, much worse for a vicar's daughter. The whispers, the ugly gossip such transgressions always invited. No, she could not have brought Blanca home to Evesham. The hurt and humiliation to her parents, whatever their private opinions on the matter, would have been too great.

Mother gathered up the ball of mauve wool and put her knitting aside. 'Penny for them.' Her gaze showed concern and Rose realised her mother had been discreetly observing her while she worked on the cardigan for Susan.

'Oh nothing important.' She chided herself for allowing her thoughts to be distracted. It was futile to hypothesise. Blanca had not lived.

She heard the click of the front door latch and Father walked in, rubbing his hands. 'It's freezing out there,' he said, taking off his overcoat and hanging it on the hall stand. 'Hello, Rose dear, how are you?' She went to kiss him, breathing in the familiar smells of Old Spice and the pipe smoke that always clung to his clothes. 'You are staying for the whole day, aren't you? I was hoping to be back by twelve but my parish visits took longer than usual. Family quarrels, debts, sickness, bereavement... Even in a quiet country town like Evesham. It makes me appreciate how blessed we are in our family.'

Maisie was laying the table for lunch. Rose went to wash her hands and the three of them sat down round the table.

'You know,' Father said, putting aside his knife and fork after a few mouthfuls,' I wonder sometimes whether the British stiff upper lip is such a good thing. People put on a brave front, burying their sadness and anger and hurt. But those difficult feelings, those guilty secrets are still there, hidden behind a veneer of respectability. They don't go away, and it seems to me that burying them only increases the suffering. Appearances are preserved at the cost of... of honest communication that could open the door to understanding and forgiveness.' He turned to Rose. 'What do you think? Did you find the Spanish people more willing to show their true feelings?'

'Perhaps their emotions are closer to the surface,' she said. 'They cry more easily. I don't know. The country was in the midst of a civil war: I was dealing with men injured in battle, fighting their own countrymen. The suffering was appalling. They showed the most tremendous courage, yet they weren't afraid of tears...' She considered for a moment, recalling the dying men calling for their mothers in a dozen different tongues. 'Actually, I don't think the foreign volunteers were so different.' Nationality had hardly come into it.

'But even away from the front,' Mother ventured, 'the special circumstances of war allow a relaxing of the usual codes of behaviour. When death, whether of loved ones or oneself, is always an imminent possibility...'

'That's true,' Father agreed. 'And now we've had five years of peace, people have buttoned up their emotions again. The old conventions have reasserted themselves.' He sighed. 'When people unburden themselves to me, knowing it's in confidence, and I see the relief on their faces... Well, I do wonder if they wouldn't be better off opening up to their nearest and dearest, if not to the world at large.'

'If people didn't judge so readily...' Rose said.

'Indeed. Humankind is harsher in judgement than God.'

Rose glanced at her father and discerned the lines of care on his face, the thinning hair and sagging jowl. 'You look tired,' she said. What she meant was *you're getting old*. Turning to look at her mother, she saw a woman moving past middle age, a woman with blotched skin and a scraggy neck. Her parents were getting old. It hit her with the force of a revelation. Why hadn't she noticed before? She worked in a home where the majority of the patients were elderly. She was intimately aware of their ailments, their failing sight or hearing or memory, their minor humiliations. Yet the ageing of her parents had passed her by. Father would turn seventy in a couple of months. He planned to retire later in the year. She knew this but had failed to absorb it. Maybe she hadn't wanted to; or maybe she'd just been too wrapped up in her own life.

'We must start thinking about your big birthday celebration,' she said, watching Father eat. The loss of several teeth in the last few years made chewing a laborious process. He was always last to finish.

'Wait till I retire,' he said, smiling. 'I believe there are plans afoot already in the parish. After nearly thirty years here, they'll want to make an occasion of it.'

'So they should.' Rose got up to turn on the light. She was sick of winter: the dismal days that seemed to be over before they'd begun; the damp January air, heavy with drizzle. It was early afternoon but before long they would have to draw the curtains. She had left her bicycle at the station in Oxford. Her ride home would be in darkness with rain lashing her face. She felt a sudden longing for the light and colour of Spain where even the winter sun illuminated and warmed the body and made the soul sing.

CHAPTER 26

Oxford, 1953

Dennis was a lanky young man with thick, horn-rimmed spectacles and a serious manner. 'I just want a quiet place to live, not too far from the school,' he said. 'I'm newly qualified so I'll need to prepare well for my classes.' He inclined his head towards Rose and she noticed he had a pronounced stoop, unusual for one so young. He surveyed the bedroom with its single bed, wardrobe, desk and chair. 'This looks perfect,' he said. 'Now, what about meals? The thing is, I'm quite fussy as to what I eat.'

'Oh I'm sorry, I should have made it clear: the rent doesn't include meals. You'd have access to the kitchen, of course.' So many men had no idea how to cook the most basic dishes. Perhaps he'd never had to cook for himself. 'I work irregular shifts,' she added, 'and usually I'm provided with meals at the nursing home where I work. So I'm looking for someone independent...'

'That's not a problem, Miss Tilly, I assure you. I'm used to preparing my own food. And I'm very tidy. You'll find your kitchen spotless.'

The neatness of his appearance – his well-groomed hair, perfectly pressed shirt and trousers, shoes polished to a gleam – made her believe him. 'Very well,' she said. 'I've already explained the terms. Once you've paid the deposit and the first month's rent, you can move in whenever you like.'

After Dennis had left, Rose flopped into the armchair facing her small back garden. The daffodil and crocus bulbs planted by the previous owners had taken her by surprise, brightening the view from the window with their cheerful splashes of yellow and purple. It was her first spring in the little house in Jericho, conveniently close to the centre of Oxford. A small inheritance from an uncle added to her savings had enabled her to buy a place of her own. The income from a lodger would help meet the mortgage payments.

She yawned; the busy night was catching up on her. They'd had to call the doctor to Ethel after she complained of chest pains. Albert had fallen on his way to the toilet. Then another resident had been found wandering about in an agitated state. Rose, on duty with only one not very experienced assistant, had been kept busy. She had cycled home from her shift this morning in time to interview Dennis. Now she must grab a few hours' sleep or she would collapse. She thought of those absurdly long shifts she had worked in the Spanish hospitals – twenty-four hours or more at a stretch, kept awake by black coffee, driven by necessity. She doubted she could do it now.

Having her own home had never been a priority, but after her parents moved out of the vicarage, she felt the need for a base of some kind. Her childhood home mattered to her far more than she'd realised. She missed the house itself, she missed the large garden with its roses, climbing plants and beds of lupins and delphiniums, and she missed the stability and permanence it represented. The accumulated memories of her growing up belonged there.

Her parents seemed out of place, diminished somehow in the modern semi-detached dwelling on the outskirts of the town where they now lived. When she visited them, she could not dispel the deep sense of loss that immediately gripped her on entering number 19 with its box-like proportions. Her terraced house in Jericho was smaller but she didn't feel hemmed in as she did in her parents' new home. *I like it here*, she thought, surveying the cosy room with its fireplace and low, beamed ceiling. With a job she loved and a proper home, she felt more settled than she had since her childhood. Even if, unlike the majority of her friends and contemporaries, she had no husband, no children. Even if grief for Miguel and Blanca continued to assail her the moment she let down her guard.

'What language are they speaking?' Mother whispered to her as they waited at the bus stop after their shopping trip.

Rose had been watching the two women a little way ahead of them in the queue, observing the way their hands moved through the air as they conversed in animated tones. She had known immediately, even before odd words and phrases began to reach her ears above the street hubbub. Their hand gestures gave them away.

'They're Spanish,' she replied. It was the first Spanish she had heard since she left in '39. The effect on her heartbeat and breathing took her by surprise.

While Mother returned to the theme of today's purchases – table linen, a hat, slippers – Rose strained to hear the two Spanish *señoras*. They'd be refugees, Republicans living in exile here in Oxford. She felt a strong urge to approach them, to hear their story. A bus was drawing up; the women boarded it. She could see them through the window, the older one seated, her companion standing. The older woman, sharp-featured, dark hair pulled back from her forehead, looked out and for a second their eyes locked.

'Come on, Rose. This one's ours.' Mother plucked at her arm as their bus pulled to a halt behind the other. She had been too slow. If she saw them again, she would not let the opportunity pass.

Helen was jumping up and down with impatience. 'Can I see, Mummy? Are they red yet?'

A mere slip, born of habit, but Rose felt a painful tug on her emotions. She was not Helen's mummy – neither Helen's nor anyone else's – even though many people remarked on how closely her niece resembled her. It was true: if you discounted the chubbiness normal for a six year-old child, their faces had the same heart-shaped contours; Helen's pale complexion flushed pink in a trice with heat or exertion or excitement, just like her aunt's, and her blond flyaway hair was every bit as difficult to control. 'Like hay,' Chantal often complained.

Rose did not correct Helen but took the lid off the pan, where half a dozen eggs were banging against each other as they boiled. She turned down the gas and smiled at her niece. 'Only pale pink but don't fret, they'll be done before you can say Jack Robinson.'

'Please.' Helen raised her arms and Rose lifted her high enough to see the eggs bubbling away in cochineal-tinted water.

'We promised to wait till Peter was back before painting,' she reminded Helen. Ralph and Chantal had taken Peter with them to church. 'In any case, the eggs will need to cool.' Six blue ones, dyed with red cabbage leaves, were already sitting in an egg-carton on the table. For Rose, spending Easter Sunday with Ralph's family was an unexpected treat; more often than not she had to work on feast days.

'That should do.' She scooped the eggs from the pan with a ladle and put them to cool in the sink, watched by Helen, whose solemn green eyes were fixed on her aunt with a look of adulation that tickled Rose. She felt a rush of gratitude to her brothers for the gift of these children to love. They were all precious to her but she had a particular soft spot for Helen.

'They're back!' Helen ran to meet her parents and brother as Lucky the dog began to bark and voices drifted through from the hall.

Taking a blue egg, Rose painted eyes, a smiling mouth and some curly hair. As an afterthought, she added a moustache. 'What do you think?' she asked the children.

'He's got no nose.' Peter picked up one of the other eggs. 'Mine's going to have a great big nose,' he said. 'And freckles. And...'

'I want a red one.' Helen waited while Rose took one of the freshly boiled eggs from the sink.

'It should be cool enough now.' The telephone rang as Rose handed her niece the egg. Ralph picked up the receiver.

'Hello Bertie, happy Easter,' she heard, and then, 'Oh I say, congratulations! When is it due?' A pause. 'September, that's terrific... but Prue's feeling a bit rotten, you say? Well, I'm sure that will soon pass. Chantal was quite poorly with Peter too, the first few weeks.'

So. Another baby in the family. Rose pushed aside the fleeting twinge of envy before it took hold. How could she not welcome the prospect of a fourth nephew or niece?

'You're going to have a new cousin,' Ralph told the children.

'It'd better be a boy,' Peter said. 'There are too many girls in our family.'

Rose reached for a blue egg and the remaining paintbrush. 'This one's going to be Humpty Dumpty,' she said, setting to work with determination.

'Can you see a stile over there?' Reggie was alternately poring over the map and gazing into the distance. They all knew how short-sighted he was.

'I can. In the corner of the field, there.' Rose pointed to a stile in the gap between two large oak trees. The four of them set off towards it, past a herd of grazing Friesian cows.

'Oh no, look what I've stepped in.' The others laughed as Phoebe withdrew her boot from a fresh cowpat and attempted to rub it clean on a patch of grass. 'We're not having our picnic in this field.'

'No, but we'll have to stop soon,' Reggie said. 'I could eat a horse.'

'Me too. Right, ladies first.' Ken stood aside for Rose and Phoebe to climb over the stile into the next field.

'No cows here,' Rose said as she stepped down. 'And that tree trunk over by the hedge looks perfect to sit on. I think we've found our lunch spot.'

Rambling in the Cotswolds or along the river had become a semi-regular activity for the four friends, usually on a Saturday or Sunday when the others weren't working. Rose, whose days off didn't always coincide with weekends, joined them when she could.

They positioned themselves in a row along the tree trunk and delved into their knapsacks for flasks and sandwiches. Rose took a ham sandwich from its wrapping of greaseproof paper and tucked in.

'How is it working out with your lodger?' Ken asked.

'All tickety-boo,' Rose replied, wiping the crumbs from her mouth. 'He's the studious type: very quiet, spends a lot of time in his room.'

Phoebe looked sceptical. 'Don't you mind having a man sharing? Wouldn't you rather have a girl?'

'Why?' Rose asked, surprised.

'Well...' Phoebe hesitated. 'You know, having a man see your underwear on the line and all that.'

Rose laughed. 'I'm a nurse, remember. You get used to all manner of intimate encounters. And in Spain the living conditions... To be honest, I've never given it a thought.' Her only fear had been that Dennis might want mothering. 'He's very tidy,' she added. 'My kitchen is always immaculate. In fact I worry about failing to match up to his high standards.'

'Really?'

'I find the knives and forks in my cutlery drawer perfectly aligned. You know, spoons and forks cupping each other. And everything has to be in its precise place on the shelf: the jars and storage tins and so on. If they're not, he moves them. I don't think he's even aware of doing it.'

'I knew someone like that in the Army,' Reggie said. 'We used to tease him something terrible. Poor bugger, he couldn't help it.'

'Oh, I'd never say anything to Dennis. I just let him get on with it. He's a treasure.'

'Do you cook for him?' Ken asked.

'No, he's perfectly independent. Prefers it that way. Actually,' she added, 'he has rather strange eating habits. The list of what he won't eat is as long as your arm, which means his diet is pretty monotonous. He's thin as a rake, but he seems healthy enough. He drinks a lot of milk.'

'And you don't worry what people might think?' Phoebe persisted. 'I mean, living with a man who isn't related to you?'

'What?' Rose spluttered with laughter. 'He's at least fifteen years younger than me. Anyway, if people are so narrow-minded as to think...' She glanced at Ken, who was struggling to contain his amusement, and shook her head. 'No, Phoebe. I don't.'

Rose woke early on September 12th, immediately conscious of the date. She never forgot. This year, Blanca, had she lived, would have been celebrating her fourteenth birthday. Rose had lit a candle for her the previous night as she did every year in a private ceremony she knew was over-sentimental. Today, however, she was determined to look forward and not back. With a free day before her evening shift, she had arranged to meet two of her old 'Spain friends' for lunch in London. Time had not loosened the deep bond between them.

She was sitting in the kitchen with her second cup of tea and a bowl of cornflakes when the telephone rang.

'Bertie just called. It's a boy!' Mother's thrilled voice crackled down the line, too loud for the small room and the time of day. 'Eight pounds, two ounces, quite a whopper, but both Prue and the baby are fine. Robert, they're calling him. I expect he'll be Bobby, don't you think?'

'Wonderful.' Rose was glad Mother couldn't see her face. Why did it have to be today? She was pleased of course, but… The pain was physical: a tightness in her chest, the muted echo of earlier pain but still potent enough to hurt. She imagined Prue comfortable in the hospital bed, attended by kindly nurses. She pictured Bertie at her side, Susan being lifted up to see her new brother; flowers and fruit and letters of congratulation beginning to arrive; the baby on Prue's breast or in a crib beside her bed. And compared it to Blanca's arrival in the world.

'I've some good news,' she told Margaret and Annie as soon as they'd greeted each other and sat down at their usual table in the little restaurant off Oxford Street. 'A new nephew, born this morning. Isn't that splendid?'

Annie saw through her smile immediately. 'Then why are you looking so sad?'

Trying to pretend was useless. 'I am thrilled, honestly. I'd just rather it were a different day. Not the same day my own baby…'

'Oh Rose, you poor thing.' Margaret's brow creased in sympathy.

'I'm alright. Really. I just needed to tell someone, I mean someone who knows. I feel better already.' It was true.

After a moment's silence, Annie said, 'You're brave, dear Rose. I've always admired your courage. Forgive me for saying this, perhaps I shouldn't, but… I don't suppose Miguel would have wanted you to suffer or miss your chances of happiness. Even if you never feel remotely the same about anyone else, just don't let life pass you by. It would be such a waste.'

'Oh I won't.' Anxious to change the subject, Rose told them about the Spanish women she'd seen at the bus stop in Oxford. She'd had no sight of them since.

'There's quite a community of Spanish refugees in London,' Margaret said. 'Including a few of the Basque children who came on that boat, the *Habana*, after the bombing of Guernica. They're better off here. Safer anyway.'

'True,' Annie agreed, 'but I've got to know some of them and you can see the yearning in their eyes when they talk of home. Exile is brutal for them.'

CHAPTER 27

Oxford, 1955

'You might not think so to see me now,' the new patient said to Rose, 'but I consider myself a lucky woman. I have the best husband in the world and three wonderful sons. I've had a good life.'

Lilian was fifty-three and dying of cancer. Although she'd had both breasts removed, the cancer had returned and was spreading rapidly. Her prognosis was poor: a few weeks, three months at the very most. Much of the time she was clearly in pain, yet unlike the majority of patients, she declined the morphine prescribed by the doctor, complaining it made her woozy and sick. Only occasionally, when the pain became unbearable, did she allow an injection. Her fortitude moved Rose. How could facing a painful death at the age of fifty-three be considered lucky?

'I've only one regret,' she said. 'That I won't live long enough to see a granddaughter. I like girls, you see. And never having had a daughter...' She paused and Rose could tell from the change in her breathing that she was in pain. 'But there it is, I have a lovely girl for a daughter-in-law. She's a physiotherapist, qualified just this year. We're all very proud of her.'

'I wanted a career when I was young,' she confided to Rose on another occasion. 'I was raised on a farm and I dreamed of becoming a vet. In those days it was almost impossible for a woman, of course. It was just a silly girl's pipe dream. Now things are different – you can go to university, you can marry *and* have a career. Do you like animals, Rose?'

'I do.' She had thought about acquiring a kitten, until Dennis informed her he was allergic to cats.

'I've always loved animals but growing up on a farm, you couldn't afford to be sentimental. Jack is much soppier than I am about the pets. We used to have a houseful of animals – cats and dogs, rabbits when the children were young. It's just Barney now. We found him as a stray and he has such a happy, loyal nature. He'll be company for Jack when I'm gone.'

She couldn't afford to be sentimental regarding her own death either. Or perhaps it was because she believed in 'the next world'. She would joke about it with Rose. 'I hope to grow new boobies up in heaven,' she had said once. But her faith in the spiritual afterlife was sincere, not just banter to stave off fear or pity. Sometimes Rose wished she could share that faith, as she had done once.

Almost every month they had a death at Elmhurst. With sick, mostly elderly residents, it was only to be expected. Rose took it in her stride. She was a nurse: death was part and parcel of the job. And after what she had experienced in Spain... But she knew Lilian's death would affect her in a more personal way. In the short time she had been there, a special relationship had developed between them, a close understanding and mutual respect. Lilian had refrained from assailing her with the usual battery of questions and comments about her personal life that others seemed to find necessary: *Are you married? Why not? Don't you miss having children? What a shame, but there's still time...*

Rose glanced out of the window and saw Lilian's husband Jack striding up to the front door as he did every day without fail. He would ring the bell at two o'clock sharp, having walked up the country lane leading to Elmhurst after finishing work. His job as a postman meant he started early and got away early. Often he would bring his lunch: cheese and pickle sandwiches in a white paper bag, which he'd eat as he sat with his wife.

'How is she today?' he asked Rose when she opened the door to him.

'She's bearing up well. Cheerful as always.'

'I hope she's not too tired to see me.' His eyes clouded with anxiety. 'Yesterday I could tell it was an effort for her to talk.'

'She slept for a couple of hours before lunch. Now she's looking forward to seeing you.' Rose couldn't help noticing how Lilian always became more animated as the hour of Jack's visit approached.

He followed her into Lilian's room. She was sitting up in bed with a pile of pillows propped behind her and Rose observed her face light up as they entered. 'I'll leave you to it,' she said as Jack embraced his wife. 'Just ring the bell if you need anything.' She would make sure a pot of tea was sent from the kitchens.

In the end, Lilian's decline was swift. She stopped refusing the morphine; she slept a great deal of the time; her words became barely coherent. Rose was glad – for Lilian's sake and even more for Jack's – that her death did not drag out too long. His distress touched her deeply. Their sons, all three of them frequent visitors over these past weeks, were also visibly overcome. Rose attended the funeral and, like most of those present, shed a few tears.

She hadn't expected to see Jack again. He had already collected Lilian's few possessions from the home, so when she was called over the intercom three weeks after the funeral to find Jack standing in the entrance hall with a bunch of chrysanthemums, her surprise must have been obvious.

'I just wanted to show my appreciation for all you did while Lilian was here,' he said, handing her the flowers. 'It made a difference; she talked often of your kindness.'

'Thank you, that's sweet of you.' She blushed, embarrassed by his gesture. 'I was just doing my job.' Jack shook his head. 'It's true I was fond of your wife,' Rose said. 'We're not supposed to have favourites but she had such a generous spirit, and she was brave right till the end.'

'I know. I miss her.' Simple words, spoken without self-pity.

Men coped less well with bereavement, Rose had often thought. Yet in Jack she detected a strength and self-sufficiency that would see him through his loss. All the same, he could probably do with someone to talk to. On an impulse, she said, 'I'm going off duty in an hour. If you don't mind hanging about, we could walk back to town together.'

'That would be grand. I've got a book to read, never go anywhere without one. I'll sit on one of those benches in the gardens if that's alright.'

Beryl, the nurse on night duty, came to relieve her at eight and she went to fetch him. Jack was deep in his book and didn't notice her approach. 'Hello.'

'Good heavens,' he said, looking up. 'Has an hour passed already?'

She glanced at the cover of the book as he marked his place and closed it. He was reading Dickens' *Bleak House*.

'I'm trying to work my way through all the classics,' he said. 'I hardly read in my youth so I've a lot of catching up to do.' He stowed the book in his haversack and rose to his feet. 'Public libraries are a first-rate institution, don't you think?'

They walked side-by-side up the lane bordered by hedges of hazel, hawthorn and bramble, Rose wheeling her bicycle. The sun was low in the sky, casting a soft pinkish light on the fields and hedgerows. A couple more weeks and the blackberries would be ripe.

'There's a pub I sometimes go to on a summer's evening,' he said as they neared the centre of Oxford. 'It's one of those right by the canal. I like to sit by the window and watch the activity on the water. If you've no other plans, perhaps you'll let me buy you a beer.'

She was touched by Jack's concern about her cycling home in the dark. 'I'll be perfectly fine,' she said. 'It's not far, and look, I've got lights.'

'We'll meet again though, won't we?' he said, as she mounted her bicycle. 'I've some photos I'd like to show you.' Rose had thought he might be at a loose end after his wife's death. She was wrong. 'Trouble is, I've only one free evening a week, what with classes and so on. I dropped everything while Lilian was ill but now I'm back to my studies. Sorry to be so awkward but if Wednesdays are any good to you…'

They began to meet regularly once a week. He was a passionate supporter of the Workers' Educational Association, she discovered. Classes on politics, social history, and literature, along with the necessary background reading, occupied several evenings a week and he also served on the branch committee. Sundays were reserved for family. He would travel by train to Birmingham to see his married son Gordon or go fishing on the Thames with the youngest, Vince, recently returned from his stint of National Service in Germany. On Sunday evenings, he liked to have a drink with his other son Lenny.

Wednesday became 'Jack's night'. Rose was surprised how much she looked forward to their outings. If Betty put her on the rota for Wednesday nights, she would try to arrange a swap with one of the other nurses. They made the most of the extra hours of daylight during the summer by taking one of the paths along the river, often accompanied by Jack's dog Barney, and as darkness fell, rounded off the evening with a drink at one of the riverside pubs in town.

He was easy company – they could walk in silence for long periods without her feeling the slightest discomfort. She imagined he was thinking about his wife and hesitated to intrude. At other times, their animated conversation stayed with her for days afterwards, challenging her to think more deeply. They talked about their families and about the trees and plants they saw, the bird and aquatic life. But they also talked about books and ideas. He'd had to leave school at twelve, he said, to help support his widowed mother. Rose admired his zest for learning and improving himself in later life. Occasionally, the fervour with which he spoke of trade unionism or the importance of education or the welfare state put her in mind of Miguel. His wide reading put her to shame.

'What, you haven't read *The Ragged-Trousered Philanthropists*? But Rose, you must. I'll lend you my copy.'

She waited while Jack loosed the twine fastening a gate into the next field. Barney had already jumped between the bars. Jack followed her through the gate and closed it again. 'I'd better put him on the lead before he goes chasing the cows.'

Rose watched him as he bent over to attach the dog's lead. Nothing in Jack's appearance was exceptional; she wouldn't have noticed him in a crowd. He was of average height, neither fat nor thin. His jaw was squarish; he had brown hair, greying around the ears and beginning to recede from the forehead; he wore horn-rimmed glasses and on cooler days a flat cap; he dressed unobtrusively in a sports jacket and flannels.

What Rose found exceptional in him was a certain sureness of purpose, as if he had spent a lot of time thinking, working out what he wanted, what he believed in, what gave his life meaning. And unlike many others who merely dreamed, he had acted on it. He had chosen his job for the outdoor life it offered and the freedom to follow the pursuits that interested him. 'I hate being cooped up,' he had told her that first evening in the pub by the canal. 'I wouldn't care to work in an office or factory, not for all the tea in China. Out and about on my rounds, I see life; I'm in the open air, come rain or shine; my mind is free to roam. And when I finish my rounds, I can please myself what I do for the rest of the day.'

They walked on. A gentle breeze was rippling the water. As children, she and her brothers had often swum in the river near their home. The idea of a river swim appealed – not now, but perhaps on the next hot day. Now the gnats were beginning to annoy her. She touched his arm. 'Shall we turn back?'

It was six months since Lilian's death. He still talked about her often – fondly and always with great respect, despite what he referred to as their 'differences'. His kiss, as they parted that evening, was so completely unexpected that Rose almost stumbled. The sudden intimacy of his lips on hers, of his male scent inhaled from close up, knocked her for six.

'I hope I'm not being too forward,' he said, gripping her arm to steady her. 'Tell me to go to blazes if you want.' He was observing her confusion with a mixture of apprehension and amusement. 'But I hope you won't,' he added.

Smiling, she shook her head. 'Oh no, I wouldn't be so rude.'

'In that case, can I kiss you again?'

She had never considered him as anything more than a friend. The spark of attraction ignited by his kiss caught her unawares, jolting her more profoundly than she let on. After the traumas of Spain, she had thought all that was behind her.

CHAPTER 28

Oxford, 1957 - 58

'Rose, you're not working on Wednesday evening, are you?' Phoebe asked as they parted company at the railway station after one of their weekend walks. 'It's my birthday and I'm having a little celebration. I do hope you can come.'

Rose hesitated: Wednesdays were sacred. 'Well, I'm not working but...'

She hadn't told anyone about Jack. There was no explicit commitment between them. 'Don't think I'm one of those men who, no sooner widowed than they're on the hunt for a new wife,' he had said after their first kiss. 'I don't intend to rush into anything, nor would I want to rush you into anything before you're sure.' Would she ever be sure? Jack had become very dear to her. Their friendship was steadily deepening with time, but her feelings for him were in a different league to the passionate love she had shared with Miguel.

'Would you mind if I brought a friend?' she asked.

Phoebe clapped her hands. 'Oh Rose, you're blushing. Don't tell me you've got yourself a boyfriend at last. How terrific!'

'He's just a good friend, someone I got to know through my job.' Rose wasn't ready to acknowledge any more – especially not to Phoebe, who was quite incapable of discretion. 'It's just that we'd arranged to meet on Wednesday and I don't want to let him down.'

'Bring him along then. The more the merrier.'

Rose had already provided Phoebe with one titbit of gossip today. Her lodger Dennis had amazed everyone by announcing he was getting married at the end of the year, to another teacher at his school. She would have to look for someone else to share her house.

Perhaps it was time to introduce Jack to her friends, she thought as she walked home from the station. There was no real reason to keep him a secret. Telling her family was a different matter. Mother would immediately jump to conclusions.

At home, Rose removed her boots with the usual sense of relief, made herself a cup of tea and picked up the phone. She hadn't spoken to her parents for over a week. Father answered. She could tell immediately that something was worrying him.

'Your mother is a little under the weather,' he said. 'Actually, she hasn't been quite right for some time. It's her digestion. The doctor has ordered some tests...'

'Why didn't you tell me?' His words chilled Rose. She should have noticed. She *had* noticed. She had noticed that Mother seemed to be losing weight and looked tired, but it hadn't registered.

'She was anxious not to worry you. She thought it best to wait until we knew more.'

'I'll come over tomorrow when I finish work.'

'That would be lovely, Rose,' he said, in a much brighter tone. 'By the way, please don't say anything to the boys – not for the moment. It's probably nothing.'

Rose took a few days off work to look after her mother when she came out of hospital. They had found several tumours on her bowel; operating would be risky and probably futile. If she had gone to the doctor's earlier... Father was beside himself. 'I should have made her go,' he said to Rose. 'But your mother doesn't complain, all her energy goes into helping others. I hadn't the slightest inkling there was anything seriously wrong – not till far too late.' Rose reproached herself too. As a nurse, she had no excuse. Six months, give or take, the consultant said, advising Mary Tilley to make the most of them.

Jack listened to her outpouring of grief and guilt. 'Don't be too hard on yourself, Rose,' he said. 'You're not responsible for her illness. I felt something similar when Lilian was ill, blamed myself for not paying enough heed to the signs. It's easy to look back and convince ourselves we could have done more, easier perhaps than recognising how helpless we really are.' His attention was always absolute. Whatever she told him he remembered, down to the smallest detail. He would observe her as if he wanted to memorise not just her words but her facial expressions, the language of her body. As if they might give clues to what lay beneath, to the part of her she kept hidden.

They were walking in the park on a typically damp November afternoon. Already at four o'clock, dusk was draining the light from a sky that had been heavy with cloud all day. On the path, fallen leaves had been driven by the wind into sodden heaps. Even Barney seemed affected by the gloom, running with less energy than usual.

'Let's find a café,' Jack said. 'I think we deserve a cup of tea and a scone.'

'I'd been thinking exactly the same,' Rose said. 'But if I can tempt you with homemade cake rather than scones, why not come to my place instead? It's not far.'

'That would be a treat.'

'I must warn you I don't often make cakes. You're lucky. I was expecting a visit from my godson Frank. He's a big, hungry sixteen year-old and needs feeding up. But as he's caught the flu and had to cancel his visit, I guess you'll do instead.'

'As a big, hungry fifty-seven year-old, I need feeding up too,' Jack said with a smile. 'I'm honoured.'

They sat facing each other across the table, waiting for the kettle to boil. He had been to her house a number of times; his presence in her small kitchen felt quite natural. She wondered what it would be like to live with him, to start every day in this easy, intimate companionship. And then for some reason her mind flipped to Miguel, the only man with whom she had lived – but in conditions so glaringly different, it was impossible to compare the two scenarios, to see them both in the context of one life. In her life with Miguel there had been no room for cosy domesticity, for the ordinary, everyday pleasures taken for granted in peacetime. They'd had to be on guard every moment, ears pricked for danger, guns at the ready.

'Rose...' Jack took her hand. 'Perhaps I'm being presumptuous; if so, forgive me. You know I care for you very much.' The kettle began to whistle on the stove and he reached out a hand to turn off the gas. 'But if I could help banish that sadness I've noticed in you from time to time, it would make me very happy.'

She looked into his eyes, so kind and understanding, and her own filled with tears. She didn't deserve him. 'There's something I ought to tell you, Jack.' She had been mulling it over in her mind for weeks, preparing herself.

'I'm ready, Rose. Whatever you tell me, I promise I won't judge you.'

She closed her eyes and took a deep breath. 'I had a lover in Spain. His name was Miguel. We lived together after the war ended – as fugitives in the mountains. The Civil Guard were on our tail and... It was my fault, I slowed him down and he was shot. I saw it happen but they dragged me away, they wouldn't let me go to him.'

As she gave way to her tears, Rose was vaguely conscious of Jack raising her to her feet and gently leading her to the sofa in the living room. He sat beside her, close but not touching; listening with complete concentration as the words poured out. She wanted him to know everything.

'Your baby died in the night, they said. I can still hear the voice of the sister who told me.' She shuddered, remembering its icy indifference. 'I can still see her standing by my bed, her face like stone. I didn't understand at first; then I refused to believe her. An infection, they said. But so sudden, it didn't make sense. I'd held her, put her to the breast. How could she be dead? Only when they showed me the paper, the death certificate... I'd already given her a name, a Spanish name: Blanca. She was so perfect, so pure... Snow-White, I thought.'

Jack held her as she sobbed and the salt tears swept her pain out to sea on a tidal wave of release. 'I guessed you'd been through something hard,' he said. 'And what could be harder than what you've suffered? My poor Rose, my darling...' He stopped. 'Am I allowed to call you that?'

Unable to speak, she nodded and leant her head against him. She felt blessed, she felt overcome with gratitude, she felt... Was it love? She could think of no other word for it. The knowledge came as a revelation. She loved Jack. Of course she did. Why hadn't she realised?

They held each other for a long time without speaking. She felt elated, delirious with relief.

Jack was the first to move. 'What about that tea?' he said. 'And you promised me cake.' He was teasing her, trying to suppress a smile and failing utterly.

'Oh Jack, you must think I enticed you here under false pretences. Will you ever forgive me?' She stood up. 'Tea and cake coming right away.'

Jack followed her to the kitchen and watched her as she relit the gas under the kettle, set out cups and saucers and swirled hot water round the teapot to warm it before spooning in the tea. She fetched the cake tin from the larder and cut two slices of her lemon cake. A jet of steam rose from the kettle's spout as she filled the teapot.

Leaving it to stand, she turned round to face Jack. 'If you like...' She bit her lip and started again. 'If you like, Jack, you could stay the night.' She busied herself pouring the tea, unable to look at him now, scarcely believing what she'd said. She was too impulsive; her mother had always told her so.

She felt his hands on her shoulders; his scratchy cheek brushed hers. 'Can you repeat that?' he said. 'I'm not quite sure if I heard you right.'

'No. No, I can't.' Rose freed herself and reached for the teapot. 'Oh, I forgot the milk and sugar.'

'Rose, look at me.'

She finished pouring the tea and faced him. 'You heard me,' she said. 'And just in case I wasn't clear enough, I'm inviting you to share my bed tonight.'

'You'll get me into trouble,' Jack said some hours later as they lay entwined in Rose's single bed. 'I was supposed to be writing about the Tolpuddle Martyrs tonight, not making love to a beautiful woman. I don't know what my tutor will say when I turn up to the class tomorrow empty-handed with such an implausible excuse.'

'Blame it on me propositioning you without prior warning,' Rose said. 'Were you shocked at my forwardness?'

Jack smoothed back her hair and kissed her on the forehead. 'I certainly wasn't expecting it,' he said. 'I was convinced I'd have to make the first move. You may not have noticed but several times I almost did – I'd rehearsed it often enough in my head – but my courage failed me at the last minute. I was afraid of offending you.'

'I might have turned you down,' she said. 'I don't know why I was so slow to recognise my feelings. I think I've loved you for a long time but I only realised this evening.'

'I realised my feelings a long time ago,' Jack said, 'but I didn't want to spoil our friendship by putting pressure on you. And then I thought: why would she want an old fogey like me? I was worried you might see me as a father figure.'

'Oh Jack, I've never thought of you like that. I have a perfectly good father already, thank you.'

They lay in silence for a few minutes, relaxed, luxuriating in the pleasure of skin against skin, the warmth of each other's bodies.

Jack raised himself on one elbow. 'You've no idea how nervous I was,' he said. 'At my age you can't take anything for granted and… well, I was desperately anxious not to disappoint you.'

'*You* were nervous! What about me? After all these years…' There had been no one since Miguel. At forty-two, she had not expected her desire to be rekindled. 'You didn't disappoint me,' she added. 'It was beautiful.'

He pulled her closer. 'I'm glad. And now, my dear Rose, we must be practical. Do you have an alarm clock?'

'Oh poor Jack, you have to start work at some unearthly hour, don't you.'

'Set it for a quarter to five. I'll slip out of bed quietly, bring you some tea and disappear. But now you must let me sleep.'

It was Jack's idea to get married on Valentine's Day. 'I'd never have guessed you were such a romantic,' Rose teased him. The ceremony was to take place in Father's old parish church in Evesham, performed by the new vicar. The pleasure it would give her parents was more important to Rose than satisfying her own preference for a registry office wedding. Jack had no objection. Since their engagement, he had met most of her family and many of her friends. She had anticipated raised eyebrows from some quarters at Jack's working class origins and lowly job as well as the age difference. But with one or two exceptions, their initial scruples melted away on acquaintance, banished by his charm and gentle manners.

'So you've taken my advice not to let life pass you by,' Annie said. 'Good for you, Rose.' Jack's sons too voiced their approval, much to Rose's relief. Even Vince, who had been particularly close to Lilian, seemed pleased. Everyone told her how happy she looked. She *was* happy.

At the wedding, Mother glowed, her smile counteracting the pallor of her skin. 'I've waited so long to see you married,' she said. Rose was glad they had fixed an early date. Mother's dress, bought for the occasion at her husband's insistence, hung pitifully on her skeletal frame.

'Will you try for a baby?' Prue asked. 'You're not over the hill yet. I've a friend who gave birth at forty.'

Rose shook her head. Jack had posed the question of whether she wanted children; she'd sensed his relief when she said no. He was fifty-eight: old enough to be a grandfather. 'I've left it too late,' she told her sister-in-law. 'I have three stepsons, not to speak of my four adorable nephews and nieces and a godson. That's enough for me.' After long years of practice, she had become adept at hiding her sadness.

For their honeymoon, they took a week's holiday in Cornwall, where they spent the days beachcombing or battling the wind on long cliff walks before seeking shelter in a café and indulging in a big pot of tea and fresh scones oozing jam and clotted cream. Their hotel had a cosy lounge with an open fire. One evening as they sat together watching the flames leaping up the chimney in tongues of molten orange, Jack said, 'There's something I wanted to ask you.' Earlier in the day, she had described to him the beauty of Spain's wild flowers and mountain landscapes, the relief she had found in the countryside from all the barbarity of war: the blood and guts; the young men dead or dying or disfigured; their screams. 'Will you revisit Spain one day?' he asked now. 'I'll take you there if it's what you want.'

'That's kind of you, Jack but no, I couldn't. It would be too steeped in painful memories. Do you understand?' Sharing the pain had weakened its grip but she knew the slightest touch of a chord would bring it surging back in full force. Despite her contentment with the new life given to her, she wasn't yet strong enough to face the trauma of going back – not even with Jack's support. Death had robbed her of Miguel, robbed her of the child they'd created. To forget them – even if she could – would be an insult. But to tear open the wounds by returning to Spain now? 'No,' she repeated. 'Thank you but no.' Was it too much to hope that one day she would be able to think of her lost ones without the heartache, without the canker of bitterness and regret?

PART 6 CONSUELO 1967 - 1971

CHAPTER 29

Antequera, 1967

Consuelo usually enjoyed the August *feria*. The lively atmosphere that always surrounded the bullfights, livestock trading and fairground entertainments perked her up – not least because it provided an opportunity to catch up with her friends. But this year the heat was overpowering and the extra weight of her pregnancy made every movement an effort. Walking in procession this morning in the *romería* for the Señor de la Verónica, all the way from the bullring where the Mass took place, through town and up to the hermitage, had worn her out. Mamá was too busy with her brothers' families to give much help.

In three weeks she would celebrate her twenty-eighth birthday. As she reached for her fan yet again, an image came into her mind of the distended belly of a faceless woman, her own birth mother, who would have been heavy with child in the August of 1939. She too must have suffered from the heat. The thought awakened a curious spark of connection that, strangely, gave her some consolation. But this was immediately displaced by another more painful realisation: that she could pass her mother in the street and not know her. Perhaps she had. Consuelo supposed that Jaén was her mother's hometown since she had given birth there. Could it be that one of the women glimpsed on their brief stay in the town for Uncle Rodrigo's funeral was her mother? And as she observed her own children, secure and happy in their rightful family, it occurred to her for the first time that her mother might have given birth more than once, that she might have younger or older siblings. The sister she had so often wished for, perhaps?

Belén and Carlos were at the window, jumping up and down and screaming with excitement every time one of the rockets went off. They were raring to join the festivities in the marquees, to visit the stalls selling trinkets and sweets and watch the entertainments. Consuelo had worked hard at her sewing machine to make outfits for the two of them. It was worth it. Belén looked prettier than ever in her pink spotted dress with all its frills and flounces, while Carlos, at the age of two and a half, was quite the little man in grey striped trousers, waistcoat, red sash and *cordobés* hat.

She hoped Enrique wouldn't be too long so that they could go out before the children became overtired. The holiday week was a busy time for the bakery: all hands were needed to fulfil the heightened demand. Antequera's famous *bienmesabe* had to be prepared in great quantities, not just for the town's population but also for the many visitors from Málaga and Granada, who were eager to sample the dessert.

Lately, Enrique had been coming home from work in a bad mood more often than not. He seemed restless and preoccupied. From the few hints he dropped, she guessed that he and his brothers had quarrelled. Consuelo wished he would confide in her instead of brushing off her questions with some dismissive comment. 'It's not a matter for women,' he would say, or 'You don't need to bother your head with men's affairs.' She would have liked to feel trusted enough to share his problems, and more importantly, to offer him some comfort.

Fortunately, his grumpiness didn't last long. Little Belén could charm him out of the darkest moods with her chatter and affection. He adored both children and the feelings were mutual. Their third child was due in three months. She looked forward to the joy of a new baby, as did her husband.

'¡Papá, Papá!' Enrique stood in the doorway, the two children clinging to his legs. Belén tugged at his hand. 'Let's go now, let's go to the fair, Papá.'

He picked them up, one in each arm and kissed them. 'Look what I've brought you.' From his pocket he produced a bag of *caramelos*. 'We'll go in just a moment,' he said, popping a sweet into each of their mouths.

He looked weary but he would suppress his exhaustion for the sake of the children, just as she would conquer her own need for rest. She took a bottle of beer from the new refrigerator and poured him a glass. He drank it quickly and turned to the children. 'If you're ready for some fun, we'll go out as soon as I've washed my face and put on a clean shirt.' They had saved a little money for the *feria*. Enrique loved to spoil the children with treats, especially at holiday times.

'*Vámonos*,' he said a few minutes later. 'The circus is in town; there'll be clowns and pretty horses. And if you're good, I'll buy you sticks of candy floss.'

That night, when the children were in bed and all was quiet, he finally unburdened himself to her. There was little future for him in the bakery, he said. With so many brothers and sisters, his share of it would be small. Federico was now an ordained priest, the *cura* of a parish near Ronda, and had no interest in the family business, but along with the girls, he would inherit a share of it. Their father was in poor health these days and the two eldest sons, Ignacio and Javier, were gradually asserting their control. Enrique was convinced they were trying to edge him out.

'But your father wouldn't allow that, would he?' Consuelo asked.

'Well, there would have to be a financial arrangement,' he explained. 'And Papá would make sure it was fair, so...' She was surprised to see his eyes light up as he spoke. 'So it might not be such a bad thing, Chelo.'

The new vigour in his voice confirmed what she had long suspected: that he wanted to move to Málaga as so many from their town had done in recent years. He had been spending his free weekends on the coast with his friends, gawping at the foreign girls in bikinis, if the other wives were to be believed. She hoped it was only gawping.

'So what work would you do if you left the bakery?' she asked.

'On the coast it's easy to find work – and much better paid than here. Wouldn't you like to live by the sea, *corazón*? We could go to the beach every afternoon in summer. The children could play in the sand, splash about in the sea...'

Consuelo had been to Málaga a few times. One of her early memories of the town was of cripples begging on street corners, many of them missing an arm or leg. There were even some with both legs amputated, who crawled along grotesquely on arms and stumps. She supposed their hideous injuries had been inflicted by the reds during the war. As Papá always reminded her, they had their beloved *Caudillo,* Francisco Franco, to thank for saving Spain from the barbarous communists. He had restored peace and order to their country. And now, it was said, tourists were bringing a new prosperity. Certainly Málaga would no longer be the shabby, down-at-heel city she remembered from her youth.

'I don't know, we'd be a long way from our families.' She was thinking more of her friends – not that she saw much of them now they were all wives and mothers, controlled by their husbands and in-laws.

'Have you forgotten, my sister Isabel lives on the coast?'

Isabel worked at the airport in Málaga and lived in Fuengirola, a small town not far away. She'd learnt to speak English and had friends from abroad. It was there on the coast she had met her Swedish husband. Sven didn't mind her working after they were married. She loved her job, especially as it gave her the chance to travel cheaply or even free to other countries. Why tie yourself down with babies, she asked? To Consuelo, her life seemed exotic and glamorous.

'But are there really so many jobs?' she asked Enrique.

'They're crying out for workers, Chelo. In construction, in hotels and restaurants, in bars and nightclubs... You should see the huge blocks of apartments and hotels going up, because the tourists keep coming – planeloads of them from all over northern Europe. Germans, English, Dutch, Swedes... They love our beaches.'

It was clear he had made up his mind, regardless of her feelings. And no doubt she would get used to a new place, although having spent all her life in Antequera, it would be strange at first. 'Whatever you think best,' she said. After all, he was the man; it wasn't her place to argue with him.

'Isabel is having a party at her house,' Enrique informed her a week later. 'She says we can stay overnight in their spare bedroom. I told her we'd go.'

The house was already throbbing with laughter and music when they arrived. Consuelo could see no other children. The guests crowding the room stood, glasses in hand, talking animatedly in some foreign tongue. The women wore dresses with low necklines and high hems, the men open shirts and tight trousers that flared at the ankles. Isabel had taken the children into the kitchen, leaving her and Enrique at the mercy of her guests. She clung to his arm, intimidated by these cosmopolitan strangers.

A woman with long flowing hair, her neck and wrists encircled by rows of beads, addressed Consuelo in what might be English. She stood mutely, looking to Enrique for help, but he just shook his head.

'Julia is asking where you're from.' Isabel had reappeared, holding Belén and Carlos by the hand. 'She'll have assumed from your looks that you were Scandinavian or English.'

'What pretty children,' another of the guests said in Spanish, patting Carlos on the head. His wife nodded at her protruding stomach. 'So when are you expecting number three?' The man made some joke she didn't understand and everyone laughed.

'Don't take any notice,' Isabel said. 'He was just commenting that we Spanish like big families. What, don't you have drinks yet? That's unforgiveable.' She called to her husband, 'Sven, get my brother and his wife something to drink, *pronto.*'

Later, the lights were turned down and people started to dance. One man was so drunk he fell over; another stripped off his shirt. Couples were entwined together in such an intimate manner, Consuelo had to turn her eyes away. She was glad the children were asleep in bed. 'Let's go to our room,' she whispered to Enrique.

CHAPTER 30

Torremolinos, 1969

'Shh, Pablito, it's only an aeroplane.' Consuelo picked up her youngest child and kissed him. The low-flying planes were the main drawback to living in Torremolinos. They roared overhead, either taking off or preparing to land at Málaga's airport. In the two years since they'd moved here, the number of flights had increased noticeably. It was good for business, Enrique said, but the noise of the engines terrified Pablo; he screamed every time. The older children were used to it and found the planes exciting. Carlos said he wanted to be a pilot when he grew up.

Some of the men working on the coast took lodgings during the week and returned home to Antequera at weekends. Consuelo was glad Enrique had not suggested such an arrangement. She worried about the effect on her husband of seeing all those scantily-clad northern European girls with their loose morals and complete lack of shame. The way they behaved shocked everyone. The young people came on holiday unsupervised by their parents and were seen kissing (or worse) in full public view. They even walked through the town in their skimpy bikinis.

In many ways it suited Consuelo to live on the coast. Without the interference of her own and her husband's families, she felt freer. Of course she also missed their help, but she didn't mind working hard in the home, especially now they had a little more money. Enrique had promised to buy her a washing machine next month. She hoped it would be one of those automatics everyone was talking about. She put Pablo down and examined the skin on her hands; it felt rough and worn from washing everything by hand. Mamá's were still smooth despite her age because she had servants to do all the work for her. It was Paloma and the other *criadas* whose hands were red and wrinkled and aged.

Enrique's job as cashier at the Hotel Palmero had been a stroke of luck. His uncle Gustavo was a friend of the manager's so it was easily fixed. Enrique liked the work and enjoyed mixing with the foreign tourists, though few of them spoke much Spanish. The boss preferred to employ workers who knew some English or German, but as Enrique's job mostly involved working with figures, Uncle Gustavo had persuaded him it wasn't important in his case. She had suggested once or twice that he try to learn another language in order to gain promotion. 'One day I will' was his usual reply. She didn't want to press him: in truth it pleased her that he would rather play with the children than study after his day's work.

Because they lived close and had a car, Isabel and Sven visited them often. At first, Consuelo had been shocked by some of their ideas, especially when they criticised General Franco or complained about the power of the Church. She worried about the consequences of expressing such dangerous thoughts. Enrique would laugh and tell his sister she was crazy but Consuelo sensed he found her views disturbing too. On the other hand, the children adored their Aunt Isabel. She enthralled them with stories of magic and adventure plucked from her imagination; when she accompanied them to the beach, they always had more fun, jumping the waves and playing the wildest games; in the park she encouraged Belén to climb the old tree with her brother, assuring her it was fine for girls to climb trees too. The grandparents would have been scandalised had they known.

Consuelo took care to hide the books Isabel passed to her. Most had been published in Mexico. She had no idea how her sister-in-law managed to smuggle them into the country. Two she liked particularly were *Los Viajes de Gulliver and El Retrato de Dorian Gray*. She felt a little guilty reading and enjoying books forbidden by the censor. But Isabel said there was nothing wicked about these books: they were classics and it was wrong to prohibit the Spanish people from reading them. Consuelo wasn't sure her husband would agree. She and Enrique never spoke about such things. Nor did she talk to her friends on the subject. As far as she knew, none of them read books. Reading was a secret pleasure, shared only with Isabel.

Alone with the children, Consuelo found the day long. In Antequera, Enrique had always come home for lunch but now he ate at the hotel and didn't return until evening. Although she was on friendly enough terms with her neighbours in their *barrio* of El Calvario, she had no close friends here. The feeling she had harboured all her life of not quite fitting in persisted, though for different reasons now. Her upbringing in a rich family had been noted and as a result, their mostly working class neighbours kept a wary distance.

It was time to fetch Belén from school. She put Pablo in the pushchair and persuaded Carlos into his coat. Winters were warmer on the coast but often a cool breeze chilled the air. Today a westerly wind was gaining strength, carrying with it an intermittent drizzle. Consuelo covered Pablo from the rain as best she could while she waited for the children to be released. Carlos had joined some of the other young boys running about the playground.

The door of the school opened and the children poured out – not in a silent, orderly line the way the nuns at her old school had dictated, but chattering and laughing – first the girls, then from a different door the boys. Belén's face lit up when she spotted her mother. She ran towards them and Consuelo hugged and kissed her.

'Come on, Carlos,' she called. The *poniente* blew rain into their faces as they walked home through the streets, Belén talking non-stop, Carlos dragging behind. Her daughter enjoyed going to school and liked her teacher, a young woman with proper training, not a nun. She was glad Belén didn't have to endure the cruelties and humiliations she had suffered at the hands of the nuns during her own education. Once she finished at the National School when she reached eleven, the choices would be fewer. Belén might have to attend a convent school to study for her *bachillerato* or else travel to Málaga.

Back home, Consuelo set to work preparing lunch. Earlier in the morning she had bought sardines at the market. They sizzled now in the hot oil, filling the kitchen with their rich, fishy tang. While they were frying, she mashed the sweet potato she had cooked before they went out and put it in a pan to reheat. She sliced some bread and called to Belén to help lay the table.

At the weekend they had promised to visit the family for a celebration of her father-in-law Ernesto's Saint's Day. She looked forward to seeing her relatives, though the journey would be tedious. Enrique's dream was to buy a little Seat car so they'd be able to drive to Antequera instead of having to travel by bus, first into Málaga and then on to their hometown. He thought they should join the waiting list now, as it could take a year. Consuelo doubted if they'd be able to afford a car even in a year's time, even if he sold his little Vespa scooter, but she determined to save every peseta she could and hide it away so that his plan might come to fruition.

The first person she saw when they stepped off the bus in Antequera was the pharmacist, Serafín. He was sitting on a bench in the plaza with two other elderly men. Of course he looked much older than she remembered him – hardly a hair remained on his head, his face had become wizened and his body shrunk – but she recognised him immediately. To her relief, he showed no sign of recognition – she had been a child still when he was detained – and feeling awkward, she turned away without greeting him. She remembered hearing on the radio some months ago of an amnesty for prisoners and guessed he had spent the intervening years locked away.

Others too had reappeared after the amnesty, she learned. Emilio, who used to teach at the town's public school before the war had been hiding in Sevilla for thirty years; his wife and children had long presumed him dead. Now they were finally reunited. But Manuela's son had not returned. He had been executed by firing squad, his sister Charo told her.

After being away from Antequera, Consuelo was struck anew by how it differed from Torremolinos. She no longer felt oppressed by the many churches, convents and mansions lining its streets but appreciated the beauty of these buildings. Approaching the church of San Sebastián, she gazed with affection at the *angelote* on its spinning weather vane. Round its neck, the angel wore a relic of Santa Eufemia.

What a contrast to Torremolinos which, except for the old part where they lived, consisted of ugly apartment blocks and skyscraper hotels built in lines parallel to the beach. Everything was geared to the tourists. They could even buy 'fish and chips' or cups of English tea with milk as if they were in their home country.

In Antequera she saw no foreigners. On the contrary, quite a few *antequeranos* had emigrated to Germany or Switzerland, where they could earn enough to send money home. In general, little had changed in the town since her early childhood: it was still a serious place dominated by religious tradition rather than bars and discotheques. Photos of the *Caudillo* and of José Antonio, founder of the Falange, adorned the walls of every public building as they always had, while above people's front doors she observed the familiar Sacred Heart of Jesus plaques. It was a relief not to be confronted with the embarrassing pin-up girls so common now in establishments on the coast. Just seeing them made her feel sullied, as if even the air around them became tainted with sin.

'It's true what they say about foreign girls,' she confided to her friend Mari Carmen, who had married a vet and moved to Lucena, far from the coast. 'The rules were too strict when we were young, that's for sure, but these girls… When I see how they behave, it makes me proud to be Spanish.'

'Oh we're all proud of our country now,' Mari Carmen replied, smiling. 'La, La, La. We won!' She sang a few bars of the song that had given Spain top place in the Eurovision Song Contest and Consuelo joined in. Everyone knew the words. Everyone had shared in the triumph of beating all the other nations, even England's famous Cliff Richard.

The new groups from England were catching on. Consuelo found the songs of *Los Beatles* irresistible. She would sing along to them on the radio, imitating the sounds without understanding their meaning. And the lively music of *Los Rolling*, with its insistent beat and raw vocals, had even prompted her to dance occasionally in the privacy of her own home. But the traditional *coplas* were still her favourites. She adored Lola Flores and Marife de Triana. Seeing their films was the greatest treat of all.

CHAPTER 31

Torremolinos/Granada, 1971

'Papá will be home very soon.' Consuelo reached over to wipe Carlos's nose while she held six month-old Luisa to her breast. Pablo was asleep but she had promised the two older ones they could stay up until their father came. It was a mistake: their bedtime had long passed and they were becoming fractious. Both children had been suffering for days from a feverish cold.

'I've been celebrating,' Enrique said with a broad smile when he finally walked through the door nearly two hours after his usual time.

She bit her tongue, determined not to complain about the late hour, and tucking Luisa under her arm, began to prepare their supper.

'What? Are you not in bed yet, *chicos*?' He bent to kiss the children and followed her into the kitchen. 'Chelo, *mi amor*, don't you want to hear my news? I've been offered a job in Granada, deputy manager of a hotel. Almudena swung it for me. It's her cousin's hotel and she put in a good word. We'll be much better off, *corazón*.' He came up behind her and spun her round to face him; she smelt the wine on his breath. 'Aren't you pleased?'

Responding to the appeal in his eyes, she smiled and kissed him. 'Of course I am. That's wonderful.' She needed time to absorb the news. This evening she felt too weary to think beyond the disruption of moving house with four little ones. Making an effort, she said, 'Granada's a proper town like Antequera. I think I'll feel more at home there.' Her lack of enthusiasm must be apparent.

'Granada is much bigger, Chelo. It's a city and the hotel is right in the centre.'

Her mind was still dwelling on the part played by Almudena. She had never met this woman but her name had cropped up several times recently in Enrique's conversation. Apparently she worked as some kind of rep with the foreign tourists. Consuelo tried to dismiss the niggling fear that her husband's relations with Almudena might go beyond what was appropriate or decent.

'When do you start?' she asked.

'Next month. We must begin looking immediately for a house to rent. Then, with luck, we'll be settled by Christmas.'

She placed a bowl of steaming lentils on the table for Enrique. 'Come and eat now, you must be hungry. I'll join you in a minute when I've taken the children up to bed.'

'Leave them to play a few minutes longer, sweetheart and sit down with me. We should eat together.'

'They're tired, Quique. It won't take me long to settle them down.'

'In that case I'll wait.' He turned to Carlos and Belén. 'Come, give your papá a kiss, then off to bed, *pronto.*'

'It's just a small hotel at the moment,' he told Consuelo later as they sat together at the table. 'The guests used to be travelling salesmen and businessmen mainly, but now the tourists are beginning to come and the owner has plans to build two more floors. The foreigners want to visit Granada's Alhambra palace. They say it's famous all over Europe. Our country is changing, Chelo. It's opening up.'

Driving along the coast road in their pale green Seat 600, Consuelo began to feel more enthusiastic about the move. She had only once visited Granada, about ten years ago when Papá had business there. What remained most strongly in her mind were the spectacular views of snow-covered peaks starkly outlined against a blue winter's sky, and then later in the day, the radiant ball of the sun turning the hills rose and then blue as it sank over the town. They would be able to afford a bigger house or perhaps a flat, Enrique said. Big enough for a couple more children, should they come along.

To their right lay the sea, fringed with beaches of sand or shingle, to their left the conglomerations of one resort after another. Bars, restaurants and hotels lined the road, while further back, parallel blocks rose up, many still under scaffolding, with cranes towering above them.

She glanced across at Enrique as he drove, hands resting on the steering wheel. In sunglasses, with his dark hair slicked back and a cigarette between his lips, he looked perfectly relaxed. The white shirt she had ironed this morning was open at the neck, the sleeves rolled up to expose his muscular arms. To her mind he was more handsome now than when she'd married him. The shy gazelle had matured into a confident buck.

She loved her husband and felt proud of their family. They had been truly blessed. Luisa wriggled on her lap and turned to give her a beaming smile. She stroked the baby's fine hair and covered her head with kisses. The other three children sat in the back of the car, Belén trying to teach her brothers a song she had learnt at school.

At Motril they turned off towards Granada. Enrique's new boss, Pepe, had invited them to eat at a restaurant close to the hotel. After lunch they would look at some houses and flats for rent and, should they find a suitable one, hand over the deposit. The plan was to move as soon as possible, preferably before the start of the Christmas and New Year festivities.

'One day we'll be able to buy our own house,' Enrique said.

'If we strike lucky in *El Gordo*.' Smiling, she asked, 'Have you bought your *décimo* yet?' Like most people she knew, Consuelo dreamed of winning the lottery and planned in her head how she would spend the jackpot.

'I'm in with the others at work,' he replied, 'and my father always buys tickets for the family. So you never know.' He reached for the stick of chewing gum she held out but the packet dropped to the floor. 'Hey, what's the matter?'

Consuelo bent to retrieve it. 'Nothing.' She passed him a *chicle* and tried to recompose her face. A fragment of the dream, so vivid when she woke this morning but banished by the day's domestic demands, had flashed before her again: that insistent female voice from the back of the church. *I'm looking for my daughter*. She tried to recall the rest of the dream, to build up each element of the scene.

She was in church with her family when the voice, echoing from the frigid walls and flagstones, rang out. '*I'm looking for my daughter.*' A stranger had entered halfway through Mass and Consuelo knew it was her mother, her birth mother. She tried to call out *I'm here!* But the words stuck in her throat and no sound emerged. Her legs had turned to rubber. She could neither speak nor move. Other heads swivelled to peer at the intruder but hers would not. Behind her she heard scuffling and angry voices. 'Out, *puta*. This is a place of God.'

A small cry, the dragging of feet across the floor, then once again that piteous plea. 'My daughter, where is my daughter?' Consuelo heard the church door bang shut; the priest resumed his intonations; the congregation settled.

On her lap in the car, Luisa was starting to grizzle. Consuelo opened her blouse and felt the draw of the milk as her child began to feed. Just a dream, she told herself, pulling her daughter closer. Yet it continued to haunt her as they drove towards Granada.

PART 7 ROSE 1961 - 1972

CHAPTER 32

Oxford, 1961

Rose looked up through the branches of a large oak at the darker smudges of cloud blowing across an otherwise ash-grey sky. The rain was easing off; with luck she would make it home before the next shower. She wheeled her bicycle back onto the path and mounted the saddle to resume her ride. This was the last stretch; in a few minutes she'd be in Iffley. She loved living by the river. Even when it rained, the thirty-minute ride to and from work along the towpath was a pleasure. Yesterday she had caught the bright turquoise flash of a kingfisher.

Letting herself into the house, she was greeted by the familiar sight of Jack's postman's cap perched on a hook in the hall. His uniform, the navy trousers and jacket with red piping, would be on a hanger in the bedroom, ready for tomorrow morning. He was an orderly man, she had discovered – not obsessive like her former lodger but particular enough to tidy up after her on occasion.

Adapting to married life, to her new identity as Mrs Drummond, had proved easier than she'd expected. She relished the everyday intimacies: sharing meals, sleeping and waking together, their bodies taking warmth and comfort from each other. The welding of their respective families gave her a particular joy. She was becoming fond of Jack's sons and he was a hit with most of her family too, the differences of class and age having been exposed as immaterial. Father hailed Jack as a humane and thinking man. There was no stopping the two of them once they embarked on philosophy or politics or history.

Jack's house in Botley had been their first home. Initially, the delight of being together dominated all else and Rose could put aside the slight unease she felt at living with the visual reminders of his previous marriage. But although she had been fond of Lilian, her ghost was too pervasive. She felt awkward sitting in 'Lilian's chair', looking at 'Lilian's favourite painting', 'the wallpaper Lilian chose'; sleeping in the same bed they had shared. One night he'd suggested they read to each other in bed, adding, 'Lilian liked me to read to her.' Rose took care to hide her pique. Jack was guileless; he would never hurt her deliberately. She wasn't jealous. It was just that she felt the house belonged to Jack and Lilian; it was filled with memories of their life together and sometimes she felt like a usurper.

Selling both Jack's house and her former abode in Jericho had enabled them to buy their large, redbrick Victorian house in the centre of Iffley village. Not only was there more room for family to stay but also – much to Rose's joy – space for a piano.

She delighted in waking up to birdsong, having green fields and meadows all around and the river so close. The centre of Oxford was only two miles away: they had the best of both worlds. She was looking forward to the warmer weather, to evenings sitting by the lock, watching the water levels rise and fall as barges and narrow boats waited to pass through, and to picnicking in meadows of wild flowers.

'I'm home, darling,' she called.

Jack appeared at the top of the stairs, book in hand. 'Did you get wet?' he asked. 'Barney and I were like two drowned rats after our walk this afternoon.' He left the book on the landing and joined her downstairs. 'I've some good news,' he said. 'Vince is coming home for a week's leave. His letter arrived this morning.'

The gleam in Jack's eyes told Rose how much this meant to him. His youngest son had joined the Merchant Navy and was often at sea for long periods. 'That's wonderful,' she said, giving her husband a hug. 'Now, come and keep me company while I prepare our supper.'

Jack followed her to the kitchen. As she reached the open door, a sudden impulse made her turn and take him by the hands. 'I feel so lucky,' she said. 'I never expected a life of domestic bliss. If anyone had told me… Well actually, some of my friends did, but I pooh-poohed their ideas.'

'We're both lucky.' Jack's face creased into that smile that conveyed better than any words how much he loved her. 'Oh, before I forget, there was a phone call for you. An old friend, she said. I took down her number for you to call back. Now, what was her name? Ah yes, Peggy.'

'Peggy?' It took Rose a few moments to remember, a few moments before the memories came flooding back. The nightmare of the Ebro; the frantic search for a safe place to set up their hospital as the bombs rained down; scrubbing away at the walls of that filthy railway tunnel with Peggy working by her side, cursing each time she tripped in the dark... She recalled her shock when Miguel – not yet her lover – was brought in with horrific abdominal injuries. His life had been saved against all the odds, thanks to Dr Jolly's exceptional skill.

'Rose, are you alright? You've gone rather pale.'

'Oh Jack, just hold me for a minute.' Spain, her past life, was never far away. She would not be allowed to forget, or only for so long. Jack's embrace gave some comfort but not enough to restore her mood of calm contentment.

'Peggy served in Spain with me, one of the other nurses. Did she say why she phoned?'

'She mentioned she'd be visiting Oxford shortly. You don't have to see her, darling. Make up some excuse if it's too upsetting.'

'No, I must see her of course, but... Jack, do you mind if we delay dinner a little?'

'You're going to phone her now?'

'No. I'm going to play the piano.' The urge to lose herself in some Chopin was compelling.

'I suppose some husbands might consider that gross neglect,' Jack said, smiling, 'but luckily I'm a tolerant man. Go and play, by all means. I'm getting used to your sudden whims.'

CHAPTER 33

Oxford, 1965

'But you *must* have a party.' Family and friends were of one mind, sweeping aside any objections on Rose's part. 'You can't reach the landmark of fifty without celebrating in style,' Prue said. 'We'll all muck in with the preparations, you won't have to do a thing.' Peter, who played bass guitar in a pop group, suggested they hire a hall. His group, The Rocking Turtles, were willing to play for free. Even Jack's sons joined in the chorus of persuasion. Rose found it hard to believe she was approaching fifty, though the signs of change in her body confirmed it.

'I hope you're not bored with our quiet, sedate life,' Jack said one evening a week before her birthday as they walked Barney on their usual route along the towpath. Their walks were shorter and slower these days. Not only was Barney getting old but Jack too had slowed down. His knees had been giving him trouble for some time, making it painful to walk very far. Cycling suited him better. He no longer delivered the mail; instead he worked in the sorting office, a change not at all to his taste. Later this year he would retire.

'Bored? Not on your nelly! I don't have time to be bored,' Rose said, laughing. More soberly, she added, 'Besides, I've had enough excitement to last me a lifetime. More than enough.'

But even as she spoke, some sixth sense intimated that her life might not continue as serene and uneventful as it was now.

'Crumbs! Just look at old Ralph,' Bertie said as Peter's band belted out a heavy rock 'n' roll number. Their brother was on the dance floor, throwing Chantal about in a fast jive.

Rose grabbed Bertie's arm and drew him over to where the more youthful crowd were jigging about to the lively beat of The Rocking Turtles. What they were doing looked much easier. Rose in her knee-length cocktail dress felt rather square amongst all the girls in mini-skirts. 'This is fun,' she said, slightly breathless as the band launched into the Swinging Blue Jeans' hit, *Hippy Hippy Shake*.

She had given in to the pressure and booked the church hall. Just as well they had a large venue, she thought now, casting her eyes over the guests – friends from every decade of her life. She spotted several of her former nursing colleagues from London, Dorothy and Archie with Frank in tow, her old rambling friends Ken and Phoebe, even Betty B, her boss from Elmhurst, now long retired.

'Susan's crazy about the Beatles,' Bertie said. 'She went down to London to see them last year, screaming along with the rest, I wouldn't be surprised.'

'If I was fifteen, I'd probably scream,' Rose said. 'They've got more life and energy than all the old bands put together.' She glanced round the room and caught sight of her father sitting at the far end of the hall with Prue. How frail he looked. A bent old man with no weight on him, shrunk to little more than her own height though he had been a tall man once. Since breaking his hip after a fall during that icy winter two years ago, he had lost confidence as well as mobility. 'I'm going to join Father,' she said.

After their mother's death, he had moved in with Ralph and Chantal. Rose was grateful to them for offering him a home. Chantal provided him with company during the day if he needed it, though often he was content to sit alone, absorbed in his books. Now, with his eyesight beginning to fail, he relied more on the wireless to connect him with the wider world.

'I hope it's not too noisy for you,' she said, taking a seat opposite her father.

'Oh no,' he said. 'I don't mind at all. Even though it is a little loud, I'll admit. I like to see you young people letting your hair down. You know...' He started to cough.

'I'll go for some water,' Prue said as he fought to control his coughing fit.

His chest was full of phlegm. The sound alarmed Rose; she had been concerned for some time about the state of his lungs. The last two winters he'd suffered one respiratory infection after another and had several spells in hospital. It must be hard for Chantal, even with the help of the district nurses. She felt guilty leaving it to her sister-in-law to care for Father, but with Jack about to retire, she couldn't afford to give up work.

Prue handed Father a glass of water and after a few minutes the coughing stopped and his breathing returned to normal. 'Sorry about that,' he said. 'I'm right as rain now.' But he didn't look it.

The musicians had taken a break and Jack was busy rounding people up to start on the buffet. Rose helped her father towards the table where some of the guests were already piling food onto their plates.

'Let me get you some drinks,' Jack said. 'There's Babycham for the ladies, though you'd probably prefer cider or beer, wouldn't you, Rose? Or a glass of wine? Let's see… It's Mateus Rosé or Blue Nun.'

Prue opted for a Babycham. She pointed to Rose's glass of Mateus. 'Is the wine Spanish?' she asked.

'Portuguese. In Spain they drink mostly red.' It was rough stuff, the wine she remembered from Spain. But no doubt the land-owning class would have imbibed a wine far superior to any she had tasted. 'And the Blue Nun is German.'

'I daresay you'd like a stout,' Jack said, addressing Father. 'Can't beat good old Mackeson's.' He opened a bottle and filled a glass for Father before pouring one for himself.

'Milk stout. I used to drink that when I was nursing my babies,' Prue said. 'The midwife recommended it.'

The ghost of a memory – no more than a faint echo – swam into Rose's mind: the tingling sensation in her breasts as they swelled with milk for Blanca. She turned away in case the pain showed. It must be the approaching menopause making her more emotional than usual.

Dorothy and Archie came over. 'You must be very proud of Frank,' Rose said as Jack poured wine for them. Her godson had recently been appointed assistant registrar of births, marriages and deaths for the local Council.

'Oh we are,' Dorothy said. 'He's done awfully well to get the job at his age.'

Rose looked around at the guests eating and drinking and talking nineteen to the dozen, all these people who had gathered here to celebrate her birthday. They had known her at different stages of her life. Whom did they see, she wondered? The happily married, middle-aged woman she was now? The impetuous, determined vicar's daughter who had set out for Spain in 1936, filled with her father's humanitarian ideals? The young nurse having to deal with all the carnage of war? Not one of them would see in her the armed guerrilla, a woman who had sacrificed safety and chosen instead to live a wild existence in the *sierra* with her lover, had seen him die, given birth to his baby, been faced with the tragedy of losing her too… Even her family knew only half the story. And Jack, though he had heard it all, had never known the wayward, youthful Rose. Yet these disparate identities were all part of her, had made her what she was. Nobody passing her in the street would guess her history. Sometimes she could scarcely believe it herself. There must be others too with unorthodox stories concealed behind seemingly ordinary lives. Perhaps she was not so unusual.

The lights were suddenly dimmed. Rose noticed that the band had taken up their positions on stage again. Prue's cake, decorated with fondant roses and the words *Rose 50* in pink icing, was placed in front of her.

'Are you ready?' Jack asked as he lit the five candles. She was given no time to answer. The band struck up and a swell of voices sang out in chorus.

Happy birthday to you, Happy birthday to you…

'It's been quite a year, hasn't it?' Jack said on December 31st as they sat together on the settee, waiting for Big Ben to chime midnight. Having had a houseful over Christmas, they were now on their own again, preparing to celebrate the arrival of 1966 with a glass of Asti Spumante and their usual bedtime snack of cheese and biscuits.

Rose nodded. The lump in her throat prevented her speaking. A year of family gatherings. Her fiftieth had been followed by a funeral, a retirement bash, a wedding… Jack's retirement and his son Lenny's marriage had been happy occasions but the loss of Father just a month after her birthday had cast a dark cloud over everything. Pneumonia on the heels of a bout of flu had proved fatal. During his last days, she'd been with him as much as the hospital would allow. Distraught, she had watched helplessly as the fever raged, knowing all too well that he lacked the strength to survive the infection.

She tried not to dwell on her loss, reasoning with herself that he'd been old, that his life had been happy on the whole, that it was normal at her age to lose one's parents. But the tears still welled up, often at inappropriate moments. He had always been there for her. She could hear in her head his wise, measured words, his kindly voice. It was hard to accept she would never hear it again. Jack was sympathetic, always ready to listen, but she felt he didn't really understand. His own father had died when he was very young and left him with few if any memories. How could she put into words Father's importance to her, what his loss meant?

'Don't be sad,' he said now, putting an arm round her.

'I'm sorry. It's hard… We were very close.'

'I know. And your father was an exceptional man. I admired him greatly.' Jack paused and bowed his head. 'You see, Rose, I didn't have a father.'

'You mean you don't remember him.'

'No, I mean… Oh darling, I should have told you this before but…' His eyes were averted as if in shame. 'I'm illegitimate.'

'Jack…' She took his hands and forced him to look directly at her. 'Do you really think that makes any difference to me? After all I told you about my past?'

She was shocked – not by his revelation but by the fact that after seven years of marriage, he could still surprise her, still have secrets. Why had he waited till now to tell her the truth? 'You didn't trust me,' she said. It came out too much like an accusation.

'You don't understand. It's not something I talk about, not to anyone. Lilian knew, but we managed to keep it from her family. We were social outcasts, my mother and I. Her family cut her off. We had to rely on charity and the pittance she earned from taking in people's washing. The shame, my mother's shame… It was scandalous in my village to be born out of wedlock. Reason doesn't come into it. When you've lived with that kind of shame, it's not so easy to free yourself from it.'

'My poor Jack.' She cradled his head against her chest, stroked the smooth skin of his scalp, the strands of thin hair that remained. Seeping through her blouse, she felt the dampness of tears – for once not her own.

When he raised his head some minutes later, it was to ask, 'Did you hear Big Ben? I didn't, but I've a feeling it must be 1966.'

'No,' Rose said in surprise. 'Really? I can't believe we missed it. And we must have missed *Auld Lang Syne* too.' She laughed and kissed him. 'Oh Jack, pick up your glass and let's drink to the New Year. To the future.'

CHAPTER 34

Oxford, 1969

Rose leaned back in her chair and observed Helen across the restaurant table. She had dressed for the occasion in a close-fitting mini-dress; her straight hair was neatly turned under at the ends – kept in place by hairspray, Rose guessed, knowing how wayward it had always been, just like her own.

'So what's more exciting?' she asked, when they had ordered and the waiter had poured them each a glass of wine. 'Your engagement or qualifying as a teacher?'

'Oh, that's an unfair question, Aunt Rose!'

'I'm sorry, I was teasing. It's a bad habit of mine.' Happiness could make the plainest of faces beautiful, she thought. Not that Helen was plain, but today she had that singular radiance bestowed by love. Even a stranger would detect it. 'Let me see your ring.' Helen held out her hand for Rose to admire the small diamond set between rubies. 'And do you have a wedding date in mind?'

'Maybe next summer, after Mike finishes his training.'

'So he'll stay in Sheffield till then, and what about you?'

'It all depends. I've been applying for jobs in the city, but with no luck so far. There are just too many of us history graduates in search of teaching posts.'

Rose would have liked someone in the family to follow her into nursing but none of her nieces or nephews were interested. Susan had opted to leave school at sixteen and go straight into secretarial work.

She raised her glass. '¡Salud! To your success in finding a job up north.'

'I've been meaning to ask you,' Helen said a few minutes later as she dipped into her prawn cocktail. 'You've never told me much about your experiences in Spain. One of our modern history lecturers had a particular interest in the Spanish Civil War. I think his older brother went out there – not to fight but as a journalist. Anyway, he used to talk about it quite often, about it being a prelude to the Second World War because many people on the left, especially those who joined the International Brigades, saw it as a fight against fascism in Europe.'

'My goodness, does it already count as history? Makes me feel old.' With any other member of the family, Rose would have found a way to change the subject. She took a sip of wine. Helen's lively, intelligent eyes were on her, expectant initially, then apprehensive in case she had touched on too sensitive a topic.

'Officially, our course only took us up to the First World War. But you know, sometimes the discussion would go deeper into politics or the lecturers would suggest further reading about the inter-war period.'

'What did you want to ask?'

'You must have been about the same age as me when you went,' Helen said. 'And I've been trying to imagine… Weren't you scared? I don't think I'd have had the guts to risk my life like you did.'

'Of course I was scared. War is terrifying – not just for those directly involved in the fighting but for the civilian population too. I'd hoped we were finished with wars – and perhaps we are in Europe – but now there's Vietnam. When I see the reports, the pictures, it brings back all the obscenity of it.'

'My mum knew a couple of Spanish refugee families; they'd settled in her village. There were thousands, weren't there, who fled to France when the Nationalists won. Anyway, these particular ones are still there, waiting to see what happens when Franco dies, whether it'll be safe to go back. They still think of themselves as Spanish. I was talking to one girl about my age – it was last year when we went to visit *grand-mère* – and she said they speak Spanish at home and eat Spanish food, yet she and her sister have never set foot in Spain. Her father was telling me about the concentration camp at Argelès-sur-Mer and how dreadfully the refugees were treated. Loads died of starvation or from the cold or they were worked to death. Mum said when she heard about what went on, it made her ashamed to be French.'

'Some managed to get on a boat to Mexico,' Rose said. 'They were the lucky ones.' She thought of Margaret, who had worked with

Spanish medics in one of the French camps until the Quakers got her out. 'It was dreadful, the end of the war after the Republican defeat. A disaster.' She sank her head in her hands. This wasn't the conversation she had anticipated for such a happy occasion.

'I'm sorry,' Helen said. 'It must be upsetting for you to remember.'

'There's no need to apologise. It's a very long time ago. You wouldn't think that after thirty years…' She raised her head and looked directly at her niece. 'The thing is, Helen, I faced some very difficult experiences, personal calamities that…' She noticed the waiter approaching. 'Oh, I think this is for us. Look, let's enjoy our meal and talk about something more cheerful, shall we?'

The arrival of their roast duck and vegetables put conversation on hold for a while as they tucked in.

'Right, now I want to hear all about Mike,' Rose said, putting aside her knife and fork for a moment. 'And I'd love to see a photo? I'm sure you must have one hidden away in your bag.' Helen's cheeks flushed pink. 'You can show it to me later, when we've finished eating. If you want to,' she added in case Helen should think her a bully. 'In any case, I have it on good authority from your mother that he's very nice-looking.'

Rose speared a piece of potato and popped it into her mouth. In England after the war, when so many women had lost their husbands or fiancés, she seemed to be the only one with not a single photo to treasure – of Miguel or of their baby. Would photos have helped? Probably not.

'So what else did Mum say about him?' Helen asked.

'Ah, that would be telling.'

Bertie and Prue's house was always noisy when the children were around. If it wasn't Peter practising on his electric guitar, it was the radio or the record player blasting out pop music. Rose could hear loud music in the background now as she and Prue attempted a conversation on the telephone.

'Turn it down!' Prue shouted. 'Sorry Rose, I wasn't talking to you.'

'I don't know how you stand it,' Rose said. 'Doesn't it give you a headache?'

'Sometimes. When I'm tired it drives me mad. You know, I think teenagers are more difficult to cope with than small children. Now Susan is planning a holiday in Spain with her friends and to be honest, neither Bert nor I are very happy about it. I wanted to ask your advice, Rose. It's one of those package holidays that seem so popular now.'

Franco's brutal dictatorship, a repressed society dominated by the all-powerful Catholic Church… For Rose, what came to mind at the mention of Spain had nothing to do with beaches and *sangría*, with package holidays on the Costa Brava. Spain under Franco made her shiver. Prue, of course, would have different concerns.

'She's nearly twenty, Prue. And she seems a responsible girl.'

'She is usually sensible, but when she gets together with her friends… Well, you know how it is. They say the drinks are very cheap and then the promiscuity… I don't want her to come back from Spain pregnant.'

'No.' Even had Prue been present in the room, she would not have guessed the reason for Rose's wry tone, her ironic half-smile. 'There's always the pill,' she said, 'if you're really worried. But I'm sure she wouldn't be so silly as to get into that kind of trouble.' Unlike her aunt. 'Where exactly is she planning to go?'

'I forget the names… Oh yes, Benidorm was one resort she mentioned. And there was another more to the south. I don't think they've quite decided yet.'

'I'll have a word if you think it would help. But in my opinion, you'll just have to swallow hard and trust to her good sense. What else can you do? She's an adult.'

'That's true, Rose. And she's saved up her wages to pay for it. Bert still thinks of her as his little girl – or so Susan complains – but you're right, there's nothing we can do.'

'Here,' Jack said, handing Rose a postcard. 'It arrived this morning, from Susan.'

The picture, slightly out of focus, showed a sandy beach with rows of thatched umbrellas, bordered by a lurid blue sea. Hotels and tall apartment blocks rose up behind, some still under construction with cranes in view. Rose turned the card over to find the location. Fuengirola, Málaga. The name didn't ring a bell. She reached for her glasses to read what Susan had written. *Dear Aunt Rose, We're having a smashing time here. It's very hot so we spend all day on the beach, in and out of the sea. There are parties and discos every night. Spain is fab.*

'I don't recognise it,' she said to Jack. 'It's not the Spain I recall.'

'Remember, this country has changed too,' he said gently.

'I know, but with Franco still in charge, even if he is old and frail... How much can it really have changed?'

'He'll want to encourage tourism,' Jack said. 'It must be good for the economy. A lot of people are going now they have these package holidays. It's not so expensive. My old workmate Ron took his family. And Lenny was talking about a holiday in Majorca next summer.'

Rose recollected Jack's offer to accompany her to Spain. Her old colleague Lilian Urmston had been back several times – to the same areas she'd worked in as a nurse. She had met people who still remembered her.

'If you change your mind about going,' Jack said, placing his hands on her shoulders and looking her in the eye, 'I'm still willing. It's up to you of course, but think about it, Rose. You never know. It might help.'

A sigh escaped her. 'I'll give it some thought,' she said.

CHAPTER 35

Oxford, 1972

Rose stood at the greengrocer's, eyeing the bright displays of oranges and lemons.

'Where are these from, Jim?' she asked.

'Cheer you up, don't they, dear.' The woman behind her in the queue pulled off her plastic rain hood. 'With all this wet weather, a bit of colour is just what we need.'

Always ready to entertain his customers, Jim picked up an orange in each hand and juggled them in the air a couple of times. He pointed to the box. 'Valencia, it says here. That's in Spain, if I'm not mistaken.'

Rose held out her shopping basket. 'I'll have two lemons and half a dozen of the large oranges.' It was late February, the winter dragging on with no sign of a let-up. She was missing the sun. In Spain, she remembered, people kept their tiny windows shuttered to protect themselves from its glare and heat, but they also lived most of their lives outdoors.

'Will these do, love?' The greengrocer held out two plump lemons.

Rose nodded. She saw in her head the dark, glossy leaves and ripe fruit of a lemon grove in Murcia, smelled their citrus scent and felt against the back of her legs the rough wool of a hospital blanket. Miguel was leaning over her, his fingers caressing her face. She closed her eyes for a moment, savouring the memories.

'Six oranges, was it?' The day, not long after, when they'd made love for the first time, lying on the ground behind the ruined *cortijo*… That day they had fed each other segments of orange. She remembered the stickiness of the juice dripping over her hands and how Miguel had licked it off, his tongue probing between each finger.

'Anything else, my lovely?'

'Oh sorry, I was miles away.' Rose hauled herself back to the present and surveyed the vegetables on display. 'A pound of carrots please, and a cauliflower.'

The travel agent's was just round the corner. She had passed it many times without giving more than a cursory glance to its colourful displays featuring seafront hotels and bronzed bodies soaking up sunshine in exotic locations. It wouldn't hurt to pick up a few brochures.

The clock on the mantelpiece chimed three. Early afternoon yet the remaining light was scarcely enough to see by. Rose switched on a lamp and sat down again next to her husband. Rain lashed the windowpanes, a patter of rapid drumbeats. Inside, the glass had misted over, obscuring completely their view of the garden. Half a dozen brochures lay open on the coffee table in front of them. She swept them up into a pile.

'Jack, you do understand, don't you? It isn't about this. I'm not interested in lying on a beach all day, let alone by a hotel pool.'

'Rose dear, I'm leaving it entirely up to you. I've reached the age of seventy without ever leaving this country. I'm a novice, I don't speak the lingo; whatever we do will be new to me. You're the boss.'

'I want to find her grave, Jack. If I could just go to the grave, say my goodbyes… They must know at the hospital, there must be a place where the babies are buried.'

'It's a long time, darling. Over thirty years.'

'I know, but there'll be records. There was a death certificate.' She took a brochure from the pile and opened it at random. 'We could book a two-week package to one of these resorts near Málaga. We don't have to stay at the hotel the whole time. There'll be buses. We could travel to Granada and then on to Jaén. Maybe the agent can find out about public transport.'

'Or we could hire a car. How far is it?' His eyes narrowed and he tilted his head upwards, chin on fist, his usual thinking pose. 'Mind you, I'd not be too happy driving on the right.'

'The roads will have improved. Still, a few hours, I'd imagine.' Rose fell silent, pondering whether to tell Jack of her other plan. If finding Blanca's grave promised to be difficult, finding Miguel's would be next to impossible. For so many years she had lived with the ache of separation, of leaving him to die alone. Images of his body abandoned on the hillside to rot or perhaps dragged off to some communal pit still haunted her dreams. Now she thought, as she had often since that day, about his family, spared those images but suffering in equal measure from their ignorance of his fate, beyond the simple fact of death.

She had considered trying to contact them after her return to England in 1939, but with Franco intent on exterminating all those of Republican persuasion, she'd feared a letter might endanger them. Now, assuming they had survived, she would not be putting them at any risk, surely? Although their first names eluded her, she still remembered Miguel's full name. Their village was small. A letter with the family *apellidos*, Velasco Robles, addressed to Cañar, province of Granada, would be sure to find them. His mother had been illiterate like so many others at that time, but he had brothers and sisters. Some at least were likely to have remained in the village.

Should she write or would it be selfish to reveal to them the traumatic circumstances of his death, opening not only her own wounds but theirs too? How would she and Jack be received if they turned up in Cañar? Would they be able to locate the family? How many of his kin were numbered among the Republicans imprisoned or executed by Franco?

'Jack,' she said, 'there's somewhere else I'd like to go. I know this is asking a lot of you but... will you come with me to Miguel's village?'

The night before their trip, neither Rose nor Jack could sleep. Their cases were packed, their new navy blue passports, air tickets and cardboard wallets of peseta notes laid out ready on the hall table.

'You're quite sure about this?' Jack asked in a whisper. 'I'm worried in case... There may be disappointments, Rose. I just want you to be prepared.'

'Go to sleep, darling. Don't fret about me; I'm expecting to be disappointed.' She might feel differently if the hospital had replied to her letter or if she'd heard from Miguel's family. There'd been nothing.

'I don't even know if my letters arrived – or if they did, whether my rusty Spanish made any sense to them. I'm steeled for...'

She noticed the change in Jack's breathing and was glad he had finally drifted off. Tomorrow would be a long day. For her, sleep was a lost cause. She slipped out of bed and padded downstairs to the kitchen. Sitting at the table with a cup of tea still too hot to drink, she asked herself why on earth she was dragging her husband on this wild goose chase. What exactly was she hoping for? Dredging up the past could only end in distress, to herself and others. Rather than face inevitable failure, they should simply relax on the beach for a fortnight like the other package tourists. Sun, sand and sea, why not? As soon as Jack woke, she would tell him.

A rep from the travel company met them at the airport. 'Welcome to sunny Spain,' she said. They were joined by two women – sisters, Rose guessed – and led outside to a waiting minibus. 'I'm going to leave you in the care of José,' the rep said. 'He'll take you to the hotel and my colleague Mandy will sort you out there.'

Even before they got into the bus, Rose could hear the driver's radio belting out a song. *Te quiero, te quiero, te quiero, y hasta el fin te querré.* He lowered the volume and jumped out to stow their suitcases in the back. 'Niño Bravo,' he said, nodding his head in time to the rhythm as they settled into their seats. 'You like?'

Rose gazed out of the window as they drove west from the airport. On their right, beyond a swathe of sandy beach, the sea, sunlight dancing on a gently rippled surface; palm trees lining the road. On their left a string of bars with tables outside, small shops, a garage. Tourists in shorts and skimpy tops sauntered across the road in front of them; local women in black, over-dressed for the heat, emerged from the shops carrying bread or groceries, while their menfolk, in short-sleeved shirts, sat in the shade of a bar veranda, playing dominoes.

'Torremolinos first time, yes?' José twisted round and grinned at them.

'It's our first time abroad,' the woman said. She turned to Rose and held out her hand. 'I'm Doreen, by the way. You don't know what to expect, do you. I've brought teabags, just in case. My daughter-in-law said the tea was awful here. Is it your first time too?'

'I was in Spain in the 1930s,' Rose said, 'but it's new to my husband.'

'You should have warned me about the tea,' Jack said. His mouth was twitching with amusement. 'I might have to make do with beer.' He pointed to a road-sign. 'It looks as if we've arrived.'

They were approaching a line of hotels strung out along the beachfront. Doreen nudged her companion. 'Golly, Jen, look at that beach! I can't wait to get down there.'

Rose stole a glance at Jack. His eyes had followed Doreen's gaze but his expression was neutral. He had agreed to her overnight change of plan without comment this morning. Now he would tease her, smile at her contrary impulses. It didn't matter. The soft velvety air, the intense blue of the sky, the not so distant mountains were striking a chord in her, awakening echoes impossible to ignore. She said nothing but her mind was busy with plans.

'We want to go to Jaén,' she told Mandy as soon as they had checked in. 'Are there buses from Málaga, do you know?'

'Where?' Mandy stared blankly at her. 'Is that further up the coast then?'

'It's north of Granada?'

'Oh I know you can get to Granada. A couple of our guests have been to see those Moorish palaces. I'm not sure they took a bus though. I'll have a word with the manager when he comes in later this afternoon.'

On the balcony of their room, they stood side by side in silence, each absorbed in their own thoughts. Rose looked out at the sea and the sweep of mountains following the far curve of the coastline.

'We could check out the beach if you like,' Jack said, putting an arm round her waist. 'While we wait for word from the manager.'

She nodded. 'I'll just unpack a few things first.' She felt restless, impatient to embark on her quest.

'Try to relax,' Jack said. 'There's nothing we can do today. A dip in the sea and a little lie-down under one of those beach umbrellas will be just the ticket.'

'You're right, as always. We should rest after the journey.' Jack rarely admitted to being tired but at seventy, he had less energy than at sixty. *She* had noticed even if he had not.

'And we must buy you a hat,' she said. 'Or your poor head will fry.'

'My brother take you to Granada OK? Monday he go. Then you take bus, Granada, Jaén. I tell him OK?'

'Monday? That's the day after tomorrow,' Jack said, half to himself. 'How much would he charge?'

'Good price and much faster than bus. He come to hotel early, seven o'clock.'

'OK,' Rose said. '*Perfecto.*'

The manager passed the back of his hand across his brow in an exaggerated gesture. 'Granada very hot. *¡Agosto uf!*'

Rose switched to Spanish. Already the words were coming back to her, more easily than expected. Were there regular buses to Jaén? How big was the city? Did he know of any hotels there?

There was a *parador*, he told her, situated in a 13th century castle on a hilltop. '*Vistas magníficas,*' he said, spreading his hands. And they must see the Renaissance cathedral, also magnificent and very close.

'Splendid,' Rose said. 'Tell your brother yes. We'll be ready at seven.'

CHAPTER 36

Jaén/Granada/Cañar, 1972

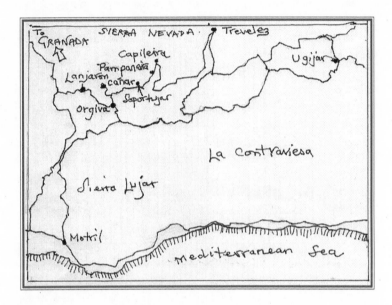

The receptionist at the *parador* eyed Rose with alarm when she asked about hospitals. 'You are sick? You need doctor?'

'No no, I'm fine. I'm a nurse.' Ignoring his puzzled look, she continued to question him. 'How many hospitals in the city?' She pointed to a street map on the desk. 'Can you show me where they are?' It may have been knocked down, replaced perhaps by a more functional building. If it still existed, would she recognise it?

He squinted at the map. 'Hospital San Juan de Dios here, La Santa Misericordia...'

Of course, they would all be named after saints, associated with religious orders. They would all, even now, be staffed by nuns. A sudden dizziness came over her, a fear she might faint. She clutched at Jack's arm and concentrated on the map in an effort to banish the memories.

'And this one, this is military hospital. Here ancient hospital of San Antonio de Padua.' He looked up. 'Many fine buildings in our city. Cathedral with famous relic of the Holy Face...'

'We could probably visit them all in a day,' Jack said over breakfast in the Arab-style dining room. 'They're not so very far apart.'

They had arrived the evening before, too exhausted by the heat and the long road journey to do more than briefly admire the spectacular hilltop location, take a much-needed shower and collapse into bed. Jaén was olive country. Once they left Granada, they had seen little else from the windows of the bus – just miles and miles of olive-covered hillsides, interspersed with the occasional small factory or mill where the olives were pressed. In the villages, some of the houses had mules tethered outside; chickens pecked in the dust; pigs – one per dwelling – were commonplace. Despite the lack of variation in the landscape, Jack had been riveted by the unfolding vistas as they wound their way towards Jaén. Only for the last hour had he fallen into a doze.

'If you'd told me I'd one day sleep in a castle,' he had muttered drowsily as the taxi stopped outside the *parador*, 'I'd not have believed you. Not in a month of Sundays.'

'That's it, that's the one.' She had no memory of the exterior, had barely noticed it at the time, but now with its forbidding stone facade in front of her, she knew immediately. Images of the interior ran through her mind like old black and white film clips. Were they true or merely imagined, the backdrop of innumerable nightmares?

'Rose darling, you're trembling.' Jack pulled her closer. 'Remember I'm here with you,' he whispered. 'You can't lose your nerve now we've got this far. Shall I ring the bell?'

The sister who opened the door to them was young, serious but not unfriendly. 'I'll take you to Sister Marta in the office,' she said when Rose explained why they were there.

Speaking through a grille in the wall, Rose re-stated her 'business' to the unsmiling older nun facing her. They were not invited into the office. When Rose asked for a seat for her husband, Sister Marta pointed to a bench in the corridor. 'He can sit there. Now, 1939 you say? You gave birth here in 1939?' She frowned. 'Date? Your name? The father's name?'

'You don't need the father's name' Rose said. 'Look for my name: Tilly.' She spoke firmly but her hands were shaking; she could hardly breathe.

'And the child, was it named?' Her voice was cold with reproof.

'Blanca.' She returned Sister Marta's stare, determined not to blink.

The nun walked over to a large wooden cupboard. Peering through the grille, Rose saw her open a drawer, pull out a stack of files and flick through them, giving a cursory glance to each.

'There's no record,' she said, returning to her seat at the grille. 'You must be mistaken. Now I have work to do.' She gestured towards the door.

'There was a death certificate. I saw it. Tell me where my daughter is buried.'

Hearing her raised voice, Jack came over and stood by her side. 'Rose...'

'I want to see her grave. You must know where...'

'I'm sorry, I can't help you. We have no record of your admission or of a birth in that name. This is a hospital; our duty is to our patients.'

'Come on Jack, we're going.' Rose turned and walked away, fighting to control her anger and disappointment.

'Wait. You could try the cemetery.'

'Where? Give me directions.' Rose stopped and retraced her steps.

'San Eufrasio. On the Granada road.'

Once outside, she collapsed into Jack's arms. 'I couldn't have done this without you,' she said.

'But I didn't do anything,' he protested. 'And I didn't understand a word of the conversation.'

'You were there.'

'So what now?' Jack mopped his forehead. 'I take it she wasn't over-helpful.'

'The cemetery. It's out of town, I think. Look, shall we find some shade before we both melt?' She pointed to a line of trees on the other side of the road.

Jack glanced at his watch. 'Why don't we find a café first? Have a cold drink and maybe a bite of lunch. Then we'll take a taxi to the cemetery. We certainly can't walk in these temperatures. It must be well over a hundred.'

'Oh Jack, I'm sorry. Dragging you round the streets like this when you could have been relaxing on the beach, cooling off in the sea every half hour...'

'Just give me a cold beer and I'll be happy.'

'It's a deal.'

'Are those...?'

'Yes.' Rose had forgotten how Spanish cemeteries often stacked their dead vertically in compartments rather than burying them in the ground. She scanned the rows of sealed chambers and imagined the body of her precious infant shut in one of them. It took all her powers of self-restraint not to scream.

'Chin up, darling.' Jack was regarding her with concern. 'There doesn't seem to be anyone about.'

She closed her eyes, focused on her breathing. *Don't be stupid*, she berated herself. Those niches, some with engraved tombstones and vases of flowers, were for the well-off. Ridiculous to imagine Blanca being granted such a space. She would have been thrown into a common pit. *Don't think about it. You should never have come.*

'Let's go, Jack. Now.' She pulled at his arm. 'It was a bad idea, I'm sorry.'

'There's someone coming.' A man was unlocking a door in what must be the administrative building opposite. She turned to look and at the same moment felt Jack's body convulse, the prelude to an explosive sneeze, followed immediately by another.

'Bless... Oh, we've been noticed.'

'Can I help you?' Alerted to their presence by Jack's sneezes, the official was now approaching them.

'Courage, my dear.' He squeezed her hand then let it go as the man reached them and repeated his question.

'I'm looking for my daughter's grave. She died in 1939 in the town hospital.' Her voice scarcely wavered.

'Come into my office.' The same questions: dates, names, civil status. The same dusty files with their thin sheets of yellowing paper, their barely legible scrawls in black ink, now much faded. On the wall behind the desk, a framed photo of Franco – arrogant, smug, invincible – looked down on them.

'I can't find anyone of that name in our records. Was she baptised?'

'There was no time.'

He rose to his feet and from the doorway, pointed to a plot of land over to the left. 'It's possible she is buried there, in the grave for atheists and apostates.'

'Don't you keep lists?'

'We do, of course. Your baby is not on the list.' He shrugged. 'You must understand, in those days there were sometimes mistakes or omissions. There were many deaths to record. Now we are more punctilious.' He held out a hand and added, 'I'm sorry to disappoint you. It was well before my time.'

Rose had known the chances were slim, but even so… It was as if Blanca had existed only in her imagination: a phantom baby. No one believed her; no one cared.

'We're on a fool's errand, Jack. Let's just go back to Torremolinos.'

'Rose, you're tired. We'll decide in the morning after a good night's sleep. In any case, I absolutely refuse to leave the *parador* without having a swim in that fabulous pool. When will I get another chance to float on my back in the water, surrounded by mountains, with eagles soaring overhead?'

Rose sighed. 'Alright, you've convinced me.'

Later, as they lay by the pool after a long, languid swim, Rose reached for Jack's hand. 'You always know what's best,' she said. 'I feel thoroughly revived.'

'I was just being selfish,' he replied. 'I've never been anywhere like this, never seen a sky so deeply, intensely blue. The mountains, the vegetation, it's all new to me. You know, I've seen films, read books set in the Mediterranean – in Greece, Italy, Spain, the south of France – but I could never really capture it with my senses. Now I know how it smells, how it feels to have the sun caressing my skin, the dusty dryness of the air in my lungs. I'm intoxicated by it all.'

'So you're not hankering after the beach?'

'Beaches aren't really my cup of tea,' Jack said. 'Give me the mountains any day. I think we should stick to the plan.'

Rose's stomach lurched as the bus turned into yet another bend. 'I hope we're nearly there,' she said. 'Many more of these curves and I'll be sick.'

Jack was staring out of the window, mesmerised by the mountains that loomed all around them, bluish in the late afternoon light. 'What's that? Oh, we must be fairly close, I should think. Did you say this village is a thousand metres up?'

Rose nodded. 'Miguel said it was often cut off in the winter. Can you imagine?' She gripped the seat in front as they swung round again. 'He loved his village. They all do, the Spaniards.' She closed her eyes and tried to shut out the sound of someone behind her vomiting.

'Isn't this where we get dropped?' Jack pointed to a sign by the roadside.

The driver pulled off the road and brought the bus to a halt. 'Soportujar,' he called to them. He pointed to a dirt road on their left. '*Cañar por allí. Cinco kilómetros.*'

'How many kilometres did he say?' Jack asked as they stood watching the bus pull out of sight round the next bend.

'Five. Don't worry, darling. There's bound to be a car or a farm vehicle soon. We could sit on that rock while we wait.' With Jack's knees giving him pain even on flat ground, she had ruled out walking.

'This feels like quite an adventure... Oh Rose, I'm sorry. I was forgetting for a moment. But I meant the journey.'

'It is an adventure. We're heading into the unknown. No place to stay, no idea if we'll even find Miguel's relatives.'

A lorry rumbled past them without stopping, then a battered Seat car. 'Perhaps we should have hired a vehicle and driven up ourselves,' Rose said. 'I'm going to stand here and stick out my thumb next time.'

A few vehicles drove past on the main road but none turned off. After twenty minutes, Rose was beginning to worry. A couple more hours and darkness would fall. At this height, even in August, temperatures would quickly drop; a night in the open without so much as a blanket could be dangerous. 'Let's start walking,' she said. 'We'll take it slowly.'

Five minutes up the track, a jeep-like vehicle overtook them and braked sharply, throwing up a cloud of loose stones and dust.

'Where are you going?' the driver shouted. 'Cañar? Jump in. If you don't mind the *cabritos* in the back.' The two baby goats were making quite a row. 'I've fetched them from a friend's *cortijo* lower down. They won't hurt you.'

'*No nos molestan nada.*'

'They're not bothering you? Good. So what's taking you to Cañar? We don't get many foreigners up here. Fewer still who speak Spanish.'

Rose took a deep breath. 'I'm looking for the family of an old friend. Perhaps you can help. The Velasco Robles family.'

The jeep swerved as their driver turned his head and stretched out a hand to Rose. '*¡Anda!* What a coincidence. Matilde Velasco is married to my brother, so we're all family. But how come you know them?'

'I'm a nurse. I was working here during the war.'

'*Ay*, that's a long time ago. You'll maybe not know then, their father Salvador was executed in '39. But Modesta is alive – eighty-six and still going strong. Of the children, Lourdes lives here in the *pueblo* with her mother, Herminia down in Órgiva. The *chicos*... unfortunately they didn't fare so well. Miguel was killed in the war and Juanma died in prison. Alfonso is the only one of the boys still alive. He moved away when he married. A girl from Sevilla. We don't see him much.' The names were familiar to Rose though she wouldn't have been able to recite them. Miguel had spoken often of his family. 'But tell me, which one did you know?'

'Miguel.'

'Miguel, he repeated. 'You were a friend of Miguel's? His mother will be... *¡Ay, fíjate!* You knew Miguel.' Rose could not see his expression, only the shake of his head from side to side in a slow recurrent motion. 'You must sleep in our house,' he said. 'And you're welcome to share our modest supper. Juliana, my wife will be delighted. And Matilde... They were very close, Miguel and Matilde. I'll ask her to come over.'

'That's really kind of you. I'm Rose and this is my husband Jack. He doesn't speak Spanish.'

'And I'm Agustín. *Encantado*.'

'Pleased to meet you too.' To Jack she whispered, 'He's invited us to stay. He knows Miguel's family.'

'Tomorrow you must visit Modesta. She has bad legs and hardly goes out these days but she's sharp as a pin. She'll be thrilled.'

Rose took Jack's arm as they trudged up the steep village street, trying to keep pace with the more nimble Agustín. She had already stumbled a couple of times on the rough, part-cobbled surface.

Jack winced. 'Can you ask him to slow down a bit?'

'These streets aren't designed for gammy knees,' she said after signalling to Agustín to wait. 'We must get you a stick, *pronto*. In fact I could do with one myself.'

'Here we are.' They had turned a corner onto a more level but even narrower street. Agustín held aside the bead curtain hanging across the doorway of his house. The door behind was already ajar. 'We live simply,' he said, following them in. 'But we'll do our best to make you feel at home. Juliana! We have visitors.'

The interior was dim and it took a few seconds for their eyes to adjust from the still golden evening light outside. 'It's nice and cool,' Jack said, wiping his forehead.

A television was flickering in one corner but no one seemed to be home. 'She must have popped round to Matilde's,' Agustín said. 'Sit down, make yourselves comfortable while I go and fetch them. I won't be a minute.'

'Is there a reason for the barred windows?' Jack asked when Agustín had gone. 'I've noticed all the houses have them.'

'I don't know, it's the custom.' Rose was busy taking stock of the room: the wide *chimenea* with an esparto basket beside it half-full of logs; the clay-tiled floor with a multi-coloured rag rug in front of the fireplace; the chestnut ceiling beams above. It all fitted Miguel's description of his home, as if little had changed in the intervening decades. Doubtless the houses were all similarly furnished; Modesta's would be no different.

'I don't believe it! After all these years.' A woman of about sixty, wearing a loose flowered dress, had appeared in the doorway. Rose stood as she approached them, arms outstretched for an embrace. 'You knew Miguel? I'm Matilde, his sister.'

'Rose, and this is my husband Jack.' The two women kissed and for a long moment Rose and Matilde stood, hands clasped, regarding each other. Rose noticed that she was not the only one with tears in her eyes. She searched for a likeness in Matilde's features, some tell-tale trait that would connect her with Miguel. What would he have looked like at sixty? Would his face have fleshed out to resemble that of his sister? Something about the mouth recalled Miguel's, though Matilde's lips were thinner. She gave up, unable to recast the images in her memory. She could picture him only as he was.

'Tell me, tell me everything.' Matilde sat down beside Rose.

Agustín, accompanied by his wife, had followed her in. 'First you must have a drink,' he said after introducing Juliana. 'This calls for a celebration. A glass of our local *vino de terreno*? It's a little rough if you're not used to it but it's all we have.'

'Do you like *morcilla*?' Juliana asked. 'From our own pig, last year's *matanza*.'

'Jack loves it.' Rose turned to her husband. 'It's black pudding, homemade.'

He smiled at Juliana. '*Gracias.*'

'I'll make a tortilla too and some tomato salad. Matilde, you must fetch José Antonio.'

Jack retired to bed soon after they had eaten but the rest of them talked late into the night, by the flickering light of oil lamps. As Rose suspected, Miguel's family knew nothing about how or where he had died.

'My mother has postcards he sent,' Matilde said. 'The last came in the autumn of '38. After that nothing, we never heard again. It broke my father's heart. What with that and two of his brothers fighting on the other side, for the rebels... But we weren't the only family divided by the war. *Ay, perdóneme.* You must excuse my tears. It's been such a long time not knowing. Our mother will be overjoyed: even bad news is better than none at all. Not having a body is the worst. It took her five years to accept he was dead.'

Seeing Agustín and Juliana's family portraits on the sideboard, it occurred to Rose that his family might have pictures of him, as a child or a young man. So often, especially in the early days, she had longed for some keepsake: a photo or other material reminder of her lover. 'Do you have any of Miguel?' she asked, pointing to the portraits of her hosts' family.

'Mamá has a few. Tomorrow I'll take you there, first thing. *Ay*, who would have thought?' Matilde rose from her chair and addressed her husband. '*Vámonos*, José Antonio, we must let our guest sleep.' To Rose, she said, 'I'll be back in the morning, sister. Come, an embrace.'

Modesta's house, the one where Miguel and his siblings had grown up, was in the centre of Cañar, close to the square with the stone fountain.

'Do the goats still stop to drink here?' Rose asked Matilde as they walked past the following morning.

'How on earth do you know about that?'

'Your brother described it to me in great detail. He missed his *pueblo* very much. In fact he promised to bring me one day, when the war was over.'

'Well, you have found your way alone,' Matilde said drily. 'Now, here we are, this is the house and look, Mamá is waiting for us at the door. I told Lourdes to warn her so that the shock wouldn't be too great.'

'*Mamá, aquí estamos,*' she called as they approached.

Miguel's mother, dressed in black like so many of the older women, was short and plump, her thinning grey hair neatly permed. Under her shapeless dress, her breasts, still large, hung down to her waist. They must once have been magnificent, Rose thought. Matilde had inherited her full figure; she was bosomy but still in good shape for her age.

'*¡Madre mía!* So this is the *inglesa*. Come in, come in.'

Another woman – Lourdes, she presumed – was standing in the shadow behind Modesta. The door opened straight into a living room furnished in much the same style as Agustín's. Modesta hobbled in, leaning on a stick, with Rose and Matilde following.

'Sit down, Mamá. You'll get tired.'

Modesta ignored her daughter and lifted her face up towards Rose. 'A kiss, *hija*. What is your name?'

'You can call me Rosa. I'm so happy to meet you.'

'And you've come all the way from England?' Modesta shook her head in wonder. 'Incredible. But you didn't come alone, surely?'

'No, I came with my husband. Agustín is taking him on a tour of the village.' Over Modesta's shoulder, Rose glimpsed Lourdes and had to stifle a gasp of recognition. Some idiosyncrasy caught in passing and impossible to pin down: a quizzical look, a tilt of the head, a slight lift of the eyebrows – she could not say which – recalled Miguel to a T.

'Come on, Mamá. Do sit down, and you too, Rosa. What will you think of us, leaving you standing?'

'Sit next to me here.' Modesta lowered herself onto the sofa and patted the space beside her. 'So, you were a nurse, Matilde tells me. He spoke of you, of an English girl. You remember, don't you, Lourdes. An English nurse. We were glad, I remember, that he'd found some happiness in that accursed war. Open the drawer, daughter; the *postales* are in there.'

Lourdes held up a wad of postcards and letters tied together with string.

'Yes, those are the ones. Read them to me, Lourdes.' Modesta was becoming agitated. 'All of them.'

Miguel wrote of the cold and the shortage of tobacco and soap but reassured his family he was in good health and that victory was close, the war would soon end. The cards were mostly addressed to his mother; he hoped his father or siblings would read them to her. On one, he wrote that he was teaching some of his comrades to read, that they even held classes in the trenches when it was quiet.

Lourdes passed them to Rose. One card portrayed a mother reading a letter, while in the background a militiaman with a rifle could be seen. Printed on it was the legend: *Your son is fighting for a humane and worthy cause. Be proud of him!* Seeing the carefully penned messages on the back, written in Miguel's own hand, brought a lump to her throat.

'This is the one,' Lourdes said, holding up a letter. 'The doctors and nurses are a marvel. In particular, there's a dear English nurse whom I hope to marry when the war is over, if she'll have me.' Lourdes looked up and her eyes were wet. 'It was the last,' she said. 'We waited for more, for some word from him or of him; even bad news would have been easier. There was nothing. But then it was the same for many families, even in this small village. People's loved ones disappeared without trace.'

'I was with him when he died.' Rose spoke quietly, fighting back her tears.

Modesta seized her hand. 'You were with him? What happened? Tell me, *hija*. Tell me it was a quick death, that he did not suffer.' Her gnarled hand gripped Rose's fingers. She seemed to be holding her breath.

'It was quick. A single shot from the *Guardia Civil*. He died instantly.' Modesta nodded and visibly relaxed. '*Ay*, I'm glad.'

Matilde stood behind her mother, a hand on her shoulder. 'We were forbidden to wear mourning,' she said. 'Only the victors were permitted to wear black for their dead.' The bitterness in her voice made it clear this gratuitous cruelty was still deeply felt. 'After the war, when my father was executed, we could not show our grief. The same when Juanma died in prison. We were obliged to dress as if we had suffered no loss.'

'Show her the card,' Modesta said. 'The card Juanma sent from Belchite.'

Lourdes rummaged in the drawer and pulled out a card stamped with a picture of Franco and the message *Arriba España, Saludo a Franco*. On the reverse, a swallow had been drawn in black ink. In its beak the bird carried a letter inscribed with the word *Madre*. 'He always had a gift for drawing,' his mother said. She was silent for a moment, nodding to herself, lost in memories of her sons perhaps.

Then, looking up, she asked, 'When was it? When did Miguel die? It was after the war, no?'

'September '39. We were in the *sierra* north of Granada, in the province of Jaén.'

'Didn't I tell you, Lourdes? I felt it: I knew something had happened to my son. I felt it here in my chest. A burning pain. You remember, don't you, *hija*? A few months after the Republic fell. Until then I never doubted Miguel was alive. A mother feels these things.' She turned to Rose. 'Do you have children?'

Rose shook her head. 'No.'

'Well, that is a pity.' Modesta's eyes, bright beads in that worn, heavily lined face, held Rose's. Had they detected the fleeting hesitation that preceded her reply? She was sharp, as Matilde had said. 'But you lived as man and wife, you and Miguel.' It was a statement rather than a question and its forthrightness took Rose by surprise. She flushed, relieved that no answer seemed to be required.

'There were many in the mountains here too. "The men of the *sierra*" we called them. They came down for food and supplies; some in the village risked their lives to help them.'

'And some lost their lives for doing so,' Lourdes added. 'The Army would shoot anyone who gave them food. Isn't that right, Mamá?'

'It's true. And in the end, some of the *maquis* were forced to hand themselves in. But there was a kind priest here in Cañar, remember him, Lourdes? If the reds went to him, he'd absolve them and tell the Army they'd repented. He persuaded them to give the men their freedom. They were the lucky ones; the majority were killed.'

She fell silent for a moment and Rose noticed the pain cross her face at the reminder of Miguel's fate. He would not have voluntarily handed himself in, she thought, nor repented to a priest, however kind.

'Those were cruel times after the war,' Matilde said. 'We lived in constant fear, especially after they came for Papá. One of our neighbours, Concha, was taken and spent twelve years in the Ventas jail in Madrid just because her husband had fought on the Republican side. She was pregnant at the time and had a two year-old son. They took the boy too, but after a year the children were sent away, to some convent no doubt. When Concha came out, she went frantic trying to find them. Poor soul, the authorities refused to tell her anything. They said she was unfit to be a mother, that the children were contaminated with the 'red gene', or some such nonsense, and had to be re-educated. There was nothing she could do. She died soon after – of a broken heart, it was said.'

'It's true, the fear was always present. And on top of that, the hunger. *Ay Dios*, the struggle to put food on the table. Many a day we went to bed hungry.' Modesta placed a hand on Rose's knee. 'You see, my dear, we'd been unable to cultivate the land during the war and then with the drought... We'd be scouring the countryside for herbs, for fennel. *Salvavidas* they called it, the life-saver.'

'Burnt because there was no oil to fry it.' Matilde wrinkled her nose. 'And dry bread or *gachas* made with maize flour.'

'On good days I'd make a fennel stew with a little potato or spinach if I could get it, maybe a small onion.' Modesta paused and her face brightened. 'Well, life is much better now: we work the land and can live well off it.'

'Mamá, Rose would like to see the photos of Miguel.'

'Of course. You know where they are, Matilde.'

'These are all we have.'

Rose held the three pictures and gazed at each in turn. The first, its edges tattered from much fingering, had been taken in the doorway of their house with his two older brothers. He looked about five, solemn-faced in short trousers held up with braces. The second, a group photo, pictured the pupils at Cañar's school with their schoolmaster.

'He fled when the rebels took Granada,' Modesta said. 'Just as well. Hundreds of teachers were executed during or after the war. Who knows where he went? Or whether he survived? That's Miguel in the second row. Nine or ten he'd have been. Lourdes is standing at the back, see? The two older boys were out working on the land. Herminia didn't go that day either and Matilde was still too young.' The photo had faded and Rose could barely make out Miguel's face.

Disappointed, she turned to the third picture and a tumult of emotion welled up in her. There was her lover, instantly recognisable, posing with two comrades in the trenches. The hope in his face almost broke her heart. She was transported back to that other life so long ago. Everything looked familiar: the uniform, the rifle slung by a strap across one shoulder, the roughness of the stone wall behind the men. She noticed the trembling of her fingers as they held the photo.

'He sent it to us in '36,' his mother said. 'We should not worry; the rebels would soon be defeated. That's what he told us and here we are now, still under the yoke of Franco.' The bitterness in her voice did not surprise Rose: she had lost a husband and two of her three sons.

Finding no words, she turned towards Modesta and embraced her silently.

'*Bueno*. I'm glad you came,' the old woman said finally. 'Now at least we have some idea where his body rests. You should stay for the grape harvest, Rosa. September 14th we celebrate our *fiesta*. The Cañar wine is very good.'

Rose smiled and shook her head. 'Thank you, but we can't stay so long.' A thought struck her. 'Did you receive my letter? I wrote some weeks ago but without knowing the name of the street…'

Modesta looked questioningly at her daughters.

'No,' Lourdes replied. 'We had no letters. But now I'll write down the address for you.'

Matilde jumped to her feet. 'We must take a photo of Rosa to show the rest of the family. I'll get my camera.' They took several – of Rose with Modesta, Rose with the two sisters, Rose alone. 'I'll get copies made and send them to you.'

After parting with tears and kisses and promises to stay in touch, they returned to Agustín's house to find Jack. 'After lunch my husband will take you to Soportujar for the bus,' Matilde said.

'That's very kind. We're going to stay in Granada tonight.'

They arrived at the Hotel Trinidad, on the edge of a leafy square, in the early evening. Rose still felt slightly nauseous after their tortuous three-hour bus journey.

'So you'll be wanting to visit our magnificent Alhambra palace,' the manager said, welcoming them with a beaming smile. He had rounded shoulders and he reminded Rose of an owl, probably because he had no visible neck: his head was sunk forward into his chest.

'Tomorrow.' She needed time to absorb the events of the last two days; to recover from the turbulent feelings they had aroused.

'*Muy bien*. If you need any information in the morning, our deputy manager, Enrique will be delighted to help you.'

PART 8 CONSUELO, 1972 - 1975

CHAPTER 37

Granada, 1972

At first Consuelo blamed her tiredness on the disruption of the move and the strain of adjusting to a new life in Granada. She had only just weaned Luisa and was not expecting to fall pregnant again so soon. It was only when her breasts began to swell and her skirt to pinch around the waist that she felt sufficiently convinced to share the good news with Enrique.

He was delighted. 'Five is better than four,' he said. 'We've plenty of room here and the rent is low. Besides, Pepe promised that if the business does well, he'll raise my pay after a year.'

Consuelo liked Enrique's boss, Pepe. The staff called him *el buho*, the owl. She could see why. He was short, with a round face and beaky nose, and if he had a neck at all, it was hidden, tucked under his hunched shoulders. He always greeted her with a smile and fussed over the children; he would surely reward Enrique for his dedication to the job. Perhaps now was a good moment to broach the idea she had been mulling over for some time.

'It's hard work with all the little ones and our families so far away,' she said. 'Do you think we might hire a girl to help in the house?' It felt like an admission of failure.

Enrique frowned. 'Belén is growing up. She could help more with the younger ones, don't you think? Besides, it's much easier here, with the shops and school so close, the automatic washing machine...'

Consuelo looked away, trying to hide her disappointment.

'*Bueno*, it's true we don't get much help from the family. I'll think it over, Chelo. Alright?'

She suspected he would rather spend the money on a television. He loved watching football, especially when Real Madrid were playing. Sometimes he came home very late, explaining that he'd been watching an important match in a bar or at the hotel. It might be better if he could watch at home. She never questioned him when he was late, preferring not to know if he patronised the *casas de putas* used by so many men, married or not. It was 'normal', people said, for men to satisfy their needs outside marriage from time to time. All the same, she hoped Enrique found enough satisfaction in their conjugal relations not to be tempted by these fallen women.

It bothered her that she often felt too tired at night to respond to her husband's embraces. She rarely rejected them but knew he would prefer her to show more enthusiasm. There were occasions when she enjoyed the act. When she was feeling relaxed and reasonably confident none of the children would wake. And if she kept her eyes from the crucifix with its sorrowful, blood-stained Christ presiding in judgement on the wall above their marital bed. It made her uneasy, but taking it down would feel like sacrilege.

Their flat was on the fourth floor of a modern block in the Realejo district, where the rents were a little cheaper. The children delighted in the novelty of being whisked up and down in the lift, which was only just big enough to accommodate the family. Each day, after taking the two eldest to school, Consuelo would shop at the market in the square, where a cluster of stalls sold fresh produce and household goods at reasonable prices. Donkeys, their panniers filled with oranges and lemons, onions or potatoes, were tethered to trees or lamp-posts; fat gypsy women sat with their baskets of snails. The large ceramic bowls of soaked chickpeas and marinated olives reminded her of her girlhood when she'd watched – and sometimes helped – Ramona in the kitchen of the *cortijo*. Even Enrique had to admit that the bread sold by the little bakery on the corner rivalled his family's.

Theirs was a friendly *barrio*. She felt more comfortable with the women here than she had with their former neighbours in Torremolinos and was starting to make a few friends – mostly among the mothers she met each day when she fetched the children from school. Not that she had much time to devote to friendships. Her work seemed relentless: cleaning, shopping, cooking, doing the laundry and ironing, as well as seeing to the children, one or other of whom generally had some minor ailment. She was too busy to pay much attention to her pregnancy. Only with the first, with Belén, had she noticed every bodily change, thrilled at each flutter or ripple of movement in her womb.

Enrique's hours were irregular. When he had a day off, they would set out together on foot to explore the more interesting parts of Granada: the cathedral and the Plaza Bib-Rambla, the hill leading up to the Alhambra, the promenade of the Carrera de la Virgen. She loved to discover the hidden corners and *plazas* of their own neighbourhood. In the huge, sandy Campo del Príncipe with its massive plane trees, a marble statue of the crucified *Cristo de los Favores* dominated the square. Women, the great majority dressed in mourning black, paused to pray there; others stood in penitential attitudes before it.

As spring turned to summer and the evenings became warmer, they would occasionally pause in their evening *paseo* to eat and drink something at one of the small bars with tables outside. It saved her preparing a supper at home and the children liked to play in the square.

Her pains started one Sunday in July while they attended Mass in the church of Santo Domingo. The baby was expected any time; her first contraction came as no surprise. She whispered to Enrique, who picked Luisa up, and with the other children in tow, they left the church. Each baby had arrived with a little less warning. On the way home, they stopped at the telephone kiosk to let her mother and the midwife know. Mamá was planning to come by train from Antequera. It was an easy journey. Rafa and his *novia* had visited them by train several times, as had one or two of her old friends.

Most women gave birth in hospital now but Consuelo had dismissed that option. She'd given birth to all the others at home without any problems. Hospital was for the sick. Fortunately, there were still midwives willing to attend women in their own homes. Josefina, a cheerful, sturdily-built woman in her forties, arrived within an hour and quickly took charge. Unlike the last, this baby was in no hurry.

The pains came at intervals, then stopped for a couple of hours, then started again but still with ten-minute gaps between.

'You have a fine family,' Josefina said as they waited, 'and soon, there'll be one more to add to your happiness. Have you decided on a name?'

'Esteban if it's a boy, Nieves if it's a girl,' Consuelo answered without hesitation. Enrique had chosen the boy's name; she had chosen the girl's. María of the Snows, like *Blancanieves* in the fairy-tale. Snow-White.

Mamá arrived in the late afternoon by taxi from the station. The heat was still fierce, but indoors with the ceiling fan whirring at full speed and the shutters down, it was bearable. Enrique kept the children occupied and later, when the air cooled down a little, took them out to run around and play in the big square.

Every so often, Josefina put her ear trumpet to Consuelo's abdomen and listened. '*Todo bien,*' she declared each time. 'A nice strong heartbeat.'

It was almost dark by the time Enrique returned with the children. She kissed them all and Mamá helped her put them to bed. The pains were getting stronger and more frequent now. The waters broke, flooding down her legs in a hot rush. At last, it seemed, the baby was on its way. In the bedroom everything stood ready. Hot water and towels were on hand.

Her eyes closed in concentration as she tried to breathe through the pain. She felt the cold metal of the ear trumpet again. And then, opening her eyes, she saw the midwife's face.

'Come on now, start pushing.' But she felt no urge to push. 'Push! Push harder.'

Something wasn't right. That frown, the urgency in her voice. But the baby was coming now. She felt her skin tear as the head emerged.

'What's wrong?' Mamá's voice addressing Josefina.

She pushed again with all her might. Was it stuck? Why didn't it turn? She fought her exhaustion to bear down with what little strength remained and felt the baby being pulled out. She waited to hear its cry, but instead she heard the midwife's panicked voice. 'The scissors, quick!'

'*Ay Dios.*'

Consuelo screamed. The baby's face was blue, its lips far too dark. It was dead. She looked again and saw the cord knotted tight round its neck. 'No!' She shut her eyes tight, refusing to believe the terrible vision they had revealed. Enrique was shouting from the kitchen, asking should he come.

'There was nothing I could do to save her,' the midwife said.

A damp cloth was being pressed to her forehead, cooling her, smoothing the hair back from her face. She felt a hand take hers, caressing her fingers. She would not open her eyes. Someone was weeping. With a shock she realised it was Mamá. She had never heard Mamá weep.

Josefina spoke sharply. '*¡Vamos, cálmate!* Pull yourself together, you should be comforting your daughter.'

Consuelo turned her face to the pillow. The weeping stopped but now her ears picked up a different cry. One of the children had woken. It was not the cry she wanted to hear: the cry of a newborn. Enrique could go to Luisa. At this moment, all her love, all her yearning was focused on the infant whose lifeless form, though glimpsed so briefly, stayed etched in her mind.

She woke suddenly, her breasts tingling, a dull ache in her abdomen. The baby. There was no baby; her baby was dead. A chink of daylight through the door, left slightly ajar, illuminating the bedroom; a faint smell of disinfectant; hushed voices from a great distance. She had no idea of the time. Black despair engulfed her, an emptiness that could not be filled.

Why? Why had this happened? Had she unwittingly offended God? She could think of nothing she had done to deserve such a punishment. Could sinful thoughts be to blame? She went regularly to confession, tried hard to be a good wife, a good mother. Somewhere she must have failed. Her thoughts turned to the children. What was she to tell them? Belén had been thrilled at the prospect of a new baby to cosset. Now…

She heard the creak of the stairs and Enrique's face appeared round the door.

'Chelo, are you awake?' He came to her side, his step hesitant, and embraced her. 'I'm sorry,' he whispered.

'Where is she? Where is our baby?'

'The priest is here; the child will be buried today.'

'I want to see her.'

'*Cariño*, I don't think…'

'I want her to have a proper Christian burial.'

'I'll talk to the priest.' Her husband's face was troubled. He took her hand and gently stroked it. 'Chelo, he says the baby cannot attain salvation but will remain in limbo. Without baptism, as you know, the stain of original sin…'

'It's a nonsense. I hate God!'

'My darling, you don't know what you're saying. Rest now. I've told the children their sister has gone to Jesus. They understand. I'll send your *mamá* up in a little while.'

Mamá's face was a sea of grief. A mask had been removed, the composure of decades stripped away to reveal raw, unbridled emotion. Consuelo felt she was seeing her mother for the first time. She was sobbing as she spoke; her words were hard to make out.

'We named her Gracia, she lived for five days. That's why…'

'Mamá, I don't understand. Who? Who are you talking about?'

'Before we adopted you. A baby girl, I gave birth to a baby girl, Gracia. After five days she died…'

'I didn't know.'

'Of course not, I had to try and forget her, to love you instead. But now… now it's all coming back to me.' She struggled to compose herself. 'I'm sorry, *hija*. I should be comforting you but you see… God knows, it's a heartache that never goes away. All these years…'

A flash of anger ignited Consuelo. 'I don't care about your baby! That was years ago. I care about *my* baby.' She didn't want to hear about Mamá's 'heartache'. Not now. Not when the pain of her own loss overwhelmed her. Nieves, poor Nieves. Strangled by the cord that nourished her for nine long months. And now they said she would have no place in heaven, an innocent baby. How could she be anything but pure?

'Shh, calm yourself, daughter. It's hard, very hard. I know, I understand. The grief almost sends you mad. I thought by...' Mamá broke off with a heavy sigh and reached out to embrace her.

She perceived a warmth she had never felt before from her mother, her touch expressing what words could never convey. Was this what a mother's love felt like?

'We had an English couple arrive last night. They'd been up by bus to the Alpujarran villages. The woman said she'd got sick from all the bends in the road.' Consuelo knew Enrique was just trying to distract her, to take her mind off the baby. 'She spoke good Spanish,' he continued, 'unlike most of the foreigners. Her husband couldn't speak a word. They were planning to visit the Alhambra today...'

Consuelo was only half-listening. The English couple were of no interest to her, neither they nor the hotel's other guests. She had more than enough on her plate with the demands of the children, a household to run... Mamá had stayed to help for the first three weeks, when she was too consumed with grief and guilt to do anything. Although everyone said it wasn't her fault, that it could just as easily have happened in hospital, still she blamed herself for insisting on giving birth at home. Enrique didn't understand. He was kind, but baffled by her continuing anguish. There would be another baby soon, he assured her. She should forget the one they had buried and look to the future.

Only Mamá understood that you couldn't reason away the loss of a baby. She had carried the child for nine long months, only to be cheated of her at the last moment. Her body remembered and was not satisfied. Her womb demanded to be filled again, one more time.

Try as she might to believe her husband's words of solace, each month when the unwelcome red stain announced another failure, her disappointment grew harder to bear. A year passed and Enrique began to fret too. 'I don't know what's wrong,' he said. 'Perhaps you should see the doctor.' She went to confession twice a week. She stood before the *Cristo de los Favores* in the Campo del Príncipe and prayed for a child. But no child came.

CHAPTER 38

Granada, 1975

Pablo was tugging at his father's sleeve. 'I can't see!'

Enrique handed Luisa to his wife and hoisted Pablo above the heads of the crowd.

'Can you see now, son?' It was the eve of *Reyes* and the children were bright-eyed with excitement. The three kings, mounted on camels, were passing through the streets of Granada, followed by carriages, musical bands and troupes of dancers. Any moment now, they would start throwing out sweets to the throng of families lining the route.

'Come on,' Carlos yelled to his brothers, rushing to pick up one of the *caramelos* that had landed nearby.

Consuelo put Luisa down. At three-and-a-half, she was too heavy to carry for long. 'Give one to your sister,' she called to the boys, who were busy scrabbling for the sweets. Belén caught one in mid-air and unwrapped it for Luisa.

Tonight the children would put out their shoes, hoping for presents from the kings. She remembered how as a young child, she had been made to cry by her brothers, who said she would be rewarded with coal, the punishment for naughty boys and girls. It had made her dread the morning of Epiphany – though when the day came, their threats proved idle. She and Enrique would never instil such fears into their children. It was up to parents to protect their offspring from cruelty, of whatever kind.

They had been saving hard for *Reyes*. Prices had gone through the roof this last year and Enrique's wages weren't keeping up. They could manage but there was little money for extras. She had not yet told her husband that in a few months, God willing, there would be another mouth to feed. She had told no one, scarcely daring to believe that at last she was pregnant again. Her monthly bleed was three weeks late and the excessive tiredness that overcame her towards the end of each day confirmed her suspicions. Soon she would break the news to Enrique and to her parents.

Consuelo stood under the shower, looking down at her belly as the water ran over it. She traced the smooth curve with her fingers and thought about her recent conversation with Mamá. Since her mother's revelation about the death of her baby girl – the reason she had been adopted – a host of questions had surfaced in her mind. Some she feared to ask but others gnawed at her, insisting on answers.

'Did my natural mother really want to give me up or...?' She could not imagine – especially since death had snatched poor Nieves from her – how a woman could voluntarily relinquish her newborn, even in the most difficult circumstances.

From Mamá's expression, she could tell it was a question she was loath to consider.

'I don't know,' she replied after a long silence. 'Your Uncle Rodrigo is the only one who might have the answer and Rodrigo – may God rest his soul – is long in his grave.'

Your mother abandoned you. The explanation she had grown up with, that she'd absorbed and carried with her most of her life might be false. Perhaps her natural mother had been offered no choice. Perhaps she had suffered as a result, with guilt adding to her sorrow.

'One must assume she was willing,' Mamá continued, 'because how could a young, unmarried girl bring up a baby on her own?'

I would have fought. I wouldn't have let them take my child. But Consuelo said nothing. It was too late, far too late.

The unflagging routine of their lives kept Consuelo busy so that the weeks flashed past. Their baby was due in early August, another summer baby like Pablo. As her time approached, Consuelo grew more fearful. What if the same happened again? Another stillbirth would be beyond her capacity to endure; she would rather die. When she confided her fears to Enrique, he dismissed them. '*Gracias a Dios*, we have four strong, healthy children,' he reminded her. 'Soon we'll have a fifth. What happened last time was a stroke of bad luck. These things don't happen twice.'

Nieves was an unlucky name, she had decided. This one, if it turned out to be a girl, would not be Nieves but María del Sol or María de la Luz. She would bring sunshine and light into their lives.

Her adoptive parents had not named her after their own baby Gracia – the one she had replaced – but had given her a different name. Consuelo meant 'bringer of comfort'. Yet she had failed to bring comfort or consolation to her mother. She was a cuckoo in the family nest and it was Gracia for whom Mamá continued to pine. Had her real mother chosen a name for her, she wondered? Like so many of the questions that haunted her, it would never be answered.

Consuelo smelt disinfectant, heard the clanking of a trolley and, opening her eyes, let them rest briefly on the row of beds opposite, some of them occupied. Of course, she was in hospital. She remembered now: remembered the sudden onset of her pains, the race against time to get here, the euphoria when she heard the cry of her living, breathing baby daughter. Mamá was bending over her, speaking into her ear. 'She's fine. Your baby is beautiful and healthy.'

Muted voices reached her from far away. She lay in the high hospital bed, her limbs too heavy to move, her head stuffed with some kind of wadding that prevented her thinking clearly.

'You lost a lot of blood,' Mamá said. 'You must rest, you're very weak.'

'How long have I slept?' Her memory of the birth itself was hazy. The baby had come quickly but then... She remembered feeling faint, the room spinning round. Her womb was being massaged, and there was blood, so much blood... She struggled to clear her mind.

'A night and a day almost. The doctor gave you medicine.'

'Where's my baby? I want to see her.'

'She's right here in the crib beside you, sleeping peacefully.'

'Let me hold her.' Consuelo tried to sit up but she had no strength. 'I can't...'

'Shh, it's too soon. But look, I'll hold her for you so you can see how beautiful she is.'

Mamá turned away and then the baby, wrapped in a shawl and still sleeping, was held in front of her eyes, so close that she could smell her infant sweetness, see every fold and wrinkle in her face and neck, each strand of light hair. She lifted her hand and brushed the baby's silken skin with her fingers. It felt warm. Relief washed over her and she sank back on the pillows, closing her eyes. The baby had come early, two weeks before she was expected. But she was alive, healthy.

'I want her to be baptised. Soon.'

'Don't worry, *hija*, everything in its time. Later you can put her to the breast, but first you must take some nourishment yourself, build up your strength. I've brought a flask with some soup.' Mamá laid the baby back in her crib and stroked Consuelo's hair. '*Ay*, it all happened so fast. A haemorrhage, the bleeding wouldn't stop. We feared... Your husband was beside himself with worry.'

'But she's alright...?'

'It was you we were worried about, not the baby. The doctor says you must eat plenty of red meat to replace the iron.'

'I want to go home.' She should be with her family, with Enrique and the children.

'As soon as you're strong enough. Later, your husband will come.'

With an effort, Consuelo shifted her body higher up in the bed, raising her head and shoulders so that she could see her daughter more easily.

'Marisol. Her name is María del Sol.' She repeated it, wrapping her tongue around the sounds, tasting the joy they carried. 'Marisol.'

Enrique stood at the bedroom door. 'The *Caudillo* is dead.' It was November 20th. Her husband had turned on the radio this morning as he did every day when he got up. He looked shocked. Consuelo stroked the baby's head, soothing her daughter as if she were the one affected by the news and the uncertainty it provoked. Oblivious, Marisol continued to suck with her usual appetite. Of course their leader's death was expected – he was old and frail – but even so, she found it difficult to take in. All her life, Franco had been in charge of their country. Spain without Franco... She hoped there would not be another war. He had plenty of enemies; they would be celebrating now.

'The President will address the nation on television at ten o'clock,' Enrique said. 'We must wait and see. Who knows? Maybe our country will change for the better.'

PART 9 ROSE 1975 – 1985

CHAPTER 39

Oxford, 1975-77

'He's dead! Franco's finally snuffed it.' Rose was loading the washing machine when she heard the announcement on the Radio 4 News.

'What's that? Who's dead?'

'Franco! Shh, let me listen a minute.'

General Francisco Franco, who ruled Spain with an authoritarian hand for 39 years, has died at the age of 82. He had been ill for five weeks and died early this morning at La Paz hospital, Madrid. Doctors said the cause of death was heart failure aggravated by peritonitis. Flags all around the country are at half-mast and the general's body is now lying in state at the El Pardo Palace. Franco, also known as the Generalissimo, will be buried next week at the Valley of the Fallen mausoleum.

'There'll be some celebrating today.' Rose abandoned the laundry and leant on the worktop to listen. 'I don't believe it! On his deathbed, he asked his enemies to forgive him and said he pardoned them. Oh the bloody... excuse my language, I think I'm going to explode. May he roast in hell!'

'Come here, darling. Don't waste any more emotion on him. Let's just drink one of those... what do they call them? Begins with *ch*?'

'*Chupitos*. Excellent idea, I'll fetch the whisky.'

'So, what's going to happen now, do you think? Will the Spaniards get democracy at last?'

'It's not going to be easy. Franco has named Prince Juan Carlos as his successor, after grooming him for years. A lot depends on what he makes of his role as king. The old guard still have all the power. Whether they'll hand it over and allow elections... But I'm out of touch with Spain, with the mood of the people. I imagine they're too cowed by the years of repression to take to the streets. And I don't suppose anyone wants another war.'

If Franco's death was cause for celebration, that of Paul Robeson two months later brought Rose a passing sadness. The encouragement he had given to the Spanish Republic and to the International Brigades in particular was legendary. One of her patients at the convalescent hospital had met him and his wife when he sang for the troops in 1938. She recalled him describing the singer's rousing renditions of *Ol' Man River, Lonesome Road* and other songs and wished she'd had the opportunity to hear him. A snatch of his recording of *Peat Bog Soldiers* was played on the News, along with an excerpt from one of his speeches on human rights.

Her sadness was shared by Jack. She remembered their mutual delight not long after they met on discovering they were both fans and owned the same recording. She searched out the LP now and they listened together, moved by his rich, deep voice.

Rose had been corresponding with Lourdes since their visit to Cañar, and true to her word, Lourdes had sent the photos. Now, with the announcement of Franco's death, Rose wrote again. A letter came back warning her to be careful what she wrote while the political situation was still uncertain. She accepted the rebuke. Whatever the real state of affairs in Spain, fear was a habit not easily shrugged off.

She was still thinking about the family's invitation, repeated in each of Lourdes' letters. *My mother is always asking when we can expect another visit from you and your husband. You can stay as long as you like. Our other sister Herminia is also keen to make your acquaintance.* Each time, Rose promised to think about it. Now she was retired, she had no ready excuse. Still she hesitated. The stirring of old memories on her last visit had unsettled her more than she cared to admit. Next autumn perhaps?

Her mind veered to a recent telephone conversation with her friend Dorothy.

'You probably don't know, but Frank and his wife have been trying four or five years for a baby. Well, now it turns out she's infertile. It came as a terrible blow to them – and to Archie and me as well. We were so looking forward to grandchildren.'

'Have they thought of adopting?' It struck Rose as a sensible solution. An unwanted child would be given a good home and loving parents instead of being sent to Dr Barnardo's or some such charity. She thought of Concha, the woman in Cañar whose children had been taken from her involuntarily while she languished in prison, and shuddered. Delivered to the nuns or to some staunchly Catholic family, those children would have been moulded to conform with Franco's ideals. But that was Spain. Here in England, things were done differently.

'They're considering it. But these days, with most girls on the pill, there's a long waiting list and unless you're willing to take on a handicapped child...'

In the long hot summer of 1976, Rose half-regretted their move away from the river. It had been one of those spur-of-the-moment decisions Jack loved to tease her about. The moment had come one evening in the winter of '74 – that winter of strikes and three-day weeks and regular power cuts. Jack was sitting in his favourite armchair, wrapped in a blanket with a woolly hat pulled down over his ears. His hacking cough alarmed her; it wouldn't go away. Observing him from the kitchen doorway, she convinced herself the dank river air was to blame for his repeated bouts of bronchitis. The next day, she quietly started house-hunting.

Only when she'd found a place she thought would appeal sufficiently did she reveal her plan to Jack. Then she took him to Headington on a pretext, hoping her instincts were right. Her intention had been to allow the house – and its location on a hill overlooking the city – to speak for itself without her mentioning the ample number of bedrooms, the green spaces nearby, the cricket ground, the cosy pub, but somehow she ended up reeling off this list of advantages to a rather bemused Jack.

'Do I get a chance to consider?' he asked, having quickly surmised the situation. 'You're a crafty one, Rose dear. But you know, I had a sneaking suspicion you were up to something.' He knew her too well.

Now they were further from the river, Jack's health had improved, his energy and enthusiasm for life renewed. He had found a WEA course on 20th century Spanish history, focusing on the Second Republic. After his first class, he had come home brimming with enthusiasm and talked Rose into enrolling too. She had also joined a choir and, encouraged by Jack, played an active role in a literacy project for adults.

But family always came first; their large combined family was her greatest joy. She and Jack were rarely alone for more than a few days in a row. Ralph and Chantal were frequent visitors. Nephew Peter – now a qualified optician – worked nearby and sometimes dropped in for a cup of tea on his way home.

Vince, Jack's youngest, still single at thirty-five, left his motorbike parked at their house during his stints at sea and usually stayed with them when he had shore leave. One morning at the end of a few days' leave, Rose heard him revving up his bike. 'Fancy a spin?' he called out to her. 'Come on, you'll love it.'

'What? You're joking, aren't you?'

'Not at all. I've got a spare helmet. Where's your sense of adventure?'

'Well, if you put it like that…'

'I won't go too fast, cross my heart and hope to die. We'll head out of town on nice quiet roads.'

'You've convinced me. Hang on while I get a jacket. No leathers, I'm afraid.'

'I'd put on some trousers if I were you,' he said, looking her up and down.

'I'll be perfectly alright in a skirt. It's loose enough.' Unlike most women these days, Rose refused to dress in 'men's attire'. Trousers would forever be associated in her mind with those dreadful corduroy breeches she'd been forced to wear in the *sierras*. Her younger relations were always lecturing her on the practicality of trousers; Prue had even bought her a pair one Christmas. They hung in her wardrobe, their label still attached.

She climbed up behind Vince on the saddle and clung tight as they bowled along at a pace not fast but not exactly slow either, through small villages, each with its agglomeration of houses, pub and church. The feel of the cool air rushing past her cheeks was exhilarating.

'Is something the matter?' Vince had come to a sudden halt in the middle of a narrow lane. He turned and pointed to a wall on their left, overhung with riotous honeysuckle. 'I always think of my mother when I see honeysuckle in flower,' he said, leaning out to sniff the delicate pink and yellow tendrils. 'It was her favourite scent. Nectar of the gods, she called it.'

Vince's face was hidden from her, but the emotion in his voice revealed how deeply he felt. He'd been a boy still when Lilian died. Rose breathed in the powerful fragrance from the hedge. 'Your mother was one of the bravest, most positive women I've ever met.'

'She was my mother,' he said simply. 'Come on, let's go.' He opened up the throttle and with a roar they were off again.

The heat reminded her of Spain: of unfailing blue skies and light strong enough to blind, the relief of plunging into cool rivers on her rare afternoons off. Now the English earth was thirsty too, the land no longer the lush green of normal summers. It pained her to see her well-tended plants shrivel, the lawn turn yellow then brown. In her efforts to keep cool, the fan Susan had brought her from Ibiza the previous year proved indispensable.

She and Jack holidayed in the Lake District, where they stayed in a comfortable hotel and swam every day in Rydal Water or Grasmere. The proximity of water and mountains calmed her; she relaxed on the sun-warmed shingle beaches of the lakes and counted her blessings. The vague unease she had felt since returning from Spain melted away.

They were making love again after months of enforced abstinence due to Jack's debility. Not for them the 'separate beds' that apparently suited Dorothy and Archie. 'We gave up the hanky-panky years ago,' Dorothy had confided once. Rose hoped she and Jack would never opt for separate beds or choose to relinquish the intimacy so important to them both.

Only days after hearing of Helen's pregnancy, news of the miscarriage reached Rose via Chantal. It was a damp November afternoon, soggy leaves littering the street, a blanket of low cloud robbing the day of light. Rose had just come in with the shopping when the phone rang.

'She's disappointed naturally,' her mother said. 'But it's very common: the doctor said something like one in four pregnancies. I lost one myself between Peter and Helen; you soon forget.' *Do you?* Rose thought. She hoped Chantal took a more sympathetic line with Helen. 'It's upsetting for them of course,' her sister-in-law continued, 'but she'll be pregnant again in no time.'

Rose waited till the next morning to ring her niece. Mike had taken the day off work. 'It was so sudden,' he said. 'She was fine when we went to bed. I woke up a few hours later and she was moaning in her sleep. Then she grabbed me and started to wail and I realised... The sheets were soaked in minutes; we couldn't do anything to stop it. I phoned the doctor. There was so much blood...'

'Oh you poor things. And how is she now?'

'She can't stop crying. I guess it's the shock. Anyway, we're hoping she won't need to go into hospital. The doctor says it's not always necessary, that with luck everything will come away naturally.'

'Can I speak to her?'

'Well...' Mike sounded doubtful. 'I'll pass you over but as I said, she's really upset.'

'At three months they're fully formed,' Helen sobbed over the phone.

Rose's heart went out to her. 'I know,' she said. 'It was your child, the loss of a life, however tiny. I'm so terribly sad for you.' She pushed away the faint echoes of her own grief for a lost baby.

'We'd bought rocking horse wallpaper to decorate the spare room and taken a book of baby names out of the library and...' Another sob. 'I just can't bear it.'

'It's partly your hormones,' Rose said. 'Your body's expectations as well as your mind's.' What words of comfort could she offer Helen? Only one magic bullet would ease her pain: another pregnancy, a successful birth, a baby to hold in her arms. 'Try to rest,' she said. 'Make sure you eat well and build up your strength. You've probably lost a lot of blood. Give your body time to recover.'

'Jack, I think I'll go up to Sheffield. Helen's feeling very low.' It was May, the month their baby would have been due. 'She's still struggling to get over her miscarriage.'

Mike had phoned the evening before. He was concerned about Helen. 'She's not coping very well; she cries an awful lot, even after all this time. I wondered if you could have a word with her. She trusts you – probably more than anyone else. She keeps saying nobody understands.'

He met her at the station. 'It's good of you to come, I'm sure it will help.' Eyes determinedly on the road, he continued in a more hesitant manner. 'We were hoping she'd be pregnant again by now. I mean it's six months and... the pressure, you know, it's difficult. She's desperate to conceive and I feel...' He sighed and fell silent.

'It must be difficult for you both. I'll talk to her.'

Helen was sitting at the table surrounded by stacks of exam papers when they arrived. 'They did their mocks a couple of weeks ago,' she said, 'and I still haven't finished the marking. I promised to give them back tomorrow. So I'm afraid it'll just be baked potatoes, a bought quiche and salad tonight. Is that alright?' The brittleness in her voice worried Rose.

'Of course. Maybe I can help?'

'Oh Mike's very good. You relax, I'll be finished with this in half an hour at most.'

After supper, Mike went out for his regular Wednesday evening game of squash. He had barely closed the door behind him when the tears started. Rose had the impression they were never far away.

'Everyone says I should be over it by now.' Helen pulled the box of tissues towards her. 'It's not like it was a *baby*,' they say. 'Just a cluster of cells. But it *was* a baby. It had a head and organs and limbs, a beating heart... You know that, you're a nurse. *You* understand, don't you?' She blew her nose and pushed the damp strands of hair out of her face. 'A friend of mine had an abortion – she was further on than me – and I wanted to kill her, honestly.'

Rose moved closer and put an arm round Helen. 'I do understand,' she said, 'but not because I'm a nurse.' She took a deep breath. 'I know because I once lost a baby.'

'You?' Helen's eyes opened wide. 'But, with Jack or...?'

'It was in Spain. I had a lover there. Very few people know – not your parents, in fact no one in the family. I told Jack. Apart from him, only a couple of my Spanish nursing colleagues and my old GP in Evesham.'

'What happened to your lover? Was he Spanish?'

Rose nodded. 'His name was Miguel. He was killed just before our baby was due, shot by the Civil Guard.' She spoke calmly, as she could never have done in earlier years. Time did not heal, though it did take the edge off the pain.

'Oh how dreadful. And the baby? What happened?'

'I had a little girl, Blanca.' Now she could not keep the emotion from her voice. 'A beautiful baby girl. They let me hold her and feed her and then... Pass me one of those tissues, will you, Helen?' She dabbed at her eyes. 'Then the nuns took her away – the nurses were all nuns in Spain – and I never saw her again. They said she had an infection and refused to bring her to me. I went looking...' She paused, remembering that she was here to comfort Helen, not upset her. 'They gave me some potent sleeping draught and when I woke, they said my baby had died in the night. She was already buried.'

'I don't know how you coped.' Helen looked utterly shocked.

'I didn't have a choice. We never do really. Awful things happen and somehow we have to struggle on.' She straightened up and patted Helen's knee. 'I'm sorry, I didn't mean to talk so much about myself. Just to let you know I understand what you're going through.'

'I wish Mike understood. And my parents. I can't help it, every time I catch sight of a baby or hear one cry or see a pregnant woman – and with the warmer weather now you see them everywhere – it sets me off. Even photos of babies do it. You wouldn't believe the number of tissues I get through.' She attempted a smile. 'It's pathetic really. I mean, compared to what you suffered, a miscarriage is nothing.'

'It's not nothing. Don't let people tell you that. But you're young and you will get pregnant again.'

'I suppose so. I don't know why it's taking so long; it's not for want of trying.'

'It could be you're trying too hard. Relax, give Mike a break.' She squeezed Helen's hand and was relieved when Helen returned her grin. 'Now, shall I make us a cup of tea? Oh and I almost forgot, there's a box of Black Magic in my bag that I meant to give you.'

'My favourites, how did you know? Look, forget the tea, let's have a glass of wine. I'm sure Mike will be stopping at the pub on his way home.'

Birth and death: how often they seemed to accompany each other, Rose thought sadly when news of Dorothy's death in a road accident followed hot on the heels of good news for Frank and his wife in their bid to adopt. A happy event marred by a tragedy.

She recalled her last conversation with Dorothy, her friend's excitement bubbling over as she related every detail of the child's troubled history. 'They'll give him a loving home, stability, everything he lacked. Now I'm having a big clear-out to make space for a playroom – you know what a hoarder I am. Well, you'll never guess what I came across in one of the drawers: a bundle of all your old letters, the ones you wrote from Spain. Don't worry, they won't be going to the skip.'

Dorothy, so cautious all her life, struck down by an act of sheer carelessness; it made no sense. She'd been laden with bags from Mothercare when the motorbike hit her, right on a zebra crossing. Poor Frank. Births and deaths, along with marriages were his livelihood. Every day he must come into contact with the newly bereaved. Now he was one of them.

What would her father have made of it, Rose wondered? How would he have explained the cruelty, the randomness of fate? If God existed, His ways were indeed mysterious.

CHAPTER 40

Oxford, 1980

Rose unrolled the brightly-coloured wrapping paper and spread it out on the table, ready to parcel up the two Fisher-Price toys: a radio that played *Raindrops keep falling on my Head* and a smiley telephone on wheels with a pull-along cord. It was the twins' first birthday and Rose was looking forward to the family party at Ralph and Chantal's. 'For every death a birth, look at it that way round,' Jack had urged a few years ago when her sadness over Dorothy threatened to obliterate Frank's good news. In this case it was two births. The letter from Lourdes telling of Modesta's death at the ripe age of ninety-three had arrived on the same day Helen gave birth to Zoe and Zach, a joyous event for all.

To Rose's delight, her niece had moved much closer. Not long after her miscarriage, both she and Mike had found jobs in Milton Keynes. 'Just as well,' Chantal said when she heard twins were expected. 'They'll need a lot of help.' They had it aplenty, from both sets of grandparents. Rose couldn't keep away: for the last year she had been driving to MK (as everyone called it) about twice a month, either alone or with Jack. It took little more than an hour from Oxford.

She and Helen had always been close but since the loss of her baby and Rose's revelation of her own secret grief, the bond had grown even stronger. They had talked a lot in the period before the twins were born. Helen was curious to know more about her aunt's love affair, the time she and Miguel had spent in the *sierras* and her harrowing experience in the Spanish hospital. 'You should write it all down,' Helen urged, but in her busy life, it did not seem a priority.

She regretted not having returned to see Modesta. Now it was too late. She wrote a letter of sympathy to Miguel's sisters with vague promises of a trip to Cañar some time in the future. From news reports and the few guarded letters sent by Lourdes, Rose tried to piece together the political situation in Spain. She read of demonstrations that often led to killings by the police, of violence by separatist groups, ETA in particular, of negotiations and power struggles. The years following Franco's death were referred to as '*La Transición*' – a transition to democracy, so everyone hoped. Lourdes wrote of an amnesty referred to as *el pacto de olvido*: an agreement to keep silent about past crimes and injustices so that the country could move on. She did not reveal her feelings about this. Rose had the impression that Spaniards from both sides wanted to put the horrors of recent history behind them and allow the country to heal its divisions. Jack, who took a keen interest in the news from Spain, agreed.

In Ralph and Chantal's living room, she sat surrounded by a gaggle of laughing, shouting, screaming, chattering children, and their parents. Babies and small children were everywhere, it seemed to Rose – an impression confirmed by statistics: the language of 'boom' and 'bulge'. Her nephews and nieces were part of the post-war baby boom. Now there was a bulge as that generation became parents. Susan sat in the big armchair usually reserved for Ralph. Her first baby was due in a few weeks' time. Peter's wife Jenny was also expecting. Their two older ones were among the children running around outside. She had held so many newborns – two generations of them – and each one reminded her of her own. She could never forget little Blanca; the heartache had become an indelible part of her.

'Another letter from Spain,' Rose called gaily to Jack as she picked up the morning post from the mat. She recognised Lourdes' loopy handwriting. The stamp had a picture of the Virgin of the Snows; she would keep it for Frank's adopted son Justin, already a keen stamp collector. Jack was at the breakfast table, tucking into his fried eggs and bacon – a habit carried over from his postie days when he'd needed to stoke up before starting his round. Rose preferred a lighter breakfast of cereal and toast, at weekends a boiled egg timed at exactly four minutes. They had become creatures of habit, both of them, she thought as she sat down and drew out the thin airmail paper from its envelope.

She began to read, translating for Jack as she went along. They were all well; Matilde's older son, a car mechanic, had found work in Órgiva; Herminia and her husband were celebrating their golden wedding; Agustín's wife had just brought some of their excellent goats' cheese – they remembered how much she liked it – but the big news...

'What's the matter?' Rose had stopped dead in her tracks. 'What is it, Rose?'

'We had another unexpected visitor,' she read, her voice faltering, 'another friend of Miguel's. His name was Tomás.'

'Go on, darling.' Jack put down his knife and fork. 'Did you know this Tomás? Rose, are you alright?'

She was reading ahead, scarcely believing Lourdes' words. Tomás was still alive. He had succeeded in escaping from the *Guardia Civil*, had seen from his hiding place nearby what happened to Miguel. Later in the night, he told the sisters, two of the *civiles* had returned and covered their brother's body with earth. Tomás marked in his mind the spot where the body of his *compañero* had fallen and vowed to return one day...

'He was with us in the mountains,' Rose said. 'I thought he'd been killed too. He was from Cazorla, he knew those *sierras* like the back of his hand.' She read on. 'He said he'd spent years in prison and in forced labour on the canal of the Guadalquivir, his health had suffered...' She put the letter down, too overcome to go on. She closed her eyes and was no longer in the familiar kitchen of their Headington house but back in the mountains of Jaén, running, stumbling on tangled roots and vegetation, banging her shins on boulders. The voices of their pursuers close behind, gaining on them with every second. Miguel in front, looking back at her, urging her to move faster but the baby... Her fall, then the shot echoing from the rocky outcrops, piercing the still morning. One shot followed by a second and then a third. Partridges rising in panic, Miguel's body sprawled on the stony ground...

'He kept his word. When he was released ten years ago, he took his nephew Daniel and showed him the place so that one day, when it was safe... He didn't expect to live much longer, he said. The prison and work conditions had broken his health.

'He was younger than me,' she told Jack. 'Strong and vigorous.' The cruelty of it brought a physical ache to her heart.

It was a miracle that he found us, Lourdes wrote, *one of those rare coincidences that life throws up*. Tomás had met a man in prison, an older man called Rogelio who came from Cañar, and remembering that Miguel was from the Alpujarra, asked Rogelio if he knew the family. It turned out he had worked with their father at one time. Soon after, Rogelio contracted TB and died, but Tomás remembered the name of the village and many years later, after revisiting Miguel's burial place, felt it would be only right to share his knowledge with the family before he passed away.

How typically generous, Rose thought. He had remained a good man into old age despite the dreadful waste of his life in Franco's prisons.

'We told him about your visit and showed him the photos. He couldn't believe it, he was crying. He spoke of your great courage and the love...'

Rose looked up at Jack and he reached out a hand to her across the breakfast table. She skipped a line and forced herself to go on. 'He said you were expecting a child, that you were near your time. So we wondered – it seems strange that you never mentioned Miguel's child. What happened, Rosa? What happened to your baby?'

CHAPTER 41

Oxford/Granada/Cañar, 1985

Rose clipped off the last dead flower-head and let it fall into her basket. This was the easy part of gardening. Digging, kneeling down to weed, trimming the edges of the lawn were becoming increasingly difficult tasks. She loved her garden, much preferred working outside to cooking and cleaning. She had considered moving to a smaller place now Jack was gone, but then where would her family stay on their frequent visits?

After three years, she was getting used to living alone. Jack had died without fuss, just as he had lived, no trouble to anyone. Sitting in his armchair with a book on his lap, he had simply closed his eyes and failed to wake up. 'I feel very tired.' The last words he had spoken before his heart stopped.

'A lovely man', everyone said at his funeral. She had wept at the words, wept at the prospect of life without his quiet companionship and support. He had given her so much without, it seemed, ever asking anything of her. What a gift to have had twenty-four years, nearly a third of her life, with him. Sorting through his rather scant possessions (books formed by far the major part), she had found a bundle of Lilian's old letters together with his replies. Some dated from before their marriage, others from when he was posted away during the war. Rose glanced at a few but it felt wrong to intrude on her husband's first marriage; besides, their poignancy made her cry.

She had offered herself as a volunteer for Age Concern, visiting isolated older people at home. 'But you're old yourself,' Susan teased. She didn't feel old, not really. The people she visited were mostly housebound, disabled in one way or another. Some had no family nearby; others had family who ignored them. Rose listened to their stories and occasionally shared small snippets of her own. Sometimes she helped them fill in forms or escorted them to the shops or the park. Their appreciation – undeserved surely because she enjoyed the work – nevertheless touched her. She felt privileged to be admitted into their lives.

'Bye bye dear, thank you so much.' Hilda, who was eighty-nine and walked with a frame, stood waving Rose off at her front door. The television would probably be her only companion for the next few days, the meals-on-wheels lady her only, very brief, visitor. Women like Hilda made Rose conscious of her own good fortune. Despite having no children, she was surrounded by loving family while Hilda, with four, was left largely to her own devices.

Rose was hurrying home to prepare a meal for Susan, who would be arriving in an hour or two with her boyfriend Alan and five year-old Samantha. Bertie and Prue had hoped the couple would get married when their granddaughter was born but Susan, always a bit of a rebel, told them they were old-fashioned fuddy-duddies: she and Alan didn't need church or state to bless their union. 'Times have changed,' Rose pointed out to her brother in support of Susan. No one these days talked of 'illegitimacy' or 'living in sin'. Thinking of the shame endured by Jack (and even more so his mother), she could not but consider it a good thing.

At the Post Office, she stopped to buy a stamp for Australia. Her nephew Robert had emigrated to Sydney a few years ago. She never forgot his birthday: the date was etched in her mind. September 12th meant a candle for Blanca, a card for Robert.

Rose waited till she and Helen were alone – the twins fast asleep, Mike fixing shelves in the garage – to moot her idea. She wasn't at all sure Helen would buy it.

'I'm planning another trip to Spain,' she said, plunging straight in, 'and I'd like to invite you along. Just for a week, I thought.'

'Oh what a fabulous idea, but I couldn't possibly leave the twins.'

'I think you could.' Helen's response was exactly as Rose had expected. 'Your parents would be thrilled to have them. And Mike is perfectly competent, isn't he?'

'Well, not that competent actually.' Helen laughed. 'He needs telling what to do. I don't know, Rose. I'd have to think about it. I mean, I've never left the children...'

'The twins are six, they're old enough. We can go in your autumn half-term. It'll be gorgeous up there in the mountains. Snow on the tops, sunny days, chestnut trees flaming red and gold. We could spend a couple of days in Granada – you'll be bowled over by the Alhambra – and then visit the family in Cañar.'

'What family?'

'Oh, I didn't tell you, did I.' Rose gave herself a mental kick. 'How stupid of me, I must be losing my marbles. You remember when I went to Spain with Jack – or maybe you don't, it was back in 1972 – anyway, we managed to track down Miguel's mother and sisters in a small village in the Alpujarra mountains near Granada.' She gave Helen a brief account of their trip. Helen listened, her eyes opening wide in amazement.

'That's incredible,' she said. 'Did you tell them about… about the baby?'

'No, there didn't seem much point. But they've found out since and that's one reason I want to go back. To explain. In case they think I'm hiding something.'

Helen looked pensive. 'You know I don't speak Spanish,' she said.

'I could translate. Here, have a look at these.' Rose had come armed with a selection of her best Alhambra and Alpujarras photos to entice Helen.

'I have to admit I'm tempted. I'll talk to Mike – and Mum and Dad, of course.'

'I don't want to put any pressure on you,' Rose said. 'It's entirely your decision.'

'Hmm, I'm not sure I believe you, Aunt Rose. You've given me a pretty hard sell.'

'Oh dear, I meant to be more subtle.' They were both laughing. 'I hope I haven't overdone it. You'll let me know, won't you? And it goes without saying, the expense is on me.' She heard the back door opening. 'Oh and one more thing: I'd rather you kept quiet about Miguel and the baby. Tell Mike if you must, but as far as the rest of the family are concerned, this is just a jaunt to Granada, a cultural holiday if you like.' Helen's quizzical look made her add, 'Whether or not you decide to come.'

CHAPTER 42

Rose, Granada/Cañar, 1985

'I've brought my Spanish phrasebook,' Helen said as they waited for their plane to take off from Gatwick on a rainy afternoon in late October. 'I'm afraid I didn't get much beyond greetings and booking a hotel.'

'Even a few words will be appreciated,' Rose said. 'Anyway, the hotel in Granada is already arranged. I've booked us into the same hotel Jack and I stayed at last time.' The safety demonstration was about to begin. 'I'm so glad you decided to come,' she whispered.

Helen nudged her playfully. 'How could I refuse?'

It was dark by the time they arrived in Granada. The hotel had hardly changed since Rose's last visit. Entering the lobby, she saw no sign of the owl-like manager but she recognised his deputy, what was his name? She wondered if he'd been promoted.

'I don't suppose you remember me,' she said. 'I came here with my husband in 1972.'

'Of course I remember you. I remember all our guests. Well, nearly all. And especially the rare ones like you who speak our language. Enrique, at your service.' Glancing at Helen, he said, 'And this is your daughter? I can see a likeness – especially in the eyes. My wife too has green eyes.' He held out his hand to Helen. 'Pleased to meet you.'

'Helen is the nearest I have to a daughter. She's my niece.'

'*Bueno*, you are both very welcome.' He took their passports and cast his eye over the names. 'I'll be going off duty soon, Mrs Drummond, but my daughter Belén will be here on Reception. Anything you need, she will be happy to help you. Now, here are the keys to your room. Carlos, my son, will bring your luggage up in a moment.' He nodded to a tall, fair-haired lad wheeling a trolley-load of boxes into a storeroom, who gave them a shy smile.

'Seems to be a family concern,' Helen said as they rode up in the lift. 'That boy was unusually fair for a Spaniard, don't you think? And fancy his father remembering you all these years. Let's hope he's given us a nice room.'

The young receptionist (Belén, they presumed) was dealing with a party of new arrivals when Rose and Helen returned from their Alhambra visit the following afternoon.

'What I'd give for a head of dark glossy hair like hers,' Helen murmured, indicating the girl.

'She's got her father's features.' Rose pointed to some armchairs on one side of the lobby. 'Let's sit down for a minute, I'm exhausted.'

'Me too, you've worn me out.'

'I hope it was worth it,' Rose said.

'Worth it?' Helen raised her eyes to the ceiling. 'I'll be dreaming of it for months to come, imagining it peopled by handsome Berber princes and alluring women in dainty slippers. I can just visualise them strolling in the gardens, listening to the tinkle of fountains and the gentle twang of lute strings, or perhaps a voice in melancholy song. I can't wait to read that book you bought me.'

'It's astonishing to think that Washington Irving was able to take up residence in the Alhambra only a century and a half ago when he wrote those tales.'

'I'll have to bring Mike one day. It's the most romantic place I've ever been.'

'Oh look, there's the owl man.' Rose gestured towards the desk, where the manager she remembered from her previous visit had appeared. 'Go and ask him for the room key, would you? I need a lie-down right now.'

'So how did you like our Alhambra palace?' Rose heard the man ask as he handed Helen the key.

'I absolutely loved it. In fact my aunt had to drag me away. It's exquisite – all those intricate carvings, the coloured tiles... How much love the craftsmen must have put into their work.'

'Thank you.' His smile was proud, as if the palaces belonged to him personally. 'You know they open for night visits too?'

'Really?' She turned to Rose, who had joined her at the desk. 'Oh do let's go back when it's dark. It'll be so atmospheric. Can we?'

'Definitely not tonight, but maybe when we come back from Cañar.'

'I suggest a nice relaxing day tomorrow,' Rose said as they headed up in the lift. 'A gentle stroll in the Albaicín – that's the old Moorish quarter we could see from the Alhambra, across the valley on the hill opposite, remember? I'd hoped to go with Jack on my last visit but they told me it was very run down, lots of broken cobbles and flights of steps. I was afraid his legs wouldn't be up to it or that he might fall.'

'It looked intriguing. Cypress trees sticking up all over the place amongst a jumble of white houses. But are *your* legs up to it?'

Rose glanced at her niece, who looked somewhat overwhelmed by the crowd gathered to meet them in Cañar. Matilde and José Antonio had picked them up from Órgiva, along with the other sister, Herminia. At the family home where, since Modesta's death, Lourdes lived alone, they were introduced to two of Matilde's children and her six year-old grandson and to Alfonso's son Ángel.

'There'll be more of us for lunch,' Lourdes said, welcoming them with warm embraces and a few tears. 'Agustín and Juliana, also Herminia's two daughters…'

'Goodness, I feel honoured,' Rose said. 'But you must let me help you.'

'Certainly not, you're our guest and I've more than enough help here.'

'My father apologises for not coming,' Ángel said. 'He would have liked to meet you but the journey from Sevilla would have been too much for him – he's eighty-one and in poor health.' Alfonso was Miguel's eldest brother, Rose recalled, the only one to survive. She was doing her best to translate the exchanges for Helen.

'I have many good memories of my uncle,' Ángel told them while the sisters busied themselves in the kitchen. 'I admired him greatly, *el tio Miguel*. You ask Aunt Herminia, she'll remember how I followed him about everywhere.'

'He taught me to read,' Matilde's son said. 'I had to work in the fields from a young age so I missed out on school.'

'He hoped to become a teacher.' Rose recalled how his eyes had shone when he spoke of his ambitions.

With fourteen of them around the table at lunch, everyone talking at the same time, Rose had to concede defeat as interpreter, but Helen appeared happy enough, responding with smiles and nods and shows of appreciation to the constant entreaties to eat more. 'Aren't you hungry? Have you tried the *pimientos de padrón,* the *chorizo,* the *papas a lo pobre*? Come on, take another *chuleta,* there are plenty. Fill her glass, José Antonio.' They had been sitting for nearly three hours by the time the last dishes were cleared away.

'Now you must see the pictures we took with Tomás,' Lourdes said, bringing out a folder of photographs. If only our mother had been alive to hear his account. Well, *gracias a Diós,* she met you, Rosa.' The photos were laid one by one on the table in front of Rose. 'That's his nephew Daniel standing next to him.' A sturdy, muscular young man, as his uncle had once been. Rose would scarcely have recognised the gaunt face and cadaverous figure of Tomás. Only in his near-toothless smile did she see a trace of their old comrade. And in another snap, something in his stance – the way his feet were planted firmly on the earth – indicated a man not to be budged against his will. The set of his mouth confirmed it: here was a man with determination and grit. Rose stared at each of the photos, too moved to speak. She remembered his large hands, a labourer's hands, he would say with pride, and how, more than once, he had gripped one of her own to pull her up some steep slope where loose stones and dry earth made it difficult to gain a foothold.

'We doubt he's still alive,' Matilde said. 'Our letters have gone unanswered.'

'He wasn't well,' Lourdes added. 'His lungs were bad and the journey here had tired him greatly.'

'What nerves the man must have had. *¡Fíjate!* Just imagine him hiding all night long in the undergrowth with Miguel's body lying close by and the *Guardia Civil* searching for him.' José Antonio shook his head and began rolling a cigarette.

'Our brother deserved a decent burial,' Herminia said, tears in her eyes. 'It makes my blood boil to think of him lying forgotten on the mountain where he fell, dug into the ground without honour or ceremony.'

After a moment's silence, Matilde looked at Rose and said, 'When Tomás told us you were pregnant...' She paused and the silence in the room hung heavy. 'Let's say, it was a shock to us.'

'Yes, and I promised you an explanation.' Rose made an effort to calm herself, to breathe more slowly. 'As I wrote in my letter, the baby died.' She felt all their eyes on her and continued. 'The *Guardia Civil* took me to their headquarters and my pains started there. It wasn't yet time, the shock must have brought them on early. In the hospital at Jaén, I gave birth to a baby girl. She appeared healthy but the next day the nuns told me she'd fallen sick with an infection. I never saw her again; she died that same night.'

'*Ay*, how you must have suffered.' Matilde reached for her hand.

Ángel was frowning. 'You think they were telling the truth?' he asked. 'Did you see the body?'

Rose shook her head. 'They said she was already in the ground.'

'And were there papers?'

'That's enough, Ángel, you're upsetting Rosa.'

'It's alright, Lourdes. There were papers, yes. A birth certificate – I named her Blanca, with my *apellido*, Tilly. They tried to drag the father's name from me but I kept silent. In the end they gave up and just wrote *desconocido*. Miguel was already dead, it hardly mattered, but I didn't want to give them that satisfaction.' Rose brushed away a tear. 'After she died, they brought me the death certificate to sign. I refused. You must understand I was demented with grief. I even suspected they'd killed her, the nuns and the doctor. I couldn't believe...'

'You think they killed her?'

'*Basta ya*, Ángel. Leave off now.'

'No, of course not, it was a hospital.' Observing the faces of Miguel's relatives, Rose regretted her words. 'My anger and helplessness made me imagine things, put irrational thoughts in my head.'

'Well now, many years have passed.' Matilde patted her arm. 'We are very sorry, Rosa. The death of a baby always brings much heartache.'

'Although we knew nothing of her, she was our niece too,' Herminia said. 'We share your sadness, Rosa.'

Helen caught her eye and stood up. 'I need some air,' she said. 'Okay if I take a stroll before it gets dark?'

'Of course.' Rose could understand her niece's desire to escape the heavy atmosphere round the table. Ángel picked up his packet of cigarettes and lighter from the table and followed Helen outside.

Lourdes too pushed back her chair. Addressing Rose, she said, 'These things are not easy to talk about. We thank you for your candour. And now an infusion of *manzanilla*, yes?'

'Trevélez is the highest village in Spain.' Rose was translating the words of Matilde's son Sebastián. Six of them were squashed together in his car as the road twisted ever higher into the Sierra Nevada. 'Famous for its ham.' Rose was glad of the frequent stops to admire a view or sample the local produce: *pan de higos* in one village, salted almonds and a glass of the *vino del terreno* in another.

'It's just breathtaking,' Helen said, her stomach seemingly impervious to the challenge of one hairpin bend after another.

On the way down from Trevélez, where lunch had started with a generous plate of the famous *jamón*, they stopped to gather chestnuts, searching among the fallen leaves that carpeted the earth in overlapping layers of ochre, red and gold. In no time at all they had filled a large sack. That evening Lourdes lit the fire – the nights up here were cold already – and they roasted the chestnuts, trying not to burn their hands or mouths as they peeled off the crisped shells and enjoyed the nutty texture and rich taste of their gatherings. The room was cosy, lit only by the flames of the fire and a couple of oil lamps. The younger generation had left and those remaining were relaxed, too tired even to speak. Agustín had already nodded off, Rose noticed, and her own eyelids were drooping. In the morning she and Helen would take the bus back to Granada before returning to England the following day.

'You have another family now, Rosa,' Lourdes said as she waved them off. 'You'll come back, won't you?'

'One day perhaps,' Rose said. 'And in the meantime I'll write. I won't forget your kindness.'

'Just one more photo, the three of you with my aunt.' Helen held up her camera and flicked off the lens cap. Please?'

'Goodness, you still have film?' Rose said, laughing as the four of them posed outside the house.

'Not much. It's the last of the four rolls I brought.'

Later, sitting on the Granada bus with the villages of the Alpujarra behind them and a straighter road ahead, Rose turned to Helen and said, 'They really do feel like family, you know. Isn't that strange?'

'Well, I suppose they would have been if Miguel...'

'Yes.' *And if Blanca had lived, these people would have been her blood relatives.* But she did not voice the thought.

PART 10 MARISOL 1986 – 1993

CHAPTER 43

Granada, 1986

'¡*Puaj!* This stuff smells horrible.' Marisol stared at the viscous brown liquid slopping about in the bucket as Mamá swished it around with a wooden stick.

'That's why we have the window open.' Her mother looked up and a few drops splattered onto the newspapers covering the kitchen floor. She reached for the other pair of gloves, lying ready on a chair. 'Here, put these on.'

'Do I have to, Mamá?'

'Of course you do, *hija*. If you get splashed, the caustic soda will burn your skin.'

Reluctantly, Marisol pushed her hands into the canary-coloured rubber gloves. They were much too big: the finger ends flopped far beyond her own. 'Why can't we just buy soap like everyone else?'

'Not everyone else, *cariño*; many of the older folk still make it. Besides, ours is much better than anything you find in the shop. Who knows what they put in that stuff?' She wrinkled her nose. 'Olive oil is the best. It softens the skin and prevents infection. Come on, you take a turn now.' Mamá handed her the stick and picked up the plastic container with the oil, trickling it in, a little at a time. 'Five litres of our used oil and we get eleven kilos of soap,' she added as Marisol began to stir. 'Think how much money that saves.'

The oil smelt rancid and fishy but at least it tempered the still pungent fumes of the caustic soda. Marisol found it amazing that this cloudy liquid, accumulated over the last few weeks after frying their fish and meat and potatoes, could produce such sweet-smelling, pure white soap.

A few minutes stirring and her arm was already beginning to ache but she didn't mind too much because it meant having Mamá to herself for a couple of hours this Saturday morning. Papá was at work in the hotel, and so was Belén. He had landed her sister a job on Reception there. Everyone said she and Carlos, who worked as a porter at the same hotel, were very lucky. Some muttered that the custom of *enchufe* was unfair and everyone should have the same opportunity, but Papá just shrugged and said that was how things had always functioned. Carlos and Pablo were still asleep – Carlos because he'd worked a night shift and Pablo because he'd been out late with his girlfriend last night. Luisa was in town, shopping for clothes with a friend.

Sometimes Marisol wished she weren't the youngest in the family. Her brothers and sisters treated her like a baby even though she was nearly twelve. They also complained that she was Mamá's favourite; that she could get away with anything. Belén said there'd been another baby before her who had died at birth and that was why she was spoilt. Marisol didn't consider herself spoilt, though it was true that if Mamá caught any of them being mean to her, she went mad. She'd been the youngest in her own family and her brothers used to make her life a misery, she said. They were always taunting her, and Francisco, the oldest of the five, often pinched or hit her. Only Rafa was kind – when the others weren't around.

Mamá shook the last drops of oil into the bucket and took the stick from Marisol. 'Nearly done.'

'Oh be careful, Mamá!' A splash of the mixture had landed on her bare foot.

'It's nothing. Just pass me the cloth.'

'I'll do it.' As Marisol bent to wipe her mother's foot, the click of the kitchen door made her look up.

Pablo, still in his pyjamas, ruffled her hair as he walked past, glancing into the bucket without much interest. 'Mamá, where's my shirt? The checked one.'

'I haven't ironed it yet, you'll have to wear another.'

'But I want to wear that one. Can't you do it now?'

'You can see I'm busy, Pablo.' Mamá pointed to the juice cartons waiting to be filled. 'I'll do it when I've finished here.'

Pablo turned to Marisol. 'You do it then. You know how to iron, don't you?'

Marisol stuck out her tongue at her brother. 'Do it yourself. I'm helping Mamá.'

'No way. Ironing is women's work.'

'Please yourself.'

'Just be patient, son. This won't take long,' Mamá said, placing the eight juice cartons, their tops evenly sliced off, in a row on the newspaper. 'Pass me the ladle, Marisol.'

'I'm meeting my friends in half an hour,' Pablo said. He took a bottle of milk from the fridge and poured some into a pan to heat.

'If you're making *colacao*, I'll have some too.' Marisol peered into the pan. There was enough milk for two though she doubted if Pablo had intended to make her a cup. Boys never seemed to think of anyone but themselves. She opened the tin of *colacao* and spooned some of the powder into two cups.

'That's it.' Mamá stacked the filled cartons on the worktop. 'Tomorrow we'll cut it into blocks and in two weeks our soap will be ready to use.' She smiled at Marisol. 'A good morning's work done.'

'Mamá, now…?' Pablo fixed his eyes on the clock in case she hadn't got the message.

'Yes, alright.' She peeled off her rubber gloves and went to fetch the iron.

She looked tired. Marisol couldn't see why women and girls should have to do all the work in the house. Lots of women worked outside as well; it wasn't like the old days. Her own mother preferred not to, but Loli's and Maite's and Carmen's had jobs as well, and their fathers and brothers didn't lift a finger at home either. 'Where are you going?' she asked her brother.

Pablo shrugged. 'Just hanging out. We're meeting at Fuente de las Batallas.'

Mamá handed him his shirt and started on one of Papá's from the pile still to be ironed. The way she had to stoop over the ironing board must be uncomfortable, Marisol thought. It wasn't designed for someone tall like Mamá. She was leggy enough to be a model, though the idea of her mother on the catwalk made her giggle. A camel had more poise. Poor Mamá, it was partly her top-heavy figure to blame.

When Pablo had left the kitchen to get dressed, Marisol confronted her mother. 'It's not fair that boys don't have to help.'

'I suppose it's not very fair. But men make such a mess and besides, it's much quicker if I do it myself. In any case, their studies are more important. If Pablo's to get a place at the University after doing his *mili*...'

'But Pablo isn't studying. He's either out with his friends or playing the drums up in his bedroom. And Luisa and I have to study too. It's not that I mind helping, I just don't see why the boys can't give a hand sometimes.'

Mamá put down the iron. 'I do think you have a case but your father wouldn't agree. He thinks domestic work is unmanly. So of course your brothers take a similar view. It was the same in my family: the boys did nothing. Mind you, we had maids... But I was expected to help with some tasks too. And like you, I resented being treated differently; I felt I was being punished.'

'Punished for what? For being a girl?'

'Punished for...' Mamá frowned and her breathing changed. Marisol had noticed before how talking about her childhood seemed to take Mamá away to a dark, unhappy place she would rather not remember. After a long silence, she completed the sentence. 'Punished for not belonging.'

CHAPTER 44

Granada, 1990

'Mamá, I can't go to Antequera tomorrow. I have to study for my English exam on Monday.' Marisol knew this wouldn't go down well with her mother and even less so with her *papá*. Family celebrations weren't something you could easily opt out of. She enjoyed seeing her cousins and was fond of some of her aunts and uncles, but others made her impatient. Their minds were closed to anything different or modern, which wasn't so surprising since most of them had spent their whole lives in or around Antequera. The *abuelos* at least had the excuse of being old.

Aunt Isabel was Marisol's favourite. She'd married a Swede she met on the coast and they'd travelled all over Europe. That probably explained why she was more progressive and didn't judge people for being different. Even now she was widowed, Isabel still went on foreign holidays. She'd go with a friend or sometimes on her own, which Mamá thought very daring. Isabel had tried to persuade Mamá and Papá to go with her to Paris but they wouldn't consider it. The furthest they'd been was Madrid.

'You can study today, *hija*; you must have some time to rest and relax at the weekend. Besides, your grandmother will want to see you. She's eighty-three, she'll be disappointed if you don't come.'

It was Papá's parents who had invited them to the restaurant tomorrow to celebrate *abuela* Maruja's birthday. They hardly ever saw *abuela* Angustias – not since her husband died and she went to live with Uncle Francisco. He and Mamá hadn't been on speaking terms for as long as she could remember. Mamá said when they were children he'd been cruel and spiteful. He looked down on her, and on Papá and the rest of their family too.

'You don't understand, it's not that I don't want to go. Just… well, you know how it is, Mamá, we'll be there the whole day. And to pass the exam I must study a lot: all the grammar, the phrasal verbs, long lists of vocabulary. English is hard, you've no idea.'

'Everyone is going: your brothers and sisters, all the aunts and uncles and cousins. Family is more important.'

'If family is so important, why don't you see more of *your* family?'

Marisol noticed how the muscles in her mother's face tensed as she replied with a frown, 'That's different. There are reasons.'

'What reasons? You make it sound like some great mystery. Why don't you tell me?'

Her mother took a deep breath before replying. 'One day I will tell you, *cariño*. Now go and study. I'll make you a *colacao*.'

Defeated, Marisol went to fetch her English books and settled herself at the table, pulling up the blanket so that the heat from the *brasero* warmed the whole of her lower body.

'Your English matters too, I agree,' her mother said as she set the tray with hot chocolate and a plate of pastries on the table. 'That's why we pay for you to go to the *academia*. It's so much easier to learn when you're young. If your father had had the opportunity to learn English or German as a boy, he'd have risen higher in his profession. Perhaps he'd have become manager of a big hotel. *Ay*, I've tried once or twice myself but I'm too old now. And why would I need English?'

There was no answer to that. Of course Mamá didn't need English: she had no interest in meeting people or going places. Being a housewife and mother was enough for her, she always said (though Marisol had caught her several times absorbed in one of her or Luisa's school textbooks – science or philosophy or history).

Marisol wanted to see the world. She'd been inspired by TV programmes about distant countries: India and Thailand, Iceland and Norway, Canada and Australia… She'd listened to Aunt Isabel's stories. And wherever you went in the world, you needed English. Quite apart from that, most professions demanded a good level of English. If she succeeded in qualifying as a nurse, she'd like to go and work abroad. Not forever – she couldn't imagine leaving Spain and her family for good – but a couple of years, maybe in England or Ireland. Maite's sister was a nurse and she'd found work in Manchester. She said there were lots of jobs over there.

Some people said she looked *anglosajón*. It was probably because she had fair hair and her mother's green eyes. Mamá used to be blonde but her hair had started to go grey in her forties so now she dyed it chestnut. In shops or in the street, Marisol was addressed as *rubia*, as if her hair colour defined who she was. The boys at school would make cheeky comments about her looks. Her brothers were lucky not having to put up with that even though Pablo had green eyes too – much greener than hers – and Carlos was fair. The other fair-haired girls in her class didn't attract so much attention either. Carmen said she should be flattered – it meant they fancied her – but she just found it annoying.

Several tables had been pushed together to accommodate their party at the restaurant in Antequera. Marisol counted twenty-one family members including the two babies, with some still to arrive. She went to kiss her grandmother, who was seated at one end of the table, surrounded by a gaggle of daughters and daughters-in-law fussing over her. Maruja was revelling in the attention, as loud and animated as her husband was silent and withdrawn. Grandpa Ernesto looked completely out of it, a thin, bird-faced old man who suffered from emphysema and spent most of his time playing dominoes at the casino with other old men, including his brother Eugenio, a retired Civil Guard. Mamá said it was because their wives wanted them out from under their feet. Her grandfather owned a bakery but he'd been retired as long as Marisol could remember. Two of his sons, Uncle Ignacio and Uncle Javier ran it now. Papá used to work there too until he decided to take advantage of the tourist boom on the coast and get into the hotel business.

The meal was a ritual that never varied: the same food, starting with *jamón*, cheese and prawns, the same conversations and family gossip. Marisol peeled a prawn and reached for a serviette to wipe her hands before taking the baby from her cousin Laura, who was sitting next to her. She hadn't seen him since his christening six months ago and he'd grown a lot. He was already taking his first steps and babbling what sounded like real words. She gave him a slice of cheese to nibble and moved the plate of prawns out of his reach.

'So when's the next one coming along?' Aunt Mercedes shouted to Laura from further down the table. That started the others off with their nosy questions and rude comments. Marisol would have liked to defend her cousin; it was none of their business.

'Nobody has more than one these days,' Laura retorted. 'Do you think I haven't enough to do with my job and the house and Julio?' To Marisol she whispered, 'If Pedro helped more, I wouldn't mind but you know what men are like.' Pedro was busy talking football with Carlos, oblivious to the remarks flying around the table. Laura took back her baby and smothered him in kisses. 'Of course my mother does her best to help out,' she added, 'but with her back problem, two little ones would be difficult. Anyway, Julio's very special. I'm quite happy to stop at one.'

Much to Marisol's disappointment, Aunt Isabel had not appeared. She was off gallivanting again, Uncle Javier said. He didn't know where, it was all the same to him. Why spend money flying to distant places, he wanted to know, when Spain was so beautiful and had the best food in the world?

Bored with the conversation, Marisol wandered over to talk to Ignacio's two girls, who were playing in a corner of the veranda while everyone waited for their desserts and coffee. One of the girls was the spitting image of her mother, with the same wide face framed by a halo of curly hair, while the other had Ignacio's delicate features and slight frame. Marisol found the resemblances fascinating to observe; they'd been studying genetics in her science class.

Some day it would be fun to draw a family tree like the one in her biology book. Not that it would be easy. Going back a generation or two, there were relatives whose names it was forbidden to utter – something to do with the war, she supposed. 'The past is past, no point dwelling on it,' Papá said. As for Mamá, she buttoned her lips at even the most innocent of questions. 'Every family has secrets,' her friend Carmen argued. But her family seemed to have more than most.

CHAPTER 45

Granada, 1993

All along the beach the bonfires blazed, groups of people silhouetted against the flames. Waving torch beams cut ribbons of light in the night sky and on the sea or fleetingly illuminated the fronds of sugarcane bordering the beach. It was the night of San Juan and Marisol had travelled down to Salobreña with a dozen of her friends to celebrate in the usual way. Jaime was strumming his guitar; now and again someone walked past with a radio blaring out music, momentarily drowning his chords. But neither the guitar nor the radios could compete with the rhythmic crash of waves breaking against the pebbly shore. Mingling with the briny tang of the sea, the odour of frying fish drifted from a nearby *chiringuito* that had stayed open and was busy serving beer. Andrés and Loli, bottles in hand, were returning now, casting long shadows before them.

Further down the beach, Marisol could just make out the tall figure of her brother Carlos with some of his friends. He had stopped off in Lanjarón for the dubious pleasure of running through the streets trying to escape the buckets of water tipped from balconies, and the high-pressure jets wielded by those lucky enough to get hold of a garage or street-cleaner's hose. Mamá had made him take a change of clothes. Just as well – there was no way you could avoid getting drenched. Marisol had gone the previous year and despite the warmth of the June night, caught cold as a result. Carlos was welcome to his soaking; for her the beach was excitement enough.

'Your turn.' Loli gave her a gentle shove and she leapt over the flames, reaching the far side without mishap. Like the others, she had written her wish on a scrap of paper and tossed it into the fire, where it had briefly flared before collapsing, a charred skin amongst the ashes. She knew that luck alone would not be enough to fulfil her wish. She would have to study hard to get good grades in her *bachillerato* and a place on the nursing course.

She had wanted to become a nurse for as long as she could remember. There were none in the family – Maite's sister was the only one she knew personally – but whenever she visited relatives in hospital and observed the nurses in their crisp white uniforms bending over patients to give comfort or care, she thought how rewarding it must be. She imagined assisting the surgeons with operations, holding the hands of the dying, soothing young children waking from anaesthetic after having their tonsils or appendix removed. Paediatric nursing appealed to her, though she wasn't sure if she'd be able to cope with children dying of cancer...

'I know what you'll have wished for,' Carmen teased Alicia. 'Or rather, who you'll have wished for.'

'Wishes are secret,' her friend replied, casting a nervous glance at Nacho in case he'd picked up on Carmen's hint. Marisol kept her own wish close to her chest. Outside the family, she rarely talked of her ambitions. With her friends, the important thing was to have fun, to be gregarious and up for a laugh.

At home, they all knew about her career hopes. 'Rather you than me,' was Belén's comment. She was still working at Papá's hotel, happy enough to have a secure, undemanding job even if the pay was modest. Her husband Sergio worked in his uncle's business and earned good money. Carlos had moved to a bigger hotel and after taking a course in *hostelería*, had decided to train as a chef. Marisol and her sisters had taunted him without mercy when he told them. At home, they pointed out, he could barely be goaded into frying an egg.

Pablo's view of nursing was similar to Belén's. 'You really want to wipe people's bums and clear up their vomit?' He poured all his passion into music. It was just as well they'd moved to the house in Zaidín. The neighbours at their old flat would never have tolerated his loud practising. 'Couldn't you have chosen a quieter instrument like the guitar?' Papá asked when he decided to take up percussion. Failing to get into music school had been a big disappointment to him. Now he worked at a shop selling CDs, gave drumming lessons to beginners and lived in hope that his band, *Los Bichos Raros*, would make it big one day.

Luisa, in her final year of Business Studies at the university, was more encouraging to her younger sister. 'Go for what you want,' she advised. 'Don't let anyone put you off.' Her parents too were supportive. 'You've got a caring nature,' Mamá said. 'You'll make a good nurse.'

Returning home in the early hours of the morning, she was surprised to find Papá downstairs, talking into the telephone in his pyjamas. He put down the phone and rubbed his eyes. 'My uncle Eugenio has died,' he said. 'You'd better grab a few hours' sleep before we set off for Antequera this afternoon.'

She had rarely seen her great uncle till he retired. The *Guardia Civil* weren't allowed to work in their home province. Uncle Eugenio had worked in Jaén for a time, then Almería and elsewhere, only returning to Antequera about ten years ago. He never talked about his work or about the war. But then nobody talked about the war, least of all the generation that had fought in it. Any questions were met with a stubborn silence: it was a taboo subject. She had heard some of her older relatives muttering about the danger of 'loose tongues' as if Franco were still alive, with spies listening around every corner. Or was it red assassins they were afraid of? Or ETA? Marisol suspected they didn't even know what they feared.

At the *tanatorio,* other retired Civil Guards, some in their old uniforms, came to pay their respects, accompanied by their wives. One of them, who introduced himself as Vicente, said he'd worked with Eugenio in Jaén many years ago, but didn't give any more detail. He walked with a limp and had to lean on his wife for support. Most of Papá's side of the family were there and Marisol took the opportunity to catch up with her cousins.

When Aunt Isabel rolled in – late as usual – Marisol and her mother both made a beeline for her. She was wearing a bright pink dress, its revealing neckline partly covered by a floaty lilac scarf draped loosely round her shoulders, and carrying a straw hat in her hand. Cousin Pedro smirked and Uncle Ignacio gave her a disapproving look.

'Poor old Eugenio,' she said. 'He never quite knew how to occupy himself after retiring. When you've led an exciting life, it's hard to get used to routine. I hope I never have to.'

'I can't imagine you will,' Mamá said. 'Where are you off to next?'

'My new friend Luigi – he's Italian – wants to take me to Sardinia,' she said. Marisol did her best to suppress the smile that came to her lips. Aunt Isabel's life, she often thought, was like one of those soppy Corín Tellado romances her mother sometimes read. Mamá was looking shocked. 'By the way,' Isabel continued, 'did you read that book I passed on to you – by the Italian writer Umberto Eco? *El Nombre de la Rosa*.'

'Not yet, the house and family keep me busy. But I will.'

Aunt Isabel turned to Marisol. 'So how's your English coming on? I imagine you must be speaking it like a native by now.'

'*¡Ojala!*' Marisol replied. 'I wish! But it is improving. And next month I'm going to London to stay with my penfriend Clare for two weeks. So I guess I'll find out.'

Mamá was helping Marisol pack for her trip to England. 'You must take a sweater,' she insisted. 'And a rain jacket of course. People say it can be cold and wet there even in summer.' Marisol deferred to her mother, though she found it hard to imagine needing a sweater in July. Her excitement about the visit had been building over the last few weeks. She couldn't wait to see the sights of London. And Clare had promised a trip to Oxford too; they could go on the train, she wrote. Now her departure was only two days off, she did wonder if she'd miss her family. She'd never been away from them for so long: ten whole days. She felt a rush of affection for Mamá. If only she could penetrate that part of her that remained always closed off.

'Mamá.' Marisol put down the pile of folded T-shirts she'd been holding and faced her mother. 'You promised years ago to tell me why you never spend time with your family. You said there was a reason…'

'I saw María Angustias at Christmas.'

'That doesn't answer my question.'

Mamá pushed the case out of the way and sat down on the edge of the bed, motioning Marisol to sit by her. 'You're right,' she said with a heavy sigh. 'I did promise to tell you.' She was silent for so long, Marisol thought that was going to be it. But then the words came pouring out in a rush. 'Angustias isn't my mother, nor José my father; your uncles aren't my brothers.' She paused to draw breath. 'I was adopted.'

Marisol stared in surprise. Yet now Mamá had revealed the fact, she wondered why she hadn't guessed. It explained so much: her strained relations with most of her family, the lack of self-confidence that made her fearful as a rabbit when faced with any unfamiliar situation. Questions surged through her mind. 'How old were you?' she asked. 'Do you remember your real parents?'

'I was a baby. Listen, *cariño*, this is between you and me. Your brothers and sisters have no idea. I'd prefer to keep it that way.'

'But Mamá, why does it have to be a secret? There's nothing wrong with being adopted. It's not your fault.' Not her fault she'd been starved of love and made to feel inferior. Why had they adopted Mamá, only to treat her as a usurper? Decades had passed and still the wounds were raw.

'I know it's not my fault, but all the same… Promise me, please.' Shame was written in the droop of her head, her shifting eyes. She wouldn't look at Marisol. 'Even your father had no idea until long after we were married.'

'Are you serious?' But Marisol could see that she was. 'Don't worry,' she said, moving closer to her mother and stroking her hair. 'I promise not to say anything.' The tension in Mamá's body seemed to loosen a little. 'But tell me, do you know anything about your biological mother and father? Who they were? Why they gave you up?'

Mamá examined her bitten-down thumbnails as if deliberating which to chew. '*Nada*. Now, let's get on with your packing.'

PART 11 CONSUELO 1992-1993

CHAPTER 46

Granada, 1992

Consuelo hated going to Francisco's house. She stood at the door, trying to steady her nerves before knocking. She was glad Luisa and Pablo had agreed to accompany her. It wasn't her brother she had come to see, it was Mamá. The Christmas holiday was a time for family and she would have felt guilty neglecting her mother at this season, especially now Mamá was more or less housebound. Rafa and his wife were here too. She hoped one of them – or Francisco's wife Milagros or son Paco – would come to the door rather than Francisco himself.

They had arrived in Antequera yesterday and were staying with Enrique's sister Ana for the festivities. Tonight's big Christmas meal would be at her house, with Consuelo's parents-in-law and most of Enrique's side of the family present. She had left Belén and Marisol helping their aunt in the kitchen while Enrique talked men's affairs with Gonzalo, Ana's husband.

'Come on.' Luisa gave a knock and then tried the door. It was unlocked; Consuelo had no choice but to follow her son and daughter in. At her call, Francisco came out to greet them. 'Ah, you're here.' He kissed Pablo and Luisa and then, with less warmth, Consuelo. 'What a long time it's been. Well, Rafa and Brígida have been here since eleven; they've gone out with Paco to walk the dogs. But Mamá is waiting to see you.'

She was sitting with a rug over her knees watching the television, turned up to a volume intolerable to anyone with normal hearing. She gestured to Consuelo to cut the sound. Approaching Mamá to kiss her papery cheeks, Consuelo smelt face powder and some indefinable scent of old age. Her hair had thinned and been left to go white, though traces of the copper-coloured dye she had used until recently still coloured the ends. One or two patches on her scalp were completely bald. How old was she? Eighty-nine? Ninety? Consuelo noticed a collection of pill bottles on a shelf. Mamá had various digestive complaints as well as a weak heart and bad legs. Life could hold few pleasures for her these days.

'How is the family?' she asked, her voice weary, indifferent.

'They're all well. Pablo and Luisa are here with me – they'll come and say hello in a minute.' Consuelo told her what each of the children was doing: Belén still working at the hotel, Carlos hoping to become a chef, playing basketball in his free time… She suspected Mamá wasn't really listening or had forgotten to whom these names belonged.

She didn't mention her big disappointment earlier in the year. They had always assumed that when *el buho* reached retirement age, Enrique would be promoted to manager of the hotel. After all his years of loyalty, he deserved no less. Then a year before Pepe was due to retire, the proprietor introduced his son-in-law to the staff. Marcos was young and brash and full of plans to change things that had always worked perfectly well. It soon became clear that he was being lined up for the job of manager. Poor Enrique was devastated. Besides the humiliation of having to work under the younger man, they'd been counting on his promotion to pay off some of their mortgage. From Angustias she would inherit the amount stipulated by law and not a peseta more.

Mamá's eyes drifted back to the television. She had aged a great deal since the last time – not that long ago, surely. The anger Consuelo had felt towards her mother for so much of her life seemed misplaced now. Observing her, what she saw was just a rather pitiable old woman, all her power gone. Had Mamá loved her? It was a question she had pondered often as a child. She still didn't know the answer.

The room was cold, an electric radiator placed near Mamá's chair giving out only the feeblest of warmth. She rearranged the woollen shawl draped around her mother's shoulders and went to examine the dial on the radiator. It was turned to the lowest setting. 'Milagros won't like that,' Mamá said, noticing Consuelo adjust the knob. 'She's always complaining about the price of electricity.'

'It's a cold day, Mamá. At your age you need to keep warm.' How mean of her, Consuelo thought. Having inherited most of Papá's estate, Francisco could hardly be short of money.

'*Ay*, I'm fortunate to have a daughter. Daughters-in-law, they're not the same.' Her hand, mottled and veiny, shook as she pulled the rug up higher. Then, speaking more to herself than Consuelo, she added, 'I wasn't always kind to you, *hija*. God will forgive me, I hope.' It was God's forgiveness she wanted, not her daughter's: an assurance of her place in heaven. 'Was I hard on you? A little perhaps, at times. But you needed discipline. A girl can't be left to run wild.'

Consuelo thought of her own three daughters, none of them running wild despite the love and tenderness she and Enrique had lavished on them.

'I remember when we fetched you from the hospital in Jaén. Such a tiny creature you were, much smaller than any of the boys. But your lungs were strong – *madre mía*, how you yelled in the car.' Of course she had yelled. Yelled for the mother she knew and loved, against this impostor. 'Until I put you to the breast,' Angustias continued. 'I still had some milk from my own baby, you see. After that, you slept all the way. So hungry you were; who knows if you'd have survived without us?'

'I'll send Pablo and Luisa in to see you.' Consuelo's patience with Mamá was running out already. Her mother had never been interested in anyone but herself.

'It's over fifty years ago and I was only four.' Rafa stroked his beard. 'I'm sorry, Consuelo. I really can't remember much at all. You could try asking Francisco, he was older. Or José María.'

She had intercepted Rafa as the group returned with the dogs, steering him away from the others before posing her question. If Mamá couldn't or wouldn't tell her the full story about her origins, might her brothers know something? Could they have overheard a long-ago conversation between their parents or between Mamá and Uncle Rodrigo? Might some clue have been dropped? Francisco had said her mother was a red. What else did he know?

'Never mind,' she said to Rafa. 'I'll try asking Francisco.' But she would not give him that satisfaction. Nor say anything to José María, who would run straight to his older brother. The two of them were so close they'd even married women from the same family. Reme and Milagros were first cousins. Better to remain in ignorance than lay herself open to Francisco's contempt.

Even before they reached Ana's house, Consuelo could hear her sister-in-law shouting.

'That'll be Gonzalo getting in the way while she's cooking,' Luisa said.

'Don't be cheeky,' Consuelo chided her.

'Well you know Aunt Ana, she's always shouting at her husband. Everything he does is wrong, especially in the kitchen.'

'It's true,' Pablo agreed. 'And he's only trying to help.'

Consuelo couldn't argue. Ana did shout a lot. And the way she criticised Gonzalo shocked her. She would never talk to Enrique in such a manner, however irritated she was by his untidy habits or lack of consideration.

Belén and Sergio had arrived while they were out. Sergio had a new car, a Citroën, which he was showing off to his cousins. It must have cost a fortune, Consuelo thought as she listened to him pointing out all its state-of-the-art features. Belén would be thirty in the New Year: it was time they started a family. She couldn't wait to be a grandmother, but whenever she broached the subject of babies with her daughter, Belén brushed off her advice. 'What's the rush?' she asked. Of course, with Sergio working for his uncle on a good salary, they were enjoying life: eating in smart restaurants, taking holidays on the coast, spending money at the hairdresser's and on clothes (Belén wouldn't dream of making her own outfits as Consuelo had done until not so long ago). The couple had bought their own flat with a mortgage from the bank. They were doing well.

Things were different these days, for sure. Luisa had a boyfriend, Arturo, but they weren't in the slightest hurry to get married. Consuelo tried not to think about what they got up to in his father's car or when they went on holiday together. Marisol said she didn't want a serious relationship, her studies were more important. She preferred to go out with different boys rather than stick with just one. Consuelo worried about the risks of such casual arrangements. Would the boys respect her daughters? She had discussed her anxieties with Enrique and he agreed with her. The pill was to blame for today's loose morals, he said, echoing his brother Federico, the priest. The girls argued that it gave women more freedom, more equality with men, and that she and Enrique were old-fashioned. Perhaps there was something in that. All the same, she couldn't help feeling things had gone a little too far in the direction of freedom; there must be some rules, some limits.

CHAPTER 47

Granada, 1993

'Mamá is asking to see you. The doctor says she's close to death.' Francisco's voice on the phone was strained. 'Will you come?'

'I can't come today, Francisco. Marisol is due back from London. We're driving to the airport in Málaga to pick her up.'

'Let Enrique go. Or ask him to drop you off in Antequera on the way.'

'Can't it wait till tomorrow?' Consuelo longed to see Marisol after her ten-day absence and resented the dictatorial tone of her older brother.

'Mother may not last till tomorrow. She's adamant that you come; she has something important to tell you, she says.'

Consuelo sighed. If Mamá really was at death's door, she could not refuse. Besides, she was curious. 'I'll come,' she told Francisco. As she put down the phone, a torrent of emotions flooded though her: shock, grief, anger, fear, all subsumed in a sense of helpless panic. Love and hate were opposites yet she found it hard to disentangle one from the other when it came to her feelings about Mamá.

'Courage, Chelo,' Enrique whispered as he pulled up outside Francisco's house.

Consuelo leaned across to embrace him. 'You'll explain to Marisol, won't you. Tell her I'll be home as soon as I can.'

It was Milagros who opened the door to her. 'Your brother has gone out,' she said, and giving Consuelo a sharp look, added, 'It's a shame you two can't overcome your differences. Life's too short. I believe families should stick together.'

Consuelo ignored the rebuke. 'Is Mamá in her bedroom?'

Milagros nodded. 'She's very weak. Later the priest is coming.'

Mamá appeared to be asleep but when Consuelo approached the

bed, she opened her eyes and lifted a gnarled hand. 'Help me sit, *hija*,' she croaked. Her breath was wheezy, her face pallid. Consuelo shifted her gently up the bed, a few centimetres at a time, until she was sitting propped against the pillows. With each movement, she winced with pain. 'There were papers,' she said. 'A name. Your mother...'

'Tell me.' Consuelo's heart was beating fast. 'Tell me, Mamá. What was her name?'

'Her name was Rosa.'

For some reason, the title of that book Isabel had given her came to mind. *El Nombre de la Rosa: The Name of the Rose.* What a strange coincidence. As if the book held a message for her.

'She was English.'

'English?' This new revelation left Consuelo open-mouthed. She had an English mother. How come? What was an Englishwoman doing in Uncle Rodrigo's hospital? Mamá's head drooped. She had better not fall asleep. 'And her surname? Do you still have the papers, Mamá?'

Angustias shook her head. 'I'm sorry, child, my memory... It may come back to me. Began with a P or perhaps a T...'

'Try and remember.' Consuelo felt like shaking her. The information was no use at all without more detail. Once Mamá passed away, there would be no one who could tell her; she would never find out the truth.

'Wait... Her year of birth, I remember that. She was born the same year as Elias, my youngest brother. *Ay*, Elias, he was always my favourite. Murdered by the reds in 1936 when he was hardly more than a boy. Twenty-one only...'

'The papers, Mamá. What happened to the papers? My birth certificate.'

'The papers? I suppose we destroyed them after... We were given new papers for you. José had friends. In any case, there was a law passed in 1941, it was all regularised.'

'Anything else you can remember? My father?'

'Ah yes, I recall now. The papers said '*padre desconocido*'.

'Father unknown?'

'Exactly. You see? She didn't even know the father. Sad to say your mother was a loose woman. How would you have turned out if she'd been allowed to keep you?' Mamá's voice was fading, her eyelids flickering.

'Allowed? You mean she wanted to keep me?' Consuelo felt faint. So her mother hadn't rejected her; she had been removed forcibly from the Englishwoman named Rosa, who was deemed unfit to bring her up.

'Mamá?' She was asleep, slumped to one side, her breathing still raspy but more regular now. Consuelo supported her back and tried to ease her down, to make her more comfortable in the bed. As she sat watching Angustias, the only mother she had ever known, a feeling of acute loneliness gripped her. She wished Rafa were here – the one brother who cared about her. He must be on his way, surely. The weight of what she knew and what she would never know pressed down on her, a solid band of iron crushing her chest. Enrique would be arriving in Málaga now, but even if he were here by her side, he could not be expected to understand. Neither he nor her children. She must bear her anguish alone.

'The priest is on his way.' Milagros was standing at the door of the room. 'She asked for him this morning. Let us hope she wakes. According to the doctor, she could pass any time.'

To her surprise, Consuelo found her eyes pricking. She wiped away a tear.

'Francisco is back, with José María.' Milagros gave her a hard look. 'Both he and Juan plan to stay with us tonight.'

'And Rafa?'

'Very likely. There'll be little room, but you can sleep at our neighbour's.'

Seated at the table with her four brothers for the modest supper Milagros had prepared, Consuelo squirmed with discomfort. Juan was babbling without pause while Francisco and José María sat in sombre silence. Rafa, unable to disguise his sorrow, nevertheless made stalwart attempts to ease the atmosphere. They pecked dutifully at the ham and cheese and *tortilla* brought to the table but none of them had much appetite. By turns one of them would go and sit with Mamá, reporting back on her state. Mostly she slept, but occasionally she would stir and mutter a few words. As soon as they had eaten, Consuelo made an excuse to escape next door. She was glad to be accommodated with the old widow, a kind and unassuming woman who respected her need for quiet.

It was still pitch dark when Rafa knocked on the door to tell her Mamá had slipped away during the night, peacefully in her sleep. She dressed quickly and followed him into the house. José María handed her a *chupito* of brandy. She gulped it down, welcoming the fiery sensation in her gullet. Her brothers were already busy with funeral arrangements, vying for use of the phone to call their wives. She would wait before ringing Enrique.

'Consuelo,' Francisco was beckoning her aside. 'Mamá asked me to give you a message. It sounds like nonsense to me, a word that doesn't even exist, but she was adamant. "*Tili*. Tell Consuelo *tili*," she said. "Tell her I remembered." Moments later, she lost consciousness.'

'*Tili*? Was that all she said?'

He shrugged. 'Take no notice, her mind was going. I promised to pass it on, that's all.'

'Thank you, Francisco.' Consuelo wandered into the kitchen and found the *cafetera*. She filled the pot with water and looked for coffee, her mind struggling to make sense of the strange word Mamá had spoken. What did it mean? And then, as the coffee began to bubble up, its significance dawned on her. *Tili* was a name, the *apellido* of her mother. Rosa Tili. She repeated it to herself, embracing it, assimilating the resonance of its four syllables. Rosa Tili. Was she still alive? She would be old but not as old as Mamá. Born the same year as Elias, the youngest of the family. Which year was that? Aunt Piedad – the only one of Mamá's siblings still living – would know. If she came to the funeral…

Consuelo poured a glass of coffee for herself and another for Rafa who had just entered the kitchen. He put an arm round her. 'Are you alright?' he asked.

She nodded and leant her head against his chest. She could feel his heart beating under the thin summer shirt he wore. Its steady pulsing comforted her.

'They'll come very soon for her body,' he said. 'I imagine there'll be quite a crowd for the vigil at the morgue this evening. And tomorrow at the burial.'

Consuelo raised her head. 'I'll call Enrique in a moment.' She paused, unsure whether to confide in Rafa, but she needed to tell someone. 'Rafa, my mother...' She pursed her lips.

'What? What about Mamá?'

'No, not Mamá. My real mother. She was...'

'Sister, it's best not to think about your *real* mother.' He drew inverted commas in the air as he spoke. 'Today least of all. You're upset, it's natural.' He smoothed the hair from her forehead, his hands gentle, loving. 'Come, drink your coffee and then you can call Enrique.'

PART 12 MARISOL 1996 – 2010

CHAPTER 48

Granada, 1996

'Are you ready, Clare? We're moving on.' Marisol nudged her English friend as each of the group in turn paid for their drinks. This was their fourth bar of the evening, the night still young. It was fun having Clare along on the *marcha*. This was her second visit to Granada so she knew the score. In England they rarely went out in big groups like this and of course there were no free *tapas*. They drank more, and without eating, they got drunk far too quickly. 'Did you like the aubergines?' she asked Clare.

'First time I've had them with black treacle but yes, kind of an interesting combination.'

'It's a typical dish here, probably from Arab times. You'll like the next bar too. They do great *boquerones*.' Clare looked blank. 'Anchovies.'

She was rubbing her eyes. Unlike the rest of them, Clare didn't smoke. Marisol could see she found the cloud of cigarette fumes around the bar uncomfortable. Not that the pubs in England were any better. It was eleven thirty; after the next drink they'd probably move on to one of the *copas* bars in Pedro Alarcón or maybe head for the disco in Sacromonte.

Alberto put an arm round Clare as they made their way along the crowded street. He'd been hanging around her all evening. She had a boyfriend Steve in England – they'd been together three years – but she seemed to be enjoying Alberto's attention so Marisol didn't interfere. Clare could look after herself. She linked arms with Marina to follow the others down San Antón.

Clare was beautiful, not at all Anglo-Saxon in her looks. A stranger seeing the two of them together would assume it was Marisol, with her light hair and skin, greenish eyes and long legs, who came from

England, while Clare would be taken for Spanish. Her complexion was as dark as any Spaniard's, her thick hair almost black and her eyes with their long, curved eyelashes were, to use her own words, 'mud-brown'. There was Italian blood somewhere down the line, she had explained to Marisol when they first met.

One of her aunts was researching their family history. She had traced the family back about ten generations and unearthed all kinds of scandalous stories, including an illegitimate son born to Clare's great-grandmother and her Italian lover. A few generations further back, one of her relatives had been hanged for murder. 'Where did she find the information?' Marisol asked. Clare said you could send off for the records from some office but it had become like an addiction for Aunt Stella; she'd travelled all over the country looking in church registers and even visiting graveyards. Marisol was intrigued. She would have liked to meet Clare's aunt and learn more.

They managed to squeeze into the heaving bar and order their drinks. 'Too late for *tapas*,' the waiter said, pointing at the clock on the wall. Everyone was shouting to be heard above the hubbub. She glanced at Clare, happily chatting away in Spanish with Alberto, Juanjo and Carmen. The group were discussing where to go next. Marisol yawned. She'd been working at the hospital from early this morning on her *práctica*.

'Are you up for the disco?' she mouthed to Clare. The English weren't used to staying out all night as they did here at weekends. On her visits to London they'd usually been in bed by midnight, except for the two occasions they went clubbing.

Clare gave the thumbs up. Marisol hoped she'd be able to match Clare's stamina tonight. Once she started dancing, she usually found a second wind; the volume and beat of the music helped keep her going. And they'd have the whole of Saturday to catch up on sleep.

'Are you two girls alright in the back there?' Papá turned his head briefly as they rounded yet another curve in the road twisting up towards Pampaneira.

'I'm totally bowled over.' Clare's eyes were swivelling this way and that. 'The views are absolutely stunning. These soaring mountains…

And all the terraces planted with fruit trees – they're using the land to grow stuff, it's incredible.'

Marisol couldn't see Papá's face but she imagined the beaming smile Clare's response would have prompted. It had been his idea to show her the dramatic panoramas and picturesque villages of the Alpujarras. Mamá had insisted on stopping in Órgiva for a coffee, sitting at one of the outside tables of the café opposite the church.

'It was the Moors who terraced the hillsides and built the irrigation channels,' Papá said. 'They knew about agriculture.'

Negotiating one tight bend after another, he kept his eyes focused on the road. 'I'm afraid you do need a strong stomach in these parts. Tell me if you feel queasy and I'll stop.' They passed a couple of small villages, their white houses clustered around a church. 'They used to be cut off up here for weeks in the winter,' he added. 'It's still a hard life, especially for the old folk.'

'They must be very tough,' Mamá said. They were entering Pampaneira now and she pointed to a lame elderly woman struggling along with the aid of a stick, hauling a shopping trolley behind her up the steeply sloping street. Another followed, bent almost double under the weight of several plastic bags of shopping.

'Are we having lunch here?' Marisol asked. 'I don't think I can take many more curves without a break.'

'We'll have a walk round first,' Mamá said. 'Perhaps Clare would like to buy some of the local produce: figs or almonds or a jar of honey?'

In the main square, groups of men sat at the café tables, guarding their hands of dominoes, smoking and nodding to each other as they played a leisurely game. Others, their faces mottled and lined from years of outdoor toil under the relentless sun, occupied the benches, short legs spread and planted firmly on the ground. A donkey waited on one side of the square, its panniers laden with firewood. This was a different world from Granada capital, Marisol thought, let alone from London. No wonder Clare was fazed by it.

Entering one of the shops, they were pressed to try the almond cheese. 'It's like marzipan,' Clare said as she nibbled it. 'But what's this *pan de higos*?'

'*Pruébelo*,' the shop-owner said, cutting a generous slice off the roll of fig bread and passing it to her. 'Come on, taste it.'

'I'll get some for my parents,' she said. 'And one of those traditional wineskins for Steve.' Mamá bought a big bag of the sugar-dusted dried figs to take home with them.

In one of the *bodegas*, they sampled the local wine and sherry straight from dark wooden barrels. Clusters of tawny gold hams were hung by their legs from the ceiling, each with its miniature white cone underneath to catch the juices. Marisol remembered the place from a previous visit several years ago with Maite and her family, who came from one of these villages.

'Let's go down here,' she said, pointing to a narrow winding street with a gully down the middle. As it gradually descended towards the lower outskirts of the village, the mountainous views opened up around them, while below, the land fell away to a deep river gorge. Because the houses were built on so many different levels, you were continually looking down on another spread of flat roofs covered in grey shingle, each sprouting one or two cylindrical, capped chimney pots. They reached the *lavadero*, an old washhouse with its double row of stone sinks.

'I remember the one in Antequera,' Papá said. 'When I was a child, the women still used to take their washing there. No one had washing machines in those days and many houses were without running water.'

From one of the arched windows, they looked down on the church and across to the shadowy, blue mountains. Closer at hand, the slopes were dotted with trees – almonds and a few *caquis* and pomegranates each with its filigree of new leaves. Amongst them the cherry trees stood out, resplendent in clouds of delicate white blossom. April was a good time to come, they all agreed. Clare was snapping away with her camera. 'There's nothing in Britain to match this,' she said, spreading her hands to indicate the landscape. 'You must have found the English countryside really boring.'

'London certainly wasn't boring. And I loved Oxford with the river and all those old colleges.' On her first visit she had wanted to see the famous sights like the Tower of London and Big Ben and Trafalgar Square that she'd only seen on TV and in books. The second time, Clare had shown her the more characterful parts of the city, those with fewer tourists: Camden market, Greenwich, the pubs and clubs of Soho. From Ealing, where her family lived, they had made daytrips to both Oxford and Cambridge on the train. 'Best was the punting in Cambridge. It was a little crazy,' she added, remembering how drenched they'd all been after spending a day on the river Cam with Steve and a friend of his. Luckily it was summer and they'd been able to dry off in the sun.

A thought occurred to her. 'You know what?' she said, grinning. 'If you come here for San Juan, I can get my own back on you for that. We'll go to Lanjarón. We passed it today, do you remember? The first village, after the water factory.'

'When is San Juan? And what happens in Lanjarón?'

'June 24th and I'm not going to spoil the surprise.'

'Next year then. I should have finished my finals by the 24th. *¡Libertad total!*'

They always talked in Spanish with Marisol's family and friends. 'Listen to her *granaino* accent,' Pablo had teased last night. It was true. Clare had picked up many colloquial expressions and even fallen into the sloppy Andalusian habit of missing consonants.

'Your Spanish is really good,' Marisol said.

'Hmm, not as good as your English, unfortunately.'

'You're kidding.' Marisol took her English seriously – she still hoped to work abroad – but now she was nearing the end of her nursing studies with exams looming, precious little time remained for English. Roll on the summer and the holiday in Scotland she and Clare had planned. The Edinburgh Festival would be brilliant fun.

At a restaurant back in the village, Papá insisted they order the typical Alpujarran fare of potatoes fried in olive oil with *chorizo* sausage and black pudding, the *plato alpujarreño*. Seeing the horror on Clare's face when the plate, swimming in oil, was put in front of her, Marisol couldn't help laughing. 'You'll survive,' she said.

'I'm just thinking of all those hairpin bends ahead of us this afternoon. Are we going higher?'

'Two more villages,' Papá said, 'but there's no hurry. You'll have time to digest your meal.'

'Just as well.'

Twice on their way up to Bubión and Capileira and once more as they were driving back down to Órgiva, they had to stop for large flocks of goats.

'I can't see my dad being so patient,' Clare said as they waited. 'He hates any kind of hold-up. Being stuck in traffic drives him crazy.'

Papá turned and smiled at her. '*Bueno*, those who live in the country have more patience. Life is slower.'

'Would you like to live in a place like this?' Marisol asked her friend?

'I think I'd find it too quiet. I'm a city girl really. What about you?'

'As a place to chill out for a week or two it's great, but living here all the time, I'd soon get bored.'

'I wouldn't mind,' Mamá said. 'If there was work for your father.'

'You could get a job in one of those spa hotels in Lanjarón, Papá. Did you see them? And the guests, walking down the main street in bathrobes and slippers on their way to or from the *balneario*?'

'Oh they have coachloads of pensioners coming from Granada or further afield to take the treatments. But to get a job... Well, I don't have any contacts; it would be difficult. In any case, I'll be retiring in another six years.'

Six years was ages, Marisol thought, especially if, like Papá, you weren't happy in your job. But her parents were hopelessly stuck in their ways. She wondered what it would take to shift them out of their rut to try something new. Clare's mother was training to be a counsellor, her father volunteered on archaeological digs; they went on walking holidays in France and Italy. Her own parents looked set to carry on with the same old habits and routines for the rest of their lives.

'Do you know what I'd really like?' Papá said. 'I'd like to open my own little hotel in one of the smaller villages. Foreign tourists love the Alpujarras. Some have even bought houses and *cortijos* here. It could work out well.'

Was it just a dream or would he prove her wrong and actually do something adventurous? 'That's a great idea,' she said, clapping her hands. 'Do it, Papá.'

CHAPTER 49

Granada, 2000

Marisol picked up the remote and switched channels to *telecinco*. She wasn't the only one in the family to enjoy the new series, *Hospital Central*, which had taken over from *Médico de Familia* as her favourite TV programme. Mamá hadn't yet missed an episode and Papá watched too if he was home.

He joined them just as the theme music started up. As they watched the drama unfold with an angry conversation between a surgeon and a nurse over the operating table, Papá nudged her. 'Is it true to life, do you think?' She was fully qualified now and working in the hospital of San Cecilio, much to her parents' pride. Mamá had insisted she frame her Diploma and hang it on the wall.

Marisol shrugged. 'Some of the time it's quite boring on the ward,' she said. 'There are lots of routine tasks – like taking patients' temperature or blood pressure, keeping records.' Papá looked disappointed, Mamá relieved. 'But we have some difficult moments too. The other day a man was brought in seriously injured after a car accident; it was a toss-up whether he'd even survive. In the end they had to amputate both his legs. His wife and parents were waiting there, his mother hysterical. I knew the odds but I had to try and calm her down… It was so hard, I mean, what can you say? Then there are the relatives who get angry with the medical stuff for failing to save their loved ones – just like in last week's episode of the programme, do you remember?'

She didn't mention the current scandals concerning the staff: the mystery of the missing supplies, the anaesthetist who was rumoured to snort cocaine on his days off. Her colleague Rocío was having an affair with a married doctor. The way they carried on made it obvious to everyone, even the patients. One of them had remarked on it, whispering his disapproval when the screens were up round his bed. Their behaviour made her uncomfortable. She was glad Victor worked at a sports centre and not at the hospital. That way it was easy to keep her private and professional lives separate.

Tomorrow was their first anniversary. She doubted if they'd make another year. They had fun together but neither of them was serious: sexual attraction and sparky banter formed the basis of their relationship. With a life partner she would need a much deeper connection. She tried to imagine how it must have been for her parents' generation: the frustration of being trailed at all times by a chaperone – aunt, sister, mother, grandmother… Couples would be lucky to steal so much as a kiss before marriage. No wonder they used to wed at sixteen or seventeen.

Sex was a taboo subject for both her parents. Mamá usually left the room or switched channels when anything vaguely suggestive ('*indecente*' she called it) came on the TV. Papá watched but you could tell he was embarrassed. Having grown up under the dictatorship when everything was censored, their prudish attitudes were only to be expected. It was Belén who had enlightened Marisol about sex. Being the oldest, she complained, was a big disadvantage in terms of freedom. The strict rules imposed on her meant opportunities to spend time alone with Sergio had to be carefully contrived. They weren't allowed to go away together even when they were engaged. By the time Luisa hit adolescence, things had changed and Mamá and Papá were more relaxed. Marisol had it the easiest. They never questioned her; perhaps they preferred not to know what she got up to.

Pablo came in with an armful of cardboard boxes he'd spotted outside the supermarket. He was packing up his possessions, ready to move out. Two of the other musicians in his band had found a three-bedroom flat to rent in the Vega and suggested he share. It would feel odd being the only one at home with Mamá and Papá. Belén had left years ago when she got married; Luisa was living with Arturo in the Albaicín; Carlos – married now – had moved to Almuñecar where he worked as a chef.

Marisol was also thinking of leaving. The idea of spending a couple of years abroad to widen her experience had taken hold. She was trying to decide between England and Germany. Improving her English was important but the challenge of acquiring some German also appealed: she enjoyed learning languages. Her long-term plan was to specialise, maybe try for a Masters.

From Pablo's bedroom came sounds of thumping and banging – not from the drums, which had already been moved to his new flat – but from heavy objects being thrown into boxes. Marisol went to see if her brother needed help packing.

He unplugged his headphones. 'I'm just about finished,' he said. 'Come in, close the door, there's something I want to ask you.'

'What's that?'

'It's something Papá said.' Pablo's voice had dropped to a whisper. 'Something very strange. He was listening to that recording we made and he said, "I don't know where you get your musical talent from, there's no one in the family. Unless... Mamá's side is an unknown, of course." I asked him what he meant and he got all flustered and told me to forget it, he didn't mean anything. Then he suddenly remembered that Mamá herself used to play the piano.' Pablo fastened the cardboard tabs on the last of the boxes. 'But why would he say that about her family?'

Marisol hesitated. She had promised Mamá not to reveal the secret of her adoption. On the other hand, now Papá had inadvertently let slip that her origins were unknown, the cat was almost out of the bag already. 'Pablo,' she said, taking care to keep her voice low, 'you must swear not to repeat this to anyone, do you agree?' He nodded, a bemused look on his face. 'Mamá was adopted.'

'Really? But why the secrecy? What's the big deal?'

'She's ashamed, you know Mamá. Anyway, you mustn't let on that I told you.'

'OK, I won't,' he said with a shrug. 'By the way, are you and Victor coming to hear us play at *Alexis Viernes* next Friday?'

'You bet. We're looking forward to it.'

The old man they called Pepito was becoming more and more agitated. If she couldn't calm him down, he would need sedation. Marisol disliked giving sedatives unless strictly necessary, but it was up to the doctor to decide.

'Damned Maxims weigh a ton,' he muttered. 'British dead everywhere. No! Leonardo's been hit, he's screaming… Ramón lying there, his guts spilling out…' Pepito groaned. 'Fascist bastards.'

She took his hand and stroked it. 'Easy now, Pepito, the war is over, no more fascists. We have democracy, we're at peace.'

Thrashing his legs under the covers, he shouted, 'Why are they telling us to hold on? We've no chance. Fucking Moors so close I can see their faces.'

Poor man, the trauma was still with him after more than sixty years. He wasn't the first she had seen reliving the terrors of his youth, the dreadful war that had blighted the lives of her grandparents' generation. Her stint on the geriatric ward had opened her eyes to the hell these men and women had endured. She cupped Pepito's face in her hands, feeling the stubbly growth on his chin. Later, if time allowed, she would shave him.

He opened his eyes and blinked a few times before managing to focus. '*Ay*, you're a pretty one,' he said. 'Must be in heaven, *je je*.' Then noticing her nurse's uniform, 'I'm in the hospital, *claro*. You know…' He cleared his throat and spat into the bowl Marisol passed him. 'For a moment I thought I was still at Jarama. Suicide Hill, they called it afterwards, where that battle took place. They sent us to reinforce the XV, the British Battalion of the Internationals. It was hopeless. Lambs to the slaughter.' Beads of sweat moistened his forehead. 'Had the Moors after us at the end, the few of us still on our feet. Charging at us in their red turbans.'

All of a sudden he started to sing, warbling in his weak old man's voice.

'Then comrades come rally
And the last fight let us face.
The Internationale unites the human race.'

He was in his own world, a world Marisol knew very little about. At school, they'd skimmed over the Civil War in one class of barely an hour, moving on quickly to the Second World War. As for asking any of her older relatives, it was completely useless: they clammed up immediately. Papá and Mamá were too young, but even her questions about the dictatorship were evaded. 'The past is behind us,' Papá always said. 'Best forgotten.' Her family would have been on the side of the Nationals, of course. Supporters of Franco. On one occasion only, she had heard Grandma Angustias refer to the events of the war. Marisol still recalled the venom in her voice when she spoke of *los rojos*, before Uncle Rafa swiftly silenced her. 'That's enough now, Mamá.'

In the cafeteria later that day with her colleagues Luz and Susi, Marisol commented on Pepito's confused ramblings. 'Half of that generation must be traumatised,' she said. 'Yet we're taught practically nothing about the war. No one wants to talk about it.'

'It was right at the end of the history syllabus,' Susi said. 'Our teacher was behind, which meant we never even reached it.'

'All I know,' Luz said, 'is that my family were split down the middle. There are relatives whose names can't be uttered. My granddad never spoke to his brothers again after the war.'

'Mine disappeared for about twenty years. Can you imagine?' Susi shook her head in outrage. 'My mother said he had to go into hiding when she was two, so she was grown up by the time she saw him again. I wanted to know more but that was all I could get out of her. He'd been a teacher, on the Republican side obviously.'

Jordi, the paediatric nurse, was sitting further down the table and moved to join them. 'There were some in my family who disappeared and never came back,' he said. 'My grandmother's sister and her husband, two of his brothers... I've a friend in the United States and honestly, they know far more about our Civil War than we do in Spain. There are historians researching it, no end of books written... As far as I know, they haven't been translated into Spanish. Anyway, according to my friend, tens of thousands were executed after the war, others tortured and forced into slave labour. You'd think people would be kicking up a fuss, seeking justice.'

'I was in Scotland a few years ago,' Marisol said, 'and I met a guy whose grandfather was in the International Brigades, fighting with the Republican army. He said there were thousands of foreigners who came to Spain to fight the fascists. Many of them died, including his grandfather. People there were really interested: they'd read books, seen TV programmes and films about the war. I was embarrassed to know so little compared to them.'

'It's like the older generation here are scared to stir things up.' Luz pushed back her chair. 'Got to go, we're rushed off our feet today.'

At home that evening, Marisol tried again with Papá. 'Were there any black sheep in your family?' she asked. *Black sheep* seemed a safer expression than *reds*.

'Black sheep? What a strange question.' After a moment's thought, he said, 'I was told one of my aunts ran off with a communist. She never dared show her face again and really I'm not surprised: I doubt the family would have forgiven her. Who knows if they survived the war?'

'Is it true Franco executed thousands and thousands of Republicans after the war ended?' Marisol braced herself for a rebuff.

Papá frowned. 'Why all these questions, *hija*? *Gracias a Dios*, we're in times of peace. Who wants to re-open old wounds? It's thanks to the *pacto de olvido* that a peaceful transition was achieved. Silence was the price we paid, and a necessary one. That way we could move forward as one people. No bitterness, no recriminations, no retribution. We've had enough of hatred and division in this country. Now we have a stable democracy and only the problem of ETA to plague us. Fortunately our President Aznar is determined to deal harshly with them.'

CHAPTER 50

Granada, 2003-2004

The banners were everywhere. *No a la Guerra*. Marisol hadn't met anyone who supported this war in Iraq. Aznar's decision to join Bush and Blair in the invasion and send Spanish troops was an outrage. She had sprayed the words of protest on a sheet and hung it from their balcony. Her parents didn't object: they agreed the war was wrong. Even if it meant swapping shifts, she had every intention of taking part in the big demonstration on February 15th. She hoped to persuade her parents to march with her. Although they had very little interest in politics, they believed it their duty to vote in elections now Spain was a democracy. Quite right too. Like them, Marisol had never been tempted to get involved, but these demonstrations were different: the politicians had no right to drag the country into war for what appeared to be dubious motives. It was vital to protest.

'I've never seen so many people,' Mamá said as they stood for a moment watching the endless stream of protesters marching down Gran Via.

Marisol waved to a group of her friends marching under a banner depicting Bush, Blair and Aznar as murderers. 'Come on.' She grabbed Mamá's arm and they joined the procession.

'Half the population of Granada seems to be here,' Papá said, pointing out some neighbours he'd spotted, the woman from the electrical shop near his hotel, Carlos's old basketball coach. Young and old, hippies from the caves and squats of the Albaicín and respectable *granadino* families, trade unionists, students, ecologists, all marched together, some in silence, others chanting and blowing horns. The support was phenomenal. A solid mass of people filled Gran Via from Triunfo right down to the Plaza Isabel la Católica. As they moved slowly forward and the front of the column headed down Reyes Católicos, others joined the tail end to form a continuous river of protesters.

Marisol felt a hand on her arm. 'Hey, I know you, don't I?' She turned to glance at the man now marching beside her. He did appear familiar, though she couldn't immediately place him. He had a slim, wiry build, floppy brown hair and lively eyes that were now focusing intently on her face. He flicked back a wayward lock of hair with a small toss of the head and it was this gesture that nudged her memory. He'd been in with a broken leg when she was on Orthopaedics.

'Yes, and I'm pleased to see you're walking a whole lot better than last time I saw you.' Smiling, she said, 'Last time you were in traction.'

'Of course! And you were wearing a nurse's uniform, right? I'd been stupid enough to fall off a rock face. I'm Antonio.'

'Marisol. *Encantada.*' She looked round for her parents but they had walked ahead and been swallowed up by the throng. 'So are you back to climbing or did you give up after the accident?' she asked as they moved on.

'Just started again last weekend up at Monachil. I'm too hooked to let a mere broken leg stop me. The last X-rays showed my bone has healed; the doctor said it was up to me.'

The march came to a halt once again and they joined in the chanting. '*No a la guerra, no a la guerra.*' Although the atmosphere was good-humoured, there could be no mistaking people's anger.

'The accident has made me more careful,' Antonio added, shouting above the tumult as whistles were blown, placards raised: *No más sangre por petróleo,* No more blood for oil. *No en nuestro nombre,* Not in our name.

Antonio was carrying a placard too, Marisol noticed now. He brandished it high and she lifted her eyes to read it: *Aznar Lameculos de Bush*, written in big black letters with a caricature of the two presidents depicted as babies on all fours. The long tongue of the Spanish president snaked out to lick Bush's arse. 'That's clever,' she said, laughing.

'It's not my own creation. I found the cartoon on the Internet and printed it off. I think it's quite fitting.'

'It is. He makes me ashamed of my country.' She craned her neck to survey the crowd of marchers in front of her as they moved forward again. 'I dragged my parents along but I seem to have lost them,' she said.

'My folks were thinking about it; they always turn out against ETA. I don't know what they decided in the end. I came with a bunch of friends, only we got separated quite early on. Not that it matters. I keep bumping into people I know. Like you.' He turned to face her and their eyes locked for a moment. He had the warmest of smiles: candid, open, a smile reflected not only in his lips and eyes but the whole of his bearing. She felt a glow light up her own face in response, as if a flame had jumped.

'Antonio!' A woman in a leather jacket and high-heeled boots ran forward and grabbed his arm. 'There you are! *Hombre*, I've been looking for you for ages.'

'Well, now you've found me,' Antonio said. 'This is Marisol.' The woman introduced herself as Bibi, then turned her back on Marisol and proceeded to talk to Antonio about mutual friends and their arrangements to meet in Diamantes after the demo.

Annoyed at being ignored, Marisol walked on. Bibi seemed to be laying claim to Antonio; maybe she was his girlfriend. Dodging between groups from different trade unions and political parties with banners strung across the road, she worked her way forward, hoping to spot her parents.

'Hey, Marisol!'

She turned to see Antonio waving his placard at her from behind a group of older women walking with arms linked. Catching her up at a trot, he said, 'I thought I was going to lose you. I wanted to say, if you're not doing anything afterwards, why don't you join us in Diamantes? There's a group of us from the university – most of us are from admin like Bibi or *técnicos* like me. We're a friendly lot.'

Another burst of chanting gave Marisol time to make up her mind before she committed herself. 'Thanks, I will.' What did she have to lose? She could leave whenever she felt like it.

'Great.' He beamed at her. 'I'm sorry if we were rude just now.'

'It's okay. *No pasa nada.* So what do you do at the university?'

'I work in *informática*. You know, maintaining the computers, sorting out the staff's IT problems, mostly in the Law Faculty. It keeps me busy.'

'I bet.' She recognised a couple of the cleaning staff from the hospital and shouted a greeting to them as they moved past. Both were pushing buggies, one with an older boy in tow, all the children wrapped up snugly against the cold.

As they drew level with the Town Hall, the procession ground to a halt, the streets completely jammed as far ahead as the Fuente de las Batallas, where the rally was taking place. Marisol rubbed her hands, trying to keep warm. Stupidly, she'd forgotten to bring gloves. Diamantes would be packed – it always was – but the warmth would be welcome. So would their famous fish *tapas*.

Antonio looked at her. 'What do you think? Shall we head off? We're not going to get any nearer.'

Marisol nodded. 'Yes, come on. I'm frozen.'

They made their way across the *plaza* towards Calle Navas. The bar was packed to bursting, people spilling out of the door and into the street. 'We'll never get in,' she said as they reached it. 'Can you see your friends?'

Antonio surveyed the crowd in the street and peered inside. 'No chance,' he said, shaking his head. 'Let's go somewhere quieter.'

'Good idea.'

'I think I know the place – if you don't mind walking a bit.'

'Fine.' She blew into her hands. 'Lead on.'

'And take my gloves, I can do without.' He pulled them off and passed them to her. 'Not a bad fit,' he said, smiling as he watched her put on the warm woollen mitts.

'You could always phone Bibi or one of your other friends,' she said. 'If you think they'll be looking for you.'

'No, can't be bothered. What about your parents?'

'They can look after themselves. Most likely they've forgotten to bring their phones anyway. They're hopeless.'

'Right, let's go then.' He tossed his head. 'This way.'

Marisol followed him, feeling rather glad they would have the chance to get to know each other away from his friends.

She'd been too insistent, too preachy. It was a stupid argument and entirely her fault. All day, Marisol had been kicking herself – and at the same time feeling guilty for even thinking about last night when her mind should have been on her post-operative patients. It had all started when the waiter brought their *tapa*. Usually she remembered to ask for one without meat but last night she'd forgotten and the *carne en salsa* – once a favourite of hers – was put in front of them. She'd only been vegetarian for a few months. Clare had finally convinced her last summer by explaining the ethical reasons why half her family and many of her English friends didn't eat meat.

Antonio had, quite understandably, been annoyed by her judgmental attitude. 'Humans are natural omnivores,' he said. 'We need meat, that's how we've evolved. Of course it's a personal choice. I'd never prescribe what you or anyone else ate.' Stung by the implicit criticism, she had bitten her lip and said nothing. 'Mind you,' he continued, 'I wouldn't allow my children to exist on vegetables.'

'You have children?' Why had the idea come as such a shock? He was about her own age, possibly a little older – certainly old enough to have children.

He laughed. 'No way. I'm speaking hypothetically.'

Then he had questioned why she could eat fish but not meat. What was the difference? Didn't fish feel pain too?

She had given him her phone number in the hope of further contact. He had not offered his. The chances of hearing from him were practically nil. She couldn't even send him a text apologising. Damn, damn, damn. There had definitely been a spark between them – until she ruined it all by being too dogmatic.

Her bad humour that evening did not escape Mamá. Always sensitive to her moods, she responded to Marisol's peevishness with patience. 'Had a hard day?' she asked, cutting a slice of *bizcocho* still warm from the oven and passing it to her daughter.

'*Gracias.*' Marisol gave up her restless pacing round the kitchen and sat down at the table. 'What have you been doing today, Mamá?' she asked with an effort.

'Nothing special. Housework, shopping, baking…'

'Don't you get bored? There are only three of us at home now, it's time you took up an interest of your own, not just serving the family. You've got a brain, you should start using it.'

'I'm sixty-three. My brain isn't as good as it used to be.'

'Oh come on! You're always making excuses. Look at Aunt Isabel. She's older than you and she's studying philosophy with the University of the Third Age. Loli's mother volunteers for the Red Cross. You could learn to use a computer – that would be a start.'

'Well, I suppose you have a point. It's true there's less to do in the home now your brothers and sisters have left. On the other hand, I want to be available for Carlos and Verónica when the baby comes. They'll need help, especially as she wants to go back to work as soon as possible.'

'I know, I know. You can't wait to be a grandmother.'

Mamá smiled. 'I won't deny it,' she said. 'I'll phone them in a moment. Verónica was due for a scan today.'

The shock of 11-M was affecting everyone. At first ETA had been blamed for the bombing of the four trains at Atocha station in Madrid. Then it had all come out that the government was lying. As a result, they'd lost the election and soon Spain would have a new president, the Socialist leader Zapatero, who had promised to withdraw Spanish troops from Iraq. Viewing the scenes of carnage on the TV, Marisol had felt sick and angry. The personal stories filled her with grief for the victims and their families. Aznar's unpopular decision to involve Spain in the invasion had led directly to the deaths of two hundred innocent people. What could be more senseless than those totally random deaths? As Papá pointed out, it could have been any of them. Only a few days earlier, Luisa and Arturo had travelled to Madrid to see an exhibition; Antonio's father had been due to attend a conference there the day after.

The attack a fortnight ago had even cast a shadow over her trip to Sevilla with Antonio, a break she'd been looking forward to for weeks. They were planning to stay with some friends of his for the weekend. Opportunities to spend whole nights together came rarely. Both of them still lived with their parents so unless they arranged to go away somewhere, sex mostly happened in the cramped confines of his car, which was uncomfortable and, more often than not, too hurried to enjoy fully.

Antonio was waiting in the hospital car park when she finished her shift half an hour late on the Friday evening. She could never guarantee to get away on time: in a hospital nothing was predictable. Marisol knew he wouldn't complain, despite being keen to arrive at his friends' place in good time. He was the most patient, laidback person she had ever known.

She dashed over to the car without bothering to put up her umbrella. He had his eyes closed as if in a trance, his head nodding to the rhythm of the music on the CD. At her rap on the window, he looked up with a start and jumped out to kiss her before opening the boot and stowing her holdall.

'I'm sorry, Toni. One of my patients developed a sudden high fever – an infected wound – and I had to make sure...'

'No problem. Come on, you're getting wet.' If the rain continued to sheet down like this, driving would be stressful.

'Take it easy,' she said as Antonio pulled out onto the ring road. As usual, people were driving way too fast for the conditions. 'That spell in *Urgencias* really brought it home to me. You see the accident victims come in and mostly they're paying the price of just a moment's carelessness – their own or another driver's.' She reached up to gather the locks of stray hair that invariably escaped and were now dripping water down her neck, and twisted them into a knot again. Why wouldn't her hair ever stay in place?

'Trust me, *cariño*. I don't want you feeling nervous.' He reached across and squeezed her hand. Noticing how cold it was, she massaged his fingers for a minute before replacing the hand – marginally warmer now – on the steering wheel.

They passed Antequera and Marisol pointed out the 'sleeping giant', as her parents always called the distinctive hills overlooking the town. 'Its other name is *La Peña de los Enamorados*.' And she told him the story of the lovers who leapt off the rock to their deaths. 'We don't go back so often now all four of my grandparents are dead but my parents still consider it home.'

'You were born in Granada though, didn't you say?'

'Yes, and I think of myself as *granadina*. What about you?' She knew Antonio's family were from Almería.

'I was nine when we moved to Granada so I guess I feel more of an *almeriense*. Most of my relatives still live there.'

The rain began to ease off and then stopped completely. Breaks in the cloud revealed a spectacle of orange and gold and mauve as the sun sank low in the sky ahead of them. Marisol felt her spirits lift and soon she was singing along to the music on the radio.

'Let me know if you want to stop,' Antonio said. 'Otherwise we'll keep going.'

'I'm fine but you'll need a break, won't you? I could drive for a while if you like.'

He shook his head. 'It's only an hour and a half from here. You should take a nap; we'll be out late tonight if I know David and Soraya.'

Marisol yawned. Today had been even more frantic than usual on her ward. 'Perhaps I will.'

'Mm, I love sleeping with you.' She was only half awake but fully conscious of Antonio's warm body stretched out next to her in the bed. She snuggled closer and wrapped her arms and legs around him.

'I thought you'd never wake up.' His lips brushed her face, covering it with the lightest of kisses. She could feel his prick hard and hot against her thigh.

'Is it late?'

'I don't know but who cares?' he whispered. 'David and Soraya won't be up before midday.' He was kissing her neck now, one hand reaching down to caress her left nipple. '*Te quiero, Maris…*' Still drowsy but increasingly aroused, she luxuriated in the sensations washing over her. She had never felt so relaxed with him – certainly not during their awkward couplings in the car. The duvet lifted as he moved under it. She felt his tongue on her and gasped. Her body was opening up to him, waves of pleasure breaking, billowing, making her cry out.

Then he was inside her and they were moving together fused in pure sensation, the force of their desire, their joy in each other connecting them, carrying them together to the finish.

Marisol smiled into the pillow. Antonio was sleeping, his head turned in her direction, mouth slightly open, breath warm against her cheek. She felt tender towards him: asleep he looked vulnerable as a child. She could watch him for hours, she thought, wondering idly what time it was. Her mobile lay just within reach. 12:10. She recalled tumbling into bed sometime around four after a lively evening of *marcha*: eating and drinking in several different bars, then moving on to a *bar de copas* and finally a disco. David and Soraya were fun and so were their friends. It was the best night she'd had in ages.

Now she could do with a shower, though her limbs were resisting the effort of moving from the bed.

A soft rap on the door followed by Soraya's voice. 'Hey, are you two awake? We're going out for breakfast in a few minutes if you're ready.'

'Give us half an hour,' Marisol called back. 'Antonio's still asleep.' She threw on her dressing gown and went to open the door. 'I was about to take a shower,' she said.

'Fine, we'll wait. There's no rush.'

Over coffee and *tostadas* in the bar round the corner, Soraya made them laugh as she described her mother's escalating hints about babies. 'She thinks she's being subtle by not asking directly, but no way! Every time we speak, another friend of hers has become a grandmother or one of my cousins is expecting or she's seen such a cute baby boy's outfit in the Corte Inglés. It started as soon as we were married. One of these days I'll have to break it to her that we don't actually want children.'

'My brother Carlos has just had twins,' Marisol said. 'My mother is ecstatic – she thought she'd never see the day. I mean, Belén, my oldest sister, is forty and definitely won't have kids. Carlos is thirty-eight.'

'What about you?' David asked.

'Well…' She didn't dare look at Antonio. They'd been going out for just over a year and hadn't ever talked about marriage. She was still determined to spend a couple of years abroad: that was her priority.

The plan had been put on hold, but only temporarily so she could gain more experience. 'Sometime in the future,' she said with a shrug. The idea of having a child with Antonio excited her but it was too soon, far too soon. 'For the moment I'm fine being an auntie,' she said. 'Paula and Paloma are the sweetest baby girls you could imagine. We were all astounded when the scan showed Verónica was expecting twins. There are none in the family.' She paused and added, 'As far as we know.' They didn't know, of course. But she wasn't about to reveal Mamá's secret to Antonio, let alone to his friends.

'Look, the keyboard is no different to an old-fashioned typewriter. This arrow here is called *Shift*. You hold it down for a capital letter. And see how easy it is to erase? You can do it backwards with this arrow or forwards with the *Delete* key here. Everything can be saved, there's no need to print it, OK? Want to try writing something?'

Mamá was staring in awe first at the computer screen, then at Antonio, then at the keyboard. After only a moment's hesitation, she started typing – slowly and laboriously. *Hola Paula, hola Paloma. Os quiero.*

'Excellent, you've really got the idea. Now, to access the Internet you have what's called a browser...'

He had the patience of a saint, Marisol thought, watching them. It was a miracle that Mamá had agreed to learn. And that he was willing to devote time to teaching her. Papá had learned to use a computer in his job at the hotel; he'd been more amazed than any of them when Mamá showed an interest. Luisa said it was because she liked Antonio. Certainly she appeared flattered by his attention.

Marisol admired his ability to focus, to be in the moment, whatever he was doing, whoever he was with. It showed respect, made the other person feel valued. She had first observed it on that anti-war march – he had stopped talking to her and given his entire attention to Bibi. When his eyes and ears zeroed in on you, nothing and no one else existed; he became totally oblivious to what was going on around him. It felt like a rich gift. She would love to be able to give that kind of single-minded attention to her patients. No chance. She had to be constantly aware of others on the ward: alert to any emergency, any change in the condition of any of them, any call or warning signal.

'Next week I'll set up an email account for you,' Antonio was saying. 'In the meantime you should decide what name to use – some version of your own preferably, with maybe a number after, like your birth year – and a password.'

'Chelo39? Will that do?'

'Perfect.'

'And for the password...'

'A mix of letters and numbers is best.'

'How about ABC123?'

'No no, that's too easy to guess. And you shouldn't tell me, or anyone else. It has to be secret.' He stood up. 'We'll get it sorted next time. I have to go now.'

Marisol went to the door with him. She was working nights this week and probably wouldn't see Antonio again until the weekend. 'Call me on your break,' he said. 'Or first thing in the morning when you finish.'

'I will.' They spent a lot of time speaking or messaging each other on their mobiles. It was a poor substitute for his physical presence. She clung to him as they kissed their goodbyes. 'See you at the weekend.'

This morning she had come across adverts from two health authorities in England: nurses were wanted in Canterbury and Birmingham. The conditions for both looked right. Her CV was ready.

'I'm applying for a couple of jobs,' she said to Mamá when Antonio had gone. 'In England,' she added.

'England? But you like your work at the hospital here in Granada. And...'

'Mamá, I told you.' Her mother could hardly claim to be surprised. 'I've been telling you for ages that I want to go and work abroad for a while.'

'But what about Antonio?' Mamá looked aghast.

'If he loves me, he'll wait.'

Mamá shook her head. 'It's your decision, *hija*. But think carefully. You don't want to lose him.'

'Of course I don't.' She turned away, unable to disguise her anguish. Leaving Antonio would be a wrench. Already she was feeling the pain before she had sent a single application. 'I'm sure he'll come and visit me there,' she said. 'And I'm not going for ever, just a couple of years. The time will fly by.' Would it? 'I have to get ready now.' She retreated to her bedroom and concentrated on gathering her things together for work. Keeping busy was the best tactic. Tomorrow she would sit down at the computer and send off her CV to the health authorities in England.

CHAPTER 51

Granada, 2006-2007

Marisol was sitting on a bench by the river, close to one of the weeping willows that bent its leafy branches down to the waters of the Cam. A pleasure boat filled with tourists motored past, followed by two punts and then a rowing team, its members working in unison, their faces dogged with intent. She took out her mobile and snapped the scene. After two years in Cambridge, she had mixed feelings about leaving.

In her bag was the card signed by her colleagues at the hospital. She opened it and reread their comments, smiled at the funny pictures Lisa and Kate had drawn. *Good luck! Don't forget to invite us to the wedding! We'll miss you!* She would miss them too – all of them, not to mention her three flatmates. Cambridge had been a good choice, better than Birmingham or Canterbury, whose offers she had turned down. Britain was desperate for nurses. More than half the staff at her hospital – doctors, nurses, auxiliaries, cleaners – were from abroad. Trust Xavier to make that cheeky comment about a wedding. Marriage was not in the offing.

They had all met Antonio, of course. Even before Ryanair started the direct flights from Granada to Stansted, he would come over for a long weekend every couple of months. Kate had reluctantly given up trying to get her off with the Irish registrar, Patrick. She wasn't interested. The English had a saying: *Absence makes the heart grow fonder.* Being away from Antonio certainly didn't make her less fond. Her feelings for him had not wavered for a moment during their separation. He was the man for her, and miraculously, he seemed to feel the same way.

She had hoped the flights from Granada would persuade her parents to visit her in Cambridge. Not a chance. Even her offer to pay their fares had fallen on stony ground; they always had some excuse or other. England was like Mars to them. Luisa and Arturo had come over once, Pablo a couple of times. She had returned to Granada for the two Christmases, for last year's *Semana Santa* and for Luisa's wedding in May.

Back on duty after her morning off, she noticed that both Elaine and Mrs Morris (as she preferred to be called) were on their own again this Sunday afternoon, usually the busiest visiting time. English families, she had discovered, differed a lot from Spanish ones. A surprising number of her patients were left to themselves in hospital, with an occasional visitor if they were lucky. When family members did come, they stayed only a short time, never for the night, except on the children's wards. It had shocked her to begin with. There were a few fortunate ones – the patients always surrounded by relatives or by a faithful spouse who kept them company all day. For most though, hospital was a lonely experience and that meant more was demanded from the nursing staff. She didn't mind. At the less busy times she made an effort to stop and chat with those patients who lacked visitors. Just a few kind words, a loving gesture could make such a difference, even speeding their recovery.

'How are you this afternoon?' she asked Elaine. 'Would you like me to brush your hair?' Elaine had thick, silvery-grey hair that she kept at shoulder length, but in bed it tended to become tangled. Marisol loved to brush it till it shone and crackled with static.

'Oh thank you, dear. That would be lovely.'

After a few minutes' brushing, she held up Elaine's little hand-mirror for her to see. 'You have beautiful hair,' she said. 'The other women here, they all tell me they are envious of your hair.'

To Mrs Morris, worried about how she would cope on her return home, Marisol offered reassurance about the services that would be put in place before they discharged her – meals on wheels, a carer to help her get dressed in the morning and prepare her for bed at night, visits from the community nurse. She would have liked to feel more confident about the provision of this help. Like so many others in Cambridge, Mrs Morris lived alone and at seventy-six, after a serious operation, she lacked the strength to care for herself. However, her bed was needed.

Moving on down the ward, Marisol's thoughts returned briefly to Antonio, who was climbing this weekend. She always worried about him, even though he had plenty of experience and his club was well equipped, ensuring its members took all the necessary precautions. She had watched him once, roped to a vertical rock-face, and decided never again. 'You should give it a try yourself,' he'd suggested, as if the terror of seeing *him* risk his life weren't bad enough. She had no intention of pushing her luck. No way.

People were always telling her she was lucky in life. It was true: she had work she enjoyed, a loving family, good health and, most important, she had Antonio. But she'd seen enough of life to know that one's luck could change at any moment. Cousin Pedro had recently been diagnosed with a brain tumour. Her old school-friend Carmen had lost her job when the firm she worked for went bankrupt. Clare was still devastated over the split with Steve nearly a year ago.

For Marisol a bright future beckoned. On Wednesday, she would be flying back to Granada. A post on the surgical ward at the Hospital Clínico awaited her in September but before that, she had a week's holiday on the coast to look forward to. Antonio's aunt was lending them her apartment in Calahonda. The longer-term plan was to find a flat that she and Antonio could afford and move in together.

'You'll still come here to eat sometimes, won't you?' Mamá's mouth formed a sad downward curve as she watched Marisol pack up her belongings in boxes.

'Sometimes, of course. I'll miss your cooking.' She squeezed her mother's shoulders as she moved past to reach for the shoes lined up ready on the floor.

'I hope you'll both come often. Pablo eats with us at least twice a week.'

'Yes, I know.' Pablo also brought his ironing to Mamá, who accepted it without a word of complaint. 'You and Papá must come and visit us too. We'll be having a house-warming once we've settled in.'

Mamá was clicking her tongue. 'You young people do everything back to front. In our day, the wedding came before anything else.'

'Times change, Mamá.' She refrained from mentioning her conversations with Antonio about marriage, their plan to wed next year if the living together 'experiment' worked. For the moment, her mother had plenty to occupy her. She was completely dotty about Carlos and Verónica's little blonde twins, now running about and chattering away. She insisted on making fancy (and quite impractical) dresses for them and tying ribbons in their hair. Not that Verónica minded. She liked to have them well turned-out, especially on Sundays, when they walked along the promenade in Almuñecar before eating at the restaurant where Carlos worked and basking in the admiration of the clientele.

Marisol was still undecided about her professional development. She had discarded the idea of training as a paediatric nurse when she discovered it would involve a year in Paris. More time away from Antonio was the last thing she wanted right now. Another specialty she had considered was midwifery. Bringing new life into the world, witnessing the joy of the parents, must be incredibly rewarding. Much more so than caring for sick people, often nearing the end of their time. She had mentioned it to Mamá, who blanched and declared it a very important job but a 'terrible responsibility'. All nursing carried a responsibility, she reminded her mother. In any case, the decision could wait. In the meantime, she would carry on improving her skills and building up experience.

Unlike her sisters, Belén and Luisa, Marisol didn't want a big, showy wedding. Both she and Antonio thought it a waste of money when they were saving hard for a flat of their own. Nor did she want her parents splashing out. They were disappointed Marisol and Antonio had chosen a civic rather than a church wedding. 'But neither of us go to church,' she pointed out. 'We're not in the least religious.' She suspected Mamá's religious beliefs were based less on faith than on superstition. Fear and guilt had imbued her Catholic upbringing; in fact she always claimed it had made her wary of priests and the Church. So why was she now muttering about their choice of ceremony being an inauspicious start to married life?

Clare, who was flying over for the wedding, thought it hilarious they had chosen the holiday of the Immaculate Conception to get married.

'It's just convenient for the guests to hold it when there's a *puente*,' Marisol explained. 'Most people get the 6th December off for Constitution Day and make a bridge to the next holiday on the 8th.' She had never given any thought as to why the Immaculate Conception should be celebrated. A holiday was a holiday. Who cared about its origins?

'A pregnancy lasts forty weeks, right?' Clare was laughing her socks off. 'So how come Mary's only took a fortnight?'

'You'll have to ask a priest. There must be some Catholic churches in your part of London.'

After the ceremony at the local Town Hall, they all piled into cars to drive to Almuñecar. Carlos had talked his boss into giving them a good deal for the wedding lunch. Most of the fifty or so guests at the restaurant were family but a number of their friends had come along too, including her former Cambridge flatmate Sarah and colleague Lisa. The three English girls behaved as if it were summer, even contemplating a swim in the sea. Papá told them they were crazy, a sentiment echoed by the other Spanish guests.

'I dare the wedding couple,' Clare said as the first appetisers were being brought to the table. 'Come on, just a quick dip. I'll order a brandy for when you come out.'

Antonio raised his eyebrows at Marisol. 'Are you game?'

'What? You're not serious?'

'Come on, the sun's still strong: it won't be that bad.'

'You don't mean *en pelotas*?'

'Who's got a towel?' he shouted.

'*Momento*.' Carlos ran inside and reappeared with two beach towels.

'I can't believe I'm doing this,' Marisol said as the two of them ran down to the water's edge, stripped off and threw themselves into the waves. She gasped. 'If I catch pneumonia, it'll be your fault. Right, that's enough. I'm getting out.'

They wrapped the towels round each other, grabbed their clothes and ran back up the beach to wild cheers.

'I insist on a hot shower,' Marisol said after downing her brandy. 'Come on Toni. You'll need one too.' She turned to her brother's boss, who was standing there grinning at them. 'Where's the bathroom?'

CHAPTER 52

Granada, 2010

After spending most of the night in labour, screeching with each contraction, Elvira had given birth to a sturdy, four-kilo baby boy. Her mother sat by the bed, gazing in wonder at the sleeping baby, her first grandchild, while the new father went in search of coffee. Marisol left Elvira to rest and went to take a break in the staff room. The night had been unusually quiet on the labour ward. Apart from Elvira, they'd had one very straightforward birth just before midnight, two in the early hours, and not long ago a Moroccan woman in the early stages of labour had arrived. Marisol loved her job. She was a qualified midwife now, with a Masters in Obstetrics & Gynaecology.

Silvia, the young *residente*, was sitting with her feet up, eating toast and reading yesterday's *Granada Hoy*. 'It's horrendous,' she said, raising her head from the paper. 'Apparently there were thousands of babies stolen from their mothers and given to orphanages run by the Church, or to Francoist families for adoption. The parents were told their babies had died. Can you imagine?'

Vanesa, the other midwife on duty, poked her head round the door. 'I saw something about that on the TV,' she said. 'To start with it was political: they took the babies of women prisoners and other known communists. But it looks like the practice carried on till fairly recently. Doctors, nurses and nuns were in it for the money. It's a massive scandal.'

'But that's inhuman.' Marisol was shocked. 'Doctors and nurses? How could they do that?' She tried to imagine informing a new mother that her baby had died when she knew full well that the child was alive and healthy – just so she could pocket a few hundred euros. Then she tried to visualise being the woman in question, smiling that magical smile of joy she saw in every new mother as she held her baby for the first time, only to learn soon after that it was dead.

A chill ran through her. She and Antonio had finally decided to try for a child within the next year. They had put it off until now – first while she studied for her Masters, then because the problems entailed in reconciling work and family life appeared overwhelming. She was reluctant to give up her new role as midwife while the beauty of it still enthralled her and made her feel intensely privileged. On the other hand, dumping her own baby in a nursery at two months, as so many women did in order to keep their jobs, felt equally unacceptable.

Her mother would be only too delighted to help out, of course. Marisol recalled Mamá's words on her last birthday. 'You're thirty-six – exactly my age when I gave birth to you.' She'd even had the cheek to say it in Antonio's presence.

'That's alright then,' Marisol had retorted.

'But you were my fifth.'

Considering the remark unworthy of a response, she had ignored it. Later, when Mamá was out of the room, Antonio had whispered, 'Does she think we're going to have five?'

Before handing over to her colleagues at eight o'clock, Marisol conferred with Isaac, the obstetrician, checked on the three post-partums and their babies and gave some encouragement to Karima, who was still only five centimetres dilated. Another woman had just been brought in; one of the two midwives on the morning shift was already examining her. On her way home, she bought a copy of *El País*, hoping to discover more about the scandal of the stolen babies. On one of the inside pages, she found a short piece, accompanied by photos and quotes from two women in Madrid who suspected they may have been victims. When Antonio came home from work at lunchtime, she showed it to him.

'I heard something about that the other day,' he said. 'It's all been hushed up for years apparently, but now the details are beginning to emerge. I'll check it out on the internet if you're interested.'

Two days later, Marisol came off a hectic night shift (one difficult breech birth, one badly haemorrhaging seventeen year-old with a hysterical mother, one umbilical cord prolapse and seven more straightforward births) expecting to crash out as soon as her head hit the pillow. Instead of that, here she was sitting up in bed with the laptop, reading the articles Antonio had bookmarked for her before leaving for work. *Take a look, you'll be horrified*, his note said. Despite her fatigue, she'd been unable to resist a quick glance. Just the first one, she told herself. Then she would pull down the blind and sink into oblivion.

The first piece was about a psychiatrist from Palencia called Antonio Vallejo-Nájera, who had worked in Germany with the Nazis and been influenced by Nietzsche. *Vallejo-Nájera affirmed that a "red gene" existed, a gene that could be appeased or cured if, from the outset, children not yet brainwashed by those beyond cure were segregated from them. That is, the separation at birth of the children of "reds" from their parents. The "red" woman participated in politics to satisfy her sexual appetites. She was defined as a juvenile close to animalism and incapable of bringing up her children.*

In the next article, Marisol read that the theft of babies had continued until at least the 1980s. An estimated figure of 300,000 was quoted. Wide awake now, she shook her head in disbelief. Three hundred thousand? That couldn't be right, surely. She read on. From the end of the Civil War and throughout the 1940s, the babies were handed out to families loyal to the Franco regime – those irreproachable in terms of religion, morality and nationalism. A law was passed in 1941 enabling the original birth details in the Civil Register to be destroyed and the children given the names of their adoptive parents. Later, as the report in *Granada Hoy* had said, money became the primary motive. Presumably, the babies were sold to wealthy couples unable to conceive.

Marisol gave up on sleep and brewed herself a cup of camomile tea. Reading about the *bebés robados* had left her profoundly disturbed. That members of her own profession – one dedicated to saving lives – could be prone to the corruption so rampant among the country's politicians made her feel tainted. She turned on the television, hoping the trashy daytime soap would take her mind off such dark thoughts and help her relax. It worked: after half an hour, she felt drowsy enough to climb back into bed and sleep.

She woke abruptly, her mind churning. Why hadn't it struck her earlier? Mamá was adopted. Her family was exactly the kind she had been reading about – loyal supporters of the regime, stoutly Catholic, conforming strictly to conventional morality. Her mother had been born in 1939, a few months after the war ended. Everything fitted. Could she be the child of Republican parents, imprisoned or even executed by Franco? What lies had her birth mother been told?

It was two o'clock, which gave her an hour before she was due at her parents' house for lunch. A leisurely shower with her favourite citrus-scented gel helped her feel both livelier and more relaxed. As the hot water ran over her body, she considered how to approach the subject with Mamá. She was convinced her mother knew more than she'd let on. Just as well Antonio was eating with university colleagues today. Mamá was far more likely to open up if they were alone.

Marisol waited till the dishes were cleared away and Papá had fallen asleep in his armchair, as he always did after lunch.

'I've been reading about the stolen babies,' she said as she helped Mamá tidy up in the kitchen. She tried to keep her voice casual.

'Stolen babies? What are you talking about?'

'Haven't you been following the news lately? After the end of the Civil War, thousands of Republican women had their babies taken away and given to National families for adoption.'

Mamá carefully positioned the pan she'd been scouring on the draining board. She did not turn round or pick up the next pan but waited, motionless as a statue, for what might follow. Marisol waited too. Mamá couldn't stand frozen like that for ever.

'Mamá, look at me.' She embraced her mother from behind and leaned round to kiss her cheek. 'Do you really not know anything about your birth mother? These women were told their babies had died. Do you think…?'

'My mother was English.' She still had her back turned.

'What?'

'*Hija*, come with me.' Marisol followed her into the bedroom. Mamá shut the door and seated herself on the stool in front of the dressing table. 'Stand behind me,' she commanded. 'Look in the mirror. Have you never wondered why our skin is fairer than most Andalusians', our hair lighter, our eyes an unusual colour?'

Marisol stared. She had been asked many times where she was from. So had Carlos and occasionally Pablo. 'Our legs are longer too,' she said.

Mamá nodded. 'Your grandmother was already on her deathbed when she told me. Until then, all I knew was that I didn't belong in the family, that I was adopted. Francisco said… I didn't want to believe his ugly words. He dragged my mother's name through the dirt, called her a whore…'

'But that's awful. No wonder you were at loggerheads.' She sat down on the bed, her brain working overtime. 'What about your father? Was he English as well?' She couldn't fathom out what a pregnant Englishwoman might be doing in Spain at that time or how her baby could end up in a family such as Mamá's. None of it made sense.

'I know nothing about my father.' For a few moments the two of them remained silent. Mamá was the first to speak. 'My Uncle Rodrigo was a doctor,' she said. 'I'd already been told I was born in his hospital in Jaén. But what my mother was doing there and why she couldn't look after me, they never disclosed.'

'The hospital would have records, surely,' Marisol said. 'It may be possible to trace your mother.'

'I very much doubt it.' Mamá was shaking her head. She looked uneasy now, as if she regretted having made this revelation. 'Anyway, what's the use? Too much time has passed, my mother will be long dead. Better to let sleeping dogs lie.'

'No Mamá, we should try,' Marisol persisted. She so wanted to heal Mamá's wound, to give her back a sense of identity, even if they were too late for a reunion. 'Did Grandma Angustias tell you anything else?'

Mamá's head was lowered, her eyes closed, fingers tightly interlaced in her lap. She seemed to be battling with herself; it took her a long time to reply. 'I was told her name,' she said eventually. 'It was Rosa. Rosa Tili.'

'Rosa Tili?' Marisol repeated. 'But that doesn't sound English. Are you sure?'

'It's what María Angustias told me before she died. She said also that this Rosa was born the same year as her brother Elias. He was killed by the reds in 1936 at the age of twenty-one, so the year must have been 1915. I worked it out,' she added proudly. '*Bueno,* it could have been the year before or after, depending which month he was born and when exactly he died.'

'Mamá, just wait here a moment.' Marisol ran to fetch a pen and notebook from her bag. 'Now, will you write her name for me?' She had remembered Clare's Aunt Stella and her discoveries about their family history. With a name and a date, it should be possible...

Her mother shrugged and wrote *Rosa*. She hesitated, sucking the pen, before adding *Tili*. 'I suppose it would be written like this,' she said.

They heard a click and Papá poked his head round the bedroom door. 'So that's where you ladies are hiding,' he said. 'I thought you'd abandoned me.'

'As if we would,' Mamá said. 'Women's talk, it wouldn't interest you. And besides, you were sleeping.' She stood up. 'Well, I expect you need to leave soon for work, Marisol, isn't that so?'

'No Mamá, I'm off tonight but Antonio will be home by now and we'd arranged to go shopping. He needs a new coat for the winter.'

As she sat on the bus home, Marisol thought about the name Mamá had given her. Rosa could be Rose. And Tili... In her head she visualised all the English words she could think of that rhymed with Tili. By the time she reached her stop, she was convinced it would be written like silly, frilly, willy (a word children giggled over) and the name Billy, which she'd seen in a book once. Tilly was by far the most likely spelling. Rosa or Rose Tilly, 1915... Her grandmother would be ninety-five. The chances of her still being alive were remote but not impossible. It was worth a try.

'Clare, turn on your camera. I can't see you.' They were talking on Skype but all Marisol could see was her own picture in the bottom right-hand corner. After a moment, Clare's familiar face loomed on the screen. 'Okay, that's better. But you look dreadful, what's up?'

'I've just got a bad cold, like everyone else. It's winter, right?'

'Oh dear. Well, try and keep warm, look after yourself. Listen, a few days ago I leant something incredible and now I need your help.' She waited while Clare blew her nose. 'You'll find this hard to believe: a quarter – or possibly half – of my ancestry is English.'

'You're joking! Though actually, you do look half-English.'

'I want to trace them, Clare, and I need to work fast because my English grandmother – if she's still alive – will be very old. I was hoping your Aunt Stella could offer me some advice. Can you give me her email address?'

'Sure. I'll send it to you. But how did you find out?'

'From my mum. I'm one of the few who even know she was adopted. Our family has so many secrets, it makes me wonder, what do we discover next?'

'So how much do you know now?'

'I have her mother's name and year of birth, nothing else.'

'That might do to start with. As long as her name isn't a really common one, like Smith or Jones.'

'Brilliant. Put me in touch with your aunt and I'll get on the trail right away.'

'Excuse me.' Clare reached for a tissue and blew her nose again. 'So, will you tell your mum what you're doing or is this going to be another secret?'

'Um… I think until I make some progress, it had better remain a secret.'

PART 13 ROSE 2005 - 2007

CHAPTER 53

Oxford, 2005

Rose struggled with the buttons on her blouse. Getting dressed, like most of the other mundane tasks facing her each day, required effort. She cursed her arthritic fingers that made every small thing take five times as long as it used to. Was that why she always felt so tired? *I can manage*, her habitual response when one or other of her younger relations suggested a residential home, might soon cease to be true. She had never imagined living to ninety. At least she was still independent, still in her own home, unlike poor Bertie with his dementia and Parkinson's, who hadn't been able to manage for some time and was now more than Prue could handle.

The death of Ralph a year ago, barely six months after his wife, had hit her hard. Helen too had been inconsolable. Rose was reminded of how distraught she had been over the death of her own father. So much illness, so many deaths: almost every month brought a funeral. Losing family and friends was the price of living so long.

In the bungalow's small kitchen, she put on the kettle to make tea and inserted two slices of bread in the toaster. How comfortable life was nowadays – or would be if she were less clumsy. A memory sprang to mind of Teruel, of being caught in a blizzard halfway up a mountain and having to melt snow on their primus to brew tea. The bitter cold that winter, her hands so numb they were as useless then as now. It was a wonder her fingers hadn't dropped off with frostbite. In the trenches some had surrendered entire limbs to it.

Often she would lose herself for minutes at a time in scenes from long ago. She might be in the garden of the family home in Evesham, catching apples thrown down from the tree by her brothers. Or in the railway tunnel above the Ebro, assisting Dr Jolly with an operation by the light of a tiny oil lantern. Or on a hillside in the Sierra de Cazorla with the *Guardia Civil* close on their tail as they prepared to move camp yet again. The past would submerge her and she would surface dazed, as if from a vivid dream. Then she would have to take stock of her surroundings, piece together the here and now.

Watching the television news didn't help. Seeing the carnage and destruction in Iraq brought back all the horrors of war that she had hoped never to see again: the bombing of hospitals, schools and markets, the children maimed or left orphaned. That her own country had taken a leading part in the invasion and continued to send troops upset her deeply. She would have liked to join Zoe and Zach and their friends on one of the big protests in London, or even a smaller one in Oxford, if only her state of mobility had allowed it; instead she'd had to make do with signing petitions and writing to her MP.

Two years ago she had still been able to walk as far as the corner shop. Now, dependent on her wretched walking frame, she was practically housebound, forbidden by the family to go out alone. 'Just pick up the phone,' they always said, and sometimes she did, but with reluctance. The speed of their lives made her dizzy. Even Helen, who had taken early retirement this year, seemed busier than ever. Not that she had anything to complain about. Scarcely a day passed without a visit; the phone often rang several times in one evening; at weekends one or the other of them would invariably come to fetch her by car.

Facing her on the kitchen table as she ate her breakfast lay the shiny new mobile phone Peter had insisted she must have always to hand. 'What's wrong with the normal telephone?' she had asked when he presented it to her a few days ago. 'Everyone has mobiles these days,' he'd replied. 'It's a really simple model, you'll soon get the hang of it.' He had promised to send Oliver round on Friday afternoon to explain all its features. Rose frowned, trying to remember what day it was. Jackie, the hairdresser, had come yesterday to cut and wash the sparse wisps of hair she still possessed. Jackie always came on a Thursday, which meant today must be Friday.

She picked up the phone and stared at its tiny keys. Peter had chosen one with extra large buttons, she remembered him telling her, evidently pleased with himself. And she could choose her own ringtone, take photos, use it as an alarm clock or a torch. 'Oliver will set it all up for you, don't worry.' She pressed the key with a green telephone image and it sprang into life, lighting up and showing a message on the screen. *Welcome to Orange.* She could make out the words even without her glasses. The two cataract operations in '94 and '95 had miraculously restored her sight – not only restored but improved it. Now, how did you turn the blessed thing off, she wondered? Oliver would know.

Her great-nephew was the sweetest of chaps. She wasn't bothered about the mobile phone but seeing Oliver always brightened her day. He was gay and had a boyfriend, Mani, whose family were from India. They had met at drama school in London. While Mani dropped out early and found work at a busy bohemian-style café ('alternative' was the word they used), Oliver, as an aspiring actor, was mostly out of work. He came to visit her often and they would talk for hours – talk and laugh and eat the chocolates he never failed to bring.

She thought about making a cake, but remembering her last attempt – the slimy puddle of broken eggs on the floor, sifted flour falling like snow in all the wrong places – quickly dismissed that idea. The everyday humiliations of old age were enough without inviting further mortification. Besides, another more important task awaited her: the sifting not of flour but of paperwork. She had vowed to go through the drawers full of old bills, documents, letters and photos accumulated over decades rather than leave them for her family to deal with when she finally popped her clogs. She should have done it years ago, as soon as her eyes were fixed. Instead, she had allowed the drawers and their contents to be transferred lock, stock and barrel when she moved from Headington.

Gripping the table for support, Rose raised herself, carried her breakfast crockery to the sink and shuffled to the kitchen doorway. In the hall, two letters lay on the mat. Without much interest – most of her mail these days consisted of bills or junk – she stooped to retrieve them, and started at the sight of a Spanish stamp. Since Matilde's death two years ago, there had been no letters from Cañar.

The drawers of old correspondence forgotten, Rose sat down to open this new letter, postmarked Órgiva. The letter was printed, only the signature written by hand, and it took her a moment to recognise the name. *Estimada Rose*, it began, *Soy Sebastián, hijo de Matilde.* Of course. It was Sebastián who had driven them along the twisting roads of the Alpujarra to visit Trevélez, the highest of all the villages. That day she and Helen had spent touring the Alpujarras remained crystal-clear in her mind. She could almost taste the *papas a lo pobre*, smell the roasting chestnuts, picture the mountains looming all around her, blue-grey in the fading light of dusk. Was that why she suddenly felt dizzy, as if she were re-travelling that road, swaying to each of its corkscrew turns? Matilde's son Sebastián was a carpenter – she remembered his lengthy explanation of why chestnut wood was best for the beams of Alpujarran houses. So what, she wondered, had prompted this unexpected letter?

First of all, he wrote, Aunt Herminia sent warm greetings and kisses to her 'dear sister-in-law'. The family still talked of English Rose and her niece, still remembered with great pleasure the two visits she had made to Cañar. And now, Sebastián continued, they had news that would surely interest her. In fact, Herminia had insisted there must be no delay in sharing it with her. They prayed this letter would find her alive and well.

Rose's hands began to shake as she read on. Permission had finally been received from the authorities to exhume Miguel's remains and return them to the family for reburial. He and his cousin Ángel had been pushing for over a year to have their uncle's bones returned so that he could be given the dignified burial he deserved. Tomás's nephew Daniel, who knew the exact site of Miguel's makeshift grave, had been helping them. They'd been lucky to have the support of the local Association for the Recovery of Historical Memory in Jaén, along with that of a sympathetic local politician and an investigative journalist from Órgiva. Miguel's was one case out of many, Sebastián explained. All over the country, mass graves of Republicans executed during or after the war had been identified and now, with the change of government, the pleas of the victims' relatives would finally be heard.

We did the digging ourselves – four of us, guided by a young volunteer archaeologist from Granada University. The recent spring rains had softened the earth, which made it easier. Just thirty centimetres beneath the surface, Ángel found the first bone and after that, digging with our bare hands so as not to shatter the fragile...

Rose put down the letter. She felt breathless. Taking from her pocket the bottle of little angina pills Dr Morris had prescribed, she slipped one under her tongue. How she wished Jack were here to hold her hand. With eyes closed, she rocked to and fro, hands clasped in her lap, as she tried to take in Sebastián's news. That after all these years, Miguel's remains should be unearthed. It was so unexpected... Why hadn't they warned her?

She opened her eyes. From the kitchen window, a shaft of sunlight fell on the worktop, bringing a rosy gleam to the apples in the fruit bowl. *Pull yourself together, Rose*, she commanded herself. A collection of bones, that's all it was. A skeleton with nothing to hold it together: no flesh or blood, and only circumstance to identify it as belonging to the man she had known and loved.

Her thoughts returned to the family, to Herminia and her children and their cousins, the children of Matilde and Alfonso. She realised how much it would mean to them to honour their uncle, Herminia's brother, with a dignified goodbye, to be able to visit his grave close by, in the village where they all belonged. She too should take comfort from the knowledge that Miguel would not lie alone on the desolate mountainside but be at home among his family, those who cherished and revered him. She felt a small shift in her conscience, as if the burden of guilt she had carried with her for so long was beginning to dissolve.

Taking a deep breath, Rose resumed reading. They had fixed a date for the re-interment. He would be laid to rest alongside his mother Modesta in Cañar's cemetery, close to the graves of his sister Lourdes and of Matilde and José Antonio. If she could still travel, they would love her to be present for the ceremony on 18th June...

No, impossible, she didn't have the strength. Five years ago she could have done it. Now, just thinking of the rigmarole of airports, planes and then that tortuous journey by road… The timbre of his voice in her head was no longer distinct after so many years but she could still remember her lover's heartfelt depiction of his *pueblo,* the fond way he described its people. It was right that his bones should return to Cañar. She felt happy for Miguel and for his family, they would be in her thoughts on the 18th, but she could not be there. In a moment, when she felt less unsteady, she would ring Helen. Right now, she did not dare move from her seat.

CHAPTER 54

Oxford 2006-2007

'Hiya Rose, is it okay if I come round? Mum said I should practise my Spanish with you.' Rose struggled to identify the voice on the other end of the line. Her hearing wasn't so sharp these days. 'It's Zoe, if you hadn't guessed.'

'Of course dear, though I'm afraid my Spanish is a little rusty. Helen did mention you were taking classes.'

'That's right. I thought it would be useful. My boyfriend's parents have bought a *cortijo* inland from Alicante and we've promised to help them do it up over the summer.'

'Oh, I see. Well, come this afternoon if you like. And while you're here, you can change a light bulb for me. I daren't get up on a chair myself.'

'I should think not at your age!'

'¿Qué parte de España te gusta más?'

'Which part of Spain do I like best?' Frowning, Rose pondered Zoe's question. Her memories of Spain were all mixed up with the war. It was hard to cast aside the images of dying men with faces half blown away, insanitary, rat-infested 'hospitals' and bombed villages, to remember the particularities of one landscape or another. '*Las playas de Alicante son preciosas,*' she said, conjuring up the feel of warm sand between her toes, the salty tang of the sea, the mountains that formed a backdrop as she walked with Miguel, one hand in his, the other clutching her *alpargatas*. Her hands then had been smooth and agile, not the twisted tree roots they resembled now. Walking and talking, spinning illusory dreams of a future together.

'*También Granada, las Alpujarras y la Sierra Nevada,*' she added.

'Mum's always going on about the Alpujarras,' Zoe said, reverting to English. 'She went there with you when I was a child, didn't she.'

Rose nodded. She felt a sudden urge to see the video again – the one Herminia's son had sent her, of Miguel's re-interment in the cemetery. The last time, with Helen, her emotions had got the better of her and she had missed half of it, blinded by tears. Since then, the disk had remained in its box on the shelf. Now she felt calmer, more in control. If Zoe were willing to keep her company, she would like to watch it once more.

'Zoe.' She turned to her great-niece. 'Will you indulge me by letting me play a short video of… well, this may seem odd to you, it's a burial actually, the burial of an old friend in one of the Alpujarran villages. It's just that I'd prefer not to watch it alone. If you don't mind…'

'I don't mind at all. Tell me where it is and I'll put it on straightaway.'

Rose steeled herself. This time she would not weep at the homespun eulogies of Miguel's relatives as they stood around the grave together with a few older people from the village who still remembered him; not look away as, one by one, they tossed flowers onto the casket.

'That was so moving,' Zoe said as the video came to an end. She loosed her hand to brush a tear from her eye – she had been gently stroking Rose's palm with her thumb as they sat side by side, watching the simple ceremony. 'I don't know who all those people were but I guess Miguel was… Hey, you're smiling.'

'So I am,' Rose said with surprise. She hadn't been aware of it till Zoe spoke. Watching the second time had left her with a deep sense of peace, as if a troublesome wound of the flesh had finally healed, the scar only a faint, barely visible reminder of past pain. As if the laying to rest of Miguel had also pacified the spirit that haunted her own mind. It brought an unexpected sense of liberation. 'Would you like a glass of sherry?' she asked. 'Yes, I know you're driving but just one won't hurt.'

Rose stood watching from the doorstep as Zoe pulled away in her little silver car. Already, evening was encroaching. Stepping back inside, she flicked the light switch in the living room and cursed. Neither she nor Zoe had remembered the spent light bulb. Lucky she had the lamp in the corner, the one with the pretty pressed-flower shade given her by Susan.

She fell heavily. Awkwardly, with most of her weight on one side. *Stupid rug. Stupid old woman.* Hadn't Peter warned her the rug was dangerous? That one day she would trip over it? She couldn't move. The pain was excruciating. And now she needed it, that mobile phone sat useless on her bedside table, far beyond reach. Was it the shock making her feel she might pass out at any moment? She imagined herself lying here all night, to be discovered dead in the morning by Sylwia, the Polish cleaner...

The doorbell. She must get up. She *must*. She moved a leg, the one that wasn't trapped beneath her. And screamed out in pain. The bell rang a second time. Tears rolled down her cheeks. There was no way she could answer the door. After the third ring, followed by a sharp rap, a deathly silence fell on the house.

'Where am I?' Her voice emerged as a feeble whisper. But without even opening her eyes, she knew; she recognised the smell, the background hum. She was in hospital. Slowly her memory returned: of the fall, the unanswered doorbell, the telephone ringing again and again a million miles away. Then, much later, Helen's face looming over her. 'Don't move, I'm calling an ambulance.'

She opened her eyes and looked around. The nurse's face was kind. 'How are you feeling, love? A bit groggy, I expect, from the painkillers. We think you've broken a hip; it was lucky your niece found you so soon. At your age, you know... We'll be taking you down for X-ray in a little while. I'm afraid you may well need surgery.'

'Oh, I'm sorry to be such a nuisance. It was stupid of me to fall...'

'Enough of that. Now, how about a cup of tea? We don't want you getting dehydrated.'

'That would be lovely.'

'Ah, here's your granddaughter come to see you.'

'I don't have a grand...' Rose turned her head.

'God, I feel so awful,' Zoe said, bending to give Rose a kiss. 'It was my fault for forgetting to change your light bulb. I came back ten minutes later when I remembered, but I suppose you were helpless on the floor by then. Lucky Mum had a key or we'd have had to break in. She'll be back in a minute, by the way.'

'I used to be a nurse, you know.' Rose allowed Kristina to help her off the commode and back to her armchair. It felt all wrong, this reversal of roles. Her days at Elmhurst did not seem so very long ago, though when she worked it out, she found that more than three decades had passed since her retirement.

'You nurse?' Kristina loosed a bright, toothy smile and winked – her substitute for the language she lacked. 'Very nice. I think long ago many things different.'

'Not so different,' Rose said. 'Neither for nurses nor patients.' Despite all the new-fangled technology, caring for the sick and disabled required the same skills, the same qualities of patience and kindness and practicality as it always had. And for the patient, the humiliation of being dependent on others for the most personal of tasks remained constant in time. For her, that loss of dignity was one of the greatest trials to be borne.

Of course she felt grateful for the care she received. The nursing home on Boars Hill was comfortable enough and it took the onus off her family. But she wanted to go home, to be surrounded by familiar objects – the clock from her parents' home, her albums of photos, Jack's favourite walking stick – and regain at least some of her former independence. The doctors, the OTs and physios were evasive, her relatives too. 'You're not exactly a spring chicken,' Dr Matthew had reminded her, as if she needed reminding. 'Better not to set your mind on going home.'

Her frequent visitors were the envy of other residents. Even so, the days crawled by. More and more, she would drift back into the past. Her thoughts dwelt often on the years with Jack, the simple happiness they had shared. She missed him still. At the suggestion of his three sons, they had taken his ashes to the Oxfordshire hills where he loved to walk, and scattered them to the wind. She too would prefer cremation, she had told her family. The idea of her flesh rotting away in the ground disturbed her, bringing to mind the mass graves of

Spain where so many brave souls had been tossed without ceremony, hidden from sight and mostly still lost to those who mourned them. 'And your ashes?' Peter had asked. 'Is there some special place you'd like them to be dispersed or buried?' What did it matter? She would be gone. 'You and Helen decide.'

A Christmas tree and decorations were going up. Was it for the benefit of residents or staff, Rose wondered? 'They're beautiful,' she told Kristina and the other care assistants who had taken so much trouble over them. This Christmas would be her last. She knew with absolute certainty, though whether this was a premonition, a wish or an active decision, she could not say. She was in her ninety-second year. The challenge of getting through each day with her worn-out body – her creaky, painful joints and poor circulation, her itchy skin and weak bladder – often seemed more effort than it was worth. Death, with any luck a painless slipping away, might be a welcome release.

'Lunchtime, Rose.' Ivan had appeared at the door, ready to supervise her slow shuffle to the dining room. 'It's shepherd's pie today.'

She always had the option to eat in her room as some of the other residents did, but mostly she preferred a change of scenery and what passed for conversation. Besides, she was supposed to walk; the bossy physio insisted she must. 'You've got a frame, use it.' Her mobile phone rang just as Ivan closed the door behind them.

'Wait there, I'll get it for you,' he said.

'No, don't bother. Whoever it is will phone back.'

He shrugged. 'Up to you.'

Her appetite was tiny these days. Mealtimes broke up the day but she rarely did more than pick at the food, which tended to be soft and bland to accommodate the dental and digestive deficiencies of the residents.

Back in her room after the meal, she checked on the missed call, as Zach had shown her how to do. Susan's name came up on the screen.

'Rose, I've a proposition to make,' she bubbled when Rose called her back. 'We're taking Samantha's little Evie to the pantomime. It's Cinderella, we think she's old enough. Anyway, we'd love you to join us. It'll be a hoot. Obviously I'll pick you up and bring you back; your wheelchair will go in the boot, no problem. You need to get out more.'

'Which day are you going?' As if she had a full diary.

'January the 6th, it's a Saturday.'

Reyes, Rose thought: the day of the Three Kings. But of course nobody celebrated that here. It was only Spanish children who had to wait till January for their presents. 'I'll think about it, Susan.' She thought about the palaver involved in dressing up to go out, manoeuvring herself into and out of the car, the wheelchair... And Evie, had she met Susan's granddaughter Evie? It seemed only yesterday that Samantha turned five and now she had a child of her own. *Be a sport*, a voice in her head (was it Jack's?) coaxed.

'I'll get a ticket for you,' Susan said. 'It's a matinee so you won't be back late.'

January 6th dawned damp and dismal, though warm for the time of year. The rain started early and pelted down all morning, misting the window, obscuring her view of the garden. Rose sat in semi-darkness, feeling like a prisoner in this small room. She was sick of its pale cream walls and pale wood fixtures, the bed with its flowery duvet, the small table and chair, the commode discreetly placed in one corner. A collection of family photos – framed and unframed – stood on a shelf, along with a few books and ornaments she had brought from home. The leaves of the azalea plant – a Christmas gift – were wilting but several of its pink flowers still survived.

This year they had spent Christmas Day at Peter and Jenny's in Oxford. So many people, so much noise, an abundance of food and drink. Children (who were they all?) rushing around, screaming, giggling, quarrelling, jumping up and down. She'd felt dizzy with it all. But everyone was so kind, treating her like a queen (the real queen was ten years younger), that she could only count her blessings.

Now there was the pantomime, and to her surprise, she was rather looking forward to it. Susan was right: she should get out more. It did her good, relieved the boredom of sitting here day after day. 'Don't even think about crying off,' she'd said on the phone last night. 'We've got tickets for the stalls, end of a row so your wheelchair can be parked right next to us.'

At lunchtime the rain slackened off briefly but by the time Susan arrived, it was bucketing down with renewed force, driven almost horizontal by the wind. 'We'll have to make a run for it,' Susan said, laughing.

'Ha ha, shall I race you?' Although Ivan held an umbrella over her as she made her lumbering progress from wheelchair to car, rain blew into her face, splashed her legs and dripped down the back of her neck inside her coat.

'You'll soon dry out,' Alan said. 'I've put the heater on high.'

'Evie, don't wipe your nose on your sleeve. Here's a tissue.' Susan sat in the back with the little girl. 'She's got a nasty cold, I'm afraid. Better not get too near.'

'You've forgotten, I'm a nurse,' Rose said gaily. 'We're used to being in contact with infection.' She twisted round to address Evie. 'I hope you don't feel too rotten, dear.'

Alan was smiling, shaking his head as if she'd made a joke.

The loss of her glove distracted Rose right through the pantomime. She must have dropped it in the road as she got into or out of the car. The maroon leather gloves had been a present from Ralph and Chantal and she was inordinately fond of them. The leather was soft and supple and they fitted like a second skin. Wearing them made her feel cossetted, as well as reminding her of her beloved brother. Of course it was silly to feel so sentimentally attached to an inanimate object, but these days small things were enough to distress her.

The following Tuesday, Rose woke with a sore throat. She couldn't pin the blame on Evie: coughs, sneezes and runny noses had been rife in the overheated theatre. It was that time of year. She asked Kristina to get her some Vitamin C, drank hot lemon with honey and stayed in her room. By the end of the week, her cold had developed fully: a stinker of a cold. She took to her bed, feeling miserable, but a chesty cough made it difficult to sleep. The doctor advised paracetamol and plenty of fluids. Helen came to visit, bringing grapes and clementines, and clucked when she said she had no appetite, not even for fruit.

'I've brought something else for you,' she said, delving into her bag. 'Your missing glove. Susan noticed how upset you were so she went back to the theatre next day and someone had handed it in.'

'That was kind.' Rose took the glove and held it to her cheek. 'Thank you dear.'

On her next visit, Helen demanded to speak with the doctor. Her aunt should have been prescribed antibiotics, the cold was sitting on her chest; it was affecting her breathing. Rose felt too weak to protest. Weak and tired. If this cold put paid to her life, so be it. To have lived through nine decades was a privilege not granted to all.

She reflected on the arbitrary span of a life. *The days of our years are threescore years and ten; and if by reason of strength they be fourscore years, yet is their strength labour and sorrow; for it is soon cut off, and we fly away.* Psalm 90: extraordinary that the words she had learnt in her childhood should come back to her now. If three score years and ten was the measure, she had long outlived it, while her child Blanca, allotted a mere two days, had been cruelly cheated. How comforting it would be to have her father's faith in an afterlife, one where she would be reunited with all those who had preceded her. Sadly, she did not believe in such delusions. Nevertheless, she felt ready to fly away. Her body felt light as a sparrow's.

March 2nd 2007

Dear Sebastian,

You may remember me from my visit to Cañar with my Aunt Rose. I'm sorry to share this sad news with you and sorry too that I'm unable to write in Spanish. I seem to remember one of your siblings or cousins spoke some English. In any case, I'm sure you'll find someone to translate.

As you may have guessed, I'm writing to tell you that Rose passed away on February 14th, a few weeks short of her ninety-second birthday. Valentine's Day was perhaps appropriate for such a loving person, don't you agree? She died of pneumonia following a bad cold and chest infection.

After the cremation, we buried her ashes in our garden and planted a rose bush there. It was my daughter Zoe's idea. Rose was a great inspiration to all of us and we'll miss her dreadfully. I'm sure you and your family will share our sadness.

The video you sent of Miguel's re-interment moved her deeply and I think brought a kind of closure. My sincere thanks for taking the trouble. It was much appreciated.

With best wishes to you and all your family,
Helen

PART 14 MARISOL 2011 - 2012

CHAPTER 55

Granada, 2011

From the speed of her reply, its breathless tone and the number of exclamation marks in her email, Marisol took Clare's Aunt Stella to be a bubbly, vivacious kind of person.

Clare told me all about you, she wrote. *How exciting to discover you have English blood!!! Of course I'll help you trace your grandmother. Actually, it's dead easy now, not like a few years ago. All the records are online and the basic information is free! If her name's not too common and you know what part of the country she's from, you'll find her in no time. I'll give you links to a couple of websites you can use. Just be careful. Some companies are cashing in on the craze for family history and charge a bomb for information you could probably get for free.*

By the way, did Clare tell you about the juicy scandals I uncovered in my family? Blimey, I was shocked at what they got up to!! Once you start digging into the past, you just never know what you're going to stumble on!!!

Marisol wasn't looking for juicy scandals; she was looking for her grandmother. At the age of ninety-six, it was unlikely she'd still be alive, but the search would surely turn up other members of her family. According to Clare, Tilly was an unusual name. The main snag lay in the lack of a location. Not that she'd let that put her off. She clicked on the first of the links.

Clare Skyped her the next day. 'My aunt said you'd been in touch. How are you getting on? I'm all agog.'

Marisol laughed. 'It was only yesterday but already… Listen to this. I went on a site called *FreeBMD* that your aunt recommended. It was brilliant. You could opt to search for names that were phonetically similar, so it came up with a Rosena and a Rosella as well as Rose. And Tilly, Tilley, Tooley, Tiley...' She spelt them out to Clare. 'There were about ten of these different versions, spread all over the country, all born in 1915.'

'Wow, you're a fast worker.'

'I'm so... on fire? Can you say that in English?'

Clare laughed. 'Fired up. I guess if there's only ten, the next step might be to go through each one in the phonebook – you can do that online too. BT online or something like that.'

'Great, I'll get started right now.'

She was disappointed to find only one – in the north of England – and when she rang, a male voice answered and said his mother had moved to a nursing home a few months ago. And no, she had never been to Spain. Marisol's initial euphoria began to dissipate. It was going to be a long search, she could see now.

'Do you think it would be easier if you went to England?' Antonio asked.

'Not really. I mean, without knowing where she lived, what's the point? Also, she might have got married back in England and changed her name. Women don't keep their surnames like here. I feel a bit stuck.'

Antonio was drumming his fingers on the table as he often did when faced with a problem to solve. 'Could there be another way to go about it, I wonder? I mean what would an Englishwoman have been doing in Spain at that time, just a few months after the war ended? It's odd, there were no tourists then, surely.'

'Hey, I've just had an idea. Loads of foreigners came to fight in the Civil War. But not just soldiers. Doctors and nurses and writers, all kinds of people.'

'True, but didn't they all leave with the Republican defeat? Or even before?'

'I guess you're right.' She let out a sigh. 'I can't see a way forward. To ring up every Tilly and Tilley and Tooley in the entire country on the off chance one of them might be related would take years and cost a fortune.'

Antonio squeezed her shoulder. 'Don't lose heart now, Maris. I've never known you turn away from a challenge. We'll find a way.'

Marisol tried to comfort the weeping *primigravida* who had been so insistent on a natural birth. After twelve hours in labour she was now being wheeled off for an emergency caesarean. 'In a few weeks, you'll have forgotten which way he came out,' she said. 'Believe me, I've heard it from so many mothers. The important thing is not to risk your own or your baby's life.'

She went to see how the two women approaching transition were doing. One was coping well; the other had become tetchy and was giving her dismayed husband a hard time. Marisol drew him aside. 'It's quite normal at this stage,' she said. 'Don't take it to heart, just hold her hand and keep encouraging her.' Work had been non-stop today; thankfully she was nearly at the end of her shift. The job was definitely becoming more stressful.

Looking up an hour later, having just tucked a newborn into the cot next to her mother's bed, she noticed with relief that Anabel and Begoña had arrived to take over the shift. After updating her colleagues, she switched on her mobile and went to get changed. Antonio had left a message. *I've got some exciting news for you. Hurry home. Kisses.* She smiled to herself, wondering what it could be. Perhaps he had the results of his *oposiciones*, due any time now. If he'd succeeded in the exam, it would mean a pay rise.

'So what's the news, *cariño*?' she asked as they embraced. 'I'm intrigued.'

'I've been very busy on your behalf,' he said, looking rather smug. 'And...' He smacked a loud kiss on her forehead. 'I think I've found your grandmother.'

'Never. Tell me more.'

'Take your coat off first and let's sit down.'

'That can wait,' she said laughing. 'Tell me. Now.'

'*Bueno*, I thought there must be some kind of information about the women who came here in the thirties to help in our struggle: a list of names at the least. So I started searching on the web.'

'Of course, why didn't we think of that before?'

Triumphantly, he said, 'I found a Rose Tilly and guess what? She was a nurse.'

'Oh darling, that's incredible. Well done!'

'She came from a small town in… I'm not sure how you pronounce it but I looked it up on the map and it's not far from Oxford. She was a vicar's daughter and…'

'Is she still alive?'

'It didn't say, but she survived the war and returned to England. I'm sure we can find out more, now we know her identity.'

'You're brilliant,' she said, hugging him. 'I love you.'

'Who are you?' Tilly, P sounded suspicious.

He was Marisol's third try after Tilly, W S and Tilly, Michael, with both of whom she'd drawn a blank. Tilly, Dawn and Tilly, L J remained on the 'to call' list. Oxford had seemed the obvious place to start, though as the English tended to move about all over the country, Rose or her relatives could be anywhere. She had come out with her set speech: 'I'm looking for a Rose Tilly. She may no longer be alive but if there was anyone in your family with that name… your mother perhaps?'

'My name is Marisol and I'm Rose Tilly's granddaughter,' she said in answer to his question, adding, 'She was a nurse. In Spain.' Marisol heard a gasp, followed by silence, except for his slightly laboured breathing coming down the line.

When he finally spoke, faltering a little, his tone was less gruff. 'I had an aunt who was a nurse; she went to Spain in the Civil War. But she had no children.' Marisol could hear the confusion in his voice.

'Her father was a vicar,' she said, 'if that helps.'

There was another long silence. 'I guess that clinches it,' he said eventually. 'My aunt's father was a vicar in Evesham, not far from Oxford.'

'Yes?' Now it was she who was flummoxed. What to say? Where to go from here? 'Well…' Stunned at her success, she nearly forgot the most important question. 'I suppose she's not still living, is she?'

'Sadly not. She died four years ago. Look, forgive me, but I'm finding all this difficult to understand. As I said, we weren't aware of any children. It's rather a shock, to put it mildly. I don't have a clue who you are. You sound… Spanish? Also, I must speak to my sister. She was very close to Rose. Then maybe the three of us should meet.'

Marisol's mind was beginning to clear. 'I can understand your shock,' she said. 'This is pretty momentous for me too. I'd love to meet you and your sister but first… My mother, she doesn't know I make enquiries about Rose. I'll have to tell her. She was adopted as a baby and never knew who was her real mother.'

'Well. Well, well.' He seemed as much at a loss as she was. 'I guess I'd better introduce myself: my name's Peter. I can see we have a lot of ground to cover. Perhaps a first step might be to exchange emails. Then you can explain more fully. At the moment, I can't really fit the pieces together. Of the jigsaw,' he added. 'Though it's possible, I suppose, that my sister Helen… But I'm sure she would have told me.'

'That's a great idea. In any case, I'm in Spain. I have a job; I can't drop everything and come over immediately. If you spell out your email address, I'll give you our end of the story and tell you about my family. There are five of us, I'm not the only grandchild.'

'Amazing. To think Rose kept this secret all her life. Well, I can fill you in too, about your grandmother and her English family. After all, if it's true, we must be related. Do you have a pen? I'll give you my address.'

'Four years,' Marisol said to Antonio over lunch. 'We've missed her by just four years. I'm kicking myself for not having started on the trail sooner.'

'It's a shame we're too late,' he agreed. 'Still, now you're in contact with her family, you can learn a lot about her. There'll be stories and photos, letters probably. It's exciting, Maris. ¡Ánimo!'

'I think I'll wait before telling Mamá. I'm going to write to Peter this evening. Then, when I have his reply, with a bit more information about Rose, I can show her the email. Otherwise, I'm worried she might tell me to drop it, not to stir things up.'

'Really? I doubt it. Surely she'll be curious. I mean, Rose was her mother.'

'Mm, you'd think so, I agree. But she can be funny sometimes. It won't hurt to wait a couple of days. In any case,' she added, 'I don't care what Mamá says, I'm not going to keep this to myself. My brothers and sisters have a right to know too.' She stood up and started to clear the table.

'I can see the sparks flying already,' Antonio said with a smile. He took her hand. 'Shall we go to bed? You've nothing urgent to do right now, have you?'

'But my mind's on other things, sweetheart. I don't…' She hesitated. It was the right time of month to conceive and after several months of trying, they shouldn't let the opportunity go. 'On second thoughts, why not? I'm sure you'll have no trouble distracting me.'

'Mamá, are you alright?' Her breath was coming in shallow gasps and she had turned very pale. Marisol kicked herself for not breaking the news in a gentler way. 'Mamá?'

'You had no business acting behind my back.' She sat on the edge of the chair with pursed lips, her spine rigid. She was twisting her hands together in her lap, playing with her wedding ring.

'I'm sorry, Mamá. You're right, I should have talked to you first.' Marisol watched her mother. Anger and curiosity were battling it out, the conflict written in her face, her hands, her tensed muscles and tapping foot. She waited, confident Mamá would be unable to resist knowing more.

'*Bueno, hija*, you'd better tell me then. You say you traced this Rosa Tilly?'

Marisol stood close to Mamá and stroked her hair. 'I did. Unfortunately, your mother died in 2007.' She switched on her laptop. 'This email is from her nephew. I spoke to him yesterday.' Mamá bowed her head. 'Would you like to read it? It's in English but you'll understand some parts, I think.'

Mamá shook her head. 'Just tell me what he says.'

Marisol took a deep breath. 'He didn't know about you,' she said.

'He was completely nonplussed when I contacted him. But...' She turned to the email and began translating it for Mamá. 'When I spoke to my sister, she told me Rose had confided in her about a baby born in Spain, a baby girl she was told had died. It appears she'd had a Spanish lover, Miguel, who was killed just before the baby's birth. Helen was absolutely...' She stumbled over the word 'dumbstruck', trying to guess its meaning. '*Totalmente atónita* when I told her about you. We assume they must have lied to Rose in the hospital and given the baby away for adoption (you told me your mother was adopted).'

'Uncle Rodrigo,' Mamá muttered. Marisol looked up and saw how her mother's mouth had tightened in anger. She was trembling.

'Do you want me to go on?'

'Yes, go on, of course.'

'What's more – and this part is really amazing – Helen accompanied Rose to Spain in the '80s and met Miguel's family. They were good, kind people, from a village near Granada, she told me. Can you believe it, Mamá? They were from our province. This Miguel, he was your father.'

'I can't take it in. Are you sure it's true? Not some hoax? Well, go on.'

'Helen is eager to meet you and your mother. She's going to write to you separately in the next few days. There's so much to tell on both sides. For the moment we'd like you to know that her life was happy on the whole. She married some years after the war (WW2) but had no more children.' Marisol broke off. 'Mamá, will you come with me to England to meet them? They're family, they have photos of your mother, they can tell you what she was like.' Mamá was shaking her head. Marisol put a hand under her chin and forced her mother to look her in the eye. 'She didn't give you up, Mamá; she was deceived into thinking you had died.'

'England... Well I would, of course, if she were still alive. Or if... if I had a sister. I always dreamt of a sister.' The pain on her mother's face was so pitiful Marisol had to turn away. 'But you go if you like, *hija*. You speak the language.' Did she detect a slight hesitation in Mamá's voice? 'No, no, it's too far for me. Besides, I can't leave Carlos and Verónica in the lurch. They rely on me to help with the twins. And your father...'

'Oh for goodness' sake, you're just making excuses. I don't understand you, Mamá, these people are your family. They want to meet you. It's two and a half hours on the plane, not the North Pole.'

'Don't bully me, Marisol. Can't you see this is a shock? All my life I've longed... I need time to get used to the idea.'

'It's a shock, of course, Mamá, but just think. This is wonderful news, to have discovered your real family. You *must* meet them – when you're ready. And in the meantime, we have to tell the others. Maybe Belén or Luisa or one of the boys would like to accompany me to England.'

'You want to drag them into this as well?'

'Come on now, Mamá. Rose was their grandmother too. Naturally we must tell them.'

'I suppose so.' She had folded her arms and was rocking back and forth in her chair. 'Well, I think I'll lie down for a while, till this headache goes. Fetch me an aspirin, will you, *hija*.'

CHAPTER 56

Granada/Oxford 2011

Marisol reread Helen's email. *To say this came out of the blue would be an understatement*, she had written. *Even more so for the rest of the family, who knew nothing about Rose's baby. Now we're all itching to meet you. Rose would have been thrilled to know that her granddaughter was a nurse. She always hoped one of the family would follow in her footsteps. If only we'd made the connection a few years ago. Your email made me cry because it would have meant so much to Rose to know her daughter was alive and well and with children of her own. What a poignant reunion that would have been.*

Marisol wasn't so sure. Knowing she'd been cheated, robbed of her child for political or financial motives, would surely have caused her unbearable pain. Any joy at a reunion would have been bittersweet, tainted with regret and anger. No, it was better this way – better for Rose at least. For Mamá maybe not.

Helen had attached a photo of Rose, taken on her eightieth birthday. *There are plenty more pictures*, she wrote. *When you and your mother come over, you can look at them all.* Marisol showed Mamá, hoping it would convince her to make the trip.

'Let me see,' Mamá whispered, leaning in close. 'Oh!' She started to cry. 'Leave me, I want to be alone for a minute.' Marisol gave up her attempt to soothe Mamá and left her glued to the screen.

Later, Papá pored over the photo for ages, a puzzled look on his face. 'She looks familiar,' he said, 'I must be mistaken, obviously.' He shook his head. 'Perhaps it's just the resemblance with Consuelo.'

The resemblance – allowing for age – was clear to all of them.

'No doubt about it,' Carlos said. 'She's like an older version of Mamá.'

'She looks to me like a strong woman,' Luisa said. 'I mean in character.'

'From what we know of her life, she must have been tough,' Marisol pointed out. Mamá's face did not reflect that strength, that backbone and spirit. The resemblance was purely physical.

'Let me have another look,' Belén said. She stared at the image for a moment, then asked, 'Do you know if she ever came here, to Granada?'

'I suppose she must have done because she visited the Alpujarra. Why?'

'She stayed in the hotel. I'm sure it was her. Papá, come here. Don't you recognise her? She said it was her second visit; the first time she'd been with her husband. She remembered *el buho*, which I thought was funny. I guess he is unforgettable.'

'Never!' Marisol said when Papá confirmed it. 'You mean, you actually met our grandmother without knowing it? That's mind-blowing.'

'She spoke Spanish,' Papá said. 'I remember her because it was unusual at the time for a guest to speak our language.' He peered at the photo again and then at Marisol. 'I can see something of you there too. In the eyes perhaps? Or the set of the mouth. And her face is the same shape as Pablo's and Luisa's.'

Marisol clicked on the flight to Gatwick and pressed *Continue*.

'Are you quite sure you'll be alright on your own?' Antonio asked for the third time. 'I'm happy to come along if you need moral support.'

'Thanks, Toni.' Marisol blew him a kiss. 'I'll be fine, don't worry.' She had waited for Mamá to change her mind or for one of her brothers or sisters to say yes but in the end Mamá had failed to summon up the courage and the others had all claimed they were too busy with work, children, commitments of one kind or another. Couldn't she wait for the October *puente*, Luisa had asked? No, she'd hung about too long already. Her next weekend off would see her on the plane to England. She keyed in the details of her bankcard. 'Done,' she said.

She had chosen to stay at the Youth Hostel in Oxford rather than at Peter's home nearby. Both he and Helen had invited her but she had politely declined; she would feel more comfortable having a place where she could retreat and take stock. Arriving late at night on the bus from the airport, she went straight to bed, hoping for a good night's sleep before the reunion next day. On the journey she'd been buoyed by excitement, listing in her head the family members she was about to meet, working out their ages, trying to imagine them. She had jotted down some of the questions she wanted to ask. Rose's life – and especially her time in Spain – was an enigma. She hoped Helen would be able to recount some of her aunt's intriguing story.

Now, lying in the hostel bunk, her mind was invaded by other, less agreeable thoughts. The couple she had known as her grandparents were abductors. They had stolen another woman's baby – whether directly or not, it came to the same thing. They must have known. *Cold* was the word that came to mind when she recalled them: María Angustias, the woman whose lips were always painted a bright carmine red and who wrapped herself in furs every winter; who fawned on Uncle Francisco and treated Mamá and her family with undisguised indifference. José, a distant authoritarian figure who barked orders at everyone and whose lips were edged with tiny gobs of white foam. She could not forgive them. And if she felt angry, how must her mother feel?

Marisol listened to the giggles of the two Japanese girls across the dormitory and the light snores of the older woman in the bunk below hers but they were not to blame for her wakefulness. The image of Rose kept returning to her mind like a song that stays on the brain in endless repetition. The face in that photo exuded warmth, its lines betraying the wisdom gained from a life marred by deep sorrows as well as the happiness Peter had implied.

She unlatched the gate and walked up the path towards the front door of Peter's house, so typically English with its neat front garden, pebbledash façade and big windows. His greeting was equally English – an awkward handshake on the doorstep, accompanied by a nervous half-smile. 'Come in, come in.' He was tall, with greying hair rather long at the back – a token to '70s fashion – and he wore glasses. Dressed in a pale blue sweater and grey trousers, he looked the part of a retired optician. 'Jenny!' he called. 'My wife is in the back garden with Helen;

they may not have heard the doorbell.' He rubbed his hands together as if they were cold. 'We thought we'd spare you the hordes for today. Tomorrow I'm afraid there'll be quite a crowd of us. We don't want you to feel like some kind of circus attraction.'

'Marisol, how lovely.' The woman who now dashed forward into the hall in muddy trainers had eyes as green as Mamá's; they were the first thing you noticed about her. 'I'm Helen.' She grasped Marisol's hand in both of hers and looked directly at her. 'It's so good of you to come,' she said. 'I've a million questions and I expect you have too, but there'll be plenty of time for that later. Come through and make yourself comfortable. Jenny's got the kettle on already.' She bent down to undo her trainers. 'Don't worry about taking off your shoes,' she said, noticing Marisol's hesitation. 'Mine are covered in mud from the garden. After all the rain… but that's England for you.'

Marisol followed her into the kitchen where Peter's wife Jenny was just lifting a tray of homemade biscuits out of the oven. She put them down and their doughy, lemony smell wafted in the air. 'Welcome to Oxford.' She smiled at Marisol. 'I hope these aren't overdone, I was in the garden. Tea or coffee?'

'Well,' Helen said when they were all seated at the dining room table with their tea and biscuits. She made a sound between a laugh and a sigh. 'Where shall we start?'

'I brought some pictures of our family,' Marisol said, pulling a folder out of her bag and laying the photos out on the table. She had persuaded Mamá to search out some old ones taken when she was a child, an adolescent, a young woman, as well as more recent family snaps, and added a few of her own, printed out specially. 'I think this is the earliest,' she said, pointing to a classic photographer's portrait in which her mother looked about six. Despite the formal pose, the black and white photo had succeeded in capturing a certain gaucheness. Studying it earlier, Marisol had also detected what looked to her like resentment, betrayed in the hint of a pout.

They examined each photo in turn, commenting on imagined resemblances, asking her questions. 'That's my father, Enrique. They married in 1962. And this one is with her first baby, my sister Belén and… Angustias.' She had almost said 'my grandmother'.

Helen took the photo and stared at it. 'Do you think this Angustias loved your mother? I'm sorry but I find it hard to understand how she could live with herself, having taken another woman's baby. Or did she choose to let that fact slip from her mind?'

'I don't think my mother received much affection from her adoptive parents. I get the impression her childhood was quite lonely. She felt she was treated differently from her brothers, despised even. She confided once that she'd invented an imaginary friend and what a comfort it was to share her secrets with this Lola.'

'So when you told your mother what you'd discovered, told her about Rose, I mean… It must have been quite devastating for her. I can't begin to imagine the bitter feelings it must have provoked to know she'd been… kidnapped.'

'She's finding it hard to fully take in what was done to her – and to her mother,' Marisol agreed. 'She's still in shock, I think.'

'You know,' Helen said, 'when I was in Cañar with Rose, Miguel's nephew Ángel took me aside one night. We couldn't communicate well – in fact I wasn't even sure I'd understood him correctly – but he seemed to have some suspicions about the supposed death of Rose's baby. There was a woman in their village, a political prisoner, who'd had her children taken away for ideological reasons. Ángel thought maybe something similar had happened to Rose. He wanted me to investigate, but without letting on to her. I'm ashamed to say I didn't take it very seriously. In any case, I wouldn't have had a clue where to start.'

'I've been reading up about the scandal of the stolen babies,' Peter said. 'It was in the papers here too. And now it's come out that the same thing happened in Ireland. Unmarried mothers were sent to mother-and-baby homes run by the Church, where they were made to work like slaves and their babies sold to rich couples.'

'The cruelty of it,' Helen said, shaking her head. 'How they can claim to be Christian beats me.'

'You haven't explained how you found out,' Peter said. 'Or how you managed to trace us.'

Marisol told them of her enquiries and of her mother's reticence. 'She was ashamed of having been adopted. All her life they fed her stories about how her natural mother was a "red" and immoral and had abandoned her. It was only when Angustias was dying that she revealed Rose's name and that she was English. We had no idea before.'

'You say her name is Consuelo?' Helen picked up one of the childhood photos and gazed at it. 'Rose had already given her a name: Blanca.'

'Blanca?' Marisol repeated. The vision of a young Rose cuddling her baby, whispering her name, made her eyes prick. She brushed away a tear. 'Blanca. That's a beautiful name.' She wondered how different Mamá would have turned out had she been brought up by her real mother, the nurse Rose. 'I'd like to see more pictures of Rose,' she said.

'Of course. Peter has some and I've brought a pile as well.'

One after another, the photos were passed to her: an entire life in snapshots. Rose as a child with her parents and brothers; Rose in nurse's uniform proudly displaying her certificate; Rose setting off for Spain; Rose with another nurse and a doctor at some desolate field hospital in Aragón; Rose in a flowery summer dress, holding one of her brother's babies. And that was just the hors d'oeuvre. Her husband Jack appeared by her side in many of the later photos, the affection between them visible. Babies and children featured often. Was it her imagination or did Rose look wistful in some of them?

'She never forgot Miguel or the baby she'd lost,' Helen said. 'It was a very private grief she carried. Few people were aware of it, but to me it was plain, a sadness that persisted all her life, despite her effort to make the best of things.'

'My mother also is very private person. Oh I do wish Mamá could see these pictures,' she added.

Helen took her hand and held it for a moment. 'This one,' she said, pulling out a dog-eared snap from the pile in front of her, 'this one is your grandfather Miguel, poor chap. The one in the middle. Good-looking, wasn't he. His sister gave it to Rose when we visited. The name of the village has come back to me now. It was Cañar. Maybe you know it?'

'I'm not sure. But I know where it is, I've certainly passed nearby.'

'This is Rose with Miguel's mother Modesta and his sisters on her first visit. She wrote the date on the back: 1972.' Helen handed her a dozen more. 'They took lots. It must have been an incredibly emotional occasion for all of them.'

Marisol studied the pictures of her great-grandmother and great-aunts: sturdy women of the Alpujarra with suffering and hardship written on their faces. Modesta wore a black dress, the traditional *luto* in memory of her husband and sons. That generation had so much resilience, she thought. To have lived through the war, battling on with half their menfolk killed, their own lives and liberty in danger too.

'I still can't get over it, that part of my family lived so close and we didn't know.'

'They still do. One of the sisters, Herminia, was still alive the last I heard, and several of their children stayed in the area. You should make contact, they'd be thrilled.'

'Oh and another amazing coincidence,' Marisol said, remembering. 'You and Rose stayed at the hotel in Granada where my father and sister used to work. Carlos too. They recognised her from the photo.'

'You're joking.' Peter looked at his sister and shook his head in disbelief. 'So many near misses. And didn't you say you were in Oxford? Which year was that?'

Marisol worked it out. '1993.'

'If only you'd known then. To think, you could have passed Rose in the street.'

'Show me that picture of your father again,' Helen said. Marisol passed it to her. 'I can't say I remember him but it was a long time ago.'

'Where did you learn to speak such fluent English?' Peter asked.

'Do I sound fluent? Thank you. I lived in England for two years, working as a nurse in Cambridge. But I still make mistakes.'

Jenny had taken herself off some time ago and now the smell of hot food drifted through from the adjoining kitchen. Helen stood up. 'How many hours have we been sitting here?' she asked, laughing. 'I don't know about you but I feel like I'm on an emotional rollercoaster: elated one minute, sad as hell the next.'

Over lunch, Helen told her about Miguel's exhumation and reburial and the video his relatives had made. 'Rose was deeply affected by it. I'll show it to you later.'

'That reminds me,' Peter said. 'Something else we watched, probably on YouTube. Remember, Jenny? The ceremony in Madrid a couple of years ago for the few International Brigade volunteers still alive and able to travel. Maybe you heard about it, Marisol? Your government gave them Spanish passports in appreciation of their sacrifice.'

'One of Rose's colleagues in the medical unit was among them,' Jenny said. 'We were sad that it came too late for your grandmother; she'd have been so proud.'

In the afternoon, Helen took Marisol for a stroll along the canal and riverbank. 'Rose loved to walk these paths,' she said. 'They bought a house – she and Jack – close to the river, at Iffley village. She said water calmed her.'

They walked in silence for a while. Marisol was thinking about Rose, who had spent her whole life in ignorance of her daughter's existence. 'I feel angry for Rose,' she said. 'Never knowing her child is alive.'

'I know. It deprived both her and your mother.' Helen paused as they passed through a gate and Marisol fastened it behind them. 'In a way, I suppose I benefitted. Rose treated me as a kind of substitute daughter. We were very close; in fact people often took us for mother and daughter.'

'Green eyes,' Marisol said, smiling now. 'We share that green eye gene: Rose, you, my mother, Pablo and me...' Would it continue down the line, she wondered?

'Rose inherited them from her father.'

'The vicar?'

'That's right. My grandfather, the Reverend Arthur Tilly.'

Marisol was reminded of that crazy psychiatrist with his Nazi notion of a 'red' gene that could justify taking babies from their natural parents on the basis of their politics. What did politics have to do with good parenting? Rose would have been a far more loving mother than Angustias. She thought of the damage done to Mamá by these people, her pseudo-grandparents, and her anger surged up again.

'Do you like blackberries?' Helen pointed to some bushes on their left. 'There are loads here, I should have brought a plastic bag.'

'I love them,' she said, making an effort to control her feelings.

'Come on then, what are we waiting for?'

They stopped and Marisol popped one in her mouth. 'Mm, they're much bigger and juicier than the Spanish ones.'

'They need rain to swell them.'

Marisol was grabbing handfuls, enjoying the sweet taste. 'We call them *moras,*' she said.

'That's similar to the French.'

'I'd forgotten, you're bilingual, aren't you.'

'Yes, my mother was French.'

'It's just occurred to me, my mother learnt a little French at school. Perhaps she'd feel more confident about meeting you if I told her you spoke French.' It was worth a try.

Back at Peter's house, Helen handed her a bundle of letters. 'Before I forget,' she said, 'you must take these. I found them among Rose's possessions after she died. They're in Spanish, from Miguel's sisters, Matilde and Lourdes. One of them mentions the baby – or rather Rose's pregnancy. A man called Tomás, who'd been with Rose and Miguel... Oh I'm sorry, you haven't heard that part of the story yet. I'll remedy that tomorrow, before we watch the video.'

Having slept later than she intended, Marisol decided not to bother with breakfast but head straight over to Peter's house. She had only one more day and there was still so much to find out, so many of the extended family to meet.

Jenny handed her a cup of coffee but before she'd taken more than a couple of sips, the doorbell rang and in a moment the kitchen seemed full of people.

'This is my husband Mike,' Helen said. 'And our children, Zoe and Zach. They're twins.'

'Twins! So they do run in the family. My brother has twins also.'

'It's great to meet you,' Zoe said. 'I was totally gobsmacked when

Mum told me about you. The whole story, what they did to Rose, it's just monstrous.'

Over the course of the morning, others arrived: first Helen and Peter's cousin Susan, with her partner Alan, son Oliver and daughter Sam, then two of Jack's sons. They all shook her hand, inspected her and remarked on what they judged to be family features; chattered away about Rose, asked her questions. She found it exhausting meeting so many new relatives all at once, remembering who was who. Names flew about the room, names of partners and children, siblings and cousins, those who weren't present today. It was impossible to keep track.

'Rose had a godson, Frank,' Peter said at one point. 'We met him at Rose's funeral and apparently he has some letters she wrote to his mother from Spain when she was nursing there. He promised to pass them on to us.'

'I'll remind him,' Helen promised. 'They would be interesting for you, Marisol, as a nurse. And for your mother too, obviously.'

When everyone except Helen's husband and the twins had left, Helen took out the video. 'I'd better fill in the missing part of Rose's story first,' she said. 'After the war ended, she and Miguel fled into the mountains – with one or two others, I think. We've only a hazy knowledge of those months, but they lived hand to mouth, it seems, dodging the Civil Guard, carrying out guerrilla actions...'

'I never knew that.' Zoe looked amazed.

'Nor me,' her brother said. 'Bloody hell!'

'It's hard to imagine Rose running around the hills with a gun.' Mike whistled through his teeth. 'She always seemed so feminine – I mean the way she dressed, that perfume she always wore.'

'4711 eau de cologne,' Helen said. 'She confided to me once that it was a reaction to her time in Spain when opportunities to wash were few and far between.'

'She was certainly a dark horse.'

'Absolutely,' Helen agreed, 'and intrepid. My God, when you consider that she must have been pregnant most of that time.'

'So she gave birth to my mother in the mountains?' Marisol asked.

'No, they were caught by the Civil Guard – that's when Miguel was killed. Rose gave birth in the hospital at Jaén after being captured and going into labour, she told me. Tomás, who I mentioned yesterday, was their friend and companion. He saw it all from his hiding place behind the trees and noted where Miguel's body fell. Years later, as an old man, he located the family in Cañar and told them what had happened. Well, to cut a long story short, they were given permission, a few years ago, to dig up Miguel's remains and, as you'll see in a minute, give him a more fitting burial in the cemetery of their village.'

Helen's words gave way to a shocked silence, broken eventually by a long sigh from Zach.

'Some brave woman, our Aunt Rose,' Peter said, his finger on the *Play* button.

'I watched the video with her,' Zoe said, 'but she didn't say a word about any of that. I kind of guessed Miguel had been a lover though. It was weird, I expected her to be upset, but no, quite the opposite. She seemed to see it as – I know this sounds strange – almost as a happy ending to the story. Like she could let go now.' Zoe stifled a giggle. 'She actually got out the sherry.' Turning to Marisol, she added, 'I wish you could have met her. She was such a sweetie.'

That night, back in the youth hostel dormitory, Marisol's sleep was disturbed by dreams of the young Rose and her Miguel tramping the *sierras* of Andalucía armed with rifles, in her grandmother's womb the unborn baby that was Blanca. Or Consuelo, as she would be known.

CHAPTER 57

Granada/Milton Keynes 2012

'No, Mamá, I won't cancel your flight. Look, it's natural to feel nervous but you can't chicken out now. We wouldn't get the money back and you'd only regret it afterwards.' It had taken Marisol months to persuade her mother. The whole family had been pressing her to go, even Papá. Helen had penned a friendly email in French that she could more or less understand; Zoe had sent a humorous card with lots of smiley faces.

'Pablo can take my place. Or Luisa.'

'No way. The others can go later. You're coming with me tomorrow so don't argue, please.' She put an arm round Mamá. 'It'll be alright, there's nothing to worry about. They're warm, kind people. And all those questions about your mother that you've had in your head since you were a child they'll be able to answer.'

Mamá sighed. '*Ay*, you're a bully, Marisol. Well, I suppose I'll have to do as you say.'

Papá drove them to the airport in Málaga. Mamá was wearing a red dress she had bought specially for the trip and a charcoal-grey woollen jacket far too warm for May even in England. Her fingertips were raw and bloody in places, the nails, painted in a colour to match her dress, bitten down ragged.

After sitting rigid and panic-stricken during take-off and the first half of the flight, she was now glued to the window, chattering away like an excited child. 'It's sunny,' she exclaimed as the plane descended through high cloud and a geometry of green fields became visible below them. Marisol smiled to herself. Mamá talked as if sun in England was as unlikely a condition as snow on the Equator.

She spotted Helen immediately they walked through the exit at Luton Airport. Now Marisol felt as nervous as Mamá had been earlier.

Introducing the two of them, she stumbled over her English, confused by Helen breaking into French to greet Mamá. '*Enchantée,*' she said with a big smile. '*Bienvenue en Angleterre.*'

'It's kind of you to pick us up.' Marisol put her arm through Mamá's and they followed Helen to the car park.

'Mike has taken himself off for the day,' Helen said as she drove towards their home in Milton Keynes. 'He's helping Zach with some DIY project. Peter should be arriving any time now.' They had agreed beforehand that only the two first cousins would be present, so as not to daunt Mamá.

'What did she say?' Mamá whispered to Marisol in the back.

'She said her husband has gone out but her brother Peter will be there. Helen and Peter are your first cousins, Mamá.'

'*Primos hermanos*, and we never knew. Incredible.' Mamá was staring at Helen's hands on the steering wheel. 'She's got long fingers like mine.'

'And like your mother's too,' Helen said, when Marisol translated her comment. '*Et nos yeux sont verts aussi.*'

'Green eyes, did she say?'

'*Sí*, Mamá. Did you notice Helen's eyes? They're green, same as ours, same as your mother's. You'll see in the photos.'

'Marisol showed me pictures of your family,' Helen said. 'Five beautiful children – you must be very proud.'

'And two grandchildren,' Mamá replied. 'Twin girls.'

'I'm envious,' Helen said, laughing. 'No sign of grandchildren for me yet.'

Peter was just parking his car when they arrived at Helen and Mike's detached house on a tree-lined estate in Milton Keynes.

'This is my brother Peter,' Helen said as he came over to greet them.

'Hello.' Mamá gave him a shy smile, then lowered her eyes.

'Come on in,' Helen said. 'You two must be tired: you probably had to get up at some unearthly hour. If you'd like to lie down for a while…?'

'No, we're fine.' Mamá was looking awed. 'What a lovely house.'

They sat in Helen's sunny living room with cups of 'English tea' and once again the photos were brought out. Mamá pored over each one in turn, devouring them like someone starved for a lifetime and suddenly presented with a banquet of a dozen courses.

Marisol translated as Helen and Peter shared anecdotes and stories. 'That's Rose at about ten, with her two brothers, Bertie and our father Ralph. Dad always accused her of being too much the bossy older sister.'

'I'm the bossy one in our family,' Marisol said, grinning. 'Despite being the youngest. Isn't that so, Mamá?'

'This one must have been taken in wartime during the Blitz, when she was helping out in the underground shelters in London.'

'That baby she's holding is her godson Frank. I hope you don't mind, Consuelo, I said he could pop round this evening. He wants to pass on some letters Rose sent to his mother Dorothy during her time in Spain. He was very keen to meet you.'

'There she is dancing at her fiftieth birthday party,' Peter said, 'outdoing the teens for stamina.'

'I miss her like crazy,' Helen said. 'Consuelo, your mother was a wonderful person – warm, loving, generous. She played the piano and sang.'

Marisol glanced at Mamá, whose mouth hung open in amazement. '*Yo también.*'

'My mother also plays the piano and sings,' she said in English, and addressing her mother, 'Now we know where your musical talent comes from.'

Helen reached tentatively for Mamá's hand. They both looked close to tears. 'Rose told me about her baby,' Helen said, her voice breaking. 'She had named you Blanca; she never dreamed you were alive. If she'd known, she would have spent her whole life searching. She and Jack travelled to Jaén to look for your grave. She never stopped grieving for you. Nor for your father.'

'Would you like to play?' Helen asked later, having noticed Mamá gazing longingly at the piano. 'We got it years ago when the twins were having lessons. Nobody touches it now. It's a shame.'

Mamá pulled out the stool and sat flexing her wrists, working up the confidence to begin. 'I'm not sure if I can remember...' She started to play, falteringly at first with a piece by Chopin, but once in her stride, she was unstoppable. Chopin gave way to Beethoven, then Brahms, then more Chopin. Marisol was amazed. It was years since she'd heard her mother play.

'Rose used to play that,' Peter said, recognising one of the Chopin concertos. 'I remember she played it one Christmas.'

Mamá stopped and turned to Marisol. 'My mother played this? Really? *¡Anda!*' When she reached the end of the piece, she let her hands fall into her lap. 'Well, that's enough. I don't want to bore you.'

'Not at all, but Consuelo, you look tired. Would you like to rest now?'

Mamá nodded.

'Thank you. If you don't mind, I will.'

Rose's godson Frank, a portly man of about seventy, seemed a strait-laced type, formal in his manners and in his dress (who on earth wore a suit and tie for a family visit?). Marisol looked in vain for some influence from Rose. Or had she formed too romanticised an image of her grandmother? His mother Dorothy was one of Rose's oldest friends, Frank told her. 'She led a sheltered life compared to Rose, and yet, ironically, she was the one to die young – in a road accident.'

The letters received by Dorothy, all stamped with *Censura Militar,* spanned the three years of the Civil War and stopped abruptly in early 1939. His mother had been worried stiff, Frank said, because no one heard a 'cheep' from Rose until she returned to England months after the Spanish war ended. Nor did she ever explain her absence.

Marisol waited till she and Mamá were alone in their room that night before reading them. Translating for her mother as she read, she tried to pick out those parts that conveyed something of Rose's personality. In her letters, Rose sounded surprisingly upbeat considering the conditions she described: heat and flies, intense cold, outbreaks of lice and scabies and typhoid, a lack of equipment and long hours working without a break.

I'm sick of the smells of iodine and blood and faeces. There's a constant stream of men with the most ghastly injuries. But Dorothy, they're so brave and determined. Nothing seems to dent their morale. They keep up their spirits by singing. Which reminds me, there's a large Scottish contingent here – we celebrated their Burns Night with Scottish ballads and revolutionary songs; some of them recited poetry. Anything will do for a musical instrument. I'd never have thought of using spoons as castanets!

When Marisol read out Rose's accounts of the terrible poverty of the people, she thought it would be completely outside Mamá's experience, but her mother nodded and said, 'Yes, we had servants from poor families. I saw how their children walked barefoot and wore rags.' Rose was full of praise for the generous, open-hearted people of Spain, their capacity for hard work and refusal to be beaten.

Please send tinned milk for the babies, sugar, soap, cigarettes, chocolate, she begged. *The children here have never tasted chocolate. Besides, we crave it ourselves to supplement our meagre diet of black coffee and bully beef sandwiches! You've no idea how much a tiny square of chocolate can raise the spirits.* In several of her letters she described the Spanish countryside she had come to love – the delicate beauty of almond trees in flower, the scent of orange blossom or of the wild lavender on the hillsides.

She wrote of the musical evening that had first sparked her attraction to Miguel. 'See? Your father was musical too,' Marisol said to Mamá. 'He played the *bandoneón*.' The following letters mentioned him frequently as she confided to Dorothy her admiration for his strong ideals, his integrity, his courage; and her sadness when he returned to the front. *He was desperate to go*, she wrote. *It was the hardest thing to watch him march off. I'm so afraid he'll be killed.* At that time, it appeared, nothing had developed between them beyond a strong attraction on both sides, an unspoken promise.

'You must take these photos of Rose,' Helen said the next day, handing Mamá a large brown envelope. 'And of course the one of your father.' Mamá was studying the picture of Miguel, holding the black and white image close to her face.

'Do you think he's a bit like Belén?' she asked Marisol. 'The dark eyes? And he has the same build as Pablo.'

'Well, maybe. But Papá has dark eyes too and he used to be more muscular when he was younger. It's difficult to tell from an old photo like this.'

'It's a shame there aren't more,' Helen said. 'Peter, did you remember to bring the video?'

'Of course,' he said, getting up to fetch it. 'Shall I put it on now?'

'I told you about the reburial video, Mamá, remember?'

The sudden switch of location from Helen's English living room to the cemetery in Cañar and a group of sombre, mostly elderly people speaking Spanish was disorientating. As the camera panned to the open grave and captured a flurry of red carnations falling onto the box containing Miguel's bones, Mamá covered her eyes. 'No, I can't watch this, I can't.' Tears were pouring down her cheeks. 'Turn it off, please. I don't want to see.'

Marisol pulled her close and handed her a tissue. 'It's alright, Mamá. You don't have to watch.'

Helen had already pressed the stop button. 'Later,' she said. 'Take it home and she can watch it later when she's had time to absorb all this. It's too much all at once.'

The formal handshakes of their first meeting had given way to warm hugs as Marisol and her mother prepared to leave. Mamá's eyes were wet again.

'Tell your brothers and sisters they must visit us soon,' Helen said to Marisol.

'Oh, they will. Ever since I showed them the photos I took last time, they've been talking about it. Pablo is keen to meet Zach and talk music. I think they'll get on brilliantly.'

'Pablo's the one who plays in a band, right? The one with the ponytail? Did Peter tell you he used to play bass guitar in a pop group? What was it called, Pete?'

'The Rocking Turtles. And you might laugh but my hair was as long as your brother's in those days.'

'Oh, I almost forgot,' Helen said, making for the stairs. She returned, holding out a pair of maroon leather gloves. 'These belonged to Rose; she wore them often. Please take them.'

Mamá hesitated, then slipped them on. They were a perfect fit.

'We should go to Cañar soon,' Marisol said as the plane banked low over the sea in its turn inland towards Málaga airport. 'You've still only met one side of your family. And the Spanish side will be easier for you.'

'*Uf*, you're always in such a hurry, *hija.*'

'What are you talking about? Haven't we wasted enough time already? You have cousins in our very own province, Mamá. It could even be that one of the *tios* is still alive. Órgiva is only an hour away by car. It's incredible.'

Mamá remained silent. She had taken the maroon gloves out of her bag and was gazing at them; stroking the soft leather, slipping her fingers in and out.

'Well I'm going anyway,' Marisol said. 'And I'm taking the other four too. You do what you like.'

'Of course I want to meet them, just don't rush me.' Mamá looked sharply at her. 'You're very tetchy today. What's the matter with you?'

'I feel a bit sick.'

'You do look off colour.' Mamá peered at her face again and Marisol saw her eyes open wide in hope. 'You're not...?'

'Yes, I know what you're thinking.' She grinned. 'You're right, I'm pregnant.' She took her mother's hand and clasped it in both of hers. 'And you know what? If it's a girl, I'm going to call her Blanca.'

ACKNOWLEDGEMENTS

For the section of my novel set during the Civil War, I am indebted to Angela Jackson, whose book *British Women and the Spanish Civil War* proved an invaluable source of background material on the nurses who worked with the International Brigades in Spain. Equally useful for building up a picture of the war from the nurses' perspective was *Women's Voices from the Spanish Civil War*, edited by Jim Fyrth and Sally Alexander. My thanks to them too.

I am also grateful to author and historian Dr Judith Keene of Sydney University for sending me a copy of her book, *Last Mile to Huesca,* which includes the diary of Australian nurse Agnes Hodgson.

The collection of Civil War documents at the Marx Memorial Library in London provided another great resource, with many first-hand accounts by International Brigaders and others, including a number of the nurses. Their memoirs and letters gave me ideas for Rose's experiences in Part 1 of this novel.

For Part 3, on Rose and Miguel's time in the sierras, David Baird's *Between Two Fires,* which included the accounts of former guerrillas, Civil Guards and villagers in the Axarquía region, was a useful source of inspiration, alongside other testimonies in Spanish.

My interviews with Spanish women and men who had lived through the Franco dictatorship were of immeasurable value and I am deeply grateful to all of them for their time and patience in answering my questions. After completing the novel, a fire in my house destroyed all my notes from these interviews – a loss that caused me great distress. I apologise if I have omitted any names from this list: Adoración,

Angeles and Josefina, Angustias, Carmen, Juan, Mari Carmen and Reynaldo, Pepita, Teresa and Victor. Also the two women from the *Bebés Robados* group in Granada, whose names I confess to having forgotten.

My interest in the lives of ordinary Spaniards during Franco's dictatorship was first aroused many years ago when I came across the oral histories recorded in the 50s, 60s and 70s by Ronald Fraser. These and two books in Spanish by Juan Eslava Galán supplemented the material from my own interviews in giving context about the times.

My grateful thanks to Allan Dorian Clark for drawing the maps that enhance this book.

I would like to thank Isabel Romero for checking the authenticity of the Spanish sections of the novel and to Paloma Ordóñez for helping me with details of nursing routines for Part 12. Thanks also to Lala Isla, who suggested background reading and who accommodated me while I carried out research at the Marx Memorial Library.

My beta readers gave me helpful feedback on my first draft. I am grateful to Sue Smith, Ann Fernández, Jane Isaacson, Lily MacGillivray, Lucius Redman and Andrew Naylor for their constructive comments. Also to Rebecca Horsfall for her critique, which gave me some useful pointers.

A heartfelt thank you to the many friends who encouraged and supported me on the rocky road to publication, with special thanks due to Candida Castro. Your solidarity made all the difference.

Last but not least, my sincere thanks to Matthew Smith of Urbane for his stalwart support and enthusiasm.

Barbara Lamplugh started out as a travel writer in the 1970s, inspired by a life-changing overland journey to Kathmandu in a converted fire-engine. Her love of adventure then took her backpacking around SE Asia via the Trans-Siberian Railway and Japan. Two travel books, *Kathmandu by Truck* and *Trans-Siberia by Rail*, were the result. Another new experience – motherhood – came next, putting an end to her extensive wanderings. However, she continued to write, turning now to fiction. In 1999, spurred by the challenge of living in a different culture, she headed for Granada, Spain, where along with the energising light of the sun, she found her dream job as a features writer for the magazine *Living Spain*, writing on topics as diverse as garlic, machismo, the life of a lighthouse keeper and the nightmarish experience of being trapped at an all-night drumming festival. Although her heart and home are in Granada, where her 2015 novel *Secrets of the Pomegranate* is set, she makes frequent visits to the UK to spend time with her children and grandchildren.

ALSO BY BARBARA LAMPLUGH

Secrets of the Pomegranate

Passionate, free-spirited Deborah has finally found peace and a fulfilling relationship in her adopted city of Granada but when she is seriously injured in the Madrid train bombings of 2004, it is her sister, Alice who is forced to face the consequences of a deception they have maintained for ten years. At Deborah's home in Granada, she waits, ever more fearful. Will her sister live or die? And how long should she stay when each day brings the risk of what she most dreads, a confrontation with Deborah's Moroccan ex-lover, Hassan? At stake is all she holds dear.

Secrets of the Pomegranate explores with compassion, sensitivity and – despite the tragic events – humour, the complicated ties between sisters, between mothers and sons and between lovers, set against a background of cultural difference and prejudices rooted in Granada's long history of Muslim-Christian struggles for power.